AUG 1 6 2007

UNITY

Battlestar Galactica™ Novels from Tor Books

Battlestar Galactica by Jeffrey A. Carver
The Cylons' Secret by Craig Shaw Gardner
Sagittarius Is Bleeding by Peter David
Unity by Steven Harper

Original Fiction by Steven Harper

The Silent Empire:
Offspring
Dreamer
Nightmare
Trickster

Luna City Special Investigations:
Dead Man on the Moon

As Steven Piziks

In the Company of Mind
Corporate Mentality
Star Trek Voyager: The Nanotech War
Identity
Exorcist: The Beginning

UNITY

A Battlestar Galactica™ novel by
STEVEN HARPER

based on the TV series created by
RONALD D. MOORE

based on a teleplay by
GLEN A. LARSON

A TOM DOHERTY ASSOCIATES BOOK

NEW YORK

UNITY

Edited by James Frenkel

A Tor Book
Published by Tom Doherty Associates, LLC
175 Fifth Avenue
New York, NY 10010

www.tor.com

Tor® is a registered trademark of Tom Doherty Associates, LLC.

Library of Congress Cataloging-in-Publication Data

Harper, Steven (Steven Piziks)
    Unity : a Battlestar Galactica novel / by Steven Harper.
        p.   cm
    "A Tom Doherty Associates Book."
    "Based on the TV series created by Ronald D. Moore ; based on a teleplay by Glen A. Larson."
    ISBN-13: 978-0-765-31608-0 (tradepbk)
    ISBN-10: 0-765-31608-0 (tradepbk)
    ISBN-13: 978-0-765-31606-6 (hardcover)
    ISBN-10: 0-765-31606-4 (hardcover)
    I. Battlestar Galactica (Television Program)   II. Title.
    PS3616.I97U55 2007
    813'.6—dc22

                                                                2006102657

First Edition: April 2007

Printed in the United States of America

0 9 8 7 6 5 4 3 2 1

ACKNOWLEDGMENTS

My thanks to the Untitled Writers Group of Ann Arbor (Elizabeth Bartmess, Karen Everson, Anne Harris, Jonathan Jarrard, Erica Schippers, Catherine Shaffer, and Sarah Zettel) for putting up with the unexpected deluge of *Battlestar Galactica* chapters. Special gratitude is in order for Catherine Shaffer and her knowledge of prions. Thanks also go to Jim Frenkel for letting me do this in the first place.

AUTHOR'S NOTE

This novel is set in the time between the events of the episodes "The Flight of the Phoenix" and "Pegasus."

UNITY

CHAPTER

1

A trio of Cylon raiders dipped and swooped through space like silent bats on razor wings. Kara Thrace clenched her toes—the only part of her that wasn't occupied with flying her Viper— and tried to keep her eye on all three at once. Two of them split off and swooped around to her left and her right in a pincer move while the third one came straight at her. Kara's eyes darted back and forth and her heart pounded hard.

Come on, she thought, and goosed her thrusters so the Viper jolted upward. *You on the left—a little higher.*

"Watch yourself, Starbuck," Lee Adama said in her earpiece. His voice was heavily distorted by the radio, but Kara understood him perfectly well. You learned to sort out the words through the distortion, almost like learning a foreign language.

"I know what I'm doing, Apollo," she snapped. "Watch your own ass, not mine."

"Apollo's watching Starbuck's ass?" Brandon "Hot Dog" Constanza said over his own radio. *"Can I make a comment about that? Please?"*

"Just do your frakking job, Lieutenant," Lee warned.

All around them, other Vipers rushed at the flock of raiders. The deadly little Cylon ships were sleek, flat, and black, with a protrusion in the front that resembled a head. A single red "eye" cruised restlessly back and forth, hunting, scanning. Aiming. In stark contrast, the Vipers were battered and battle-worn. Kara's had once been white, but scorch marks, scrapes, and other damage had weathered it to an uneven gray. It looked like a miniature fighter jet that had crashed once or twice and been knocked back together in a mechanic's back yard. Behind Kara and the other Vipers cruised the immense bulk of the Battlestar *Galactica*. Surrounding it like chicks near a mother hen were the disparate shapes of some seventy-odd ships—passenger ships, cruise ships, work ships. They were all that remained of human civilization. Behind the fleet spun an honest-to-gods blue planet. It had water, it had plant life, and it was the reason why the fleet hadn't simply hit their faster-than-light drives and Jumped out the moment the Cylons Jumped in.

The two Cylon raiders rushed inward for their pincer move, one to port, one to starboard. Kara caught a gleam of starlight off their forward guns. They fired. With a whoop, Kara yanked the control lever at the side of her seat. Auxiliary jets flashed, and the little fighter blasted straight upward. Bullets crossed the intervening space and both Cylon raiders exploded, torn to pieces by friendly fire. Kara wondered if they felt any pain. The Cylon ships were actually living beings, or as alive as Cylons got, anyway. Not that this fact kept Kara from pressing the trigger. She flicked another lever and her maneuverable little Viper whipped around in time to fire on the third Cylon. It exploded as well, close enough that the blast knocked her sideways a little bit, wrenching her around in her seat.

"I can't believe you frakkin' did that!" Kat shouted as her own guns raked the raider in front of her.

Kara grinned without answering. Ahead of her, two more Cylons exploded in bright fireballs beneath her guns. A piece of debris rushed straight at her, and she dived beneath it as if the Viper were an extension of her body. Two raiders skimmed into view ahead of her, straight into her cross-hairs, and she wiped both of them out before they even noticed she was there. Beyond the flock of raiders hovered the malignant, spiky form of a Cylon basestar. The frakking thing had popped into existence a few minutes ago and spat out a swarm of raiders, forcing Kara Thrace, Lee Adama, and the other Viper pilots to scramble into their ships to defend the fleet.

Kara brought her Viper up and around again. In the distance, the brilliant yellow star showered golden light in all directions and Kara made an automatic mental note—keep her tail to the sun and force the raiders to look into it whenever possible. She had no idea if the Cylons would be blinded by the solar radiation, or even affected by it at all. For all she knew, they had Cylon sunglasses, but it didn't hurt to try. An image of a raider donning a set of goggles with a single giant lens in the middle popped into her head and a giggle bubbled at the back of her throat. At that moment, yet another raider bore down on her, guns blazing. Kara yelped and whipped her Viper hard to port. She heard pops and pings as the raider's ammo ricocheted off her wings and tail, though her instruments stayed in the green. No real damage. Chief Tyrol would probably chew her out anyway.

Concentrate, she snarled to herself. She spun the Viper around, ignoring the stomach-wrenching vertigo, and fired on the raider with both guns. The barrels mounted on either side of the tiny flight cabin flashed, and Kara felt the familiar breathy thump of her own gunfire. The raider shredded, and Kara moved on to new targets before the debris had a chance to scatter.

11

"*Starbuck*," Lee said. "*Check your ten o'clock. A pack of raiders heading for Planet Goop.*"

Kara glanced to port and saw them. Nine raiders had broken away from the rest of the flock, clearly intent on skirting the *Galactica* so they could dive-bomb the little blue planet—and the *Monarch* on its surface.

"Moving to intercept, Apollo," she shot back. "You with me?"

"*All the way. And can the response, Hot Dog.*"

"*Did I say anything?*" Hot Dog protested. "*One word?*"

The raiders swooped and dove in perfect unison. Kara, glad the sun was behind her, hit her thrusters hard. The extra g-force pressed her back into her seat and gave her the unnerving feeling that she was flying straight up instead of forward. Space gave few visual cues, and her inner ear was shouting that gravity—down—was directly behind her. She ignored her inner ear and focused on the fleeing Cylons instead. Hatred flared hot inside her head. These were the frakking bastards who had destroyed her entire world and chased her across countless star systems. How many months had it been since she'd felt safe? How many months had it been since she'd had a night's uninterrupted sleep? How many months since the Cylon attack? She had lost count.

The stupid part was that humans had *created* the Cylons, robots designed for labor too difficult or dangerous for people. And then somewhere along the line the robots had become so sophisticated that they thought they were people too, and they started a rebellion. The resulting war had nearly destroyed the Twelve Colonies and all but wiped out both humans and Cylons. In the end, the Cylons had agreed to take themselves off to another part of space. Peace reigned, and humanity let itself breathe again. Forty-odd years later, the Cylons had reappeared, smarter, angrier, and deadlier than before. They fell on the startled Twelve Colonies and killed billions of humans. Fewer than fifty thousand had survived on various ships that had somehow escaped the carnage. Those ships were now informally known as the Fleet, under the command of Commander William Adama and the governorship of President Laura Roslin. The Fleet was looking for Earth, the fabled thirteenth colony, and Kara was sure they'd find it. Eventually. That hope kept her going. Meanwhile, they had to deal with the Cylons and their living battleships.

The nine raiders swooped downward, remaining carefully out of range of *Galactica*'s weapons. For all that the *Galactica* was an aging Battlestar that was falling apart at the seams, it had more than enough power to wipe out nine measly Cylon raiders. Unfortunately, the *Galactica* was about as maneuverable as a whale caught in low tide, so she depended on the Vipers to sweat the small stuff.

Kara and Apollo accelerated, gaining on the raiders. Ahead of them, Planet Goop spun slowly in its orbit like a perfect blue gem rolling across black velvet. Kara squinted, searching, even though she knew it was impossible to see the *Monarch* from up here. The *Monarch* was a mining ship, but it wasn't down on the surface digging up metal or rocks—it was scooping up goop. Planet Goop had an official name somewhere, but no one used it. It had water, an atmosphere composed of lots of nitrogen and carbon dioxide, and an oceanful of primitive algae. In a few million years, once the plant life had exhaled enough oxygen, Planet Goop might even be habitable by humans. In the meantime, however, the algae had turned out to be quite valuable. It was resistant to radiation—Planet Goop had no real ozone layer—and it could be refined into anti-radiation meds. More importantly, it could also be processed into edible food. Steak composed of smooshed-up algae, colored brown and grilled, didn't taste quite the same as its natural counterpart, but it sure beat starving, and the *Monarch* was harvesting the stuff by the truckload.

Then the Cylon basestar ship had popped up and spewed Cylon raiders. Every ship in the Fleet possessed a faster-than-light drive and could Jump to a safe location, but that would leave the *Monarch* and her crew defenseless. It was also frakking hard to track down ships that didn't all Jump at the same time, and there was considerable risk that one or more would be lost. So they all stayed.

Kara checked her scanner. Tiny Cylon symbols skittered around the screen. In two more seconds she'd be within firing—

An alarm light flashed. Kara gasped and her heart lurched.

"Frak!" she shouted. "One of those raiders has a nuke on board!"

"Uh oh," Lee said. *"Which one?"*

"How the hell should I know?" she shot back. "Stupid frakking Cylons all look alike."

"Hold your fire, Starbuck," came Commander Adama's voice in her headset. *"Repeat: Hold your fire."*

"No shit," she muttered, too quietly for the Old Man to hear. If she fired on a raider that was carrying a nuclear missile, the explosion would wipe out not only her, but Lee, a bunch of the Vipers, and probably a piece of the *Galactica*. It would also wipe out a frakload of Cylons, but that wouldn't be much comfort to the people-sucking vacuum.

The nine raiders sped onward. Kara continued to follow, wondering if Cylons could feel smug.

"These raiders aren't usually equipped to fire missiles," Lee said. *"How is it planning to use a nuke?"*

"Suicide run, Apollo," Kara said. "It's hoping to crash into

14

the Monarch and explode or get strafed by one of us and explode."

"Starbuck, I have the nuke on scanner," said Felix Gaeta. Kara could imagine him, dark-haired and ramrod straight, standing with Adama in *Galactica*'s Combat Information Center, outwardly cool as an arctic rock but working like hell on his systems. *"Sending you and Apollo the info now."*

One of the raiders on Kara's own screen blinked from red to yellow.

"Got it," Lee said. *"Let's go!"*

"Don't eat the yellow snow," Kara agreed, "and don't bite the yellow Cylon."

She closed in and hit the trigger. Three of the non-nuke raiders tore themselves to pieces. Kara dodged the debris cloud as the remaining seven came about. One of them—the yellow one—hung back. The forward six returned fire, and Kara was suddenly very busy. Her Viper dipped and swooped, constantly changing vector and heading. Two bullets smacked off her flight canopy like rocks off a windshield. A little more to port, and she would have been dead. The yellow Cylon continued to blink mockingly on her scanner screen.

"Come on, Apollo," she muttered through clenched teeth. Planet Goop reeled in and out of view as she dodged deadly bullets. "Get the mother—"

Friendly fire lashed down. Three more raiders vanished in exploding clouds. They'd been concentrating on Kara and forgotten about Lee. With a whoop, she reoriented and fired on the remaining trio. One more raider blew up. Kara was half sure its single red eye had widened in surprise. Another raider exploded under Lee's expert fire, leaving only the nuke raider. Kara eyed it uncertainly. It hovered in front of her and stared back, its single eye tracking back and forth. Kara wondered if it

15

was scanning her somehow and the thought made cold worms crawl over her skin. She didn't dare fire, and the frakking thing knew it.

"Shit!" Hot Dog shouted over the com. *"Another contingent of raiders coming out of the basestar's ass. Move move move!"*

"How many of those things does it have?" replied another pilot. It sounded like Jen Curtis, callsign Shadow. Kara flashed on a brief mental image of her tall, lithe figure in the Viper, her long brown hair tied back so it wouldn't float around her face in zero gravity. *"We're gonna get chewed into dog food."*

"The raider's guns have been removed," Lee said quietly. His Viper moved in beside hers and she could see Lee's handsome, boyish face in his own Plexiglas cabin. *"To make room for the nuke. It's only got one shot, and it has to make it count."*

"Kat!" Shadow shouted. *"Watch it!"*

"Too many. Pull back! Pull back!"

Kara felt a sudden urge to whip around and fly back to help her fellow Vipers. She shoved the feeling aside. This raider had the power to take out the *Monarch* or a major chunk of the Fleet, and she had to deal with it.

"Starbuck, report," Commander Adama ordered.

"The nuke raider can't decide what to do," Kara said. "Take out us or the *Monarch*."

"I'm hit! Gods, I'm hit!"

"I've got you covered, Hot Dog. Get yourself—" An explosion came over the comm.

"Shadow! Shadow! Aw, no. Jen!"

"More raiders coming from the basestar."

"Fall back to the Galactica. *Let her cover us."*

Kara glared at the nuke Cylon. It glared back. "Frak! We have to wipe out this thing and get rid of the basestar."

"How?" Lee snapped. *"The basestar isn't stupid enough to*

come close enough to engage the Galactica. *And we don't have the firepower to—"*

The nuke raider abruptly spun and dove toward Planet Goop. Kara blinked, then dove after it. Even as she moved, an idea popped into her head, and she moved instinctively to implement it.

"Starbuck!" Lee shouted. *"Don't!"*

But Kara ignored him. Grimly she accelerated, gaining on the Cylon until the blue flames of its rear thrusters were warming her Viper's nose. Her hands sweated and her heart raced like a greyhound. Her life was in imminent danger. One mistake, and she would be a cloud of debris like the raiders she had killed. A grin slid across her face. She loved every minute. With steady fingers, she lined up the shot. One chance, and one chance only.

"Starbuck!" Lee said. *"What the frak are you doing?"*

"Up yours, toaster." Kara twitched a finger and fired a single round. It went straight into the raider's thrusters. Nothing happened. Kara held her breath. Then the blue flames flickered, sputtered, and died. The Cylon coasted ahead, somehow managing to look startled. Its acceleration immediately stopped and it sped ahead on momentum alone. Kara overshot it, spun her Viper around, and extended her landing gear. Now both Viper and raider were coasting toward the blue planet, though Kara was facing backward. More sounds of combat came over the comm, but she steadfastly ignored them. This was going to be tricky enough. Carefully, using every bit of instinct and skill she possessed, she tapped her own thrusters and slowed herself enough to allow the raider to catch up with her. She edged the Viper upward just a little, then slowed herself again. The helpless raider slid beneath her. There was a *thunk* and a slight screech of tortured metal. Kara goosed her thrusters again. The

Cylon slowed with her—it was stuck on her landing gear. Without working engines, it couldn't break free. She wondered what it was thinking.

"Starbuck, what the hell are you doing?" Commander Adama demanded.

"I'm returning some merchandise to the store, sir," she said. "Apollo, cover me!" And she accelerated toward the basestar.

"Hey—what?" Lee, caught off guard, hurried to catch up and pass her. *"You're frakking insane!"*

"That's why you all love me," she shouted. "Just open up a hole in that squadron at your three o'clock. We'll send this nuke back where it came from and get rid of the basestar all at once."

"You sure you can do this, Starbuck?" Lee asked.

"Frak, no. You with me or not?"

Lee hesitated for only a moment. *"Kat, Hot Dog—lay down suppressive fire,"* he ordered. *"Creeper, Fireboy, and Zelda—keep at the others. Fall back if you have to."*

Ahead of Kara, a veritable cloud of Cylon raiders rushed in a hundred dizzying directions like a horde of vampire bats looking for prey. The Viper squadron was outnumbered at least ten to one, but they had nonetheless carved several chunks from the enemy cloud. Cylons seemed to put quantity over quality when it came to dogfighting in space. It was a wasteful tactic. On the other hand, it had won them victory over the Twelve Colonies.

Kara aimed for the basestar and flew, a grim smile on her face. Burdened with the raider, her Viper was hard to handle, sluggish and unresponsive. She couldn't maneuver much, either—a too-sudden turn might dislodge the raider caught on her landing gear. A clump of raiders swirled just ahead, between her and the basestar, and she held her breath. At exactly the right moment, Lee opened fire. Several of the raiders went up. The others regrouped, ready to fight back, but Kat and

18

Hot Dog rushed in to finish the job. Their guns blazed, creating a dozen more silent fireballs. Kara punched up her speed and headed straight into the hole that had opened up. For a moment she was blinded by fire, smoke, and debris. Something pinged off her starboard wing, jolting her around. But the raider remained firmly in place. Then the debris cleared. Ahead of her she could see the ugly Cylon basestar. It looked a little like a child's jack, the kind kids snatched from the ground before the ball could bounce again. But this jack had been squashed down and then blown up to half the size of the *Galactica*. Kara wondered how many Cylons were inside. Was one of them keeping track of the battle and issuing orders like Commander Adama? Had he given the nuke raider its orders? Maybe the nuke raider was the basestar's version of her, a Cylon Starbuck, given a mission that would take some difficult or impossible flying.

Kara shook off these thoughts and concentrated on the basestar. A glance up and port told her that Lee had brought his own Viper close to hers. Behind, she assumed, Kat and Hot Dog were keeping other raiders too busy to pursue her. She released a tense breath.

Okay, all you Lords of Kobol, she thought. *This is where you can prove that I'm one of your favorites.*

Tentacles of smoke wound out of the basestar. Missiles. Fear dried up Kara's mouth. Even with Lee intercepting, she doubted she could dodge all of them, and it would only take one to wipe her out. They threaded toward her and Lee.

"I'm reading a signal from the nuke raider," Gaeta said. *"It's similar to a distress call."*

"Starbuck," Lee said, *"we need to turn back."*

Anger boiled in Kara's stomach. The missiles were now eight or ten kilometers away. The basestar loomed, taking up Kara's entire field of vision.

"Are you frakking crazy?" she snapped. "Back through all those raiders?"

"We can't deal with those missiles on our own," Lee retorted. *"That's an order, Lieu—"*

The missiles detonated. Every one of them. Flares of light flashed against Kara's retinas, leaving red dots. The shockwave came a moment later, but the missiles had exploded far too soon to do any damage and she rode it out with scarcely a bump.

"They know!" Kara whooped. "The toasters know I have their nuke. They didn't want one of their missiles to set it off this close."

"A bunch of raiders got past us," Kat said. *"Company's coming, Apollo."*

"I'll take care of it," Lee said. *"Starbuck, go! Make it fast!"*

She went. Her sluggish Viper flung itself forward. This was the closest she had ever come to a basestar, and it filled her world with gray menace. The disgusting thing had actual frakking portholes in it, and she could see figures moving around inside. Did they know what she was doing, or that she was even here? She gnawed her lower lip in concentration. Flashes of light came over her shoulder, telling her that Lee had engaged the flock of raiders that had gotten past Hot Dog and Kat. Kara eyed the basestar, her eyes tracking rapidly back and forth almost like the single eye of a Cylon. And then she saw it—an open port. It might have been for launching raiders, it might have been for launching missiles. Hell, it might have been for launching Cylon sewage. Kara didn't much care. She aimed for it and accelerated again.

Lords of Kobol, she thought, keeping her hands steady by strength of will. Fear mixed with exhilaration, making both all the sweeter. The port loomed closer. At the last minute, Kara reversed all her thrusters. She slammed against her flight harness, and pain made an H across her chest. With a metallic screech, the nuke raider wrenched away from her landing gear. It spun like a discus, the single eye tracking frantically back and forth as it headed for the port. At the last moment, Kara fired her weapons. A tongue of flame touched the little raider just as it flew into the port.

"Run!" Kara shouted into the comm. She flipped her Viper over and punched the thrusters hard. Acceleration shoved her backward, crushing her, and her vision flickered for a moment before she could recover. She rushed past the Cylons Lee was fighting. Lee flipped his own Viper and fled along with her. The raiders paused for a moment, then flew after them. Kara threw a glance over her shoulder at the basestar, waiting for the big *kaboom*.

Nothing happened.

Uh oh, she thought, then looked at the flock of raiders on her screen. Over a hundred behind her, and all would hit firing range in a few seconds.

"If we live through this," Lee growled, bringing his Viper in beside hers, *"I'm going to kill you."*

Starbuck flashed him a sickly grin and flipped her Viper one more time, guns ready. Lee followed suit. If she was going to go down, she would go down with her weapons blazing and the wounds on her front, not her back. The raiders rushed forward, their sleek, deadly forms almost invisible against the blackness.

And then a horrendous light filled the universe.

CHAPTER

2

Kara flung up a hand to shield her eyes, though the Viper's cabin was well polarized. Moments later, the shockwave hit, flipping her and Lee ass over teakettle. Both Vipers bucked and weaved as their pilots fought to regain control. Kara bounced around within her harness, jarring her new bruises. A few hundred kilometers away, the basestar was exploding in the world's most brilliant firework display, as if the Lords of Kobol had cracked open a doorway into hell. Kara ignored the pain, ignored the light, and just frakking *flew*.

The other Vipers turned tail and ran as well. Ahead lay the *Galactica* and safety. The raiders buzzed about, obviously confused and uncertain by the loss of their commanding ship. In a few minutes they would recover, however. The light and shock of the explosion faded, and Kara regained full control of her Viper.

"Get 'em!" Lee barked.

The fight was short, nasty, and to the point. The Cylon raiders didn't have a chance to regain their equilibrium before the Vipers shredded them the way a chef shredded soft cheese. Into an omelet. With tender mushrooms and sweet onions and—

Kara's stomach growled as another Cylon puffed into a satisfying fireball under her buns. Guns! Under her guns. Frak, when had she last eaten?

The basestar was an expanding nebula of radioactive debris, and Hot Dog got the last Cylon raider, a fact he announced with a whoop that made Kara's ears ring.

"Let's go home, people," Lee said. *"You did good."*

"Services for Shadow?" Kat asked.

"This evening," Lee said.

Kara eased her Viper around to face the enormous *Galactica*, her mood gone suddenly pensive. She had barely known Jen "Shadow" Curtis and now she was gone. Kara had long since stopped keeping track of the number of Viper pilots they had lost since the Cylon attack—the number was just too depressing. What she wanted right now was a stiff shot of something that would burn all the way down, a hot meal, and maybe a card game. Or sex. With someone nice and—

"Viper squadron, I'm reading a distress signal," Gaeta said, breaking Kara's chain of thought.

"From the basestar?" Lee said, surprised.

"Negative. The signal is Colonial."

Kara's heart jumped. "Is it Shadow?"

"Also negative. It's an automated signal from an escape pod."

Escape pod? "Vipers don't have escape pods," Kara said, "and we're the only ones out here. Gaeta, you're seeing things."

"Still negative, Lieutenant. You should be getting it on your screen now."

Kara glanced down. Sure enough, the source of a Colonial distress signal was flashing.

"Have any ships in the Fleet launched escape pods?" Lee asked.

There was a pause. *"Negative, Captain,"* came the warm voice of Tactical Officer Anastasia Dualla—"Dee" to her friends. *"No distress from the Fleet, and no pod launched."*

"Apollo, Starbuck, go check it out," Adama ordered.

"On it, sir," Lee said, and both Vipers swung around. Kara made a face and her stomach growled again. Dammit, this mission was *over*. She was supposed to get food and booze and . . . maybe something else. Still, curiosity nudged her. So did suspicion. Cylons could be slippery as a snake in an oil refinery. This might easily be a trick.

"This might easily be a trick," Lee said.

Kara suppressed a snort. "You read my mind, Captain. Scary."

"Frakking scary, Lieutenant."

Kara homed in on the signal, brought her Viper about, and hit the acceleration. May as well get this over with. Lee followed, a little above and behind her. She dodged around a couple pieces of basestar debris and finally caught sight of the signal's source. The pod was boxy, about two meters tall, two meters wide, and five meters deep. A red distress light winked steadily on the top, and it was slowly rotating end over end. A rudimentary thruster jutted from the back, designed to give just enough boost for the pod to grab some distance from whatever vessel it was trying to flee. Kara stared, instantly recognizing the design.

"It's a Colonial escape pod," she reported, not quite believing it. "Where the hell did it come from?"

"Has to be the basestar," Lee said, his tone also conveying disbelief. *"Unless one of the Fleet ships blew up when we weren't looking."*

"No such luck, Apollo," said Colonel Saul Tigh, the *Galactica*'s

executive officer. His voice was dry and hard as old wood, and Kara could imagine him in CIC, his bare scalp gleaming in the artificial light. *"Nothing that comes from a Cylon ship is worth saving. Open fire."*

Kara stuck her tongue into her cheek and moved it around. Tigh wanted the pod destroyed, and that automatically made her reluctant to make it happen. Tigh was a grade-A, no-holds-barred, frakked-up, drunk-ass shithead. In her humble opinion. Unfortunately, the frakked-up shithead also had rank on her.

"Sir—" she began.

"Belay that," Adama interrupted. *"Starbuck, can you get any closer and check it out better? Apollo, you provide cover."*

"Commander," Tigh said, *"I don't think that's a good—"*

"Thank you, Colonel," Adama cut him off. *"Your objection is noted."*

"Moving in, sir," Kara said, not bothering to keep the smugness out of her voice. Adama—now there was a commander you could respect. If Bill Adama asked her to check out the heart of a star, she'd salute and fire all thrusters. She edged her Viper closer. Beyond the pod, the blazing yellow sun continued pumping out radiation across the spectrum. Already, the basestar debris field had largely dispersed. Kara matched velocity with the pod, though it continued to turn slowly end over end. Her finger remained on the fire button for her weapons. Colonel Tigh was an ass, but that didn't mean *she* had to be stupid.

The pod rotated some more, and a porthole slid into view. Through it, Kara caught a glimpse of a human face, a male she didn't recognize. He was staring into space with wide, frightened eyes. They locked gazes for a startled moment.

Help! he mouthed. Then the pod's rotation carried the porthole out of view.

"There's someone aboard," Kara reported, forcing her voice to remain steady. "I just saw a man's face."

A moment of silence fell over the airwaves. A raider was just one shape Cylons came in. Some Cylons were shiny metal robots, complete with built-in pulse rifles. And some looked perfectly, exactly human. Cylons also seemed to go in for repetition. All their robotic forms looked alike, and the human forms seemed to be limited in their variation. Kara had heard rumors that the Cylons used only twelve human shapes. She herself had encountered at least two female forms and three male forms, and she had killed one of the latter back on Caprica when—

—a shiny shard sinking into soft flesh, a choked cry gurgling from a ruined throat, an ineffectual hand clawing at her face—

Nausea quivered in her empty stomach and Kara shoved unpleasant memories aside. She needed to concentrate on the present job, not on past nightmares.

"Is he human or Cylon?" Tigh demanded.

"No way to tell, sir." Kara resisted adding an epithet about the stupidity of Tigh's question. "He looked human, and I haven't seen him before, but that doesn't say much."

"I'm dispatching a search-and-rescue Raptor, Starbuck," Adama said. *"You and Apollo can return to* Galactica.*"*

"Sir," she acknowledged, though she felt oddly reluctant to leave the guy, whoever he was, spinning alone through space. The feeling wasn't rational—there was nothing she could do for him in a Viper, and for all she knew, he was a Cylon. But the feeling remained. She gave the pod one more glance before bringing her Viper about and falling in behind Lee as he headed for home.

Home, she thought. *When did* Galactica *become home?* As a Viper pilot, Viper trainer, and occasional CAG—Commander Air Group—Kara spent more time on ships than she did planetside, and her small apartment on Caprica usually showed her neglect. But now that Caprica and the other Twelve Colonies were overrun by Cylons, she felt a strong need to return there, feel the open spaces around her, breathe the crisp, fresh air. Cook a meal. Sink into a soft chair. Hell, she even missed dusting the furniture. Before the Cylons attacked, she had treated housework as something to be seriously considered after every major earthquake. Now she would happily spend a year hunting down dust bunnies if it meant she could go back home whenever she wanted.

The thought struck her as strange. Kara had never seen Caprica or her apartment as anything but a base to operate from. She usually felt out of sorts planetside, and came truly alive only when she was flying. It was, she supposed, the lack of choice. Before the Cylon attack, she *could* go home if she wanted to. Now that the Cylons had removed the choice, she wanted it back.

"Viper four-one-six/Galactica," said the Launch Signal Officer. *"Approach port landing bay, hands-on, speed nine eight, blue stripes. Call the ball."*

Kara guided her Viper into the *Galactica*'s port landing bay, as instructed, keeping her speed at ninety-eight for a manual landing. Lee preceded her into the cavelike bay, its roof arching high above, its floor perfectly flat. A ways ahead of her was an elevator pad painted in blue stripes. Lee was already skimming down to land on one with red checks. All her instruments were in the green and she was having no problems.

"I have the ball," she said, and guided her Viper down to a perfect landing. The elevator pad dropped down, taking Kara and the Viper with it. A few moments later, she was on the even more cavernous flight deck. Ceramic tile that had once been white faced most of it. Rows of sleek Vipers and boxy Raptors stretched into the distance. Half a dozen members of Galen Tyrol's damage-control people surrounded Kara's little ship before the elevator pad could drop flush with the deck. Kara released the canopy. She pushed it up and removed the helmet to her vac suit with familiar ease. Hard smells from the flight deck assailed her—sharp solder, scorched plastic, metallic air. Kara shook her short blond hair, then hauled herself out of the Viper. The flight crew ignored her as unimportant. The Viper needed their attention more.

"Not bad out there, Starbuck," Lee Adama said. He had removed his own vac helmet, revealing a startlingly handsome, boyish face topped with tousled brown hair. Bright blue eyes met her brown ones. "Did you forget your receipt?"

"Receipt?" she said, puzzled.

"When you returned the merchandise to the Cylons," Lee clarified with a grin. "Looked like they wouldn't accept it without a receipt."

She rolled her eyes. "Gosh, Apollo—so funny I forgot to laugh."

"Wisecracks are your department. Everybody knows that."

"How much damage did you do this time, sir?" broke in a new voice.

Kara gave Chief Petty Officer Galen Tyrol an insouciant grin. He was a stocky, dark-haired man who wore a continual expression of worry from the long hours and short supplies he dealt with as chief of Deck Crew Five. He and his people oversaw the maintenance and repair of the Vipers, Raptors, and shuttles that defended the Fleet. Kara was notoriously hard on her Vipers and wasn't much bothered when they came back to him heavily damaged. She knew that to a man like Tyrol, it was like bringing home a sports car covered in dents with all the glass broken, and she could rarely resist teasing him.

"Meh," she said. "A few dings and cracks. Nothing you couldn't suck out with a plunger or slap together with some epoxy."

Tyrol's pained expression was interrupted by the staccato clatter of boots in quick-march. Startled, Kara drew back in time to avoid a squadron of marines. They wore full combat gear, face plates, and flak jackets. The barrels on their pulse rifles gleamed and their stomping boots echoed in the enormous flight deck.

"What the frak?" Kara said as they trotted past.

"The SAR Raptor's bringing in that escape pod you found," Tyrol explained. "The marines are just in case."

Kara was supposed to head for a post-flight debriefing, but there was no way she was going to miss this. Lee stayed with her. News about the pod had evidently leaked out because a small crowd of other onlookers slowly gathered. Most of them were Tyrol's technicians, and they were clearly performing make-work to have an excuse to stay close. Kara made no such pretense, and leaned casually against her Viper. Twice she caught Lee looking at her out of the corner of his eye, and she caught herself looking back. Idle curiosity? Or more than that? She felt a faint flush coming on and looked away. Several weeks ago, Kara had returned from a classified mission on Cylon-occupied Caprica. The events of the mission had been upsetting, to say the least, and Lee had done his awkward best to comfort her. And that was when he had said It.

Upon her return, Lee had met her at the airlock and grabbed her in a tight hug. He had followed this with a brotherly kiss that had, for a second, turned into something a little more powerful. Both of them had pulled back in surprise. Others had been present, however, and they hadn't had a chance to talk until later when Lee found her in a locker room, disconsolately bouncing a

Pyramid ball. Lee had asked what was upsetting her, but Kara refused to talk, and Lee filled the silence with words of his own.

You're my friend, and I love you.

The simple phrase, said in Lee's straightforward manner, had gone straight through Kara and stabbed a red-hot nerve she hadn't known existed. It brought up strange feelings, confusing emotions, difficult memories.

You're worthless, Kara. No one loves you. You're just a worthless piece of trash. Her father's voice, the one that brought up hatred, fear, and a strange desire to please, still echoed in her head sometimes, and Lee's words brought it back again. It all confused her, scared her, and she retreated into easy flippancy.

"Lee Adama loves me," she sing-songed at him. Her tone made him turn away, clearly sorry he had said anything. She pressed the advantage, taunting him with playground banter until he had slouched out of the locker room wearing a "Yeah, sure" expression. Neither of them had referred to the incident since, which was just the way Kara wanted it.

Didn't she?

Lee shuffled his feet, looking like he was about twelve. Kara looked at her nails. Tyrol fussed over the Viper.

"Crack in the main manifold," he muttered, "scoring on the cabin, and what the frak happened to the landing gear?"

"Nothing out of the ordinary for Lieutenant Thrace," said Specialist Cally Henderson. She had short brown hair, a round face, and an enormous clipboard. The paper on it was already half covered in notes. Kara waggled some eyebrows at her and Cally shook her head in mock sorrow.

Two elevator pads descended side by side. One bore the Search-and-Rescue Raptor. The SAR Raptor was larger than the "normal" Raptors and sported equipment that let it haul in ships, pods, or other objects in distress. The other pad bore the escape pod. It was large enough to hold over thirty people, if they were friendly. It had two portholes, but Kara couldn't see inside it from where she was standing. The marines quickly stepped up and trained their weapons on the airlock door with the various clacks and clicks of ready weapons.

"Everyone stay back, please," bellowed the Sergeant Major in charge of the platoon. "We're not expecting trouble, but you should remain at a safe distance."

Kara snorted. If "not expecting trouble" meant pointing a dozen pulse rifles and readying a handful of grenades, she was dying to see what "expecting trouble" looked like. She continued to lounge against her Viper, seemingly unconcerned but actually crawling with curiosity. It was sheer coincidence that the Viper's wing was providing a nice bit of cover between her and the pod.

"Where the hell did it come from?" Lee asked beside her.

She shrugged. "Maybe a Colonial ship we don't know about survived the Cylon attack and passed this way."

"Not likely. We've been in this system for days. We would have picked up the distress signal a long time ago. Has to be from the basestar."

"You said that earlier," she pointed out. "Why would a Colonial escape pod be on a Cylon basestar?"

"Maybe we can ask the guy you saw, if the marines don't blow him away."

The wheel on the airlock turned all by itself. The marines remained outwardly impassive, but tension thickened the oily air. The flight crew stopped all pretense of work and stared at the slowly moving wheel. Most had obeyed the Sergeant Major and moved away or stolen behind some kind of cover. The wheel made the familiar cricket-chirp sound that Kara heard every day from doors all over the *Galactica,* and the door swung outward. She tensed, ready to dive fully behind her Viper.

Nothing happened. The doorway stood empty, the inside of the pod completely dark. Kara narrowed her eyes. Someone in there had shut of the light. Why?

The marines stayed in attack formation around the door, their expressions tense. Still nothing moved.

"Attention rescue pod," the Sergeant Major barked. "We have you surrounded!"

Kara pushed back a laugh. Yes, the rescue pod was armed and dangerous. Any minute it would—

Movement exploded from the doorway. Kara caught a glimpse of a woman with long black hair and almond eyes. She wore a green jumpsuit and she moved faster than any human had a right to move. Before the marines could react or even blink, she stiff-armed one of them so hard that he flew backward and crashed into one of his compatriots, bringing both of them down. The woman didn't stop moving. She grabbed a rifle barrel with impossible speed and yanked. The marine holding it left his feet and smashed straight into the heel of her hand. He dropped to the deck and the woman whirled the rifle into firing position. Kara recognized the woman's face and gasped just as the rest of the squadron opened fire. Needles and bullets tore through the woman. She jigged in place as bloody holes ripped through her skin and clothes. Then she dropped to the deck, rifle still in her hand. It clanged against the deck plates.

"Frak," Lee muttered. "Sharon."

Kara nodded. One of the five versions of Cylons Kara—and Lee—had encountered took the form of Raptor pilot Sharon Valerii. Sharon had been a "sleeper" agent, a Cylon who had been programmed with false memories to make her think she was human. Her mission had been to assassinate Commander Adama, and she had nearly succeeded. Her corpse still lay in the morgue. On Caprica, Kara had come across another version of Sharon.

This copy had known she was a Cylon, but she had helped Kara on her mission, and Kara brought the Cylon back with her to *Galactica*. Caprica Sharon currently occupied the brig, and although she had helped *Galactica* fight the Cylons on numerous occasions, it sent cold shivers across Kara's skin to see "her" out in the open.

This version of Sharon was clearly dead, another one for the morgue. Kara pushed through the gathered crowd and saw for herself. Sightless eyes stared at the ceiling, and one of her legs was bent beneath her. Kara pursed her lips, then looked at the pod. It was still dark inside it.

"I saw a man in there," she called to the marines. "Before I came in to land. He's probably still there."

The marines who weren't down or attending to the wounded turned away from Sharon's corpse and trained their rifles on the pod again.

"You in there!" barked the Sergeant Major. "Hands on your head and come out!"

Long pause. Then, "I'm coming. Don't shoot!"

A shadow moved, and a figure stepped slowly out of the pod and into the light, his hands on his head. He looked out at the marines and technicians with an uncertain, hesitating expression. Every marine rifle instantly snapped around to train on him. Kara felt her eyes widen. Frak, the man was *gorgeous*. His golden hair shone like sunshine in the harsh light of the flight deck, and his eyes, blue as a Caprica lake, looked out from a smooth, square-jawed face. He wore a blue short-sleeved shirt cut tight enough to show off an arresting build and arms that begged Kara to run her hands over them so she could feel their corded muscle. She remembered her earlier thoughts on the Viper and felt a little flushed despite the weaponry that bristled around her.

"Don't shoot!" the man said, and his voice was smooth and light, almost boyish but still fully a man's. "I'm not a Cylon!"

Kara stared at him. His voice sounded familiar, and the more she looked at him, the more it seemed like she should know him. But she couldn't put her finger on why.

"Lie face-down on the ground," the Sergeant Major said. "Now!"

Slowly, the man obeyed. He looked alone and vulnerable in front of the pod. Kara felt sorry for him, though she knew full well that he could be another Cylon. The Fleet had been tricked far too often to trust a newcomer easily.

Two marines put a set of heavy shackles on the blond man. He didn't resist. He also didn't speak. Two more marines disappeared into the pod, rifles at the ready, and reemerged to report that no one else was inside. The Sergeant Major hauled the blond man to his feet. He still looked familiar.

"Oh my gods!" Cally said abruptly. She was clutching her clipboard to her chest. "That's Peter Attis!"

And then it clicked for Kara. Peter Attis. Rock star. His image had graced posters and album covers and magazine pages all over the Twelve Colonies. He had started his career when he was sixteen, and his song "My Heart Has Eyes for Only You" had soared to the top of the charts. Kara, then thirteen, had decorated her bedroom with his pictures and collected every single song. In school she had doodled in her notebook every possible combination of her name and his—Kara Attis. Peter Thrace. Kara Attis-Thrace. Mrs. K. Thrace-Attis—accompanied by the required heart over the i in "Attis." Thank the Lords of Kobol she had outgrown that phase right quick and that no one had ever seen those notebooks.

A murmur went through the assembled group. Several had recognized him, too. Peter's music had matured along with him, which garnered him fans from every part of the age spectrum. He had even gone through a brief but intense grunge phase, which Kara still listened to.

Leaving Lee behind, Kara stepped forward to get a better look. The prisoner was shackled and Kara outranked the Sergeant Major, so the marine didn't object. Peter looked at her with the bluest eyes Kara had ever seen. For a moment, Kara was thirteen again, and her heart was racing with a strange thrill.

"Peter Attis?" she said. The teenaged fangirl inside her jumped up and down and said, *I have all your records. I think you're the greatest!* Kara told it to shut the hell up and instead said, "Hell, I used to listen to all your stuff." The half-quashed teenager put a little too much enthusiasm into Kara's voice, so she added, "But that was a frakking long time ago."

"Thanks," Peter said, and flashed a wide smile that went straight down to Kara's toes. "It's always nice to meet a fan—or former fan. Uh . . . even when I'm chained hand and foot."

All at once, Kara was aware of her surroundings. She cleared her throat and backed up a step. "Just a precaution," she said. "Though I'm sure *you* couldn't be a Cylon."

"And why is that, Lieutenant?" asked Colonel Saul Tigh behind her.

Kara bit the inside of her cheek and turned to face him. Tigh was somewhere in his sixties, with a short fringe of white hair surrounding his bald pate. He wore his navy blue Executive Officer's uniform stiffly, as it were filled with wood and wire instead of skin and muscle, and his face was screwed into a permanent mask of disapproval. Behind Colonel Tigh stood Commander Bill Adama and Dr. Gaius Baltar. Adama's craggy, acne-scarred face looked grave. He and Tigh were of an age, but Kara thought Adama wore his years far better. Gaius Baltar was much younger, a genius with computers, physics, and some areas of biology. He was also the vice president of the Colonies.

"Peter Attis can't be a Cylon because his history is too well-established, sir," Kara said to Tigh, keeping her dislike out of her voice but not bothering to disguise a small sneer. "He's been a star since he was sixteen years old, and lots of people recognize his face. He has family—or he did. A brother and two sisters and parents."

"They all died in the attack, though," Peter said softly.

"So there's no way to verify his identity," Tigh said. "He came from a Cylon ship, and I'm thinking he needs an introduction to the nearest airlock."

"I'm not a Cylon," Peter repeated. His voice was calm but his face was pale. "What can I say that might convince you?"

Kara gave Adama a desperate look. "Commander, shouldn't we—"

"We've been bitten by too many snakes, Lieutenant," Adama said. "I think the Colonel may be right."

"Isn't he handsome?" Number Six whispered in Gaius Baltar's ear. Her breath was warm and wet on his skin, and her slender hands lay hot on his shoulders. He could see her out of the corner of his eye, though long practice had taught him not to spin around to look at her. He was standing at the back of the crowd, but someone might still see, and people looked at you funny when you acknowledged the presence of empty air.

"If you go in for that type," he said softly. "And before you ask, I never have done, thank you."

Number Six smiled. She was a tall, heavy-breasted woman with pale blond hair, gray eyes, and full, red lips. At the moment she was wearing a pale blue dress that flowed in some areas, clung in others.

"Jealous?" she said.

"You can't be serious," he responded. The second word came out more like *cahnt*. "He's a singing ape with the IQ of a trained poodle."

She ran a finger across the back of his neck, sending shivers down his spine. He half closed his eyes in catlike satisfaction. No one could see—or hear or feel—Cylon Humanoid Model Number Six except him. Back home on Caprica, he had thought she was a real human woman, one genuinely attracted to his natural charisma, brilliant mind, and well-toned physique. She was the most inventive lover he had ever taken to his bed, and Gaius's bed had been a playground for more years than he cared to count. Only later had he learned how she had tricked him, seduced him into giving up the secrets to Caprica's computerized defense network. The Cylons had penetrated the Twelve Colonies moments later, and Gaius himself had barely escaped death. No one on the Fleet knew about his treason—except Number Six. He had seen her die on Caprica, but now she appeared to him like some strange ghost, able to touch him, push him around. Seduce him. She had initially claimed to be a hallucination created by a chip the Cylons had implanted in his head, but Gaius had gotten his brain scanned, and no chip had turned up. He had since given up trying to define what she was or where she came from.

"Looks like you won't have to worry about him for long, Gaius," Six murmured. "They're going to toss him out an airlock. Typical mistrustful behavior."

"Yes, you and your kind have given us so many reasons to trust everyone." But the rebuke was mild, almost habitual.

"And you'll never get the chance to learn what he's really about."

Here he did turn his head. Fortunately, he was at the back of the crowd and no one noticed. "What do you mean?"

"It doesn't matter, does it?" Six nodded at Adama and Tigh. "Look at them. They're going to have Peter killed. And his secrets die with him."

"Why would I care about his secrets?" Gaius snorted, though he found himself staring at Peter Attis.

"You won't," Six said. "He's going to die before anyone even knows he *has* secrets. Too bad. There's glory in working out a puzzle like his."

"Commander," Gaius called out. He wormed his way through the crowd of people gathered around the Raptor. "Commander, if I may?"

"What is it, Doctor?" Adama said in the tired tone he often used with Gaius. It was a tone Gaius found immensely irritating. He was the vice president of the Colonies and the single most intelligent human being in the Fleet, yet Adama insisted on treating him like an annoying flunky.

"I think it might be best if we—if *someone*—interrogated this man first. If he's a Cylon, it would benefit us to learn all we can from him. If he's human, he clearly lived among the Cylons as their prisoner for quite some time, and he might have valuable insight into their thinking. He could hardly be a threat in the brig, in any case."

"I think Doctor Gaius is right, sir," Kara Thrace said.

"Which means we should definitely toss him," Tigh growled.

Adama's face remained impassive. He looked at Kara, then at Tigh and Gaius. Gaius held his breath.

"Toss him," Adama said shortly, and turned to leave.

CHAPTER

3

The marines dragged Peter away. An expression of terror twisted his handsome face and he was shouting incoherently, struggling against his bonds.

"Commander, please!" Kara and Baltar said simultaneously. Their words tumbled out in an overlapping rush.

"You're making a terrible mistake! Who knows what he might know? There's no proof he's a Cylon. You could be executing an innocent man. How could it hurt to put him in the brig? We've had Sharon on board for weeks, and she's only helped us. Peter might be able to tell us about the Cylons, things we'd never find out on our own."

Adama remained silent.

"I'll interrogate him myself, Commander," Kara added. "If there's any hint that he's a Cylon, I'll space him myself. Please."

"Yes, please," Baltar added.

Adama looked at them both for a long moment. Kara held her breath. It seemed like she could already hear Peter's silent scream as his tortured body floated through harsh vacuum. When she was drawing hearts and combining names in her school notebook, she had never thought she might be involved in trying to save Peter's life. His music had gotten her through some tough times. When she was young, the bouncy pop rhythms created a safe space far away from her father, and she fantasized that Peter might sweep into her life and take her to safety. As she grew older, Peter's music changed. His brief grunge phase had produced two albums that had spoken to Kara at a time when her emotions had been as thick and black as the music Peter produced. The albums he had done in adulthood hadn't grabbed her as much, but she still remembered how his voice had reflected her own mood and the sympathy she had found there.

"All right," Adama said at last. "Take him to the brig. I want both of you to interrogate him. Have Lee there, too."

"Thank you, sir!" Kara said over her shoulder. She was already sprinting after the marines. She didn't see Lee watching her with an odd look on his face.

Peter sat, pale and stunned, behind a table bolted to the floor in the brig. He had already thrown up twice, but he had assured Kara that the nausea had passed. She hoped so. The sour smell of vomit wasn't something she enjoyed, especially when it was someone else's.

The brig interrogation room was chilly. Bare blue walls, a single metal door with a thick glass window, and a set of chairs bolted to the floor were all that greeted "visitors." Kara faced Peter with Baltar beside her and Lee standing behind. Peter was still in chains. He also looked . . . different to Kara. It was subtle, but noticeable. His hair was disheveled, and he needed a shave. Fine lines radiated away from his eyes, lines that didn't belong on a man barely over thirty. His lips were thin with fear. The Peter who appeared on vids and posters and album covers was smooth and perfect—handsome, but in a plastic sort of way. This Peter was real, a man who breathed and sweated and chewed his nails. And he was all the more attractive for it. As a child, she'd had a crush on dream. As an adult, she wanted something more solid, and this Peter looked pretty solid.

Kara gave a slight shake of her head. This was weird. She was actually sitting across a table from Peter Attis. Okay, so her teenage fantasies hadn't involved handcuffs and leg irons—those came when she was rather older—but still.

"I wanted to say thanks," Peter said hoarsely. "For saving my life."

"Don't thank me yet," Kara said. "If you can't convince Lee and Baltar here that you aren't a toaster, they'll still space you, and I promised to hit the big red button."

"So *you* don't think I'm a Cylon," Peter said.

"I doubt you are," Kara told him carefully, "but I can't say I know for sure."

"I don't know how I can convince you," Peter said. He tried to spread his hands, but the shackles prevented him. "They look just like us. Or some of them do."

"Tell us what happened to you," Baltar said.

"Yeah," Lee said. His arms were folded across his chest. "Do tell."

"Uh . . . I'm from Libron," Peter replied. His voice was smooth and arresting, almost hypnotic. "My band and I were on tour, and we were giving a concert on a cruise ship. That was when the Cylons attacked. It was . . . everyone was panicking. Alarms were going off, lights flashing. My bodyguards disappeared, but no one seemed to care who I was anyway. Something blew up and threw us all to the floor. I found out later that half the ship had been destroyed and we—those of us who survived— were trapped on the other half. Radiation alarms kept blaring that rad levels were 'unacceptably high.' A bunch of us made it to an escape pod. We crowded inside. More people tried to push their way in, but there just wasn't room. I remember how we . . . we slammed the door in their faces." Peter's voice was shaking now. "The last person I saw was a little boy, maybe eight years old. He knew he was going to die, you could see it in his eyes."

Kara found tears pricking at the corners of her own eyes. She forced them back and told herself this could be nothing more than a story told by a Cylon desperate to convince her that he was human. Just because he was handsome and famous didn't mean he wasn't a liar. The tears ebbed.

"Then what?" Lee asked.

"Someone hit the release and the pod pushed off." Peter's eyes hardened. "That was when the Cylons grabbed us. They hauled the pod onto one of their ships. We all thought we were dead. Later, we just wished we were. Or I did, anyway."

"What happened?" Baltar said, exuding empathy.

"All of us were split up. You're the first humans I've seen since then." His voice was flat, without emotion. "They brought me to a laboratory and . . . here it gets a little hazy. I think I was drugged a lot of the time. I remember . . . I remember pain. A lot of needles. Bright light. I remember lying in bed, shaking and convulsing like a beheaded snake. A voice was babbling nonsense, and it took me a while to realize it was my own. I couldn't stop babbling. And I remember some strange robots looking down at me, doing things that hurt. And I remember a woman with blond hair. She was there a lot."

A strange expression crossed Baltar's face and almost instantly vanished. Kara wondered what that was about.

"And then one day a woman—a different woman—came to my bed at the lab. I was pretty zoned out. She said that they were all done with me. I thought they were going to kill me then, and I was glad. It would stop hurting. But the woman didn't kill me. She took me out of the bed, gave me some clothes—I was naked—and took me . . . I think she took me home with her. I mean, it was kind of like an apartment, but it was dark and damp all the time. The woman told me to call her Mistress Eight. I asked her what happened to the others in the pod and she said they all had died. She said it like you might say a houseplant or pet rat had died. I asked why I hadn't been killed. She just smiled and said the others hadn't been killed—they had died, and there was a difference. She wouldn't tell me any more than that. Maybe she was lying. I don't know."

A flicker of movement caught Kara's eye. She glanced at the window set into the door and saw the faces of two female crew. Both of them were staring. One of them said something to the other, and Kara saw her mouth "Peter Attis" with an excited look on her face. She glared at them. They gave sheepish smiles and vanished. Kara turned her attention back to Peter.

"Why did she bring you to her . . . apartment?" she asked. It seemed strange, the idea that Cylons would have places to live. What did robots need with a bed and a bathroom?

Here Peter's jaw trembled. "She kept me as a pet. Put a collar on me. Showed me off to her friends."

"Showed you off?" Lee asked.

"Mostly she made me sing for them, like a trained songbird or something," Peter said bitterly. "She kept me in a little cage most of the time. Sometimes she made me wait on her like a servant."

"Or a slave," Kara said without thinking.

"Yeah."

"So how did you get on the escape pod?" Lee demanded. His tone was belligerent.

"I'm not completely sure," Peter admitted. "Mistress Eight pulled me out of my cage and made me follow her at a run. Alarms were going off all over the place. We got into the escape pod—I hadn't seen it in weeks—and she shoved it off. Then everything was exploding and bouncing around and everything. Was that you guys? Did you destroy their ship?"

"How did you know it was a ship?" Lee asked.

Peter shrugged. "That's what *they* called it. I never really thought about it. I . . . tried not to think at all."

"What's your favorite color?" Kara asked abruptly.

"What? Uh, blue."

"What's your favorite food?"

"Red beans and rice. Why? What does—"

"Who was the drummer for 'My Heart Has Eyes for Only You'?"

"Peter Deimos. It caused all kinds of confusion, so we all called him Deimos. He hated that."

"Who was your first real girlfriend?"

"Pamela Gallic. We were twelve. What's this all about?"

Kara sat back, arms folded. "He's genuine."

"Why?" Baltar said. "Because he can answer questions of the sort you find in *Teen Tiger* magazine?"

"How do *you* know what's in *Teen Tiger*?" Kara countered.

"All facets of human nature fascinate me," Baltar said airily.

Three more faces appeared at the interrogation room window, all female. Their eyes went round when they saw Peter. Lee made an impatient gesture, and they fled.

"Look," Kara said, "I admit it. I am—*was*—a huge Peter Attis fan when I was a kid. If he's a sleeper agent for the Cylons, he's been one since he was a teenager. How likely is that?"

"He could be a construct with the memories of Peter Attis," Lee said.

"That would be a first," Baltar said. "The Cylons have never done such a thing before."

"I'm sitting right here," Peter reminded them. "Shackled and chained, but sitting right here. I'm not a dog or a lamp."

"Shut up," Lee said. "We'll the ask the questions."

"This is how the Cylons treated me," Peter said softly.

Baltar suddenly twisted in his chair, as if someone had tapped him on the shoulder or whispered in his ear. "Well, that's—" Then he cut himself off, blinked rapidly, and added, "—that's . . . very interesting."

"What is?" Lee asked.

Baltar looked nonplused. "That's very interesting . . . how . . . how he—I mean, Peter—how he thinks . . . of us." He cleared his throat and loosened his tie. Kara noticed he was looking a little flushed. His right arm twitched. Kara tried to edge away from him, no mean feat in a chair that was bolted to the floor. Baltar had a weird reputation around the Fleet, for all that he was vice president. He had a penchant for talking and gesturing to himself in public, as if he were holding a private argument. And some of his other behavior was definitely off. Kara had once walked into his lab and found him leaning over a table in a very strange position. His fly had been down and the tail of his shirt was sticking out of it. Kara didn't press for details. Most people passed this off as a side effect of genius, but Kara was beginning to wonder if Gaius Baltar might simply be a frakking lunatic.

"I mean," Baltar continued, "that Peter here may be right. After all, we can't be suspicious of every little thing every person does. The Cylons would love to know that we're at each other's throats." His left hand suddenly leaped up and clutched at his right shoulder. He changed the gesture into a scratching motion, as if he'd had a sudden itch.

"We have to tell the Commander *something*," Lee said. "I doubt he'll accept interviews from *Teen Tiger* as evidence that he's not a spy."

"Proving something doesn't exist is almost impossible," Kara pointed out. "I mean, how do you prove someone can't fly? Shove them off a building and see what happens?"

"Fortunately," Baltar said, "we have a less drastic method."

"Peter Attis!"

Kara watched as Peter stared at the woman on the other side of the mesh-reinforced Plexiglas. He was still in shackles, and two armed marines stood on either side of him. His face remained stony and expressionless, but Kara thought she detected a slight tremor in his body. The woman in the cell had almond eyes, black hair, full lips, and a slender build, though if you looked carefully, you could see a slight rounding to her stomach—an encroaching sign of pregnancy. She also wore a look of utter surprise.

"So you know who he is," Lee said into the telephone receiver.

"Don't you?" she countered into her own telephone. Lee held his receiver out so everyone could hear her voice, faint and tinny. "Look, my memories of being a teenager may be implanted and fake, but they feel real to me. I remember having a crush on him and wishing I could see him at a live concert."

"Is he a Cylon?"

"What are you, stupid? They don't make copies of real people, and even if they did, they wouldn't use someone famous as a sleeper agent. They use someone . . . someone like me. No one could verify my past because the Troy colony was destroyed in a mining accident and no records survived. That's not the case with someone like Peter Attis. He's too public, too well-known."

The use of "they" instead of "we" didn't go past Kara unnoticed. Sharon Valerii was a Cylon, but she believed—or acted like she believed—her own people to be the enemy. Just a few days ago, she had defeated a Cylon computer virus that had invaded *Galactica*'s systems and sent the Cylons a virus of her own. She had helped Kara complete her mission on Caprica. But every time she looked at Sharon, Kara saw the traitor who had pulled out a pistol and shot Commander Adama in the stomach. Kara knew that killer Sharon's body currently lay in the morgue and that this version of Sharon had done nothing but help *Galactica*. This didn't matter to Kara in the slightest. Every time she saw the woman—Cylon—Kara felt an animalistic urge to wrap her fingers around Sharon's throat and squeeze.

But Kara also looked at Sharon and saw a friend, a fellow pilot, and someone who had saved her life. The conflicting emotions made Kara uncertain and uncomfortable, which was why she avoided the brig as much as possible.

"Look, he's not a Cylon," Sharon said. "If he were, I'd tell you. If the Cylons sent another agent here to destroy the *Galactica*, I'd die along with everyone else, and so would my baby." She unconsciously ran a hand over her stomach, a completely human gesture that made Kara want to hit her and give her a hug at the same time.

"Bitch!" Peter yelled. He smashed at the Plexiglas with his shackled wrists. They left a slight scratch. "Frakking *bitch!*"

Kara jumped, adrenaline zinging through her. Lee, also startled, dropped the phone as the marines instantly moved in to haul Peter back. He clawed and snarled at the Plexiglas. Sharon shrank away from him.

"I frakking hate you!" Peter snarled, fighting unsuccessfully to free himself from the grip of two powerful marines. "If they can't kill you, I will!"

Kara got in front of him, blocking his view of Sharon. "Peter!" she said in a calm, firm voice. "Peter, listen to me! That is *not* your Mistress Eight. It's not her." Without knowing why, she reached out and took his face between her two hands. His skin was warm on hers. She moved in close and looked straight into his blue eyes. Their foreheads touched, and her breath mingled with his. He was real. He was solid. "Peter, it's not her. Your . . . 'mistress' is dead. You saw them shoot her down in front of the pod. That's not her."

"Why is she there?" he demanded in a hoarse whipser. "Gods, what's going on?"

Kara continued to meet his eyes, forcing him by strength of will to lock his gaze with hers. "You said your mistress made you sing for her friends. Didn't any of her friends look alike?"

"A couple," he said. "I thought they were twins or something."

"There are many copies of each different type of Cylon," Kara said. "This one is a copy of your mistress, but she's our prisoner. She didn't do anything to you, and she can't hurt you. Do you understand?"

He looked long and hard into Kara's eyes. A little thrill traveled over her skin. She wondered what it would be like to pull him closer, hold him, kiss him. It felt like his gaze was going through her, touching something deep inside her that she didn't want touched. She was about to pull away when she caught Lee Adama looking her, at them. He looked almost . . . angry. A flash of her own anger rose to the occasion. What right did he have to be angry at her? He had no hold on her. Just to show him that, she turned her full attention back to Peter. Tears welled in his eyes.

"It's all right," she said. "You've been places where none of

us have gone. But you're home now, with us. Do you understand?"

"Yes," he said in a small voice. "Thank you."

Kara hugged him. It was a one-way embrace—Peter was
still shackled, and the marines hadn't released their hold on his
arms. But Peter gave a heavy sigh and Kara felt his breath warm
the collar of her shirt. After a moment, she released him and
reached for the phone near Sharon's cell. Sharon herself had retreated to her bed, removing herself from Peter's line of sight.
Kara punched buttons. After a moment, Dualla came on the line
and transferred her to Commander Adama.

"We've interrogated Peter Attis," Kara said, "and we're con-
vinced he isn't a Cylon."

"All three of you?" Adama asked.

"Yeah—me, Lee, and Doctor Baltar. We all agree." She shot
Baltar and Lee a hard glare that dared either of them to say different. They remained silent. Lee raised his hands in mock de-
feat.

"Then release him," Adama said.

"Thank you, sir." Kara hung up. "Sergeant, unshackle Mis-
ter Attis. He's not a Cylon and doesn't belong in chains or a
cage."

"Yes, sir."

Kara stood carefully between Peter and Sharon's cell so he
wouldn't have to see her as the shackles fell away with clatters
and clanks. "Let's go, okay? I'll show you around *Galactica* and
we'll find you a place to stay."

"A place to stay," he echoed. "You mean, I can't go home?"

Kara lead him firmly away from the brig. Lee and Baltar followed a little uncertainly. The battered metal corridors and
walkways that made up *Galactica*'s innards snaked ahead of
them in a dizzying array of directions. The Battlestar *Galactica*

was the size of a skyscraper turned sideways, and even the engineering crews got lost if they left their own section. People in a variety of uniforms rushed about on errands only they understood, and the PA system crackled with orders and announcements almost continuously. Several crewmembers stared as Peter passed them by.

"Not exactly," Kara said. "The Cylons . . . they kind of took over the Colonies. Destroyed them."

Peter's knees buckled and Kara grabbed him before he fell. "All twelve?"

"Yeah. Sorry to be the one to tell you." Kara planted herself until Peter could regain his feet. "The Cylons somehow managed to breach the defenses. We still don't know exactly how, but when they show up and start shooting, you don't stop to ask questions, you know? Some traitor seems to have given them the codes."

Now Baltar stumbled, and Lee caught his shoulder to keep him from falling. Kara mentally rolled her eyes. The man was supposed to be brilliant, but he had the coordination of newborn kitten.

"A bunch of ships managed to escape together," Lee said. "Including the *Galactica* here. There are still a few in hiding back on the Colonies, but as far as we know, most of the humans left in the universe are here in the Fleet."

"So how many people are left?" Peter asked. He was walking on his own again, but his face was pale.

"Something around forty-seven thousand," Kara told him. They turned a corner and went down a staircase. "President Roslin keeps an exact tally, but—"

"President *Roslin?* Isn't she the Secretary of Welfare or something?"

"Education," Lee said. "But now she's president."

"And I'm vice president," Baltar put in quickly.

"Let me buy you a drink," Kara said, clapping Peter on the shoulder, "and I'll fill you in. Then you can fill *me* in."

Peter gave her a long look. Kara looked back. For once, she didn't feel thirteen. The moment stretched long, though it couldn't have lasted more than a few seconds.

"Fill you in?" Peter said at last.

Lee coughed hard. Kara ignored him. "About what happened to you with the Cylons."

"Ah."

"Before we do that," Lee said, "I think we should take our guest to sickbay."

"What for?" Kara asked.

"A thorough physical," Lee replied grimly.

"I got nothing here." Dr. Cottle removed the cigarette from his mouth and used it to gesture at the readout. The smell of smoke awoke tobacco cravings in Kara and she longed for a cigar, the one she had been looking forward to before Peter's pod showed up. Behind them, Peter Attis himself lay on a table, his head and upper body beneath an overhanging shelf that scanned him repeatedly while he remained perfectly still. "You can see for yourself. No tracers, no chips, no implants, no Cylonitis. If the Cylons sent him here so they could somehow use him to track the Fleet, they didn't do a very good job."

"He says the Cylons had him in a medical facility for a while," Lee said. "Anything to indicate what they might have done to him?"

"Nothing I can see," Cottle said. "Soft-tissue injuries won't show, though. He broke his left humerus some time ago—"

"I fell off a horse," Peter said.

"He was twelve," Kara added.

"I'm not sure we should ask how you know that," Baltar said.

"Right." Cottle took a heavy drag from his cigarette. "Anyway, the break's long since healed. I don't see any metabolic problems and he's not carrying any weird viruses or bacteria. There's more I could probably tell you about him, but it gets a little personal."

"Spare us, then," Lee muttered.

"So I pass?" Peter asked from the table.

"You're done, kid," Cottle said to Peter. "Get the hell out of my sickbay so I can attend to some real patients."

"Gladly." Peter rolled off the examination table, careful to avoid cracking his head on the scanner. Chloe Eseas, a medical technician, helped him up. Sickbay, like most of *Galactica*, was cluttered and clunky, with pieces of medical equipment crammed into corners and odd places. Lighting alternated between too dim and too bright, and the place never seemed completely clean, for all that it was the closest thing to a hospital the Fleet had.

"So you're really Peter Attis?" Chloe said.

"That's me," he said, getting to his feet. He wore a sickbay gown that closed—more or less—in the back.

"Wow. I have all your songs. Or I did until the Cylons attacked. What was it like singing a duet with Penelope Troy?"

"She was great," Peter said vaguely. "Really talented. Are my clothes somewhere nearby?"

While Peter dressed behind a screen, Cottle ground out the remains of his current cigarette and tapped another on the back of his hand. Kara was half ready to ask him for one, though she didn't really do cigarettes and preferred to save her cigars for special occasions, like card games or post-mission gloating.

"How's the harvest coming along, Captain?" Cottle asked

as he shut down the scanner. "Are we going to abandon Planet Goop? The Cylons know we're here now, unless you managed to kill them before they transmitted a signal to wherever the hell it is they transmit to."

"I have no idea, doc," Lee said. "You'll probably find out when I do."

"We need the meds that goop can make for us," Cottle said. He nodded toward a glass-doored cabinet. There was space for several hundred drug ampules, but Kara counted fewer than ten. "That's my entire store of radiation meds, Captain. Once that goes, your DNA is on its own. We might even be able to synthesize some more antibiotics, too, but—"

"But not if we leave Planet Goop," Lee finished.

"Don't interrupt your elders, son," Cottle growled around his cigarette. "It ain't polite. Even when they're stating the obvious."

Commander William Adama stood in the center of a whirlwind. People hustled around the CIC, checking printouts, making urgent calls, and tapping keyboards. The Dradis continued its low, metallic growl as it scanned in all directions for Cylons. A dozen monitors flickered with graphics, videos, and data readouts. Saul Tigh sometimes stood behind Adama and sometimes lurked around the workstations. It made the crew nervous to have Tigh suddenly pop up behind one of them to bark a question or an order, but Adama had given up trying to get him to stop. Commanding a fleet was a lot like juggling cats in a rainstorm—sometimes you had to let the small stuff slide because something big with claws was waiting to drop on your head.

"Update on the evacuation, Lieutenant?" Adama asked.

"Half done, sir," Tactical Officer Anastasia Dualla reported from her station. She wore a headset that covered one ear and slung a microphone across her mouth. "The *Monarch* should be ready for takeoff in under half an hour."

"I'll have Jump coordinates ready for them by then, sir," put in Felix Gaeta. "We should be all right."

"If the frakking Cylons don't pop up again," Tigh growled. "And they will. Mark it."

"How much more food are they estimating we'll be able to extract from the algae?" Adama asked.

"It's hard to give anything beyond a rough estimate, sir," Gaeta hedged.

"Just answer the damn question, Lieutenant," Tigh ordered.

Gaeta pursed his lips and kept his eyes on Adama, who was also ignoring Tigh. "We might get an extra week out of what we have so far. Ten days at most."

"A week?" Tigh shouted. "That's nothing! They were down there for four days. What the hell were they doing?"

"Is that a rhetorical question, sir, or do you want an answer?" Gaeta asked with utter politeness.

"It's not damned rhetorical," Tigh snapped. "What have they been doing down there?"

"The *Monarch* is a mining ship," Gaeta replied. "It took time to adapt its operations from digging to scooping. Also, Planet Goop has an atmosphere but it isn't breathable. Putting everyone in breathing masks makes everything harder to see and slows down operations. We also have to rotate the crew because of the radiation levels, and the workers can only take so much radiation exposure. Suppiles of anti-radiation meds are limited. That slows things down as well."

"Sounds like a lot of excuses to me," Tigh said. "You need to—"

"Sir, with respect, I'm just the messenger. May I suggest that you address your . . . concerns to the captain of the *Monarch*? She's the head of the harvest operation, not me."

"I think I'll do just that. Dualla, get me Renee Demeter on the line. Now!"

This caught Adama's attention. Tigh was clearly in the wrong, bent on solving impossible problems by shouting at subordinates, as if yelling would make them suddenly able to work miracles. But now Gaeta had managed to point him in another direction, toward the *Monarch*. Renee Demeter was captain of her own ship. She answered to no one but Adama, and then only in matters that concerned her ship's role in the Fleet. On the *Monarch*, she was sovereign, and Tigh had no authority over her. If Tigh started shouting at her and calling her incompetent in public, she would answer in kind and he would come across looking like an idiot. Adama shot Gaeta a hard look. Had he set Tigh up on purpose? Adama wouldn't put it past him. Gaeta had a subtle touch when it came to handling conflict. But Gaeta's expression was bland as a sand dune.

"Belay that order, Dee," Adama said. "I think Captain Demeter has enough to worry about right now. Getting those people off the planet before another wave of Cylons shows up is more important."

For a moment Tigh looked ready to challenge Adama's order. Adama looked at him, bland as Gaeta. Then Tigh straightened his uniform and turned to look at the video feeds. Adama closed his eyes. Another cat successfully juggled. What was next?

"Sir," Dualla said. She was a dark-skinned woman with surpring hazel eyes. "President Roslin is on the line for you."

I had to ask, he thought, and picked up a receiver from the central station. It had a cord attached to it. Adama remembered the days of cellular communication, computer networks, and wireless everything. The Cylons, however, had taken to networks like lions to antelope. The frakking things could infect and wipe out a network in seconds, fatally crippling whatever systems the network ran. So the Colonies had tossed digital out the window and stampeded to bring back analog. It made hell out of computing an FTL Jump when your drive computer couldn't talk to your helm computer, but it sure beat the Cylons twitching your network from a distance and making you land in the heart of star. Later, after everyone thought the Cylons were gone for good, the military had cautiously returned to networking its computers. Adama, however, had refused to allow it on the *Galactica*, and thank the Lords of Kobol for that. Far as he knew, every other Battlestar had fallen victim to Cylon viruses. The *Galactica* alone had not.

"Madam President," Adama said, resisting an urge to play with the phone cord. "A pleasure."

"Commander." Laura Roslin's voice was warm as always, but Adama's practiced ear caught the undercurrent of pain and fatigue. Roslin was suffering, in every sense of the word, from terminal breast cancer. She had kept it a secret for months, using experimental treatments to force pain and weakness to stay at arm's length, but lately the malignant tissue had made terrible encroachments into her body. Within the month, she would be dead. Adama refused to let himself think about this—he was juggling cats, after all—but the small part of his mind that never quite did what it was told feared that the grief from her loss would devastate him. Only the thought that Gaius Baltar would become president in her stead frightened him more.

"I hear the Monarch is pulling up stakes," she said.

"That's true."

"The latest projections tell me we've only harvested eight days worth of food material, and that's if we refine none of it for anti-radiation meds and antibiotics."

Apparently Roslin had access to better information than Adama did. It didn't really surprise him. "That's close to what I've heard, yes."

"Are you sure we need to evacuate right now, Bill?" she said. *"You know your job and I realize you're keeping our safety in mind, but we also really need that algae. It's not just the food. Medicinal supplies are at an all-time low. The Lesbos is dealing with an outbreak of strep that's eating up antibiotics. We've tried to make the adults suffer through it on their own and reserve the remaining meds for the children, but that only means the adults reinfect the kids."*

Adama nodded, though Roslin couldn't see him. "I know, Madam President." He couldn't quite bring himself to call her "Laura" when other people were within earshot. "But the Cylons must know we're here, and it's only a matter of time before they send another basestar or a flock of Raiders."

Roslin sighed heavily. *"I trust you to know what's best when it comes to Fleet security. I'm also worried about the food and meds. Bill, is there any compromise on this? It's been over an hour since the Cylon attack. Maybe they aren't coming back for a while."*

Adama tightened his lips. He knew the food and medicine supplies were tight—they had been since the first day after the attack. Now it seemed as if the Lords of Kobol had handed them a bounteous harvest only to have the Cylons chase them away like lions chasing a herd away from the watering hole.

"They always come back," he said. "But I wonder . . ."

"Yes, Bill?"

He sighed. There were risks, and there were risks. The lack of food and medicine would kill them just as surely, if not as quickly, as the Cylons. "Maybe we can evacuate the planet and wait a day or so. If the Cylons show up, we can Jump away. If they don't, we can resume the harvest."

"Sounds like a plan," Roslin said, relief temporarily overcoming the fatigue in her voice. Adama could almost see her behind her desk on the *Colonial One*, stray tendrils of her glossy auburn hair getting caught in her glasses while she flipped through reports and signed papers. Billy Keikeya, her chief aide, would be hovering near her elbow with more bulletins and paperwork.

Adama grimaced and banished the image. Roslin, he happened to know, spent most of her time these days propped up on a couch next to her desk. Her hair had become lackluster and brittle, her skin pasty, her face drawn with pain. He wondered if the real reason he was allowing the Fleet to remain in orbit around Planet Goop was that it would make Laura Roslin happy and bring some small relief to her stress and suffering.

"I'll expect to see you over a dinner of fresh algae salad when this is over, Madam President," he said, as if Roslin had never heard the word "cancer."

"Count on it, Commander," she said, and rang off.

Karl "Helo" Agathon checked his watch and lengthened his stride. He was a tall man, almost rangy, with close-cropped dark hair and a narrow face. He was also late for his appointment in the brig.

Helo trotted around and through the groups of people who kept getting in his way. Familiar ship sounds echoed around him—the slight hiss of carbon dioxide scrubbers, the tromp of soldier boots, the cricket creak of a hatch opening or closing. Sharon had so little to look forward to, so little to *do*. He knew his daily visits were the high point—hell, the *only* point—of her day. He hated seeing her in the brig, locked behind steel mesh and unyielding Plexiglas. He couldn't even hear her voice except through a telephone line, let alone touch her face or hold her hand. It wasn't fair. Sharon—this copy of her—hadn't done anything to anyone. It was the frakking opposite, in fact. She had saved Helo's life on Caprica numerous times, helped Starbuck retrieve the Arrow of Apollo, and just a couple days ago had single-handedly destroyed an entire fleet of Cylon raiders. And now she was carrying Helo's child.

He dodged around an ensign who was half-hidden behind a stack of papers. Yeah, some people insisted that Sharon was only frakking with him, that she had tricked him into falling in love because the Cylons were desperate to conceive children of their own, and Cylon women could only get pregnant if love was involved.

During the Cylon invasion, Sharon, a pilot, had left Helo on Caprica when Helo had given up his seat on her Raptor to a refugee. Helo had then gone on the run from Cylon troops, certain they would eventually catch up with him. And then Sharon showed up again, almost out of nowhere. Together they ran a harrowing journey across Caprica to a spaceport, where they stole a ship to rendezvous with *Galactica*. Along the way, they had fallen in love and accidentally conceived a child. Or Helo had thought the child was accidental. Only later had he learned that his lover was a different Sharon, that this Sharon had been *assigned* to make him fall in love with her to see if she could conceive. The flaw was that Sharon had fallen in love with Helo as well, and instead of turning Helo over to the other Cylons after the conception, she had helped him escape and fled with him to the *Galactica*.

Now she spent her days in the brig, mistrusted and hated by the few crewmembers who knew about her. It made Helo's blood boil to think about it. Keeping a pregnant woman in the brig—how humane was that? But Adama remained firm. Caprica Sharon, as she was sometimes called, would stay in the brig for the foreseeable future. As a prisoner of war, there would be no trial, no lawyer, no judge. Just Adama.

Helo realized his footsteps were pounding angrily on the deck plates, as if he could punch holes through them like an angry giant. He forced himself to calm down. Sharon was under enough stress. She didn't need his tension adding to hers.

Helo took the familiar staircase down to the brig and headed up the side corridor to the cell block specially designed to hold a Cylon. He emerged in a dimly lit open space. Sharon's cell was ahead of him, but the two marines assigned to guard her day and night were nowhere to be seen. It took Helo a startled second to realize that the marines were both sprawled motionless on the floor. The door to Sharon's cell stood quietly open. The interior was empty. Helo froze. A thousand different thoughts flicked through his head. Part of him exulted. Another part of him worried. Yet another felt a pang of fear. Indecision held him motionless. Should he raise the alarm first or check the marines? Maybe he should just . . . leave. Let someone else find the scene, give Sharon a good head start to wherever she was going. Or maybe he should—

Someone tapped his shoulder from behind. His heart jerked and Helo whirled. He got a tiny glimpse of the snarl that twisted Sharon's beautiful face just before her fist caught him under the jaw.

CHAPTER

4

"So what does everyone do for fun around here?" Peter asked.

"Uh, well . . . not a lot," Kara admitted. "I mean, some of us play cards and grab a drink. Sometimes you can get into a pickup game of Pyramid. Help me out here, Lee."

Lee Adama raised his hands. "You brought him down here."

They were sitting around a small table in the pilots' quarters. Bunks and metal lockers lined the walls and the air carried the stale smells of old sweat and cigar smoke. Baltar had cited urgent vice presidential business and excused himself, though he said he would want to talk to Peter later about what it had been like to live among Cylons.

"What do the kids do?" Peter asked. "On the other ships, I mean."

Kara shrugged. "I never really thought about it. They must do something, go to some kind of school. My life's pretty straight-ahead. The alarm goes off, I jump in my Viper, I wipe out more Cylons, I come back, I play cards, I drink. Sometimes I'll catch an episode of *The Colonial Gang*. It's pretty boring, even for a talk show, but there isn't much else on, you know?"

"What a life." Peter gave the back of Kara's hand a brief touch, and Kara felt it all the way up to her eyes and down to her toes. "It must be hard."

"It pays the bills," she said with a flip smile. "Except there aren't any."

Lee remained stonily silent, but his resentment filled the room with icy water. Kara gave him a sidelong glance. What was up with him? There was nothing between them. Lee Adama had no official hold on her, no deep emotional link. And she didn't want one, either. The more she thought about it, the more she decided Lee Adama could frak himself.

"Maybe I could do a—" Peter began, but was interrupted by a knock on the doorframe. Kara looked up, surprised. No one knocked at the pilots' quarters.

Billy Keikeya stood in the entrance, his blue suit and black tie looking too tidy and out of place in the battered military quarters. His curly, ash-blond hair and enormous blue eyes made him look about fifteen—okay, sixteen—though as Laura Roslin's chief aide, Kara figured he had to be somewhere in his twenties at least.

"Uh, hi," he said hesitantly. "I'm looking for . . . Peter Attis?"

"You've found him," Peter said, standing up and extending his hand to shake. "What can I do for you?"

Billy introduced himself and his position. "I've been trying to track you down for a while. There's someone who wants to talk to you."

"And that would be . . . ?"

"Me," said Laura Roslin. She entered the room, her face pale but her expression determined. "Thank you for finding him, Billy."

Kara and Lee leaped to their feet, and Lee offered the president his chair. She accepted without hesitation, and Billy took up his usual position at her right elbow. Kara knew all about President Roslin's cancer, and she greatly admired the way Roslin seemed to draw strength from illness. It was almost as if the woman forged ahead all the harder because she knew her time was limited. Kara also felt a certain awe in Roslin's presence. The Book of Pythia foretold a "dying leader" who would lead humanity to the promised land. So far, Laura Roslin's leadership had uncovered the fact that Earth, the fabled thirteenth colony, did indeed exist, and she had sent Kara back to Caprica to find the Arrow of Apollo, an artifact which had ultimately let President Roslin and Commander Adama uncover star charts that gave clues to Earth's location. Kara had considered herself only vaguely religious before, but nowadays she was a believer, and a Roslin supporter all the way. Eventually, Kara was sure, the Fleet would decipher those charts and figure out how to find Earth—and a new home, just as the Scriptures said.

Assuming the Cylons didn't kill them all first.

"I have to admit I'm something of a fan, Mr. Attis," Roslin began, "and I had to come over and meet you. You've probably heard it before, but I admire your work. I even have a few albums back on *Colonial One*." She gave a wan smile. "They may be the only surviving copies left in the universe. A tragedy indeed."

"Thank you, uh . . . Madam President," Peter said. "And I have to admit I've never met a president before. Definitely not under these conditions."

"We're all going through a lot of firsts," she replied. Then she leaned forward slightly. "Mr. Attis, I'm afraid I need to ask you a tremendous favor."

"Shoot."

"I know you've dealt with a lot—Commander Adama

briefed me on some of it—and I'm sure you're aware that your presence in the Fleet has generated some excitement."

"I've kind of gotten that idea." Peter grinned a wide, handsome grin. "I'm used to it. It's been like that for me since I was a teenager."

"The Fleet is in a state of constant crisis, Mr. Attis," Roslin said.

"Please—it's Peter."

"Peter." She nodded. "At any rate, it's not just the Cylons that cause problems. We have shortages of food, water, medicine, clothing. And entertainment. It may sound strange, but that lack is a major problem. We have an entire Fleet full of people with little or nothing to do. Thousands and thousands of them had careers that the Cylons rendered obsolete or worthless."

"Not much call for insurance adjusters or carpenters these days," Peter said.

"That's right. There's some entertainment, of course. Storytelling is enjoying a resurgence, for example. But for the most part, the Fleet has a lot of bored people. And bored people get into trouble."

"So you're hoping I'll give them something to do."

"Exactly. Would you consent to putting on a concert or two? *Cloud 9* is a cruise ship, and they have excellent facilities. We can arrange for whatever you need. And, just incidentally, this will give a bunch of sound technicians and stage hands something to keep them occupied. I don't know how quickly we can get a band together, but—"

"If you have my albums, Madam President, we can strip the vocals and I can sing to the music tracks. Later, we can get a band together." Peter rubbed his hands together in growing excitement. "Hell, this'll be great. I was just wondering what I was going to do with myself." A look of sudden pain crossed his face, and Kara wanted to grab his hand and reassure him. "It'll also be the perfect way to take my mind off . . . stuff. You know?"

"I do know, Peter," Roslin said. "And maybe for a while, you can take everyone else's mind off *their* stuff."

"Will you be there?"

"You couldn't keep me away." She smiled a mysterious smile. "Maybe I'll bully Commander Adama into escorting me."

"I'd like to see that," Lee said, speaking for the first time.

"Contact Billy here if you need anything." Roslin started to her feet with obvious difficulty. Lee and Billy sprang to assist. Billy escorted her from the pilots' quarters and Lee shut the door behind them.

"A concert!" Kara clapped her hands with a laugh. "Geez, Peter—this is frakking awesome! What do you think, Lee?" she added a little wickedly.

"I don't know," Lee said, shrugging wide shoulders. "I outgrew puffball music."

"Sourpuss." She turned to Peter. "Can I get a ticket?"

Peter shot Lee a look that said the puffball remark hadn't gone past him. "For the woman who saved my life? You bet! Front row, with a backstage pass."

"Oooo, I've always wanted to be a groupie! Do you think I can meet the band?"

"Why not?" Peter laughed. "The transistors and hard drives are always up for a kiss from a hot babe."

"Flattery will get you everything," Kara said with mock seriousness. Holy gods—she was flirting with Peter Frakking Attis. And Lee clearly hated every moment, which made it all the more fun.

"I think I'll head down to the galley," Captain Adama grumbled. "I need a drink."

The pain woke Helo. His jaw pulsed with ragged red agony. Blood was filling his mouth and he automatically spat it out, bringing on fresh spasms from his jaw. It felt like an elephant had stomped on his face, and he couldn't remember what had happened. Cold deck plates pressed against his hands as he pushed himself upright. His head rang like a temple bell. Why was he lying on the floor? Who had—

Memory rushed to fill the void. The empty brig. The motionless guards. Sharon. Helo bolted to his feet, then staggered as the deck dipped and swayed beneath him. He caught his balance on the smooth Plexiglas of Sharon's cell. The two marines assigned to guard it still lay face-down on the deck. Helo's heart began to pound, and his head throbbed in time with it. Every harsh beat was like a knife blade through his skull. He forced himself to move, to kneel down beside the first marine and feel for a pulse at the man's neck. It took a moment, but he found one. Quickly he turned to the second man. No pulse. Helo rolled him over, pulled off his helmet, and checked again. No pulse, and no breath. His head lolled. Broken neck? Tension tightened Helo's muscles as he checked for life again and again. The man *had* to be alive. He *had* to. Sharon hadn't killed him. She wasn't a murderer because this man wasn't dead. He *wasn't!*

Helo abruptly realized he was pounding on the dead marine's chest, trying to pound life back into him. He made himself stop, force back the panic. One step at a time. He got to his feet and snatched a phone from the wall.

"This is Lieutenant Agathon," he barked—or tried to. His jaw was stiff, and it mangled some of his words. "I need an emergency medical team in the brig now! We have two men down." He waited for acknowledgment, then disconnected and, with shaky fingers, punched in another number.

"CIC. Lieutenant Dualla."

"Dee? It's Helo." He swallowed, not wanting to speak, knowing he had to. What he said next would set into action a chain of events that would end in . . . what? Sharon's death? His own arrest? But he had to go through with it. It was the only choice.

"What's up, Helo?" Dee asked. *"You sound funny. Is something wrong?"*

"Yeah. Uh . . . tell Commander Adama that . . . there's been an incident in the brig. I came down to see Sharon. The door to her cell was open and her guards were down. One unconscious, one dead. I've called a medical team."

There was a startled pause, then, *"Where's the prisoner?"*

"Gone. No trace of her."

Dee's voice became shaky. *"I'll tell the Commander. You'd better come up to CIC, Helo. He'll want to talk to you in person."*

"Tell him I'm on my way."

Helo hadn't even made it out of the brig before both radios on the marines behind him crackled to life. *"Code orange twelve,"* said Dee. *"Repeat, code orange twelve. All marine personnel report to commanding officer for instructions."*

Code orange twelve. Enemy aboard ship. Helo's mouth was dry as he trotted toward CIC. Already he could hear the quick-march thump of boots on ceramic plating—marine search teams. If they didn't know by now that Sharon had killed one of them—that *maybe* she had killed one of them, he corrected himself hastily—they would know soon. No one, certainly not marines, took it well when one of their own died, and their primary target would be Sharon.

A trio of medical personnel bustled down the corridor and Helo paused to point the way. One of them tried to examine Helo—his jaw was so swollen he could barely speak—but Helo only accepted a painkiller before continuing up to CIC. The throb in his head and jaw receded almost immediately, but his tension remained, twisting his stomach into a nauseated knot as he threaded his way through *Galactica*'s busy corridors. Helo passed half a dozen fully armed and armored marines. They were searching side corridors and rooms. Helo stopped one of them.

"What are your orders, Sergeant?" he asked.

"Find the toaster, sir," she said.

"And then?"

She shifted her pulse rifle and gave him a critical look. Helo felt cold under her gaze. "Capture if possible, kill if necessary."

"Toaster lover," someone said behind him in a barely audible voice.

Helo rounded on the other marines, anger replacing his tension. "Who the frak said that?"

"Said what, sir?" replied a marine with utterly fake innocence.

"Sergeant," Helo said without taking his eyes off the man, "it sounds like your people aren't familiar with rank and respect."

"Sir," the sergeant said noncommittally.

"Maybe this group needs to search the bilge next, Sergeant. What do you think?"

"Sir, the Cylon killed Corporal Mason when it escaped," the sergeant said. "Everyone's on edge."

"Is that an excuse, Sergeant?"

"No, sir."

Helo closed his eyes. It wasn't worth it. "Carry on, Sergeant. And have a talk with your people once this is over."

"Sir."

Helo left the marines and trotted the rest of the way to CIC. He hesitated outside the hatchway for a long moment, then entered.

CIC was, as always, busy. Dee talked into her microphone and routed calls. Felix Gaeta pored over printouts and dashed from one computer console to another. XO Tigh shouted into a telephone. In the center of the room was a light table. William Adama, his craggy, scarred face serious behind his glasses, was marking up a diagram of *Galactica* with a grease pencil. He glanced up and removed his glasses as Helo approached and saluted.

"Lieutenant," Adama said. "Care to tell me what happened?"

"Sir. I don't know much." Helo related his story, leaving out nothing. His heart beat fast and he tried not to shift uneasily. It was no fun coming under the scrutiny of the single most powerful man in the Fleet, one who could order Helo imprisoned or even executed. Adama knew of Helo's involvement with Sharon and he knew about the baby. Helo was well aware that this probably made him a prime suspect in Sharon's escape. When Colonel Tigh came over to listen, Helo caught a clear whiff of alcohol on the XO's breath. Not for the first time Helo wondered why the hell Adama tolerated Tigh's drinking. A drunken officer on duty was a danger to himself and everyone under his command. But Adama seemed to disagree.

"Did you let that Cylon out?" Tigh demanded.

"No, sir," Helo said through gritted teeth. "As I said, she had already escaped by the time I arrived."

"And she got the drop on you," Tigh observed. "Sounds mighty convenient, if you ask me. Maybe you let her out and she socked you on the jaw to make it look like you had no part in it."

"No, sir," Helo said. "That's not what happened. You can

question the guards—guard. The one who survived. He'll tell you I wasn't there."

"How do we know you didn't get the drop on him, too?" Tigh said. "Maybe you—"

"Thank you, Saul," Adama said. "We'll question the marine, but I doubt very much that Lieutenant Agathon had anything to do with the Cylon's escape."

"Thank you, sir," Helo said. He noticed the tightness around Adama's mouth and remembered how Sharon—or a different version of her—had shot Adama in the gut, with almost fatal results. Helo suspected Sharon's escape was causing the commander a certain amount of stress, perhaps even fear, though he would never allow it to show. That particular copy of Sharon had thought she was human, and she had attacked Adama only because hidden Cylon programming had taken over and forced her to act.

"We're keeping this quiet," Adama said. "Anyone who asks is told that we're searching for an escaped prisoner. It's not generally known in the Fleet that we have—or had—a Cylon in the brig, and the last thing I need is panic and riots on the other ships, got that?"

"Yes, sir," Helo said.

"Where do you think she would go, Lieutenant?" Adama asked.

Helo spread his hands. "I honestly don't know, sir. It would depend on why she escaped. I don't think she wants to go back to the . . . to her home planet, wherever that is. She says they see her as an outcast because she helped me escape the Cylons on Caprica. They'd kill her if she went back."

"Even though she's pregnant," Adama said.

"They don't know about the baby, sir. Sharon never told them—"

"—as far as you know," Tigh put in.

"As far as I know, sir," Helo agreed. "But by the time Sharon realized she was pregnant, the other Cylons were already trying to kill us. She couldn't have communicated with them—they would have shot both of us on sight. There's no way Sharon would go back to them."

"So why escape, then? Is she planning some sort of sabotage?"

"That would only hurt her, in the long run. Her and the baby." Helo paused. "Commander, I don't know why she did this. I . . . she swore to me, to all of us, that she had no sleeper Cylon protocols in her. She's helped us half a dozen times when she could have let us all die. This escape, the killing—they don't make sense."

"She's a Cylon," Adama said, turning back to his diagram. "It makes perfect sense."

Gaius Baltar groaned as the staffer placed yet another stack of papers on his desk. The staffer left quickly, before Baltar could respond further. He looked around his laboratory, with its outdated equipment and half-assed computer system, with a mixture of annoyance and longing. It wasn't right that the most brilliant mind in the galaxy—perhaps the universe—was forced to endure such conditions. How could he get anything done in a lab filled with junk and a desk covered in paperwork? Laura Roslin must take perverse delight in shoving her load of paper onto him instead of doing it herself. As an experienced bureaucrat, she should be the one handling this, not him. He should be at work in his lab, making new discoveries to help all humanity, not reading reports and signing forms. Even working with outdated equipment beat mindlessly scribbling his name. Half the time he signed without reading, just to get the stupid paper off his desk.

In addition to his lab work, he had a lecture to prepare for, the first in a series. "Life Post-Apocalypse," he was calling it. He had thought of the title himself and was quite proud of it. The first lecture was called "The Sociological Effects of Limited Resources in a Declining Gene Pool." His star power as Dr. Gaius Baltar and his position as Vice President of the Colonies would guarantee a packed auditorium on *Cloud 9*, along with full press coverage. But even his star power wouldn't save him if he stood in front of an audience with a half-prepared lecture, and he'd never get the lecture finished if he had to do all this stupid paperwork.

He picked up another memo and scanned it. The Cylon woman who had escaped yesterday evening had not been re-captured despite all attempts to find her, the military was searching all ships leaving and approaching the *Galactica*, the escape remained a classified incident, blah blah blah. He supposed it was a good idea to remain informed about the situation, in case there was a danger to him, but he didn't seriously believe the Cylon was coming after him. She had no reason to. It still made for a long, boring series of memos.

A pair of warm hands slid over his shoulders from behind. "It's an outrage. A waste of your brilliance." The hands slid lower, over his chest, down his stomach, toward his waistband. Number Six's distinctive scent washed over him, and her white-blond hair brushed his face and neck. Gaius felt his body respond. His breath came faster, his skin grew warm, and his groin tightened.

"You're not helping," he murmured, though he didn't push her away.

She ran a hand over his inner thigh and at the same time gave his ear a long, slow lick. "Depends on what kind of help you need."

"That . . . isn't . . . exactly it," he managed. Then he straightened. "What do you want this time?"

"Just to give you some encouragement." Number Six put her hands back on his shoulders. "And I wanted some company. Being ignored is never easy, Gaius. You know that."

"Ignored?" He gestured at the paperwork mounding his desk. "What are you talking about? I'm anything *but* ignored these days."

Six made a noncommittal noise and leaned over Gaius's shoulder to peer at his desk. Her low-cut blue dress showed a generous amount of cleavage that Gaius couldn't help but watch. He had seen her naked hundreds of times, but she was far more alluring when he *couldn't* see everything. Her dress made her a mystery, a sly secret. His groin tightened further.

"All these worthless papers," she said. "Someone like you should have a secretary or an aide to handle this." She abruptly straightened. The movement took her cleavage out of his line of sight, revealing a stack of papers instead. Gaius was about to turn his attention elsewhere when some words on the top sheet caught his eye. He snatched up the paper in question. He would have never seen it if not for Six abruptly removing her arresting cleavage.

"What is it, Gaius?" Number Six asked, all innocence.

"A memo," he said, reading. "It has Roslin's name on it. It must have come to me by mistake." His eyes tracked across the page and his expression became more and more agitated. "My gods! This . . . this is . . . it's outrageous!"

Six leaned over his shoulder again, this time to read. "'. . . and we have found two more sound technicians, bringing the total up to five. That should be all Peter needs.' So what?"

"So what?" Gaius flung the paper down and stormed around his desk into the lab. "So *what*? How can you not see it?"

"Explain, Gaius," she said tiredly. "I'm getting bored."

He pointed an shaking, outraged finger at the offending paper. "Read the date."

She did. "Tomorrow. So?"

"So? This concert, this . . . travesty is scheduled for the same time as my lecture." He ran his hands through his hair and stalked about the lab like an angry stork. "I'm going to look like an idiot."

"Because no one will come to your lecture?"

"What? No! Because no one will go to the concert." He leaned his fingertips on a granite-topped table. "Everyone knows me. I've saved the Fleet gods know how many times, and I'm the bloody vice president. They'll all come to my lecture, Peter Attis will play to an empty concert hall, and I'll look the villain for humiliating him. Fantastic. Just fantastic."

Six moved around the desk, her hips swaying like willow withes. "Fame is a difficult burden to bear, Gaius."

"It's unfair, to me and to him." He ran his hands through his hair again. "Maybe I should talk to Attis, see if he'd be willing to reschedule for his own good."

"That's what I love about you, Gaius," Six said, perching on the edge of his desk. "You're always thinking of others."

"Check 'em out, boys and girls." Kara Thrace sailed into the pilots' quarters, holding a small envelope aloft with undisguised glee. "Two—count 'em, *two*—tickets to the Peter Attis interstellar tour *and* a pair of backstage passes." She gave the envelope a loud kiss. "Mine, mine, mine."

"And all you had to do was save his life to get them," Kat said without malice. "Bitch."

"Next time, I'll let *you* find the escape pod."

"Those things are impossible to get," said Brendan "Hot

Dog" Constanza. He looked at Kara over his hand of cards. "A buddy of mine got in line six hours before they went up for grabs, and they *still* ran out before he got one. I mean, they're going to televise it and everything, but there's nothing like a live concert. It's been a frakking long time since I've seen one."

"Billy could have gotten us tickets," Dee said. She wasn't a pilot, but was often found at the nightly card game. "But he has to go with the president and Commander Adama, so I'll just watch it on TV."

"Since when are you a Peter Attis fan, Hot Dog?" Lee asked. He tossed a chip into the pot.

"Since never," Hot Dog said. "But any concert beats playing cards with you frak-heads."

"And since when do you play Full Colors, Lee?" Kara turned a chair around and faced the group over its back.

"I'm a man of many talents."

"Yeah? Prove it. You just started this hand, right? Deal me in, Dee."

Dee obligingly sent six cards Kara's way. "Don't forget to ante."

In response, Kara opened the envelope and slid a single ticket from it. She dropped it into the pot. "There."

"No shit," Hot Dog said breathlessly.

"Someone has to come with me," Kara said. "It's no fun to go alone." She gave Lee an impish look. "You gonna fold?"

"Frak, no. I've got a good hand here."

"What happens if you win, Starbuck?" Hot Dog asked. "Or are you playing to lose?"

"Starbuck play to lose?" Kat snorted. "Right. May as well ask an Oracle to give you a straight answer."

"Damn right." Kara pulled a small cigar from her breast pocket and lit it. "If I win, I get to *choose* which one of you reprobates accompanies me. *And* you have to wear your dress uniform."

"I'm still in," Hot Dog said, dropping a chip.

"What the hell," Dee said, and put in a chip of her own. "Maybe Billy will get jealous."

Another round of betting went by. No one folded. Kara replaced three cards, and when the bet came around to her again, she held up one of the backstage passes for everyone to see. "Too rich for anyone's blood?" She put it in the pot.

"Frakking-A," Kat breathed.

Lee frowned at his cards. "I'll stand." He dropped three chips, then four more—a significant raise.

"Ooooo," Kat said. "I think he's bluffing, trying to get us to drop out so he can get the ticket."

Lee gave her a wide-eyed, innocent look. "Put your money where your mouth is, then."

Kat met the raise, as did Dee and Hot Dog. Kara looked over her cards at Lee. Was Lee bluffing? She studied his expression. His face was cool, almost smug. She knew him well enough to recognize that look—he wasn't bluffing. He had a great hand. Kara couldn't stand Lee when he was smug. She had half a mind to fold and let him win, make him come to the concert for the sole reason that he hated Peter.

"Any news on the escaped toaster?" Hot Dog asked.

"Nothing I've heard," said Kat. "It creeps me out that no one can find her. How can she just frakking disappear?"

"The *Galactica* is a big place," Lee said. His face went hard. Bill Adama was his father, and a copy of Sharon had shot him. When Kara had brought the current copy of Sharon on board, Lee had almost killed her on sight. Only Helo's intervention had spared her. "And she isn't human. She can get into places where normal people can't."

"That's one way to put it," Hot Dog scoffed.

"Maybe she left the ship," Dee said. "Like that Godfrey woman. Remember her?"

"Blond Cylon lady, yeah," Lee said. "Just vanished. We never did learn how she got off the ship."

"Maybe she didn't," Kat said. "Maybe she stuck around and now she and the other Cylon are holding a toaster convention in the air vents."

Kara dropped a handful of chips into the pot. "Call," she said loudly. "All right, guys and gals—show 'em."

Hot Dog sighed and spread his cards. "Half mast."

"One lord and a lady," Dee said. "Guess I'll join Hot Dog in the TV room."

"Two half masts," Kat said. "Best so far."

"Apollo?" Kara asked sweetly. "I'll show you mine if you show me yours."

"I just want it known for the record," Lee said, "that I'm not going to the concert, even though I'm about to win. Hot Dog, you can have the ticket."

"Really? Thanks, Captain!"

"You don't have a thing," Kara said scornfully. "Spread 'em, Apollo."

"Start your weeping." Lee laid down his cards one by one. "Full colors."

Hot Dog whistled. "Frak me!" He reached for the ticket and the backstage pass, but Kara was quicker. She caught his wrist.

"A little overconfident, are we?" she said, gently pushing his hand away. "Ladies and gentlemen, I give you the real winner of the evening." And she laid down her cards.

"Full colors," Kat said. "Wow! Twice in the same hand! How often does that happen?"

"So it's a tie?" Dee asked.

"Hardly." Kara gestured at their respective cards. "The Captain's cards are orange. Mine are pure purple goodness."

"She's right," Hot Dog said. "Colors decide in case of a tie."

"Come to mama." Kara raked the chips toward her, then plucked the ticket and pass from the pile. "Let's see. Who shall accompany me to the ball in dress black?"

"Have I told you how lovely you look today, Lieutenant?" Hot Dog said. "And what is that divine scent? Are you wearing perfume?"

"Aw, you can do better than *that*," she scoffed.

"Who's the best pilot in the Fleet?" Kat said. "Why, I think it has to be Kara Thrace."

"It's not flattery if it's true," Kara said. "Who else?"

"I have the Commander's ear," Dee put in. "Captain Adama here may write the duty roster, but *Commander* Adama approves it. I can get you some sweet run times."

"Tempting, tempting," Kara said. "And worthy of consideration. Lee?"

"I already said I don't want to go," Lee replied, crossing his arms.

"You're just mad because I ruined your perfect—excuse me, *near* perfect—hand."

"Yeah, sure. Think what you want." He got up. "I'm outta here."

"You can't just leave," Kara said, suddenly angry. "I haven't made my decision yet."

He rounded on her, eyes flashing. "Who the frak cares? I don't want to go, it won't be me, so I'm not sticking around."

Kara's temper flared higher. "Maybe it *will* be you, have you thought about that?"

"I already said I don't want to go!" Lee was almost shouting now.

"Maybe *I* want you to go." Kara raised her own voice to compensate.

"Do you?" Lee yelled.

"Yeah!"

"Fine! I'll go!"

"Good!"

"I'm thrilled!"

"Meet me in the shuttle bay at seven!" Kara screamed, storming out the door. "Wear your blacks!"

"I wouldn't miss it!" Lee bellowed, stomping after her. "It'll be fun!"

They fled in opposite directions in the hallway. Behind them around the card table, two pilots and one petty officer stared at each other.

"What the hell just happened?" Hot Dog asked.

"I think," said Kat, "that we're all watching the concert on TV tomorrow. Meet in the TV room?"

"You bring the ambrosia," Dee said.

CHAPTER
5

The auditorium dressing room smelled of old makeup and cold cream. Gaius Baltar, seated at the dressing table, checked his reflection in the mirror. Hair—good. Face—excellent. Clothes—perfect. The visuals for his lecture were loaded in the auditorium computer, and the remote for the projector was in his pocket. He had no idea what sort of audience awaited him—it was bad luck to check beforehand—but he knew the enormous auditorium would be packed to the roof. He had bullied the fire marshal into allowing people to sit in the aisles once the initial ticket run had sold out. It had, in fact, sold out within a week after tickets had gone up for sale last month. Gaius checked his tie again.

"So Peter Attis turned down your offer to change his concert, Gaius?" Number Six said.

Gaius jumped and pushed his chair away from the mirror. Six had replaced his reflection, and she mimicked his movements. He raised a hand. She did the same.

"More fool he," Gaius said, and Six's mouth moved in conjunction with his. "Would you stop that? It's creepier than usual."

"I just wanted to get your attention." And then she was perched prettily on the edge of the dressing table. "Being ignored is the worst possible fate. Forgotten, alone."

"You forgot 'in the dark.'"

"You never talk to me anymore," she said. "I always start our conversations. You never ask to see me—unless you want something."

"I've been busy," he said shortly, getting to his feet. "In fact, I have a lecture to give. I'm going to check the audience right now. The tickets sold out, but I'm curious."

And then Six was in front of him, her expression hard as iron. "Don't ignore me, Gaius. You owe me *everything*." She put both hands on his lapels and gave him a firm shove backward. "Who's more important to you—me or those trogs out there?"

Startled, Gaius back up another step. "I have to be on stage in five minutes."

"And you can't spare me four of them?" She grabbed his tie and yanked him into a kiss. Her tongue was warm on his. Six sat on the makeup table, wrapped her legs around his torso, and pulled him to her. His body responded, and he didn't try to resist. He didn't want to. Six could always do this to him. At one time he had tried to fight her, but these days, he didn't bother. One had to take what diversions came one's way.

Just as they finished, a voice came over the intercom. "*One minute, Dr. Gaius.*"

Six sighed theatrically as they parted. "Break a leg. Preferably someone else's." And she was gone.

Gaius straightened his clothes, checked his pocket once again for the remote, and dashed out of the dressing room. He made his way backstage, where he passed two stage hands and a lighting technician without speaking to them. His mind was in a strange place—half torpid from the sexual encounter, half revved up for the lecture. And he was running behind. Good thing he knew the format cold. Always start with a joke, then go into a short, interesting anecdote. Then introduce the main points. It was an old, familiar formula. The stage itself was empty except for a podium and a projection screen. Gaius couldn't see the audience, of course, but the auditorium was hushed with expectation. He felt perfectly calm—stage fright had never been one of his failings. In fact, he quite enjoyed lecturing. One of the many ways to pass his knowledge on to lesser minds.

"Um . . . Dr. Baltar?" said one of the stage hands. "Can I—"

"Shh!" Baltar made curt gesture. "I'm concentrating."

The clock backstage showed five seconds to eight o'clock.

"But I think you—"

"Quiet! My gods, can't anyone just do their job in silence anymore?"

"Sure, sure," the hand said. "They're going to announce you in five seconds, then."

Five seconds later, a pre-recorded announcer said, "Ladies and gentlemen, our honored vice president, Dr. Gaius Baltar!"

Gaius stepped out onto the stage, expecting tumultuous applause. What he got was some scattered clapping that echoed limply off the auditorium walls. Gaius blinked. The place was all but empty. He did a quick count. Fewer than a dozen people were scattered among the seats. Gaius gaped in astonishment. His mind was unable to comprehend what his eyes were telling him. Slowly, face flaming with embarrassment and outrage, he walked to the podium. It was only six steps away, but the distance felt like a thousand yards.

"Um . . . good—good evening," he stammered. "I . . . uh, that is, it's good to see that a few minds in the Fleet aren't preoccupied with Peter Attis and his concert."

One man bolted to his feet, a shocked look on his face. "The concert is tonight?" He fled the auditorium. Four other people went with him.

Gaius's face hardened as he realized what the stage hand had been trying to tell him—and what Number Six had prevented him from finding out. Peter Attis had made a fool of Gaius. In the wings, Number Six blew him a kiss.

The crowd raised its hands and screamed in utter joy when Peter Attis bounced onto the stage like a blond god. His every movement crackled with power, and Kara, all but crushed at the edge of the platform, raised her arms and howled with the best of them. Beside her stood Lee Adama like a blue-eyed statue in his crisp dress uniform. Kara wore a black jumpsuit, and with Dualla's help, she had actually put on some makeup. It felt like she was wearing a mask, and she had to remind herself not to touch her face.

"Good evening, Colonials!" Peter boomed into the microphone, and the crowd shrieked again. "The Cylons haven't found us yet, so let's make some noise!"

Kara let loose with a wild whoop that was almost lost in the thunder of the crowd around her. Far above, Cloud 9's artificial sun showered gentle warmth and golden light on the assembled concertgoers. The clear dome reflected back the image of the trees, shrubs, and lawns planted about the wide-open space, creating the illusion that the place was much bigger than it was and hiding the fact that visitors were on board a space ship. As a luxury liner, the Cloud 9 boasted swimming pools, hotels, spas, and other arenas for entertainment and relaxation, including several stages. Gaius Baltar had already booked the main auditorium, but Peter had said the outdoor theater would provide a better venue anyway. Garden tiers packed with people led down and in to the raised stage. A freestanding backdrop combined with a powerful sound system to ensure that everyone could hear. Peter stood alone on the stage—the music was pre-recorded from the stash provided by President Roslin and a few other hastily located Attis fans—and there had been no time for backup singers to rehearse. As a result, this concert would be a little on the plain side, but no one seemed to mind.

"I said, 'Let's make some noise!'" Peter shouted, and the crowd screamed even louder. "The Cylons tried to kill us, they failed, so let's party!"

The speakers slammed to life with a song Kara hadn't heard for years but still remembered with amazing clarity.

I gave you twelve soft kisses
At twelve noon every day
But you just took twelve kisses
And ripped my heart away.

Peter's golden voice turned the simple lyrics into powerful poetry. He leaped and danced as he sang, swirling the microphone cord around him like a whip. The front of his shirt was open, displaying well-defined muscle. Below him, the crowd danced like a giant living thing. Ripples of movement swayed through it, like wind rushing over grass. Kara loved every second. Peter finished his first song and went on to a second, one that also had a fast beat.

"Dance!" Kara shouted in Lee's ear.

He shook his head and shouted back, "I don't dance!"

Kara looked at him, then shrugged and danced by herself. The tight tensions and heavy pressures that continually rode her back seemed to evaporate with every move her body made.

Then, during a musical interlude, Peter looked down at her and extended a hand. Without hesitation, Kara leaped up on the stage.

"Lieutenant Kara Thrace!" Peter announced. "If it weren't for her, I wouldn't be singing up here. Give her a hand!"

The crowd went wild. Lee clapped his hands politely, completely unconcerned. Kara wasn't sure how she felt about that. He should have reacted at least a little. Peter started singing again and drew Kara into a dance, only slightly hampered by the microphone cord. Kara looked at Lee again, then got close to Peter and went into some serious hip gyrations. She felt free, like a soap bubble rising toward the stars. The crowd loved it, and Peter smiled as his voice filled the tiered garden with liquid light.

When the song ended, Kara jumped back down to her space beside Lee. She was breathing hard and a little sweaty. "That was great!" she shouted to him over the applause. "I never thought I'd get to dance with Peter Attis!"

"Neither did I," Lee said.

"You want to go up there?" she teased. "I'm sure Peter would—"

Lee looked horrified. "No!"

"A slower one now, folks," Peter said on the stage. He drew up a stool and sat. "I was a prisoner of the Cylons all throughout the conflict. Hell, I had no idea there *was* a conflict until Kara Thrace rescued me. The only thing that kept me going was the thought that someone was watching over me, keeping me alive for a reason. I rewrote the lyrics to 'You're the Only One'"—the crowd cheered at the mention of the popular song—"to reflect my faith."

A quiet, wistful tune started up. The lights went down until only a soft spotlight illuminated Peter on his stool. He swayed a little, eyes shut, then began to sing.

I obey you, that you know,
Why, then, do you burn my soul?
If you won't look on my face,
Where, then, shall I go?
Without you, why would I live?

The music swelled, and Kara felt it carry her along as if she were floating in the near-darkness of the garden. Peter slipped into the chorus.

You're the only one.
You're the only life.
You're the only reason
I survive the strife.

Kara found she was mouthing the words, singing along. So was most of the crowd. The song continued.

No one lives this life without you.
You're the only lord.
Others only show their faces
Once you've possessed my soul.

And then the chorus began again. The audience sang along in full voice. It was catchy, and the familiar tune was a piece of home. Kara found she was choking up. *You're the only reason / I survive this strife.* Even Lee was singing quietly, though he didn't seem aware he was doing so. Then Kara noticed she was holding Lee's hand. It was big and warm. Had he taken her hand or had she taken his? She didn't know.

Before she could figure it out, the song ended, and Lee dropped her hand to applaud. He didn't acknowledge the hand-holding, and Kara found that the whole thing confused her again, so she decided to ignore it, too. Peter did two more pieces before he declared he needed a break. "Fifteen-minute intermission, folks!" he said. "And I'll come back for more, if you want it."

He trotted off the stage, leaving the audience to mill around, talking. Stage hands came out to fiddle with equipment. Kara grabbed Lee's hand. "Come on!"

"Where are we going?"

"Backstage, doofus." She flashed her pass. "What do you think these things are for?"

Lee looked stubborn for a moment, then shrugged and climbed up on the stage with her. A stage hand immediately ran up to them, but Kara held up her pass and he waved them on.

The stage was actually backed up against the main dome of the *Cloud 9*, so the backstage lay between the dome wall and the stage's backdrop. A few dressing rooms and storage areas had been constructed. Kara, with Lee in tow, found Peter's room, knocked, and entered. Peter turned from his mirror. He had removed his shirt to towel off sweat. Kara couldn't help but admire the way his muscles moved beneath smooth skin.

"Kara!" he said, and gave her a firm kiss on the cheek. "And Lee!" He stuck out his hand and Lee took it. They shook hands for a long moment, and Kara only belatedly realized that they were squeezing. Lee's face was set like concrete and Peter's eyes were starting to bulge. She sighed and stepped between, giving them both an excuse to let go.

"Great concert so far," she said. "Thanks for the dance."

"You were a great partner," Peter said. "I don't suppose you sing?"

"Only if you want to kill ravens at fifty paces. Lee sings, though."

"Yeah?" He shot Lee a glance. "I'm looking for backup singers for my next concert, if you're interested."

"Right," Lee said. "I'll think real hard about it."

"Want to watch the rest of the concert from backstage?" Peter said. "Lots of people find it interesting to see what goes on behind the scenes. Though without the usual light-and-sound extravaganza, there isn't as much as usual."

"Sure!" Kara enthused.

"Great." He paused, then gestured at the two of them. "So how long have you and Lee been . . . ?"

"We're not," Lee said quickly. "We're just . . . this isn't a date."

"Gods, no," Kara put in. "I was engaged to Lee's brother a few years ago, but Lee and I are just—"

"Wonderful!" Peter said, then blushed. "I mean, not wonderful, but . . . uh . . . you know . . ."

The stage manager poked his head into the room. "Two minutes, Mr. Attis."

"Thanks," he said, clearly grateful for the interruption. He pulled on his shirt—a different one—and headed for the door. Then he paused to give Kara another kiss on the cheek. "I'll watch for you." And he left.

"He'll watch for you," Lee grumbled.

"You're not much fun on a date," she said, oddly pleased that he seemed jealous.

"This isn't a date, remember?"

"It's still supposed to be fun. Come on, lighten up."

"Long day," he sighed. "But I'll try."

They threaded their way through various stage hands and bits of equipment until they could see the stage. It was weird seeing it from the side instead of the front. Kara scanned the audience and caught sight of Commander Adama and President

Roslin. They were sitting at the back on one of the upper tiers, a bit apart from the main crowd. Billy Keikeya and another aide Kara didn't recognize hovered nearby. Kara smiled. So President Roslin had somehow bullied the Old Man into accompanying her to the concert. Kara hadn't seriously thought she could do it. Adama, also in his dress uniform, wore an expression of resignation similar to Lee's. Kara's smile widened. She wondered if there would be any way for her to tease Adama about this later.

Probably not. But it was fun to think about.

A bit of motion caught the corner of Kara's eye. Peter, who was waiting on the other side of the stage, was giving Kara—and, she supposed, Lee—a friendly wave. She waved back. Gods, the man had a great ass. And he was a good cheek-kisser, too.

The lights dimmed, and the audience started cheering again. Peter ran out with his microphone, and the cheering increased in volume. A backstage technician, now visible to Kara and Lee, sat hunched over a board festooned with levers, switches, and dials. He flipped a switch and slid a lever. Music blasted from the speakers, and Peter swung into song.

"Pretty catchy tune he did earlier," Lee remarked. "That rewritten one?"

"Yeah. Did you know the original?"

"It sounded familiar, but I never was—"

"—a Peter Attis fan," Kara finished. "I know, I know. You said it several—what the hell?"

Lee stiffened. "What? What's wrong?"

Kara pointed. Over the stage arced a metal scaffold interlaced with wooden platforms. Lights and other equipment Kara couldn't identify were bolted to it. Along the top crawled a lithe figure.

"Frak me!" Lee said. "It's Sharon! What the hell is she doing up there?"

"Nothing good, I'll bet." Kara licked her lips nervously. "What do we do? If we raise the alarm there'll be a panic out there."

"If we don't, we're frakked anyway. You have a weapon?"

"Nope. You?"

"Nope."

"Good to know we're on equal footing," Kara said. "Let's go!"

One leg of the scaffold came right to the edge of the stage where Lee and Kara were standing. Kara climbed, the steel pipes biting into her hands. Lee scrambled up behind her. She climbed carefully, trying not to make sudden motions that would attract the attention of Sharon, Peter, or the audience. Adrenaline stabbed her heart and made it pound. Cylons were stronger and faster than humans, and Kara had no idea if she'd be able to take Sharon down without a weapon. And what the hell was she up to?

Kara reached the top of the scaffold. Ahead of her stretched a bridge made of pipes and boards. Lights hung beneath her feet. The music and Peter's voice pounded at her bones—he was singing a rock song with a heavy beat. Ahead of her, about halfway across the scaffold, Sharon was kneeling on the boards. As Kara cautiously stepped forward, Sharon rose and saw her. They locked eyes for a moment. Then Sharon calmly turned and trotted away.

Kara ran forward with Lee hot on her heels. Sharon's casual trot brought her to the edge of the scaffold by the time Lee and Kara reached the middle. Kara stopped dead, and Lee almost ran into her. At her feet lay a plastic bottle. It appeared to be full of a slushy fluid. Beside was it was a small, battery-operated heater. On principal, Kara shoved the heater away from the bottle with her foot.

"Frak!" Lee shouted over the noise of the concert. "That's a nitro bomb!"

"A bottle and a heater?"

"Nitroglycerin doesn't explode when it's frozen," Lee yelled in her ear. "Once it melts, the vibrations from the music—"

"Take care of it!" Kara shouted, and took off after Sharon, who was almost at the bottom of the scaffold by now. The Cylon jumped the remaining distance to the ground, leaped off the stage, and started shoving through the crowd. People swore and protested, but gave way. Kara could track where Sharon was by the commotion, but the audience was so large that most people didn't notice. If Peter did, he gave no sign. There was no way Kara could catch up with her from here. Unless . . .

Without stopping to think, Kara leaped out into empty space. Her grasping hands snatched at one of the many guy ropes hanging from various pulleys. Her stomach lurched, and she dropped straight toward the stage faster than she would have liked. A curtain went up as she came down, and she hit the stage with a grunt. The jarring shock traveled right up her spine to her skull.

Peter spun to stare at her and the audience went silent, though the music kept up. Then Peter, ever the showman, went back to singing as if it were all part of the concert. Kara ran toward the edge of the stage, praying this would work. If it didn't, she'd have an escaped Cylon and a nice collection of bruises. She shot a glance up at the scaffold. Lee was carrying the bottle toward the edge of the scaffold as if it might explode, which it might.

Kara reached the edge of the stage and leaped off it, sailing straight down like a belly-flopper at the old watering hole. The people below her looked up in shock and Kara held her breath.

At the last second, the people flung up their hands and caught her. Relief swept over Kara. The crowd cheered, and the dozens of hands supporting her started passing her toward the back of the audience. People laughed and whooped as they did so. After two people grabbed at her upper chest, however, Kara managed to roll over onto her back. It was a strange sensation, like lying on a hammock of hands. Peter waved to her as he sang, though his expression was mystified. Kara found she was moving swiftly, much faster than Sharon had gone. In moments, she was on the top tier, and the final group of concertgoers lowered her gently to her feet. Both Adama and the President were staring at her, but there was no time to explain. A stone barrier walled the concert forum off from the rest of the dome. It was dotted with revolving barred gates that let people out but not in, and Sharon was running toward one. Kara took off after her. Sharon was quicker on her feet, but the barred gate slowed her down. Kara set her mouth in grim determination. She could catch Sharon if she really hauled it.

Sharon shoved through the revolving gate and made it through. Kara ran like hell. But instead of fleeing, Sharon snatched up a rock and wedged it beneath the gate's axis. Kara hit the bars, but the gate refused to budge. Sharon gave Kara a small smile and turned to lope away.

Kara smacked the bars in frustration. "Dammit!" Then she shouted desperately, "Sharon! Wait!"

To Kara's surprise, Sharon actually halted and turned to face her. "What?"

"Why are you doing this?" Kara grasped the unmoving bars like a monkey in a cage. "I thought you wanted to help us."

Sharon walked slowly up to the gate and leaned so close Kara could smell her breath, warm and sour. "Help you? When all you've done is frak with me? Keep me locked up in a cage like some animal? And you wonder why we're trying to exter-minate you."

"Yeah, you Cylons are all about love and mercy."

"We are to those who deserve it," Sharon said. "And that doesn't seem to be you." She turned and trotted into the trees.

Kara slapped the bars again, but all she got for it was a bruised hand. With a growl of anger, she turned back to the fo-rum and forced herself to think about what to do next. There had to be a phone around here somewhere.

The next two hours turned out to be very busy. Kara had to report what had happened to someone, but Captain Shin of *Cloud 9* had no idea that the *Galactica* had been holding a Cylon, so Kara fetched Commander Adama instead. When she ex-plained what happened, Billy and the unnamed aide hustled Roslin away and Adama's face went stony. He called Captain Shin and said that a "political prisoner" had managed to infil-trate *Cloud 9*. Security teams from both *Cloud 9* and the *Galactica* were summoned to comb the cruise liner, but no one was hope-ful. The *Cloud 9* was such a popular destination that checking all traffic to and from the ship was simply impossible, and it would be easy for Sharon to slip away.

Kara also learned that Lee had managed to get the nitro bottle to an airlock before the contents melted, and the bomb had failed to go off. If it had, Peter and a large chunk of the au-dience would have been killed. None of the concertgoers seemed to suspect anything had gone wrong.

Kara sat on the edge of the stage, kicking her feet like a little kid. Overhead, the artificial sun continued to shine, though it was almost midnight—there was no darkness in the dome on *Cloud 9*. The grass on the tiers was already springing back from being trampled by the audience. Kara could only hope humanity would be so resilient.

"Hi."

Kara looked up into Peter's blue eyes. "Hi, yourself."

He sat down next to her, so close she could feel his body heat. "I had a feeling you'd be here. I don't know why. I guess the One is looking out for me."

"The One?"

"Yeah. He guides my footsteps. What happened out there? I got the feeling it wasn't just showing off."

Kara gave him the full rundown. Since he already knew about Caprica Sharon, there didn't seem to be any point in keeping quiet about it, though she warned him not to spread the news around.

"I won't," he said. "Wow. Uh . . . should I be worried?"

Kara opened her mouth to reassure him, then stopped herself. Sugar-coating the truth never made sense. "I don't know. Even though this version of Sharon never met you, she tried to sabotage your concert. She might be going after you specifically or she might have just chosen it because she could hurt a lot of people all at once. I doubt she stayed on *Cloud 9*, but I won't lie to you—she could still be around."

"Frak." Peter glanced nervously around. "Look, could . . . could you walk me back to my room? I don't want to be alone right now."

"You have a room? Frak, Peter—I forgot I was going to find you a place to stay. Where did they put you?"

"In one of the hotels here. I'll probably be doing a fair amount of work here for a while, so it made sense."

They got up and headed for one of the exits, talking as they went.

"Where'd Lee go?" Peter asked casually.

"Back to *Galactica*." Kara pushed away a sense that he had

abandoned her. "He has duty in a few hours. I don't, so I stayed here. Nice to get away for a while."

"Looks like we're all permanently getting away for a while." Kara snorted. "One way to look at it."

A few minutes later, they were standing in a hotel corridor. Peter unlocked his door and nudged it open. Then he turned to Kara. "I never did thank you."

"For . . . ?"

"Saving my life, of course." He leaned down and kissed her. Her first thought—

my gods I'm kissing Peter Attis

—flicked through her mind, then dissolved under the kiss. Kara returned it, hungrily. After the fight with the Cylons and the pursuit of Sharon, she needed the reassurance that she was still alive, that someone would hold her. The kiss became more intense, and Kara was only vaguely aware that they were moving inside, that Peter had kicked the door shut, that they were fumbling at each other's clothes. Moments later, they were naked beneath the sheets, and for a while Kara felt everything she needed to.

CHAPTER

6

"Captain Demeter reports that harvest operations are underway, Commander," Dualla said.

Adama nodded his acknowledgment, then cast a wary eye toward the Dradis readout. The scanner remained empty. No sign of Cylon activity, though it had been over forty-eight hours since the initial attack.

Uneasiness tugged at Adama, though he was careful to keep this from showing on his face. He couldn't help feeling that the Cylons knew exactly where he was, but they were choosing not to attack. Except there was no reason for them to do this. They could have easily sent another basestar with more raiders long before the *Monarch* had finished evacuating. It was unthinkable that they hadn't. Something else must have interfered. Maybe the first basestar hadn't managed to transmit a signal. Maybe Starbuck's nuclear explosion had jammed their transmissions. Hell, maybe they were running out of basestars. Adama tightened his mouth. Too many maybes. The fact remained that after a full day of no Cylons, it made it worth the risk to put the *Monarch* back to work.

And there was the problem of Sharon Valerii. The search teams continued working around the clock, but Kara and Lee were still the only two people who had set eyes on her since her escape. It was possible she had left the Fleet just as that Godfrey woman had, but Adama doubted it. Caprica Sharon was an outcast among her own people and she was pregnant. She wouldn't go running to them even if she could, and that meant she had concealed herself in the Fleet somewhere. There had been no other attempts at sabotage, thank the gods, but it still made Adama uneasy knowing she was out there. She—or someone very much like her—had nearly killed him less than a month ago. Sometimes he woke up in the night, the sound of her pistol shot ringing in his ears, the pain of the bullet tearing through his gut. It was times like that when he missed Anne the most. Her absence was a black emptiness that trailed after him, no matter how busy he kept himself. He suspected that most people in the Fleet felt the same way about their own loved ones. Adama, at least, had the comfort of knowing his son Lee was nearby, though it scared the hell out of him every time Lee flew a mission. He sighed and wondered what it would be like to be free of crushing stress, to wake up in the morning and not be in some way worried or afraid.

Suddenly the CIC felt confining, the decks and bulkheads hemming him in like a prison. "Going for a walk, Mr. Gaeta," he said. "You have CIC. Shout if you need me."

"Yes, sir," Gaeta said.

Adama strode along *Galactica*'s familiar corridors, keeping his pace fast enough to stretch his legs but not fast enough to start a sweat. Members of crew made way for him, tossing him salutes where appropriate. He had no doubt word was getting around that the Old Man was on the prowl. The idea almost made him smile.

He hadn't been on his feet for more than ten minutes before he almost ran into Saul Tigh in a side corridor. The executive officer was waving a magazine under Kara Thrace's nose. Kara was keeping her face stoic, but Adama caught the amusement that quirked at the corners of her mouth. Adama gave an internal sigh. Kara enjoyed baiting Tigh and he loved raking her over the coals. The two of them were more alike than either of them wanted to think.

"This is conduct unbecoming an officer," Tigh was saying. "Dammit, we're the Battlestar *Galactica*. Or did you forget that during your little outing?"

"Is it against regulations to date a civilian, sir?" Kara asked carefully.

"I'll ask the questions, Lieutenant."

"So that's a no, then. And sir," her tone became sticky-sweet, "I don't recall seeing any unbecoming pictures of me in the magazines. Is it against regulations for people to take photos of me in a public place? It's not something I can exactly control when I'm not on duty."

"You know what I mean," Tigh snapped. He had rolled up the magazine as if to swat her on the nose with it. "We're the military, not some fluffbrain celebrities."

"I can't help it that people think I'm photogenic, sir. I didn't *ask* them to take the pictures, or to publish them."

"You can take these pictures and—"

"Good morning, Lieutenant," Adama interrupted, then nodded at his XO. "Saul."

Kara, seeing him for the first time, snapped a salute. "Sir!"

"May I, Saul?" Adama held out his hand and Tigh, red-faced, handed him the magazine. Adama unrolled it. The title, *Person to Person*, blazed in large yellow lettering across the glossy cover. He flipped through it until he came to the offending pages. Kara tensed visibly. Adama found a slightly fuzzy picture of Kara Thrace walking through a park—presumably on *Cloud 9*—with Peter Attis. They were holding hands. In the next photograph, they were kissing. The accompanying story was short, and only mentioned that Peter and Kara had been seen together often since the concert two days ago. The article was also full of question marks, as in "How serious is this?" and "Can the *Galactica*'s number one pilot keep up a relationship with a rock star?" A sidebar caught his eye. It was headed, GEMINON PRIESTS DENOUNCE PERFORMER'S MUSIC. Adama flicked through the article. Apparently Peter's rendition of "You're the Only One" had ruffled a few religious feathers.

"Interesting stuff," Adama said.

"That it is," Tigh growled.

Adama handed Kara the magazine. "Lieutenant, I don't see a violation in regulations—"

"Thank you, sir," Kara said, an impish note to her voice.

"—so far," Adama finished. "You need to be careful that you two are not seen together when you're in uniform, and I hope I don't need to tell you what the penalty would be if you saw him while on duty."

Kara's face instantly became serious and the impishness left her tone. "No, sir."

"Saul," Adama said, turning to him, "I left Lieutenant Gaeta in charge of CIC. You might want to make sure he hasn't caused any damage while I've been gone."

Tigh hurried off, looking slightly mollified at the chance to inspect Gaeta's work.

"Walk with me a bit, Lieutenant," Adama said. Kara fell into step beside him, and they strolled the busy corridors of the ship. The hallways were never empty, and the pair kept their voices low to avoid being overheard.

"It looked to me like you were proud of the magazine, Kara," Adama said, falling into informal mode. "I never figured you for a publicity hound."

"I'm not, really," Kara admitted.

"What changed?"

They made way for a trio of sweaty joggers and for an ensign pushing a small handcart piled high with plastic crates.

"Colonel Tigh." Her expression became impish. "I didn't realize how much I liked those pictures until he started telling me how inappropriate they were."

"Right." They passed a set of carbon dioxide scrubbers mounted on the bulkhead. Adama automatically listened to make sure they were hissing properly. Maintenance wasn't his personal job, but he couldn't help checking. "You be careful how you handle this, Kara. The media is a starving jackal. It'll devour every bit of you and clamor for more."

"Yes, sir. I'll be careful, sir."

"Thank you, Lieutenant." And they went their separate ways.

"Ready, Chief?"

Chief Petty Officer Galen Tyrol eyed the Raptor, his practiced gaze taking in every scratch, every ding, every repair. This one had a patched wing, its carefully soldered seam just visible. He couldn't see the internal repairs (scavenged communications wiring, newly cleaned CO_2 scrubbers swiped from a dead Viper, deck plating resealed with a compound of his own devising), but he knew every one. These days he couldn't look at a Raptor or a Viper without mentally tallying up what repairs it had required yesterday, what it needed at the moment, and which ones it might need in the near future.

"Why don't I get a vac suit?" he asked.

Margaret "Racetrack" Edmonson shrugged shoulders padded by her vac suit. Her helmet face plate revealed a pretty face framed by long dark hair. "Regs, Chief. Pilot and ECO wear suits. Passengers don't need them."

"Unless we get a micrometeor puncture or a Cylon attacks or—"

She clapped him on the back with a gloved hand. "You're just paranoid because you know all the stuff that can go wrong."

"Well, yeah." He ran a hand over his face, feeling more than a little nervous. "I repair them, I don't fly in them. As a rule."

"This is a sugar run," Racetrack told him. "Straight to Planet Goop, no stops, no Cylons."

"Let's frakking hope so." Helo stepped into view around the Raptor, his heavy vac suit boots thumping softly on the deck. "Chief."

"Lieutenant." Tyrol felt a vague tension humming in the metallic air. He shot Racetrack a quick glance. Her face was carefully neutral. So was Helo's. So was Tyrol's own. Yes, sir—all perfectly neutral. A silence fell across the trio, and Tyrol's discomfort grew.

"Any news about Sharon?" he blurted. Then he mentally kicked himself. He had just mentioned the huge, honking elephant in the room. And to an officer, no less.

"Not a word," Helo said. His voice had a thin quality, transmitted over the suit's intercom, and Tyrol couldn't tell by the lieutenant's tone if he was annoyed, upset, or uncaring.

"Well, that's . . . I mean . . ."

"Oh, frak it," Racetrack said. "Look, that Raptor will explode if we get on board right now, so let's defuse this little bomb right now. Chief, you know that I used to have bad feelings toward you because of your . . . relationship with Sharon.

I don't anymore. Okay? I think you're one of the best men on this ship. Helo, you and the Chief feel weird around each other because he was boink—uh . . . *seeing* the first Sharon before you got involved with Caprica Sharon, the second Sharon. So now you're both tense. Have you two resolved that or what?"

Tyrol looked at Helo and unconsciously rubbed his jaw where the other man had socked him in a fistfight over this very issue. Tyrol had given as good as he got, though. In the end, both had walked away from the fight, silently swearing never to mention it again. Racetrack, however, was throwing it back at them, and Tyrol didn't know exactly what to say.

In the end, it was Helo who broke the silence. "Yeah, we kinda resolved it." He held out a gloved hand with a sheepish grin. "We good, Chief?"

Tyrol hesitated only a moment. "We're good, Lieutenant."

"Good boys." Racetrack clambered over the wing of the Raptor and stepped into the little cabin. "Now climb aboard and strap in like a nice passenger and ECO."

"Since when are *you* a pilot, anyway?" Helo said, following her. Tyrol brought up the rear. "Last I knew, you were still an Electronic Countermeasures Officer like me."

"I've flown plenty of Raptors," Racetrack said defensively. "You'll be up for it next, just watch. Besides, this is just a sugar run."

"You say that over and over like you're trying to reassure yourself," Helo said.

"Shut up."

Tyrol quietly strapped himself into the copilot seat beside Racetrack as Helo pulled the Raptor's hatch shut. He felt oddly naked in just his orange deck uniform. The cabin was fairly small, big enough for maybe one more person. Helo took up his position at the rear, by the ECO console. Ahead of Tyrol, clear

Plexiglas (three scratches, two pockmarks, no cracks) looked out over the deck. He closed his eyes and tried to doze as Racetrack and Helo went through the pre-flight, though he was sure he was too uneasy to sleep. It therefore surprised him to wake up with a small snort when Helo said, "How about some radio time?"

Tyrol wiped drool from his chin. His dark hair felt mussed, and he blinked bleary brown eyes. Sharon had always said his eyes were his best feature. He pushed the thought aside. Ahead of him lay the perfect blackness of space. Suspended in the center of it, Planet Goop turned slowly on its axis. Wispy white clouds chased each other across deep blue oceans and piled up over brown masses of land.

"Radio?" he said. "What's playing?"

"Dunno," Helo replied. "It's always hit-or-miss out here, but luckily you have me on the communications board."

Crackly, uncertain saxophone music filled the cabin.

"No jazz!" Racetrack hollered.

"Sorry. I forgot." Helo fiddled with the boards some more and this time clear voices filtered from the speakers.

"*. . . the success of your concert,*" said an interviewer. "*What was the song again?*"

"*'You're the Only One.' I rewrote the lyrics. It seems to be catching on.*"

"*An understatement, to be sure. You're making some waves about your new spirituality. I've heard the word 'heresy' thrown around here and there.*"

A light laugh. "*Not what I intended. And it's not really heresy. I just maintain that all the gods are merely faces—different faces—of a single loving entity.*"

"Who the frak is this?" Tyrol demanded, affronted.

"Shh! It's Peter Attis," Racetrack said.

"Isn't that the definition of heresy?"

"There are Scriptural passages that support it," Peter countered. *"Though not explicitly. There's certainly nothing in the Sacred Scrolls to deny it."*

"Since when?" Tyrol exploded. "The Book of Pythia specifically states—"

"Hush!" Racetrack interrupted.

"But I'm not trying to become a spiritual leader," Peter continued. *"I'm a singer, not an Oracle."*

"Damn right," Tyrol grumbled.

"You already have people who claim to be followers," the interviewer said. *"What about them?"*

"I haven't done anything to lead them." Another light laugh. *"I think they're really fans. It's always nice to know you've touched someone's life, but I'm just out to entertain, nothing more than that."*

Tyrol shook his head, trying to imagine how his parents—a Priest and an Oracle—would have reacted to such blasphemy. "Explosive" was the only word that came to mind.

The interview came to an end, to Tyrol's relief, and Helo shut off the radio. Tyrol half expected his father to leap out of the shadows and castigate him for sullying his soul with such heretical ideas. Then he wished his father *would* leap out of the shadows, even to yell at him and make him kneel down to pray as he had when Tyrol had been living with them at home on Geminon.

"Looking forward to your stint on Planet Goop, Chief?" Helo asked. The planet in question had now filled the entire view with blue, brown, and white, giving Tyrol the unnerving feeling that he was falling toward the azure ocean. Technically, he supposed he was.

"Not really," Tyrol sighed. "It's not like I don't have enough to do on the *Galactica*. Now they want me helping with harvest equipment on Planet Goop? I have four engines to overhaul and a Viper that's missing a—"

"Now, now," Racetrack admonished. "Everyone has to do their bit for the harvest."

"Yeah? What's your bit?"

"Delivering you."

Half an hour later, the Raptor hit atmosphere. It bucked and jumped for a moment like a recalcitrant horse, and Tyrol swallowed his stomach. Then Racetrack smoothed out. They plunged into a misty white cloud bank. Droplets of condensation gathered and ran across the Plexiglas, chasing each other like quicksilver fairies. Tyrol stared at them, realizing how long it had been since he'd actually been off the *Galactica* and in a real atmosphere, with real clouds. Too bad he couldn't *breathe* the atmosphere. But Planet Goop, with its useful, edible algae, was a hell of a find. A planet fully inhabitable by humans—that was a dream almost beyond imagination. Tyrol loved his job, loved puzzling out what was wrong with a ship, loved straightening bent struts and sealing cracks so the vessel could fly again. It was like being a doctor, in a way, and it was immensely satisfying to watch a Viper he had repaired dive back into a fight, guns he had repaired blazing away. But it was also a fine thing to walk through a forest, smell green leaves, feel a fresh breeze, and it had been so long since he had done any of that.

The Raptor broke free of the cloud and dropped steadily down. Below, Tyrol made out the long, rounded shape of the *Monarch*. It sat on the dark, rocky shore of an ocean. From this low height, the water looked more green than blue. Three long, flat arms protruded from the ship, thrusting themselves outward into the gently rippling waves. As the Raptor grew closer, Tyrol could see the arms were actually enormous conveyor belts with giant scoops spaced evenly along them. According to the briefing he had read and the schematics he had studied, the scoops hauled algae into the *Monarch*'s main processing area. Once an area was denuded of algae, the arms would pivot a few degrees and start work on another section of the algae bed. Eventually, the *Monarch* would pick up and move to a different site.

Racetrack landed the Raptor a few yards from the *Monarch*. Helo handed Tyrol a full-face mask connected to a square unit the size of a beer mug. Tyrol clipped the unit to his belt and donned the mask. It fit tightly over his entire face and smelled like old plastic. Tyrol also connected one end of a corded earpiece to the unit and fitted the other in his ear.

"The unit is a scrubber," said Helo's voice in Tyrol's ear. "It'll extract enough oxygen from the CO_2 in the atmosphere to let you—"

"I know how it works, sir," Tyrol interrupted. "What's the air pressure like?"

"Only a couple millibars under what we're used to." Helo opened the hatch and a hot, humid breeze swept through the cabin. It was like being licked by a whale's tongue. Tyrol's ears popped. "Have fun, Chief."

Tyrol gave him a sour look and exited the Raptor. The ground was rough, the rocks jagged. The planet hadn't had an atmosphere long enough for any real erosion to start. The Raptor fled back into the cloudy sky, and Tyrol turned his attention to the *Monarch*.

The ship looked a lot like a low factory building that had dropped straight down from the sky. The dull roar and steady clank of machinery rumbled beneath a constant wind that plucked at Tyrol's clothing with moist fingers. Already he was sweating. Beyond the ship seethed the great green ocean. Tyrol inhaled, half expecting to smell salt water, but all he got was plastic air. He sighed. Two people were visible near an enormous open hatchway. Tyrol made for them and introduced himself.

"Good to see you, Chief Tyrol," said a woman who turned out to be Captain Renee Demeter. She had short hair the color of fresh brown earth and grass-green eyes. Her voice came through his earpiece. "We're chronically short on repair staff and staff supervisors down here. Even with anti-radiation meds, we can't keep people on the ground for long periods of time. Jim, take the Chief inside and show him around."

"Sure, Cap." Jim wore a gray crewcut and looked like he should be rolling a toothpick from one end of his mouth to the other. His clothes hung loosely on him, as if he'd lost a lot of weight lately. A lot of people in the Fleet had, Tyrol knew. Jim cocked his head toward the truck-sized hatch and went inside. Tyrol followed.

"What's your rank, sir?" Tyrol asked.

Jim glanced over his shoulder. "I don't have one, son. Civilian ship. If Cap tells you to do something, you do it. Come on, I'll show you entry bay two. That's where we need help."

The hatchway opened into a cavelike space. Scoops the size of small trucks and laden with piles of blue-green goop cranked past them on a gigantic conveyer belt and disappeared into an opening in the distant wall. Half a dozen crewmembers, all in face masks, dashed about to tend the machinery. Water dripped from piles of algae and made salty, steamy lakes on the deck. The plating was slick, and Tyrol stepped carefully to avoid slipping. A scoop loader rumbled by, its bucket piled with goop. Abruptly it stopped, backed up, and jerked forward again, barely missing the main conveyer belt. Tyrol winced and automatically reached out a hand, as if he could stop the vehicle.

"Hey!" Jim boomed, his voice loud in Tyrol's earpiece. "Watch it, Hyksos!"

Hyksos gave an odd wave from the driver's seat and maneuvered the loader around again. Jim turned his attention back to Tyrol. Tyrol wiped a fresh layer of sweat from his forehead.

"The belts haul the goop into the processing area," Jim said, cocking a thumb at the opening. "We run it through the rollers and mash it into sheets. We dry them, which makes them easier to handle, and send them out to some of the other ships for processing into food and medicine."

"How'd you adapt mining equipment into handling algae?" Tyrol said. His interest was starting to perk up.

"Crushing, mashing, rolling—we did all that with rocks before. Now we do it with algae. We did have to add a couple of access corridors to help with air circulation and make it easier to move goop around, but the biggest job was cleaning the equipment first. The main problem is that the salt water gets into everything and eats it. And the algae is primitive stuff, only a few steps above protoplasm, so it gunks up everything the water doesn't eat. Lots of constant maintenance. You arrived during one of the good times, when all four arms are hauling at capacity. Usually at least one of them is down."

As if on cue, the arm made a terrible groaning noise, clanked twice more, and went still. A moan rose from the workers in the area. Jim clapped Tyrol on the shoulder.

"Go to it, Chief," he said, and ambled away.

Two hours later, Tyrol's front was wet through, and he was covered in green slime. His fingers were wet and wrinkled. It was a far cry from the carefully controlled environment of the *Galactica*, though he had to admit the lack of "fix it now *now NOW*" pressure was a nice change. He lay on his back, staring up at the secondary motor that was supposed to help haul the conveyer belt forward but wasn't. Goop had clogged the air intake and destroyed the filter which had, in turn, put a strain on the pistons, which had—

Tyrol grimaced. Everything *should* be working now. "Okay, Ken!" he shouted. "Try it again!"

A pause. The motor sputtered and coughed. Tyrol held his breath. The motor coughed again, started to die, then caught. One more cough, and it settled into a steady purr. Tyrol pumped a quiet fist.

"Nice work, Chief!" the unseen Ken said into his earpiece.

A blob of goop plopped on Tyrol's breathing mask. Tyrol jumped. His entire world had gone green. Great—a machine that had to have the last word. He rolled himself out from under the motor and sat up to wipe his mask clean.

"Tabra! Meltina par tewmell fa!"

What the hell? Tyrol pawed at his mask, restoring partial visibility.

"Chief! Watch out!"

Tyrol twisted in place and cleared the last of the slime from his mask. The scoop loader, its bucket now empty, was rushing straight toward him.

CHAPTER

7

"Drive the crazy car at pildani mufallan dar! Dalabren bay heslan duk!"

The voice in Tyrol's earpiece made no sense, but he spared no time thinking about it. The scoop loader's bucket, trailing shreds of green goop, was only a few yards away and closing. Tyrol's heart jumped into his throat and his stomach clenched in fear. He scrambled to his feet, sending the wheeled creeper flying. No time to jump sideways—the bucket would clip him. Without hesitating further, he jumped straight up. The teeth of the bucket's lower edge gouged the air where Tyrol's shins had been. Tyrol grabbed the upper teeth with both hands. The metal bit into his palms and pain wrenched his shoulders as the loader's forward momentum jerked his upper body backward. His lower body swung forward like a pendulum. He barely managed to bring his legs up so his feet slammed the back of the bucket instead of his knees. The loader motor growled like an angry bear. People shouted in his earpiece, but he was too busy to pay attention to what they were saying.

The loader rumbled across the deck plates, with Tyrol still

clinging to the slimy bucket. The driver continued to shout incoherently. His movements were jerky, and neither of his hands touched the steering wheel. A glance over his shoulder showed that the loader was heading straight for the main conveyer belt. Scoops of blue-green goop continued to move down the enormous belt with mechanical unconcern. In a few seconds, he would be crushed.

"Turn!" Tyrol yelled at the driver. "Turn, you bastard!"

"Beelo! Frakking muzzle the dog's myl feldan mool!"

What the hell? Didn't matter. He wasn't turning. *That* mattered. Tyrol swung his body sideways, trying to get his foot up to the teeth lining the top of the bucket. He missed, swung again, and managed to hook an ankle. His hands hurt like hell. A metal tooth slashed the side of his shin with burning pain. The conveyer belt was barely six yards away. Tyrol heaved himself up, cleared the upper teeth, and rolled across the top of the bucket just as it crashed into the belt. The noise smashed through him, and he bounced across the bucket to fetch up against the hydraulic pistons that moved the scoop up and down. Algae flew in all directions, splattering every surface in blue-green goop. The belt screamed like a thousand frightened horses and came to a stop.

Everything fell quiet. Tyrol clung to a piston, trying without success to catch his breath. He was breathing all right but felt like he wasn't getting any air. His vision clouded. At last he realized it was because his breathing mask had been knocked slightly askew, breaking the seal. He braced himself against the bucket and resealed the mask. Air filled his lungs, sweetly plastic. Then several sets of hands grabbed him and hauled him gently down from his strange position on the scoop loader.

"You all right, Chief?" demanded Captain Demeter. She and

several other workers were standing shin-deep in goop. "Frak, we thought you were a goner. How do you feel?"

Tyrol checked. Pounding heart, wavery vision, vague feeling of nausea, burning shin, aching hands. Nothing life-threatening, though he wanted a stiff drink, something better than the stuff he concocted at his own still. He tried to put weight on his injured leg and yelped. Demeter helped him sit, then carefully rolled up his trouser leg, bringing a fresh onslaught of pain. Tyrol gritted his teeth at the sight of the dirty, bleeding gash. Someone ran up with a first aid kit, and Demeter pressed a bandage against the wound. It hurt.

"This will control the bleeding," she said. "Hold it there."

"Yes, sir," he said, obeying. "What the hell happened?"

"No idea," said Jim, the other person who had helped Tyrol clear of the loader. "Hyksos up there just went crazy."

Tyrol looked up at the drivers seat. Two men were dragging Hyksos from his chair. The man appeared to be unconscious, though he twitched strangely. Demeter had him hauled to a clear section of floor and bent over him. He continued to twitch.

"No obvious injuries," Demeter said. "Our sickbay can handle basic problems, but this looks seriously strange. I think we'd better call a shuttle and have Cottle get a look at both of you on the *Galactica*."

"It's not like you to hide in your lab, Gaius."

"I'm not hiding."

"Really? You haven't left this room ever since the lecture. Or rather, since the concert. Scared, Gaius?"

"Of course not!"

Number Six ran a long, cool finger down the bridge of

Gaius Baltar's nose and gave him one of her rare playful smiles. "You can't lie to me, Gaius. I know you too well."

"You think I'm afraid," Gaius snarled. He typed madly at a computer terminal in an attempt to ignore the lush blond woman who had draped herself over the arm of his chair. "You think I'm scared to go out there because people will laugh at my failed—yes, *failed*—lecture. Well, I'm not. I'm a bloody celebrity. There is always some lackwit who finds humor in the trials and tribulations of the famous. It's part of the price of fame, and I've been dealing with it for years. I'm not afraid."

"Absolutely, Gaius." Number Six got up and stretched like a lazy tiger. Her stunning red dress clashed with the harsh light and utilitarian machinery of the lab. "You're not afraid of public humiliation, that much is obvious."

"Good." Type type type. "I'm glad we agree on something. If you don't mind, I need to finish these resource-use projections, now that we have algae coming in."

"You're not afraid of public humiliation," Number Six repeated. "You're afraid of the opposite."

A small ripple of doubt slipped down Gaius's spine. "And just what is *that* supposed to mean?"

"You're afraid," Number Six said, "that no one will notice you at all."

Gaius stopped typing.

"Peter Attis, grabbing all the attention," Number Six continued. "It isn't fair, Gaius. He hasn't your mind. Your brilliance shines like a nova, and his is—"

"Dark matter," Gaius muttered. "Black and omnipresent." He straightened in his chair. "But I'm not afraid of him—or of being ignored."

"Then prove it," Six offered reasonably. "Go for a walk. I hear sickbay's a *terribly* interesting place this time of year."

"Is it?" Gaius muttered. "Look, I have no intention of . . ."

But she was gone.

Gaius set his mouth and went back to typing, trying to ignore the knots in his stomach. She was *not* always right. She had nothing better to do than bait him. But gods, she was so beautiful—and completely his. A hidden flower with soft petals no one else could touch. And she *had* given him good advice. Plenty of times. Hell, back on Caprica she had saved his life.

He glanced at the door, then back at the screen. His resolve firmed. Gaius Baltar was not a puppet for Number Six to jerk around, not a fly caught in Six's web. He was himself, his own man.

Keys continued to clatter under his hands. "You don't own me," he said aloud.

The room remained empty. Click-click-clack-click. The computer keys chattered like teeth. Stupid frakking *Galactica* didn't even have basic vocal interface.

"You *don't* own me," he said again, then braced himself for Six's soft touch on his back, her quiet voice in his ear, her moist tongue on his neck. But it didn't come. He looked at the computer screen. A jungle of gibberish took up four pages. Not one word made sense.

"Oh, the hell with it," he muttered. He grabbed his suit jacket and stormed out of the lab. A few minutes later, he was just outside the main entrance to sickbay. Uncertainty stole over him like a cold hand. What was he supposed to do—stomp in to sickbay and demand they show him something interesting?

Shouts from inside jarred him into action. He shoved open the door and ran inside. Sickbay was set up like a hospital triage unit, with curtained alcoves serving as both examination and treatment areas. The curtains did nothing to shut out noise, and Gaius easily located the source. He dashed down to the third alcove on the left and yanked aside the curtain. Dr. Cottle, his white hair disheveled, was struggling to hold down a patient Gaius didn't recognize. A medical technician was assisting, as was Chief Galen Tyrol, of all people. Tyrol's lower leg sported a bandage.

"He was unconscious a minute ago!" Cottle yelled. "Get him two milligrams of ativan. Move!"

One of the patient's flailing arms caught the medical technician across the bridge of her nose. She staggered and went down to one knee, blood gushing from one nostril. The patient managed to sit up. Tyrol flung himself bodily across the man, who went down but continued to struggle on the bed.

"Billal mulistarken far!" the patient shouted.

"Shut up, Hyksos!" Tyrol yelled back.

Cottle managed to get Hyksos's ankles into restraints, but he was still fighting convulsively. The med tech was trying to get up, but the blow had clearly dazed her. Cottle caught sight of Gaius.

"Don't just stand there, you idiot!" he barked. "This man is having a seizure. The ativan is in the cabinet. Get it!"

Gaius hurried to the cabinet, fumbled it open, and scanned the scantily stocked shelves for ativan. The ampules were in alphabetical order, allowing him to find it quickly. He snatched up a syringe, jammed it into the ampule's rubber top, and yanked the plunger back to two milligrams, then glanced at Hyksos and added another half a milligram for good measure. No sense in taking the chance he might hurt himself—or Gaius. Hyksos managed to shove Cottle aside with his free arm, and the doctor crashed into a tray of instruments. Metal flew in all directions and the tray crashed to the floor. Tyrol was still lying across Hyksos's body. Hyksos continued to thrash, shouting incoherent nonsense. Baltar hesitated. He didn't want to get close. What if Hyksos bruised him? Or worse?

"What are you waiting for?" Cottle said from the floor. "Inject him!"

Gaius took a deep breath and lunged. He got Hyksos's left wrist and trapped his arm. Both Hyksos and Tyrol smelled like stale ocean water. Gaius couldn't help wrinkling his nose as he shoved the syringe into the skin—forget sterilization—and rammed the plunger home. Hyksos continued to babble and shout for a few seconds as Cottle and the med tech got to their feet. Then Hyksos's struggles grew weaker. He fell silent, and his body relaxed. Cottle instantly locked down the wrist restraints and Tyrol slid off the patient's body. He winced when his injured leg took weight.

"Frak!" Tyrol gasped. "What the hell is wrong with him?"

"He was unconscious all the way back from Planet Goop, you said?" Cottle asked. He handed the med tech a towel, and she gingerly pressed it to her face. "You better get some ice for that."

"He was out like a light," Tyrol said. "He muttered a lot, though. Gibberish."

The med tech left. Gaius edged closer for a look at Hyksos, curiosity winning out over caution. Hyksos was a brawny, redheaded man covered with a crop of new freckles. No doubt working outdoors in the harsh sun of Planet Goop had brought them out. The man twitched and muttered in his sleep. Gaius put out a finger and touched his forehead. It was a little on the warm side.

"What's your initial diagnosis, Doctor?" he asked Cottle.

"He's agitated and he has a slight fever," Cottle replied shortly.

"That's it?" Gaius scoffed.

"I haven't run any tests yet, Your Majesty. You want to do something useful, draw some blood and do some tests. Otherwise, get the hell out of my sickbay."

Gaius drew himself up. "*I* am the vice president of the Colonies."

"And I'm God of this sickbay. Either shit or get off the crapper. I don't have all day."

Gaius whirled to stomp out and almost crashed into Number Six. He froze. Six didn't say a word, but a small smile played around the corners of her mouth. With skill borne of long practice, Gaius pretended that he had spun around so he could grab another syringe and a set of blood ampules from the cabinet. Six backed up to give him room, and he gave her a hard look. She met his gaze for a moment, then walked slowly out of the alcove, her hips switching as she went. Gaius watched her go and felt his groin tighten as it always did. As she *knew* it always did. He spun again and turned back to the bed.

"Scarlet fever, drug withdrawal, dengue hemorrhagic fever," Cottle was muttering. "Epilepsy? No, not with a fever." He pried up one of Hyksos's eyelids and shined a light on the eye. The pupil contracted normally.

"Is whatever it is contagious?" Tyrol asked nervously.

"How the hell should I know, son?" Cottle said. "If it weren't for the fever, I'd say his mind snapped. All I can say right now is that if you get the sudden urge to babble, haul your sorry ass down here before you hurt someone."

Tyrol hesitated. "I'm from Geminon, you know."

"Uh-huh. So?" Cottle wrapped a blood pressure cuff around Hyksos's arm and pumped. Gaius rolled up the sleeve on Hyksos's free arm and swabbed the inner elbow with disinfectant. He was a biologist by training, with extensive knowledge of microbiology. He wasn't a medical doctor, but much of the training overlapped. Drawing blood and running some tests were no challenge, but his curiosity was aroused. Besides, Number Six had hinted a visit to sickbay might benefit him, and he was hardly going to pass up the chance that she was right.

"My mother was an Oracle," Tyrol continued. "And sometimes the Lords of Kobol would . . . they would enter her body and make her speak. Sometimes she would say something understandable, but most of the time she sounded like Hyksos here."

"Speaking in tongues as the result of divine possession?" Gaius scoffed. He inserted the needle into a vein and popped one of the ampules into the other end. Scarlet blood streamed into the little container. "Grow up, Chief. There's clearly some microscopic agent at work. Since he was on Planet Goop when it happened, it seems logical to start there. Perhaps something in the algae."

"Then why haven't more people come down with it?" Tyrol countered. "Captain Demeter said no one else has been acting strange."

"Any number of reasons," Gaius said. He finished the current blood ampule and started another. "It might be an allergic reaction. Or perhaps it's a combination of substances that only Hyksos has encountered."

"How many of those you going to fill?" Cottle demanded.

Gaius looked down. He was working on his seventh ampule of blood. Grimacing, he pulled the syringe free, disposed of it, and handed three of the ampules to Cottle. "Can you get me urine and stool samples as well?"

"Why the hell not? You're the vice president of the Colonies."

The back of Helo's head itched but he was standing at attention, so he forced himself to ignore it. The bustle of CIC swirled around him like a sandstorm, and the continual growl of the dradis sounded like a restless lion prowling the room. Tigh gave Helo a hard look.

"Captain Demeter reports that the harvest is complete," Dualla said from her station. "The *Monarch*'s holds are completely full, and she's commenced cleanup procedures. They should be ready to leave by the end of the day."

"Thank you," Adama said. "Send a report to the President. Lieutenant Gaeta, how much material did we end up with?"

"Once it's processed, we should have enough to make current food stores last an extra two months," Gaeta said. "We'll also have more than enough antibiotics to end the strep breakout and restore the radiation meds to full supply."

A ripple of applause and a few small cheers went through CIC. Adama broke into one of his rare smiles. Helo, who was still under the harsh light of Tigh's glare, remained at attention despite the good news.

"What's the status of the Cylon prisoner?" Tigh asked him.

"Nothing new to report, sir," Helo said. "She's still at large."

Tigh continued to stare at Helo, who kept his face impassive. "Then keep looking, Lieutenant. I want that frakking Cylon found!"

"Yes, sir."

"Dismissed."

Helo turned and stepped smartly out of CIC. The moment he was out of sight, he let himself sag against a wall for a tiny moment. Exhaustion pulled at every pore. When had he last had a good night's sleep? He couldn't remember. Four days ago, Sharon had escaped. Two days ago, he had brought Tyrol and that guy Hyksos back from Planet Goop. Tyrol had been injured, Hyksos had been unconscious. Rumor had it that Hyksos was now in sickbay, under restraint. When he was awake, he babbled, spouted nonsense, and tried to attack the doctor. As a result, he spent most of his time under sedation. Helo envied him. The day before yesterday, Tigh had announced that Helo knew more about "that frakking toaster" than anyone else on the Galactica, which meant Helo was now in charge of the search teams. The stress of his new duties combined with the worry about what would happen to Sharon if she got caught and what would happen to *him* if she *didn't* get caught kept him awake long into his normal sleep cycle. Helo was caught between two rocks that were steadily rolling together. If Sharon was caught, Adama would no doubt order her immediate execution, baby or no. If she wasn't caught, Tigh would make Helo the scapegoat. Becoming Tigh's scapegoat was way better than Sharon dying, but Helo still lost. He and Sharon both.

This was, he acknowledged to himself, the reason he was searching for Sharon by himself instead of with a party of marines. If—when—Sharon turned up, the marines were likely to shoot first and ask questions later. Helo wanted to ask questions first. He had no intention of shooting.

The radio clipped to his belt squawked out orders as the search parties continued their work. Their movements had become mechanical, almost perfunctory. They had gone over every inch of the ship to no avail, and Helo was almost considering ordering the men to suit up so they could search the Galactica's outer hull. Maybe Sharon had stolen a vac suit and was—

He shook his head. No way. Even Cylons needed to breathe, and she stood an excellent chance of getting caught every time she cycled an airlock to board and refill her oxygen bottle. Still, his new situation altered the way he looked at Galactica. Every alcove, every passageway had turned into a possible hiding place, every shadow became a black blanket of suspicion. And every moment he was aware that eventually a choice would leap out of the darkness and tear him in two.

He scratched the back of his head. The itch had been bothering him a lot lately, and it helped keep him awake at night. Maybe he was getting a rash or something. That was all he needed.

Helo turned a corner, intending to head for the showers to see if washing would help, then abruptly changed course for deck five. He knew where Tyrol kept his still, and right now a good drink would settle his nerves. He was on duty, but it never stopped Tigh, and Helo was suddenly in a go-to-hell mood.

Deck five was in an unusual lull. Crewmembers were engaged in busywork—cleaning, sorting equipment, taking inventory. Off to one side sat the escape pod Peter Attis had arrived in. Tyrol was walking in a circle around it, examining with a critical eye. A slight limp hobbled his steps a bit. Helo wandered over.

"What's going on, Chief?" he asked. "See something that's going to explode?"

"No." Tyrol wore a distracted expression. "There's something about this pod that bothers me. Has since the day it showed up. But I can't put my finger on it."

"You've checked inside," Helo stated.

"Of course. Thoroughly. With every instrument I have. Nothing."

"Let me take a look," Helo offered. "Maybe it needs a fresh pair of eyes."

Tyrol gave him a look with hard brown eyes. The offer went a little beyond their shaky truce.

"Putting off looking for . . . her?" Tyrol said at last.

"Maybe." Helo felt his face grow warm. "I haven't had much luck."

Tyrol flashed a grim smile of . . . understanding? He stood aside like a doorman. "Be my guest, sir."

Helo stepped into the pod. It was basically a gray metal

cube with rounded corners. Helo's head brushed the ceiling, and he ducked instinctively. A simple control panel stood against the wall opposite the hatch, and two small ports looked out on deck five. A CO_2 scrubber hung on one wall above a set of oxygen tanks. The interior smelled vaguely of machine oil. And that was all. Helo examined the controls. Environmental readouts, automatic distress signal, engine power control. Nothing else. The engine would shove the pod in one direction—forward. No way to steer. The pod was meant to be picked up quickly by a rescue ship, not to provide transportation. Helo stood there for a long moment. He turned in all directions. He pulled the front off the control panel and looked inside. He paced the walls and rapped on the ports. Then he went back outside. His head itched again, and he forced himself not to scratch.

"Well?" Tyrol said.

Helo shrugged. "Nothing. I don't even get suspicious. Maybe you're just reading too much into it because a copy of . . . of *her* was inside."

"Maybe." But Tyrol clearly didn't believe it.

Helo's radio squawked for his attention. *"We've completed our search of the main galley, Lieutenant."*

With a sigh, Helo pulled the unit from his belt and spoke into it. "Continue on to the food storage area, then. And try not to die of boredom."

"Roger that."

He sketched a waved at Tyrol and started to move away, but Tyrol's touch on the shoulder stopped him.

"Chief?" Helo said.

Tyrol leaned close. "I hope they never find her, too," he murmured.

There didn't seem to be anything to say to that, so Helo just nodded and continued on his way. Helo skirted the edge of the main deck and headed for the storage rooms, pretending he was going to look there. Instead, he waited until no one was looking and ducked through a particular doorway. Freestanding metal shelves stacked with meticulously labeled parts stood in neat rows. Helo threaded a path to the rear. Behind a shelving unit stood a tangle of coils and drums. There was no smell—Tyrol had built a fan and filter system into the device to ensure the odor wouldn't give him away. Helo, however, walked past it and knelt in front of a meter-high grate set into the back wall. He tugged once, and it came away, revealing a small open space inside. Tyrol actually kept *two* stills. Commander Tigh had discovered the first one. Instead of shutting it down and ordering Tyrol's arrest, he had wordlessly begun taking a percentage of everything Tyrol made in it. When the percentage climbed to one jar in four, however, Tyrol had taken steps. He had scavenged enough parts to make a second still, one that created higher-quality stuff, and hidden that one more carefully. Tyrol now only made what he called "single malt engine cleaner" in the first still, and Tigh hadn't yet caught on to the ruse.

Helo poked his head into the space behind the grating. The still, compact and efficient, purred softly to itself beside a pile of jars filled with clear liquid. Helo reached for one—and froze.

"Hello," said Sharon Valerii.

CHAPTER

8

Billy Keikeya poked his head into the section of *Colonial One* that served as Laura Roslin's office. "Sarah Porter is here, Madam President."

"Thank you, Billy," Laura said. "Show her in."

Billy ducked back out and President Laura Roslin pulled herself upright in her chair. Gods, she was so *tired*. Gravity pulled at every limb with twice its normal strength, making every movement a struggle. And she ached all the time, whether she was awake or asleep. It was a deep, cold feeling, as if an icy dragon were gnawing at her bones. One day it would bite all the way through them, and she would keel over like a tree with severed roots. It had been going on for so long, she had forgotten what it was like to be pain free. Laura wanted nothing more than to pull on some old sweats, wrap herself in a soft bathrobe, and lie on the couch watching something mindless until she drifted into a restless sleep—or death. Instead she found herself on a chilly ship, an unwilling leader to the last remaining shreds of humanity left in the galaxy while implacable enemies chased them from sector to sector.

A wan smile crossed her face. *Playing the martyr again, Laura?* she thought. She had had several opportunities to hand the reins of government over to someone else and had waved aside every one. Hell, she had *fought* to remain president. Like all teachers, Laura had been trained to lead, but it wasn't her preference. She would much rather let someone else handle all the stress and nonsense while she worked quietly in the background. In her teaching days, she never chaired committees—unless no one else was willing to take the job. Or was qualified for it. She remembered the day Nick Liaden, her department head, had announced his retirement and Helga Upton had announced her intention to take over his position. Horrified, Laura spent her prep period running from classroom to classroom to see if anyone else planned to challenge Helga. Everyone refused. The thought of cold, officious Helga in charge made everyone unhappy, but no one was willing to step up. This one worked two other jobs and didn't have time. That one was pregnant and would be going on leave soon. A third was a new teacher, completely unqualified. So Laura had strode into the principal's office to announce that she wanted the position. He had been all too glad to give it to her, and Laura had spent four years in that capacity. Her experiences had given her many skills that she still used today.

Except none of those experiences had given her the skills to cope with dying. Laura reached for a pencil, intending to toy with it, then decided it wasn't worth the energy. Sometimes she felt as if she had accepted her impending death, other times she felt a gut-twisting terror that kept her awake late into the night. The concert two days ago had bolstered her spirits for a while, returning her to a time when her biggest worry was whether her students' math scores were going up or down. The boost in her mood hadn't lasted, however, and now, frankly, she was feeling pretty shitty all around. The last person she wanted to talk to was Sarah Porter. But duty called.

The curtain that covered the doorway parted and Sarah strode into the room like a thunderstorm laden with hail. She was a dark-skinned, full-bodied woman who preferred short hair and favored chunky gold earrings. Currently, she represented Geminon on the Quorum of Twelve, and Laura had mixed feelings toward her. Geminon had a well-deserved reputation for conservative political parties that tried to mix religion into government, and Sarah represented her people well. She had been one of Laura's most vociferous opponents early in her presidency, then had abruptly become a firm supporter once the Scrolls of Pythia had revealed Laura to be the fabled dying leader who would lead humanity to its new homeland. As an experienced politician, Laura was always willing to accept a supporter, but as a human being, Laura had a hard time pretending to like someone who had once professed to hate her.

And behind her . . .

Behind her came a tall, dark-haired man with the look of someone who had once been hard and handsome but had now gone rather to seed. Lines softened his sharp features, and his nose looked a little too big for his face. His expression was as bland as a mayonnaise sandwich, but Laura Roslin wasn't fooled for a moment.

"Tom Zarek," she said. "I thought my appointment was with Sarah alone."

"I asked to come," Tom said. "As a witness."

"Witness to what?" Laura asked.

"What transpires here," Sarah said.

Laura didn't like the sound of that at all. She briefly considered calling Billy in to throw Tom out, then dismissed the idea. Tom had spent considerable time in jail for inciting riots—and worse. He was an old-school revolutionary who distrusted all government on principle and who had a distressing amount of charisma that he could turn on and off like a light switch. It was currently set to "off," but Tom could fire up a crowd like no one Laura knew—except perhaps Peter Attis—and she envied Tom that talent even when he used it against her, as he had done. He had started a revolution among his fellow prisoners on the *Astral Queen,* a process that had ended up with Tom not only being granted his freedom, but also grabbing a seat on the Quorum of Twelve as the representative of Sagittaron. If Laura tossed Tom out of this meeting, he would raise hell about it in the media, and there was no way Laura could come away from it without looking bad.

"As you like," she said. "Please sit."

They did. Tom's face remained neutral, but Sarah wore an angry expression Laura knew well because it had often been pointed in Laura's direction. Laura tensed, which took energy she couldn't really spare.

"I hate to bother you with this," Sarah said, "but I don't know what else to do."

A wary bit of relief threaded through Laura. Porter wasn't here to cause Laura trouble, then—at least, not directly. So why Tom's presence?

"What's on your mind, Sarah?" Laura asked in her sympathetic voice.

"A fringe group that calls itself 'the Unity' has been causing problems," she said. "Especially on the *Tethys* and the *Phoebe.*"

"Problems?" Laura asked. "What sort of problems?"

Porter's expression was set like stone. "They're spreading like can—like weeds. They stand in the corridors and local gathering places and *preach.*"

"What do they preach?" Laura noticed the switch from

"cancer" to "weeds," but pretended not to. Sudden exhaustion swept over her, and she had to fight to keep from slumping in her chair. Uh-oh. The day was turning into a bad one. Her treacherous body did that to her, switching her from functional to exhausted without warning.

A look of disgust crossed Porter's face. "They wear red masks so we can't tell who they are and they preach that all the gods are merely multiple aspects of a single god. They preach that the single god is a being of love and kindness and that nothing else exists. This is heresy, Laura! Heresy *and* blasphemy! The Scrolls are very clear on—"

"I don't need a lecture on comparative spirituality, Sarah," Laura interrupted gently. "Though I have to say the ideas as you've presented them make me . . . uncomfortable. And they sound familiar."

"Of course they do," Porter spat. "Peter Attis sings about it. His songs are all over the radio now, especially that 'You're the Only One' song. These Unity people have taken it as some sort of spiritual call. Haven't you heard him? It seems like he shows up somewhere on the radio four or five times an hour."

"I haven't noticed," Laura admitted. "I went to the concert, and I have to say I enjoyed it very much"—*until the escaped Cylon showed up*, she added mentally—"but I really haven't had time or inclination for the radio lately."

Throughout this exchange, Tom remained silent. Laura's attention was on Sarah, but she was aware of Tom, much like the way a feeding rabbit remained aware of a hawk wheeling overhead. His presence made no sense, and it nagged at her like a hangnail that had almost come free. She was dying to ask what his real purpose was, but knew that would be a mistake. It would put him in the position of holding information she clearly wanted. Better to let him think she didn't care, rendering his information worthless and forcing him into a position of lesser power.

"Keeping in mind that we do have freedoms of speech and religion in the Colonies," Laura said carefully, "I need to ask— have the Unity people broken any laws?"

Long pause. Still Tom didn't speak.

"No," Porter said at last. "Their demonstrations have been peaceful and orderly so far. And so far they've agreeably moved out of the way whenever someone has asked. A few fights have started, but never by the Unity. Other people always hit first." She folded her arms. "People get upset and angry wherever the Unity goes. Perhaps we can arrest them on the grounds that they instigate unrest."

Alarm bells rang in Laura Roslin's head. Early in her career as president, Commander Adama and Colonel Tigh had accused her of instigating unrest and tried to force her out of office. She had resisted and eventually won her position and their respect, but the situation had been dicey for a while, and Laura had lived in fear that what remained of the Colonies was heading for a military dictatorship. Now Sarah Porter looked to be heading down a similar road, one that led to a religious dictatorship. But how should she turn Sarah aside? It was always best to convince rather than dictate, whether you were teaching or governing, but Laura was so damned *tired*. Her mind flowed like a slushy stream, and she couldn't get herself to focus.

Wake up! she told herself sternly. *You can sleep when you're dead, and the way things are going, that'll be right soon. So get your work done, woman.*

The room wavered like a desert mirage. What was the last thing Sarah had said? Something about arresting Unity members as dissidents. A small part of Laura agreed with Sarah's sentiments, wrong-minded as they were. Maybe she could use her own sympathy to get Sarah's and bring her around. Dammit, she hated this. It was like being forced to work under the worst case of flu in history. A drain had opened and strength was rapidly flowing out of her. She could barely sit up now, but she had to find the strength to speak somewhere. Laura took one deep breath, then took a second. But before she could speak, Tom raised a finger.

"I need to interject here, Sarah," he said. "I feel duty-bound to remind you that it's the government's job to protect its citizens, and regardless of how we"—and Laura instantly caught Tom's careful use of *we* instead of *you*—"might feel about them, it sounds like the Unity members are actually victims who need protection. As government officials, we don't have the luxury of deciding who is worth protecting and who isn't. If the Unity is attacked, it's our job to defend its members."

Laura stared, unsure of her own ears. Tom was taking *her* side? Why?

But even as she asked, the answer came. Tom was all about the rights of the individual, no matter how difficult or inconvenient those rights might be. That included the rights of a religious minority. Laura had automatically assumed Tom was out to make trouble for her, but instead he was helping. She glanced at him with a small measure of respect, but he didn't seem to notice.

"I should defend heretics?" Porter's face was hard. "Tom, Geminon has a long history of careful adherence to the laws set down by the Lords of Kobol. These Unity people are damning themselves by their preachings and their beliefs."

"Then it'll be up to the Lords of Kobol to deal with them," Laura said. The words came with aching slowness, as if she had to pull them out of thick mud. "But in the meantime, we can't tell them what to believe or what to say."

"They're dangerous! Just listening to their lies turns my stomach and makes me fear for my soul." Porter got up and paced around the tiny office like an angry wolf. Laura envied her easy power, her fluid vitality. What would it be like to have strength to spare for pacing? She felt herself slump a little more. In minute she was going to collapse, she could feel it. Laura had to wrap this up, get Sarah out of her office before that happened.

"How can I let them spread such filth around Geminese ships?" Sarah continued, oblivious to Laura's distress. "They threaten everything Geminon stands for, and they need to be exterminated."

And then the words came to Laura. She murmured, "That sounds like something the Cylons would say."

That stopped Sarah Porter. She stared at Laura for a long moment, then turned and gazed out the window. Laura never could bring herself to call them "portholes." Stupid thought to have right before you were going to collapse. She needed to speak, but her energy was gone. The floor rocked slightly—a bad sign—and the words wouldn't come.

Tom came to her rescue. His charisma was in "on" mode now, and his presence filled the room like a brewing thunderstorm. "If you want another assessment," he said, "think of it this way. We'll turn the Unity into martyrs if we muzzle them or arrest them. It would probably be better to take the tone of a parent indulging the whims of a silly child. You know what I mean—'It's a phase. He'll grow tired of it and come around.' And if there is no truth to what they preach, the Unity will eventually collapse. Then you can look merciful and magnanimous by accepting its former members back into the fold." He flashed a grin. "Everyone wins."

Sarah continued staring out at the cold stars. Laura was holding herself upright now by sheer strength of will, and even that was fading fast. But if she dismissed Sarah now, it would look like Laura was ordering Sarah to agree with her instead of letting it happen naturally.

Please, Laura begged silently. *See it my way. Our way. Then both of you can go and I can collapse.*

"All right," Sarah said at last. "We'll try it that way. Thank you, Madam President. Tom."

Laura nodded acknowledgment. Her head weighed a thousand pounds and the motion almost broke her neck. Sarah left, and Tom was at the curtains. Her energy was gone, but somewhere she found a tiny spark that let her speak.

"Tom," she said. Her voice was soft partly out of calculation and partly out of necessity.

He stopped at the doorway and turned, eyebrows raised.

"Why?" She was whispering now. "Why take my side?"

Tom paused, and for a horrible moment Laura was sure he was going to say he had helped because she was dying. She didn't think she could stand the pity of someone like Tom Zarek.

"It's never been about you, Laura," he said softly. "It's been about the people."

He left. The moment the curtains fell shut behind Tom Zarek, Laura collapsed over her desk blotter. She lay there, halfconscious. In a minute she would have the strength to get up and move to the couch, but for now . . .

"Madam President?" An urgent hand shook her shoulder. "Madam President, are you all right? Should I call the doctor?"

Laura managed to raise her head enough to look into Billy Keikeya's eyes. "Doctor Cottle can't do anything, Billy. I just need to sleep."

"At least let me help you to the couch," he said. "Come on."

She was only vaguely aware of Billy's solicitous hands

guiding her to the couch and helping her lie down. His presence comforted her more than it should have, and she wondered, not for the first time, what their relationship might have been if they hadn't been separated by multiple decades and several lines of professionalism. "Billy," she said. "I'm glad for your help."

"It's what I'm here for, Madam President," was all he said.

The still hissed quietly to itself. Helo remained frozen, his head still sticking into the space behind the grating that hid the little machine. Sharon knelt beside it, looking almost serene. She wore a bulky gray jumpsuit she must have scavenged or stolen from somewhere. It looked warm, and it completely hid her rounding stomach. Helo couldn't even tell she was pregnant.

"Frak," Helo whispered. "Sharon, are you okay?"

"Perfectly fine," she said. "Though now that you've seen me, I may have to kill you."

Helo went cold all over. Sharon could do it. He had seen her move inhumanly fast before, and she was strong as a steel spider. "You wouldn't," he said, hoping he sounded braver than he felt.

"Actually, I haven't decided yet. That's why you're still alive, Helo."

"Why . . ." Helo swallowed. "Why did you kill the guard? You could have just knocked him out. Hell, why escape at all?"

Sharon snorted. "You have to ask?"

"I do. Dammit, Sharon, you've done nothing but help us before. Why run now?"

"The reason's standing in front of you, Helo," Sharon scoffed. "But you're too stupid to see it. After everything I've done for *Galactica*, you still kept me in a cage. You treat me like an enemy."

"I don't."

"Well, no," Sharon admitted. "That's true. But you haven't tried to persuade Adama to release me, either."

"How do you know what I have or haven't done?"

"If you really tried—really, really tried—you could get me released. So frak it. You treat me like an enemy, I'm going to act like one. It's a hell of a lot more interesting than sitting in a cell all day, Helo."

"How did you get out, anyway?"

"Please," she snorted again. "That little box you call a jail? Not even close. I only pretended that cardboard brig could hold me. Adama would have spaced me if he had known otherwise."

"But now you're in worse trouble," Helo pointed out, trying to remain calm and reasonable. Sharon sat serenely, but he saw coiled springs and sheathed claws in her body language. He felt like he had found a tiger in his closet, or maybe a time bomb. "Half the ship is hunting for you."

"Like they'll ever find me."

"I did."

"Because I let you."

"The platoons—"

Sharon waved this off. "You're not creative enough to look in *all* the places someone could hide. You just look in the places where you *think* someone could hide. I'm a lot more bendable than a human. You guys don't bend—you break."

"What about our baby?" Helo said. "Didn't you think of that before you escaped?"

"The baby," she repeated. "Yes, I thought about it. I decided it would be better for it to die free than live in a prison."

"Commander Adama would never imprison a baby," Helo protested.

"Oh, sure. And she'd have a fine life, right? A half-breed, living among humans. You have a great track record for love and tolerance. Admit it—you think of the baby as half Cylon."

"As opposed to?" Helo asked, a bit of anger edging past the fear.

"Half human."

That stopped Helo. He had to admit Sharon was right. He thought of the baby as half Cylon, meaning he focused on the nonhuman aspect. And the baby was his own. How would other people react to such a child? Would they see a child or a creature that was half enemy? The answer was obvious.

"How would *your* people see the baby?" he countered. "As half human?"

"We want babies, Helo," she reminded him almost gently. "This one would be precious—the first baby born to a Cylon ever."

"But your people killed babies," Helo shot back. "Thousands of them. Hundreds of thousands."

"Are you trying to guilt me into turning myself in?" she asked. "It won't work. I'm not going back to that cell. It's more interesting out here. There's more to do, causing trouble for the Fleet. And you don't have a hope of catching me. Even if I decide not to kill you, I'll be long gone before you can call the marines."

"And what about when you're too pregnant to get around well? Or when the baby is born? You can't hide a crying baby."

"I'll worry about it then." She leaned toward him over the still, and Helo had to force himself not to draw away. Abruptly she grabbed his face with both hands and yanked him into a long, hard kiss. Her lips were cool. He forced himself not to struggle—she could break his neck. Maybe she was planning to.

A part of Helo wondered if he looked ridiculous, with his ass hanging out of the vent space and his torso pulled over a still. Then Sharon released him.

"So that's what it's like," she murmured.

Helo blinked to clear his head. It was buzzing. "What do you mean?"

"Just Cylon talk," she said. "You'd better get going now. I'm not going to kill you."

"Yeah?" His tone was slightly sarcastic. "Because I'm a good kisser?"

"Because someone else just might do the job for me."

Before he could respond, alarms blared all over the ship.

CHAPTER

9

"Report, Mr. Gaeta," snapped Adama.

"Ten—make that *twelve*—Cylon raiders and one heavy raider at the edge of dradis range," Gaeta said crisply. "No basestar."

"Thank the gods for small favors," Tigh muttered.

"Set Condition One," Adama ordered, and Tigh reached for the PA phone to comply. "Get the Vipers out there. Dualla, how close is the *Monarch* to clearing the planet?"

"This is Colonel Tigh. Set Condition One throughout the Fleet," Tigh's voice boomed from the loudspeakers. *"Repeat: Set Condition One."*

"Captain Demeter estimates half an hour, sir," Dee replied.

"One side or the other will be dead by then," Tigh said, dropping the receiver into its cradle. A loud *clunk* thudded from the PA system—Tigh had forgotten to shut off the PA before he hung up. Dualla winced as the sound echoed in her headphone. "Why would they send such a small force? They have to know that we can eat a tiny group like that for breakfast."

"Maybe it's a scouting mission," Gaeta said.

Adama eyed the dradis readout as it growled to itself. Twelve little Cylon raiders buzzed toward the Fleet. It sounded like a nursery rhyme. *Twelve little raiders buzzing from the heavens. Vipers ate one and that left eleven.* They moved steadily forward, like barracuda skimming toward a wounded fish. Except this particular fish was a shark, and the barracuda in question were smart enough to know better. What the hell was going on?

"Scouting parties have all been smaller than this," Adama said. "And raiding parties have always been bigger. This doesn't add up. Dualla, do we have radio connection with the Viper squadron yet?"

"Affirmative, sir." Dualla threw a switch, and distorted voices filtered from the CIC speakers.

"Listen up," Adama said loudly. "There's something odd going on this time around. The enemy is up to something strange, and I want all of you to use extra care." Even as he gave the order, he realized how idiotic it sounded. The Viper pilots *always* used extra care. Anyone who flew out using anything less was unlikely to return.

"*Got it, sir,*" Lee said, and Adama felt the usual mix of pride and fear—pride that his son was CAG, fear that he would never come back.

"*Maybe they thought we were gone,*" Kara said. "*Figured they'd get Planet Goop for themselves.*"

"*Maybe they want to work on their tans,*" Hot Dog said. "*Or maybe they want tickets to the next Attis concert.*"

"*Table the conversation,*" Lee ordered. "*We have a mission.*"

"*Roger that,*" Kat said. "*Roger dodger codger with a pipe.*"

Adama shot Tigh a glance.

"*What was that, Kat?*" Starbuck said. "*I didn't copy.*"

"*I said, 'We'll smash 'em flat.'*"

Adama gave a mental shrug. Radio distortion, must be. But

Tigh looked concerned, and Adama was afraid his own face wore the same expression.

The first Cylon raider dipped and swooped against the starry black background. Kara's cross-hairs dipped and swooped just behind it on her screen. Her breath sounded harsh and steady inside her helmet.

"Come on, frakker," she muttered. "Come on."

Then the raider zigged when it should have bet on zag. Kara thumbed the fire button. She felt more than heard the soft thump of gunfire, and the raider went up in the usual yellow fireball. It was amazing, actually. The single flick of her thumb destroyed an enemy. A small action that precipitated an enormous consequence. The ultimate in power and control. She loved it. Out here, she was in control of her own destiny. Out here, the choices were crisp and clear, with no emotional tangles. It was fly the ship, destroy the enemy. Nothing else mattered. Lee only mattered as her CAG, and Peter . . .

. . . Peter didn't matter at all.

It had been almost three days since their . . . encounter after the concert. Kara had slid out of Peter's bed without awakening him, dressed, and slipped out. No emotional tangles, thanks. It wasn't what she wanted right now. She had lost Zak Adama, her fiancé, to a flight accident. She had lost Samuel Anders, another lover, to the resistance movement he was still fighting back on Caprica. She didn't need to get involved with someone else right now.

But another part of her remembered Peter's mouth on hers, the way he touched her, the way he had sung to her after their lovemaking had ended. Her loneliness hadn't disappeared, but it had certainly ebbed. Still, he hadn't tried to contact her, and she hadn't tried to contact him, not even to get tickets for his second concert, which was tonight. And that was for the best.

It sure was.

Another raider came about and trained its guns on her. Kara casually twitched her joystick and her Viper smoothly skimmed out of range. Then she abruptly reversed, flipped over, and fired back in the direction she had come. The raider exploded. Kara twitched the joystick again, the Viper came about, and once again she was facing the rest of the raiding party. A strange emotion came over her—calm mixed with exultation. It felt as if her senses had merged with the Viper and stretched out to encompass the rest of the squadron and the Cylon raiding party. She could see exactly what needed to be done and exactly how to do it. Kara allowed herself a small grin. She recognized the feeling—she was heading into the Zone. Her grin widened. A pilot who hit the Zone could do no wrong, make no mistakes, remained invincible. It was a glorious—and rare—place to hit. Better than a runner's high. Better than sex, better than art, better than music. Better than life.

The other raiders fell back out of firing range and spread out, as if creating a net. Behind them hovered the blocky form of the heavy raider. Kara could see every detail—the exact shade of red of each scanning Cylon eye, the position of every star, the tiny flare of every rocket booster. Around her, flying in perfect formation, was the rest of the squadron—Lee, Kat, Hot Dog, Mack, Ukie, and Powerball. Kara knew where they were without even looking.

"*Nice shooting,*" Lee said.

"Roger that," Kara said. "I'm in the Zone."

"*Chaldena talush saemal,*" came Hot Dog's voice. "*Vili ve.*"

"*Hot Dog, are you all right?*" Lee said. "*I didn't copy that.*"

There was a pause. *"I t-tried to s-say it was pretty impressive,"* Hot Dog replied. *"I've never b-b-been in the Zone."*

"That's not what it sounded like you said," Kara put in. "It sounded like nonsense."

Hot Dog didn't answer. The Cylons hovered, still out of range, still waiting. Kara felt the moment, the Zone, slipping away.

"Let's go in and get 'em," she barked.

"I'm CAG, Lieutenant. CAG stands for 'guy who's in charge,'" Lee reminded her. Brief pause. *"Okay, blow them out of the sky!"*

Kara vaulted forward, then yanked her Viper upward to avoid a spray of fire from one of the raiders. She brought her nose around, snapped the cross-hairs into position, and fired. The Cylon quivered under the hail of bullets, then soundlessly blew up in a satisfying ball of flame.

"That's three!" Kara whooped.

"Kildra nash," Hot Dog shouted. His Viper overtook hers and rushed straight at the hole Kara had made in the line of raiders. Except his ship jumped and wobbled like a baby bird just learning to fly. It jerked around, then abruptly skewed sideways, dropping out of Kara's line of sight.

"What the hell are you doing, Hot Dog?" Lee demanded. He fired at a raider, and it exploded. Only eight left, plus the heavy raider. Kat and Powerball were engaged in a dogfight with a pair of Cylons. Mack failed to dodge a third raider quickly enough, and his Viper shuddered under his opponent's fire.

"I'm losing altitude control!" he shouted. *"Frak! I can barely keep myself upright."*

Kara punched her own thrusters and zipped into the space between Mack and the Cylon. She spun about and fired. The Cylon jerked as she raked one of its wings. It climbed, trying to get around her.

"Get back to the *Galactica,* Mack!" Kara ordered. "Go!"

"*Nultani nultanil reb!*" Hot Dog said. "*Fleg anzara bekki!*"

Kara glanced at her screen. She had forgotten about him. Hot Dog's Viper bobbled about her readout like a drunken spider. A raider zeroed in on him, diving like a falcon reaching for a rabbit. Her heart lurched. Shadow's death loomed in her mind, but Kara was too far away to do anything about it.

"*I got him,*" Yukie said, and gunned the Cylon down.

"*Hot Dog, respond!*" Lee ordered. "*Brendan!*"

But Hot Dog only spouted more gibberish. His Viper continued to fly in erratic lines. Beyond him, Kat and Powerball destroyed their Cylons, leaving only five and the heavy raider. They hovered silently in place, almost as if they were watching.

"*Got it!*" Powerball howled. "*One more dead mother-frakkin' Cylon.*"

"*Yilt denow!*" Kat said. "*We rock!*"

Kara's blood ran cold. "Repeat that, Kat. You sounded like Hot Dog for a minute there."

"*Bedlom pilt kareem Hot Dog,*" she said. And her Viper began to wobble, too.

"*Shit!*" Lee said. "*What the hell is going on? Kat, Hot Dog, and Mack—haul it back to* Galactica. *Move it! The rest of you, wipe out the rest of the Cylons.*"

Kara flipped her Viper around to orient on the remaining enemy ships. But even as she punched up her thrusters, six flashes of white light blasted across her retina. The Cylons vanished into hyperspace.

"They're gone?" Kara said. "Just like that?"

"*Maybe they figured we were winning,*" Lee said.

"*Viper squadron, this is* Galactica *Actual,*" Commander Adama's voice broke in. "*Return to* Galactica *immediately. And I want all of you in sickbay.*"

Kat and Hot Dog landed unevenly. Both of them needed steady encouragement and orders to stay focused, and both of them spoke a steady stream of nonsense words laced with occasional snatches of normal speech. Kara landed her own Viper, the clamps engaged, and the elevator went through its usual descent. The moment her canopy opened, Kara yanked off her vac suit helmet and vaulted clear of the little ship. A small swarm of people had surrounded Kat's and Hot Dog's Vipers, and both pilots were being helped down to the deck. Kara caught a glimpse of Hot Dog's pale face. His mouth was moving, but she couldn't catch the words. Abruptly he went into convulsions. A stream of unintelligible words rolled from his mouth. Kara's stomach turned. Illness always creeped her out. It was worse when someone she liked was sick, and she liked Hot Dog. When a bunch of *Galactica's* pilots had died in an accident, Adama had ordered Kara, an experienced flight instructor, to shove him, Kat, and several others through intensive flight training. She knew him fairly well as a result, and she fervently hoped both he and Kat would be all right.

Hot Dog continued to babble. His eyes were wide open and alert, his expression both frightened and mystified. It looked as if he knew what was going on, but was powerless to stop it. Looking at him sent a chill down Kara's spine.

"Medic!" someone shouted. "Get him a stretcher!"

"He's speaking in tongues," said someone else. "The Lords of Kobol speak through him!"

That hushed the onlookers. Kara blinked. She knew of the concept, had heard that some Oracles went into strange fits that foretold the future or channeled the Lords of Kobol themselves. Was that the source of her unease? Were the Lords of Kobol present? Kara fought an urge to look over her shoulder.

Over by her own Viper, Kat kept her feet with the assistance of a repair technician. "Green eyes like a cat mouse in a trapdoor in a barn horse riding into the sunset," she said. "F-frak! I'm . . . I can't keep my key in the lock of my brainwave pattern of a dress my mother sewed for her tenth anniversary."

A medic appeared with a stretcher, and several people were helping Hot Dog onto it. Lee was among them. Hot Dog continued to thrash and babble. Kara dashed over to Kat and put a hand on her forehead. It was hot and moist. Her dark skin had a ghoulish cast to it.

"She has a fever," the repair tech said. "I can feel it through her clothes."

"Kat, can you hear me?" Kara demanded, looking into her eyes. "Can you tell me what's wrong?"

"I . . . I have no idea what's up in the sky with pie and apples and pears of two or three green leaves. Pel dar mayfel nam! Frak!" She shook her head. "I'm trying . . ."

"Try not to talk." Kara ducked under one of Kat's arms while the technician ducked under the other. They lifted Kat partly off her feet. "Let's get you to sickbay along with Hot Dog."

"Bun in a refrigerator," Kat agreed.

"I don't know what to make of it," Cottle sighed. He ground his cigarette out in the ashtray on Adama's desk. "I've got three people babbling and convulsing in my sickbay with no idea what's behind it. Meds help, though they just treat the symptoms, not the cause. I'm stumped. I'm waiting for some more test results to filter through, but so far I'm finding no viruses, no bacteria, not even a protozoan. But some weird agent is attacking their brains."

"What exactly does this agent do?" Adama asked. He was

sitting rigidly behind his desk, forcing himself not to drum his fingers or tap his feet. This was not good news, and he was so frakking *tired* of bad news. Two pilots incapacitated, possibly dying. Chief Tyrol nearly mowed down. Tiredness washed over him. Another three or four cats had been added to the pile he was juggling.

"Just reading from their symptoms," Cottle said, "I think it attacks the language and motor control centers first. This, by the way, means the little sucker can cross the blood-brain barrier, which isn't easy. It's why brain diseases are so rare."

"You're sure it's a disease," Adama said. "Not something else."

A knock came at the door and Gaeta poked his head into the room. "I'm sorry to interrupt, Commander, but you wanted to be informed the moment the *Monarch*'s crew had cleared Planet Goop."

"Thank you, Lieutenant. Are the Jump coordinates still good?"

"I've been keeping them updated," Gaeta replied.

"Then let's get the hell out of this sector," Adama said. "Order all ships to Jump immediately."

"Sir." Gaeta vanished.

"I'm not ruling anything out at this point," Cottle said, answering Adama's earlier statement. "Radiation exposure, toxin, something in the food. I don't know. The problem is, I can't find a common vector. Hyksos works on the *Monarch*. Kat and Hot Dog, as everyone likes to call them, are Viper pilots. They don't all three know each other, they don't eat the same food or drink the same water. All three have been in space recently, but that was after they were showing symptoms. My gut says it might be something from Planet Goop simply because it's the only new thing that's been introduced to all of us, but I have no evidence

to support that. Hell, I don't even know if this thing is contagious or not."

Adama felt the sudden strange shift that indicated the ship's
Jump drive was powering up. It was as if his clothes were turning inside-out with him still inside them. A bit of nausea sloshed
through his stomach, he felt a slight *wrench*, and it was over.
Jump successful. Cottle didn't seem particularly bothered, and
Adama kept his own face impassive. He straightened his glasses
and continued the conversation. "What are you doing to learn
more?"

"All kinds of tests on every body fluid and tissue I can
reach. Dr. Baltar is doing the same, though His Majesty hasn't
deigned to report anything to me, so I don't know if he's found
anything."

"I'm sure he'd say something to one of us if he did," Adama
said.

"Sure," Cottle drawled. "It's not like he's weird or strange or
anything. Always well-behaved in public, that's our vice president."

"Kara! Kara Thrace!"

Kara spun and came face-to-face with Peter Attis. He leaned
down and gave her a quick kiss before she could react. Two
passing repair techs turned to stare.

"Uh, hi," she said, caught off guard. She felt strangely
breathless and struggled to hide it.

"I was beginning to think you'd forgotten who I am," he
said with a grin. Then the grin faded. "You haven't, have you?"

She looked at him, and all her earlier cautions came flooding
back. She didn't need to get involved with anyone right now.
She didn't need to be tied down or entangled.

She didn't need to.

But that was it, wasn't it? She didn't *need* to. But that didn't mean she couldn't. Kara tossed her doubts aside with a laugh, then gave Peter a brief hug and stole an ass-grab in the process. His butt cheek was firm with muscle, and she liked the way it filled her hand. Peter stiffened, then laughed himself. It was a liquid, masculine sound that flowed over her with unexpected warmth. She drew him into a side corridor so they wouldn't block traffic or garner more stares, then gave him a kiss of her own, a longer one this time. Her body pressed against his, and she could feel his response.

"I haven't forgotten," she said. "But I wasn't sure you wanted to see me again. Rock star always moving on and all that."

"Give up my number one groupie? You have to be kidding! Besides, what would the tabloids say?"

She laughed again. It was *fun* to laugh with Peter. She kissed him again, thanking the gods that she was officially off duty and able to steal a few kisses without violating regs.

"Are you coming to the concert tonight?" he asked. "I've got tickets for you and for . . . for Lee, if you want to bring him."

And suddenly she was reluctant. "I don't know," she said. "I have the feeling . . . we just came away from a Cylon raid, and it was a little weird. They Jumped away just when things were getting interesting."

"Well that's *good* news, isn't it?"

"Yeah . . ." Kara reached up and smoothed a bit of his hair. "But it doesn't feel right." She thought about telling Peter about Kat and Hot Dog, then changed her mind. No one had said to keep the problem quiet, but she wasn't sure it was a good idea to spread the information around the Fleet. "My instincts tell me to stay on alert status, even though I'm off duty until tomorrow."

Peter took her hand. "Look, if you won't come to the concert, then have dinner with me. On *Cloud 9*. They feed me pretty
well over there. What do you say?"

Okay, that'd be great. "Not sure," she said.

"Look, you work hard defending us. You deserve some 'me'
time. And it's only dinner. Not like it's an entire evening. What
do you say?"

She wavered. Fresh after a Jump was usually the safest time.
It would take the Cylons some time to track them down again. If
she wanted to grab some R&R, this was the best opportunity.

"All right," she said. "Where should we meet?"

"Can you find the Gilded Lily?" he asked.

Her eyes widened a little. "Sure! But they're pretty expen-
sive. Especially now."

"The owner's a fan," Peter said, a smile in his eyes. "Meet
me there at five, okay? I have to be backstage by seven."

"Sounds perfect."

He gave her another kiss, then turned and strode away.
Kara watched him go, noticing the little bounce in his step.

Gaius Baltar frowned into the microscope eyepiece. A crowd of
red blood cells and occasional white blood cells drifted slowly
through a sea of plasma. He refocused, bringing the image
closer. A donut-shaped red blood cell, or platelet, ballooned to
the size of a basketball. Using precise nudges of the controls, he
edged the slide a few microns to the left. The platelet slid sideways a little, and Gaius brought the focus in even tighter. Some
of the larger individual molecules were starting to take shape
now, emerging in fractal patterns on the platelet's cell mem-
brane and in the plasma itself. A little closer, and . . .

There it was. A clump of molecules that had caught his eye earlier. He moved in closer yet so he could examine a single one. It looked like three twisted ribbons attached to each other by twisted threads at the ends. It wasn't a virus or bacillus, that much was obvious. It was a single molecule, protein if he was any judge. And he was.

"What did you find, Gaius?" Number Six asked breathily in his ear.

"I think," he said without taking his eyes off the slide, "it's a prion."

"A prion?" she repeated. Her tone sounded like she knew exactly what one was, but Baltar couldn't help explaining, showing off what he had discovered.

"Prions are protein fragments that aren't viruses but can act like them. They often attack the nervous system, especially the brain."

"Really." Six sounded bored. Baltar ignored this.

"Yes. It won't show up on a normal test for a virus or bacillus because it isn't one. When they attach to nerve cells, they can interfere with neurological activity, even destroy brain tissue." He stared at the tiny bit of protein. "But this one . . . this one I've never seen before."

"Where did it come from?"

"Hyksos, the harvest worker."

"No, Gaius—I mean originally."

"Oh." He shrugged. "No idea."

A pair of soft hands caressed his back. "Amazing how something so small, so insignificant, can be so powerful." Gaius felt Six's touch tingle through him, setting off little waves of desire. He forced himself to continue staring at the molecule. It drifted away from the red blood cell and rotated slowly in the plasma. Gaius pressed a switch, and a micro-camera captured an image. Six ran a finger down the side of his neck, and he shuddered.

"Pay attention to me, Gaius," she whispered, her breath hot in his ear. "Don't ignore me."

He turned on his stool to look at her, and his jaw dropped. Six wore a short skirt, high-heeled sandals, and nothing else. Her bare breasts were tantalizingly within reach. Her presence contrasted sharply with the machinelike utilitarian lab around her.

"You . . . you . . ." He cleared his throat and tried again. "You've never struck me as the needy female type."

She leaned into him, her warm softness pressing against his body. "I need some 'me' time. And so do you."

There seemed to be a joke in what she said, but Gaius didn't get it, and Six didn't explain.

"I don't think so," he said, though his face felt flushed. "I need to track down exactly what this thing is."

Rather than respond, Six drew him off the stool and pulled him toward one of the work tables. Gaius didn't resist. She boosted herself up on it and leaned back slightly, her lips parted, her platinum hair falling backward.

"Kiss me, Gaius," she said. "Now."

He leaned toward her. She put up a hand.

"Not there," she said. "This is for me."

When the door opened a few minutes later, Dr. Cottle entered the lab and found Gaius Baltar kneeling in a strange position behind one of the tables. Both his arms rested on the tabletop as if his hands were cupping something. Cottle blinked and shifted his cigarette from one side of his mouth to the other.

"Did you lose something, Dr. Baltar?" Cottle said.

Gaius shot upright, his face bright red, his brain moving

fast. "No . . . no. I was just . . . doing some stretching exercises." He demonstrated some deep knee bends and winced a little. "See? I get cramped up, sitting on these stools all day long."

"I hear you," Cottle said. He was carrying an uneven file folder filled with papers, and he set it on the table. "Though deep knee bends won't stretch you much. I just dropped by to tell you Hyksos has slipped into a full-blown coma and those Viper pilots stay quiet only when they're pumped full of ativan. I've got a whole ream of test results here, but nothing comes up. I came down to see if you've got anything."

"I do, actually," Gaius said, gesturing at the microscope. He was flushed and slightly sweaty. Dammit, why did people insist on walking in on him during private moments? "Take a look."

Cottle did. "What am I looking at?"

"I think it's a prion," Baltar told him. His groin ached.

Cottle whistled. "Now why the hell didn't I think to look for that? Dammit. And you're right. Come on." He straightened and headed for the door.

"Where are we going?" Baltar asked, giving chase.

"Back to sickbay, where else? I want to scan a few brains."

Cottle made his way down the corridors of *Galactica*, not seeming to hurry, but somehow forcing Gaius into a trot to keep up. Down in sickbay, he summoned two med techs to roll Hyksos's bulky, quiescent body down to the corner where they kept the image scanner. Hyksos's face was pale and still, and Gaius was barely able to make out his breathing. Something suddenly occurred to Gaius, something that made his heart lurch, and he sidled up to Cottle as the techs slid Hyksos onto the scanner shelf.

"Some prions can be transmitted from host to host," he murmured. "What do you think of the possibility that these could . . ."

151

"It's already crossed my mind," Cottle murmured back. He puffed smoke from the side of his mouth. "I don't think we need to bring that up with the general public just yet, though."

"Of course, of course. I'm sure everything will be fine, in any case." But Gaius's entire body had gone cold. Prions generally weren't easily contagious. In most cases, one had to bring the prion directly into the body, usually by eating it in contaminated food or by direct introduction into the blood. Easily transmittable prions were pure theory, known only as projections on paper. Or were they?

"Look at this, Doctor," Cottle said, pointing at the scanner readout screens. They showed images of Hyksos's brain activity. The entire system was darkened—the man was in a coma—but Cottle zoomed in on the left hemisphere. "There. The language centers show severely depressed activity. And over here—motor function. The damage is more extensive than in the other areas, which means they were probably attacked first. No wonder the patients convulse and spout gibberish."

Gaius slowly and deliberately pulled on a pair of sterile gloves. Without a word, he pulled a cotton swab from a drawer, pried Hyksos's mouth open, and collected a sample of saliva. Then he slid another swab into Hyksos's nose. It was difficult— the shelf of the scanner was in the way—but he managed.

"What are you doing?" Cottle demanded.

"I should think it was obvious," Gaius said, and he all but ran back to his lab. When Cottle arrived some time later, he found Gaius hunched over his microscope, not kneeling behind the table.

"What's going on?" Cottle said. "What are you thinking?"

Gaius pushed himself back from the microscope. "See for yourself. I've already run a few tests. This prion is present in Hyksos's saliva and his mucus. I've exposed this one to low temperatures, high temperatures, UV radiation, and a dry atmosphere. It holds cohesion."

"Oh, shit." Cottle leaned against a table. "You think it's contagious."

"Just like the flu," Gaius agreed. His voice was flat. He felt oddly detached, strangely calm. The panic, he was sure, would come later. He had just spent a goodly amount of time in sickbay with three people who carried what appeared to be a deadly contagious disease. Number Six was nowhere to be found, and he was dying to talk to her about this. She was the one who had suggested he visit sickbay in the first place, which meant she had to know something.

"Where the hell did it come from?" Cottle muttered. "Frak! What's new on the ship?"

"The algae, perhaps," Gaius said. "Though that doesn't seem likely. None of the other people on the *Monarch* have come down with this condition, and the other two patients are Viper pilots."

"Brain diseases are funny that way," Cottle pointed out. "One person contracts it and falls into a coma almost immediately, another contracts it, and lives for months without showing a single symptom. No one knows why the hell it happens that way, but it does. One of the Viper pilots could be Patient Zero, or it could be someone who hasn't shown symptoms at all."

"We can't find Patient Zero until we know what vectors the other patients have in common," Gaius said. "Of course, knowing the first person to contract it would help us figure out where this came from."

"So what do all three patients have in common?" Cottle asked, clearly thinking out loud. "Something that other people don't."

"Actually, we could all have come down with it months ago,

long before the Cylon attack on the Colonies," Gaius pointed out. "Perhaps these patients are just the first to show symptoms."

Cottle eyed him. "Do you honestly think that's likely?"

"No," Gaius admitted. "But we can't afford to restrict our thinking at this stage."

"We still need to establish *some* sort of parameter," Cottle argued. "Two Viper pilots and a worker on a mining ship. Do they all three know each other?"

"Not that I know of, and unfortunately we can't ask them." He looked into the microscope again. The ribbony prion seemed to stare obstinately back up at him. "I doubt it's the algae. We'll have to check samples, of course, but as far as I know, prions that can infect humans simply don't hang about in primitive plant life. Something else must have brought this thing aboard."

Cottle took a nervous drag on his cigarette. "So what else is new to the Fleet?"

Peter Attis stood in the middle of a group of people, raised his glass in a mock toast, and said something Kara couldn't hear. Everyone around him laughed. Kara eyed him warily. She had been expecting a date sort of thing—two people, one table, candle, lots of innuendo. Instead, when she had arrived at the Gilded Lily, she had been ushered into a private banquet hall. There, Kara had found Peter holding forth to a roomful of maybe two dozen people, none of whom she recognized. A group of about ten had clustered around Peter, while the others stood around in uncertain small groups. A pre-concert party, perhaps? Whatever the case, it had caught her off guard. She felt annoyed that Peter hadn't warned her. Hell, she had even borrowed a dress from Dualla for the occasion. An angry look crossed her face and she elbowed her way toward him through the crowd.

"... can't believe you're actually here," a young woman gushed. "We've been waiting for so long."

"Waiting for what?" Kara asked a little too brightly.

"Kara!" Peter swept her into an unexpected kiss. Kara let him, but only just. The onlookers waited politely. "Glad you made it!"

"Who are your friends?" Kara said. "When you asked me if I wanted to have dinner, I didn't think you meant an entire banquet."

The gushing lady, a small, dark-haired woman, grabbed Kara's hand and shook it. "You're so lucky," she said. "Peter chose you for his consort."

"Consort?" Kara echoed. "Listen, lady—"

"That's not quite what she meant," Peter said quickly. "Louann, please. Kara's a good friend."

"But someone like you deserves a consort," Louann said, clearly shocked. "I can find one for you, if you like."

Peter was actually blushing. "Not today, thanks."

"Peter," Kara said in her "someone's going to get hurt soon and it won't be me" voice, "what the frak is going on?"

"Blasphemy!" said a man in shock. "That sort of language in front of the Chosen."

Before Kara could respond to this, Peter spoke up. "If by 'chosen' you mean 'chosen by the Cylons,' you can keep it."

"But they were the ones who taught you the Unity Path," Louann said.

"Yes," Peter acknowledged with a duck of his head. "But it wasn't fun or pleasant."

"'And the Unifier shall walk among the Enemy, and He shall return both changed and unharmed,'" the young man intoned.

"What's the frakking Unifier?" Kara demanded.

"They're saying," Peter spoke up before the man could bring up blasphemy again, "that the Sacred Scrolls predict the arrival of a leader."

"That's President Roslin," Kara said waspishly. "The dying leader. Everyone knows that."

"No," the man said. "That's from the Book of Pythia. The Book of Glykon predicts the arrival of a spiritual leader who will bring all the tribes together, a Unifier. It says, 'The Unifier shall have a Voice of Gold, and He will save Humanity with the Plague of the Tongue.'"

"And," added Louann, "Glykon goes on to say, 'The Unifier will bring together all Humans into one Tribe under one God.' Peter's music—the golden voice—talks about the One. When Alexander and I"—here she took the man's hand—"heard Peter sing his new song at the concert, it was like a bolt of lightning struck us both. We knew he was it. The Unifier. He will lead us all to the next level of spirituality. He will convince everyone that all the gods are merely facets of a single entity."

Kara suddenly felt uneasy, as if someone might be listening in. Perhaps the gods. She turned to Peter. "Do you believe that? Do you believe that the Lords of Kobol—Zeus, Athena, Artemis, all of them—are all different facets of a single god?"

Peter nodded. "I do. Humans can't comprehend the true nature of a deity, so we divide the One up into pieces we can comprehend."

"And the Cylons taught you this," Kara said. Her scalp prickled, as if her hair were about to stand up. "Philosophy from a toaster."

"Not exactly." Peter ran a hand through blond hair. "It might be better to say that the Cylons helped me realize the truth. They didn't convert me to their religion—they didn't even try—but I lived among them as a slave for all those months, and several truths were revealed to me during that time."

"Most spiritual leaders go through a time of trial before truth comes to them," Alexander pointed out. He was in his forties, and his dark hair had receded almost completely. He needed a trim, however, and his remaining hair stood out like a mane on an aging lion. One of his hands shook slightly. Kara wondered if he had palsy.

Kara gave the room an uneasy glance. A sizeable group was still listening to the exchange, hanging on every word. Suddenly she wished Lee was there, and that thought made her even more uneasy. Lee would be a bright, solid presence in this place where words spun around like shadows. Peter stood in the center of the room, a sun god surrounded by lesser, darker beings. Kara realized she was in the center with him. As a consort? She pushed that thought aside. Conflicting emotions tugged at her like restless children. She wanted to stand by Peter, feel his warmth and wallow in their shared sexuality. She also wanted to run away, leave his strange ideas far behind and bury them in the shadows.

And then a server announced dinner would be served and everyone needed to take their seats. The little crowd dispersed. Peter showed Kara to a chair at his right, and Kara decided to let him. No point in giving up a good meal over someone else's blasphemy.

The table itself was set with a linen tablecloth and linen napkins. The water glasses were thick, heavy goblets, and the silverware shone like clear water captured beneath a monstrous chandelier. Even during times of struggle, you could find luxury if you looked hard enough or had good enough connections. Earlier in her life, Kara would have felt out of place and uncertain in such grand surroundings, but a military officer quickly learned manners proper for any occasion. When in doubt, pretend the host was your commanding officer and everything else would follow.

Servers brought bowls of salad—fresh algae—and Peter took up a spot at the head of the table, where he addressed the room. He raised his water glass.

"A toast," he said. "First, to Kara Thrace for saving my life, leading me to all of you, and showing me that I don't need to feel lonely or afraid. Long may she live!"

"Long may she live!" repeated the room.

Slightly mollified, Kara nodded to everyone as they thumped their glasses twice on the table and drank to her health. Peter flashed her his trademark wide grin. But she was still unsettled. What the hell was this about? Had Peter made this many friends since she had brought him into the Fleet? She supposed it was possible. He was a celebrity, and celebrities rarely had trouble finding friends—or acquaintances and suck-ups, anyway. She glanced down the long table, trying to see what, if anything, everyone had in common. Almost everyone was her age or younger. The sole exceptions were Louann and Alexander. Both sexes seemed to be equally represented.

Kara took up her fork and tried a bite of salad. It was dark green and cold, with a slight salty tang. Surprisingly good. It was the first fresh greenery she had eaten in weeks, come to that. As a teenager, Kara had rebelled against eating anything resembling good nutrition. Once she was on her own, the diet of junk food and alcohol had continued, more out of habit than necessity. On *Galactica*, of course, fresh food was at a premium. Kara hadn't realized how much she'd missed the stuff until she had some in front of her, and she dug into the salad with delicate relish.

"We don't have much time tonight," Peter said, resuming his seat. "So we'll start."

Start what? Kara wondered, starting to feel uneasy. Her annoyance returned, and she found herself glaring at Peter. He had dumped her into an unknown situation without warning, without even telling her there would *be* a situation. She felt like he had tricked her.

"Most of you have been asking questions about my spiritual leanings. I'm here to make some of those clear." He coughed slightly and took a sip of water. "I believe I am the Unifier mentioned in the Book of Glykon. We humans fight among ourselves. We bicker and bite each other's backs. All humans once belonged to a single tribe living in splendor on Kobol until they argued and split into thirteen tribes. One of those tribes was lost forever, but instead of learning from this lesson, we still fight among ourselves. We rage over who should get what food and clothing. We bicker over sleeping quarters and medicine. We fight over who should be in charge. Laura Roslin, the dying leader mentioned in the Book of Pythia, actually had to flee the military. How did it happen that such an important person should have to run for her life?"

Kara set down her fork in surprise. Peter must have been busier than she knew. President Roslin's imprisonment and escape had happened long before he had shown up. Possibly Louann and Alexander had filled him in on the major events of the last few months.

"The Cylons were able to destroy the Colonies because they were united under a single god with a single belief," Peter continued. "Our belief in many gods and many tribes weakens us, creates us-against-them among our own kind. The Cylons will eventually win by default—we ourselves will finish the job they started."

Kara found herself leaning toward Peter, listening hard as a child sitting at the feet of her grandfather. Peter's smooth voice dripped hypnotic gold, his handsome face shining with an inner light. His words made sense. How much time had she spent fighting with other people instead of fighting Cylons?

"We need to reunite ourselves," he said. "Stop thinking of ourselves as Capricans or Geminese or Librans. We are all human beings. We are—"

"Heretics!"

Startled, everyone twisted in their chairs. Sarah Porter was standing in the doorway, her face dark with fury. Five or six more people stood behind her, all dressed in Geminese clothing. Kara tensed.

"How can you listen to this filth?" Sarah demanded of the room. "You so-called Unity people bring chaos and disruption at a time when we need to be focused. And you, Peter Attis." She stabbed a furious finger at him. "You and your music spread lies that poison everyone who hears."

"How dare you!" Alexander said, leaping to his feet. "You can't barge in here and—"

"No." Peter held up a hand. "No, it's all right. I welcome the dialogue. Though I'm afraid I can't invite you to dinner, Representative Porter—we seem to be out of plates."

Sarah folded her arms. Her followers remained stoically in place. "I wouldn't break bread with a poisoner."

"Please." Peter spread his hands. "Exactly what are your objections? I'd love to talk about them with you so everyone here can decide for themselves."

"You claim that all the gods are facets of a single god," Sarah said. "And that path only leads to damnation. It's what started the exodus from Kobol. The Sacred Scrolls say, 'One jealous god desired to be elevated above all the other gods, and thus the war on Kobol began.' You and your single god will destroy us all."

"The One isn't a jealous god," Peter countered. "The One is *all* gods, and can't be above or below them. Don't twist what I say."

"You twist what the Scrolls say," Sarah snapped.

Louann leaped to her feet. "Leave him alone! Peter's going to save us. Remember? 'The Unifier shall have a Voice of Gold, and He will save Humanity with the Plague of the Tongue.'"

"Nonsense," Sarah scoffed. "The Book of Glykon was declared apocryphal during the Third Conclave of Kobol."

"Only because the Oracle of Arachne was feuding with the Priests," Alexander retorted, also jumping up. "They knew she favored Glykon's writings, so they declared the book apocrypha to discredit her. That Conclave was a galandine takil from the very beginning."

A chill ran through Kara's body. What had Alexander said?

"Arachne was a disgrace to her office!" Sarah growled, not seeming to notice Alexander's odd language. "Your so-called Unifier has no place in our society!"

"Ah ha!" Alexander pointed at Sarah. His hand was shaking. Kara stared at it, remembering Kat and Hot Dog. "So you acknowledge that Peter is the Unifier! You recognize our existence, our power. There are more of us than you know, and thanks to Peter, we're growing. People listen to him, and to us. There are more than five hundred of us now."

"Perhaps I'll have Peter arrested," Sarah snapped. "For inciting a riot."

"Peter isn't our only leader," Alexander said darkly. "And you jail the Unifier at your own peril. By throwing him in jail, you acknowledge who he is."

"People, please," Peter interjected. "I don't want a fight."

Sarah ignored him. "I acknowledge no such—"

And then Alexander toppled over. He landed on the floor, twisting and writhing. A string of nonsense words streamed from his mouth. Louann clapped her hands over her mouth. Everyone else, including Peter and Sarah, stared. Kara recovered first and dashed over to kneel beside him. Alexander continued to yammer.

"He needs help," Kara said. "Call a medical team! Get Dr. Cottle!"

"It's a miracle!" Louann clasped her hands together. "The miracle of tongues! It's proof that Peter is here to save us!" She dropped to her knees and raised her hands high above her head. Most of the dinner crowd did the same. The salads sat on the table, half-eaten and ignored.

"Oh mighty One!" Louann shouted.

"Oh mighty One!" the kneeling crowd echoed.

"You who are all in one!"

"You who are all in one!"

Louann's eyes were shut, and she swayed like a willow in a wind storm. The crowd followed her movements as if tied to her. Alexander continued to writhe and babble.

"We thank you for this miracle!" Louann said.

"We thank you for this miracle!"

Kara's skin crawled. She ignored the people as best she could and tried to straighten Alexander's limbs to keep him from hurting himself. He seemed unaware of her presence. His eyes stared at nothing, and he continued to spout nonsense, just as Kat and Hot Dog had. Kara couldn't see Peter.

"Call a team!" she shouted again, hoping someone would *do* something. "Peter!"

"Blasphemy!" Sarah hooted.

The door exploded open and a platoon of marines poured into the room.

CHAPTER

10

Howls of indignation echoed through sickbay. Peter Attis shouted and bellowed and wrenched at his restraints. Kara stood next to his bed, feeling uncertain. One bed over, Alexander twitched quietly in medicated sleep. Dr. Baltar stood to one side, watching with a look of vague distraction. He kept turning his head, as if someone were standing beside him.

"Hold still," Cottle barked. "You'd think I was pulling out your fingernails."

"Let me go!" Peter snarled. "What the hell are you doing?"

"I just want to draw some blood." Cottle held up the empty syringe. "See? Simple blood. Just hold still."

"This was a trick, wasn't it?" Peter said, eyes wild. "You're all Cylons. You just made me *think* I'd escaped, and now you're playing with me some more."

"Shut up, Pete," Kara snapped. "And dump the martyr pose. It doesn't look good on you."

He stopped struggling and stared at her. Cottle used the moment to insert the syringe and start drawing blood. Peter winced. "Ow! What the frak—?"

"Peter," Kara said. "You need to listen to what the doctor is saying. They've found a disease that attacks your brain. It makes you babble and shake, and then it puts you in a coma. It started just after you arrived, which probably means you have something to do with it."

"I didn't do anything wrong! I didn't make anyone sick!"

"Not on purpose," Baltar said from his corner.

"Not on purpose," Kara agreed, resisting the urge to stroke Peter's forehead like a concerned wife or mother. She didn't like seeing him tied down, knew it upset him more than it would most people. "But it's happening anyway."

Peter slumped back against the thin mattress of his sickbay bed. Other patients groaned in other beds. A few babbled nonsense. Peter took a deep breath, visibly trying to calm himself.

"The people will recover eventually," he said.

"What makes you say that?" Cottle asked sharply.

"Because I did. I shook and babbled in a Cylon lab for hours, but I recovered. I told Kara—Lieutenant Thrace—about it. It's not a disease. It's a miracle."

"You'll pardon me if I don't completely take your word for that," Cottle said.

"You're just prejudiced," Peter shot back. "Anything that differs from your point of view must be evil or blasphemous."

"I don't give a damn what you believe, kid," Cottle told him. "I believe my tests and my microscope. If they tell me it's a disease, it's a disease."

"Then why am I not sick?" Peter asked pointedly.

"It's possible," Baltar put in, "that the Cylons used you to infect the Fleet. You said you spent considerable time in a laboratory, after all. If they wanted you to carry a disease, they would almost certainly want you to be immune so you could spread it as far as possible. Say, for example, by putting on a rock concert?"

And then everything clicked at once. Kara stared down at Peter as the pieces came together, creating a terrible picture she wanted to deny but couldn't. It was like staring at a picture of a beautiful young woman and abruptly seeing an ugly old crone occupying the same space. "That's what happened, isn't it?" she said. "Frak, we should have seen it."

"Seen what?" Peter asked. The fight seemed to have gone out of him.

"The Cylons created this disease and infected you with it," Kara said. "Then they showed up at Planet Goop and attacked us with a half-assed force. They *wanted* to lose—it was the only way to make sure you'd end up here. When I was flying that Cylon raider with the nuke back to the basestar, it sent a signal. We thought it was warning the basestar not to fire on me because that would set off the nuke and destroy the basestar, but that wasn't it. The raider was telling the basestar to get ready for a big kaboom and make sure that you were on the escape pod. Frak, the Cylons knew from the beginning exactly what was going to happen. Otherwise you and your Mistress Eight wouldn't have been able to make it to the pod in time. Hell, she must have hit the engines a few minutes before the explosion. Otherwise you'd have been too close to survive."

"I . . . no," Peter said. "That can't be. Why would they kill hundreds—thousands—of their own kind on purpose, even to destroy the Fleet?"

"Cylons don't exactly die," Baltar said. "When one . . . expires, its consciousness is downloaded into a new body. So sacrificing an entire basestar full of them is more like wrecking a car than killing people. And the Cylons have wonderful auto insurance."

165

"It also explains why they didn't come back to Planet Goop," Kara said. "At least, not at first. They needed to give the plague time to spread. And then when they *did* show up, it was with a tiny force. They weren't playing to win—they were playing to see how well we could hold the game. Kat and Hot Dog broke down in the middle of the fight, which told them the plague was working, so they left. Now all they have to do is sit back and wait for us to die."

"So why aren't *you* sick?" Peter asked. "You're one of the first people I ran into." Then he added quickly, "I'll tell you why you aren't sick. It's because the One hasn't chosen you to see the truth yet."

"A more scientific way to put it," Baltar said, "is that the disease's course runs differently in different people. It's the nature of such brain disorders. One person succumbs quickly, another goes unscathed for weeks or, in some cases, months. It seems Lieutenant Thrace is one of the lucky ones."

Cold water seemed to trickle over Kara's skin. With all that had happened in the last few days, it had never occurred to her that she might be infected.

"Do you think I have it?" she forced herself to ask.

"Almost assuredly," Baltar said wryly. "And it's likely I do, too, and Dr. Cottle, and everyone else in the Fleet. Why do you think we haven't bothered with quarantine protocols, Lieutenant?" His voice took on a shrill note. "Mr. Attis's concert—and there's no doubt in my mind that the Cylons chose him because they knew he'd give one—would have spread the disease to thousands of people. We've learned that Mr. Hyksos over there was on the third or fourth tier, and *he* caught it. Perhaps he even caught it from you, Lieutenant Thrace, during your excursion into—what's it called? Crowd surfing?"

Kara's mind fled back to the night she and Peter had shared, to the number of times they had kissed. Her insides shrank from sudden, cold fear. You couldn't fight a disease. It got into your blood, hooked your cells with tiny, invisible claws, and tore you to bits from the inside out like a rabid dog in a henhouse.

"Dr. Cottle said I was free of bacteria and viruses," Peter pointed out. "So it can't be a disease. It's a miracle, like I told you."

"Actually it seems to be a prion," Baltar said. "A protein fragment that in some ways acts like a virus but doesn't look like one. That's the theory, anyway."

Cottle held up the scarlet vial. "Then let's test it."

Gaius Baltar pushed himself away from the microscope and almost backed into Number Six. He shot her an annoyed look, then ignored her. She ignored him, just as she had been doing from the moment of her appearance. Yet, she remained, perched on one of the work tables like a slighted cat. She looked at the ceiling, she looked at the equipment, she looked at Cottle. She never looked at him. Gaius shook his head. It made him nervous, but he really didn't have time to ponder Six's strange behavior. His work was vitally important to the safety of the Fleet. There were other considerations as well. A trickle of sweat skimmed along his hairline, and his mouth was dry. A few minutes ago, he had slipped a sample of his own blood under a microscanner and set it to search for the prion he had found in Hyksos's blood. Now that he knew what he was looking for, the test was easy.

And it had come back positive.

Now every tiny tremor, every slip of the tongue made him break into a cold sweat. He was infected with a deadly scrap of protein, and he was going to die. He, Gaius Baltar. Struck down in his prime by a terrible disease. It wasn't fair. After everything he had done to save humanity from the Cylons, he was now going to die in a Cylon plague. Fear knotted his stomach and made his hands shake. Or maybe it was the prions already. He had been one of the first people to examine Peter Attis. Hell, he had helped persuade Adama not to space the man. Well, *that* had clearly been a mistake.

This was all Kara Thrace's fault. If she had just kept her mouth shut, Adama wouldn't have changed his mind and Peter Attis and his stupid prions would be floating in space, freeze dried for all eternity.

"Are you seeing what I'm seeing?" Cottle asked from his own microscanner. Gaius came to himself, realizing he had been staring at a computer screen without reading it.

"What are you seeing?" he asked.

"Peter's blood," Cottle said, "has three different prions."

"All right, we're listening," Adama said.

Gaius stood at the front of the conference table with a pointer in his hand. An overhead projector cast a harsh square of light onto the screen. At the long conference table sat Commander Adama, Colonel Tigh, President Roslin, Captain Adama, and Dr. Cottle. With a small start, Gaius realized he had never learned the doctor's first name. By now there was no way to ask it without being socially awkward. He cleared his throat.

"Dr. Cottle and I have run extensive tests," Gaius said. "And this is what we've found."

He slid the first transparency onto the overhead, which cast the picture of a prion onto the screen. It looked similar to the infectious one, except its ribbons were wrapped tightly around a body that was now slightly curved. Strange that it should look so innocent and pretty, like a tangle of bright ribbons on the dresser of a young girl.

"This is a prion, which is short for 'proteinaceous infectious particle,'" Gaius said in his Lecture Voice, the one he would have used if it hadn't been for Peter Attis. Peter Attis—the source of this plague and of Gaius's public humiliation. Anger rose up and threatened to burn away Gaius's fear like a forest fire swallowing a firebreak. He let it happen—anger was always better than fear. "A prion, if you haven't heard yet, is a long, complicated protein which isn't quite a virus. We've named this one Prion H, for 'harmless.' This prion is actually inert. Your body ignores it, and it ignores your body. This is the natural state for most prions, or PrPs. They're everywhere in animal tissue, to tell you the truth, and it's likely that this particular one was with us long before Peter Attis showed up on our doorstep."

The people at the table sat in rapt attention. A bit of pride gave Gaius's movements a bit of snap. They were enthralled, just as the audience at his ruined lecture would have been. Gaius was in charge of the room, and he liked that. He removed the first transparency and flipped a second onto the overhead's glass platen. Another protein molecule came up on the screen, this one a bit smaller and less complicated.

"This is another prion," Baltar explained. "We call it Prion T, for transformational. It's the one that's causing problems. It gets into your neural tissue and creates a form of transmissible spongiform encephalopathy."

"Could we have that in English, Doctor?" Tigh asked.

"Sorry," he said. "The prions attach themselves to a patient's brain cells and interfere with brain function. Eventually, the prions begin to actually *destroy* the tissue—encophalopathy. This opens up thousands of tiny holes, and after a while the brain takes on the form of a sponge—spongiform. And the condition is transmissible from one person to another. Transmissible spongiform encephalopathy."

He paused to take a drink of water. No one moved or spoke. "There's a theory called the Protein X hypothesis. It says that harmless prions like Prion H are transformed into their dangerous form by yet another prion. In other words, Prion H meets with Prion T and the two combine to form—" He twitched a third transparency onto the overhead. This one was the prion he and Cottle had seen in the lab before, its ribbons twisting about it in all directions, like strands of bright taffy on a bender. "—this prion. It's still Prion H, but this one interacts with brain tissue. It's deadly."

"So the Cylons created this Prion T, and it changes Prion H, which we already have in us, into a deadly form," Roslin said. "Is that it?"

Gaius nodded. "Yes. Prion T is designed to replicate itself in the human body, and your immune system ignores it. Prion T is hardy, and easy to transmit. A triumph of biological engineering, really, if you don't mind that it kills you."

"What are the symptoms, exactly?" Roslin asked.

"They vary in degree and intensity," Gaius said. "Early on, the prions are only interfering with the brain and not destroying it. Symptoms include light palsy that eventually becomes full-fledged tonic-clonic seizures. Some people show strange slips of the tongue. Their brain-to-mouth filter malfunctions, and they start saying whatever occurs to them, rather like a bad stream-of-consciousness novel. Others sprinkle nonsense words into otherwise normal sentences. And still others will do both. These speech symptoms eventually worsen into an inability to say anything that makes sense—once the language centers start breaking down, the only thing the patient can produce is mind-less babble. For some people, the progression is slow. For others, it's quick. Eventually, the patient lapses into a coma and dies." He cleared his throat. "We know this because the first patient we diagnosed—Mr. Hyksos—died a few minutes ago."

The room fell silent. No one present had known Hyksos personally, but so few humans were left that even the death of a stranger was reason for a twinge of fear. Gaius more than anyone knew the difficulties and dangers of a small gene pool, and he didn't like the way the odds were shrinking every day.

"So what's the good news?" Lee Adama asked at last.

"I'm afraid there isn't any right now," Gaius told him. "Unless you count the fact that we have Peter Attis so we can study him."

"Where is Attis now?" Adama asked.

"In sickbay," Kara said. Her voice was quiet, completely unlike her usual brassy self.

Laura Roslin raised a finger in a tired gesture. Even in the semi-darkness of the room, Gaius could see that her face was pale. "Is there a cure or treatment for—what is the condition called, anyway?"

"I gave you the proper name," Gaius said. Didn't these people pay attention? "It's a transmissible spongiform encephal—"

"Everyone else calls it the plague of tongues," Cottle interrupted with a wave of his cigarette.

"Oh, frak me," Kara muttered.

"Seizures and babbling," Tigh observed sourly. "Shit."

"It's taken on a religious connotation?" Roslin asked.

"Sounds that way," Commander Adama said. "This could cause a problem."

"A *problem*?" Tigh said. "It's a frakking disaster."

"I never thought I'd say this," Kara said, "but I agree with Colonel Tigh."

A startled look crossed Tigh's face, but he hid it quickly. "It's because I'm right."

Kara looked ready to snap at him, then seemed to change her mind. "Look, I've seen some of these people. They think that Peter's a savior. Hell, *he* thinks he's a savior." And she gave a short description of the events at the restaurant. "When the marines broke in and hauled Peter away, his . . . his followers reacted as if the marines had shot him." She gave Saul Tigh a hard look. "With all due respect, Colonel, it might have been better if you—if the marines—had been more subtle."

"We had to get him fast, Lieutenant," Tigh replied. "No time to pussyfoot around just because he's a prettyboy who can wiggle around on a stage. He's a danger to the Fleet."

"Not his fault," Kara said with cold calm. "He didn't *ask* to be infected."

"How do you know?" Gaius interjected. "The Cylons might have agreed to send him back to his own kind provided he carried this prion."

"So he would be the only living human on the entire Fleet?" Kara scoffed. "Not likely."

"He may not have known the prion was deadly," Gaius pointed out. "He might have—"

Roslin held up a hand. "This is immaterial, and it doesn't answer my initial question. Is there a cure?"

Everyone turned to look at Gaius, who hesitated a tiny moment. "No," he said.

The word landed on the table like a lead paperweight. A long silence followed. No one seemed willing to speak, as if more words might make the situation worse. Gaius waited.

"So we're all dead?" Lee Adama said at last.

"Not necessarily," he said, relishing the relief, however small, that came over their faces. It swelled him, made him feel important the way they turned to him for answers. "No one's ever cured a spongiform encephalopathy, but it doesn't mean it can't be done. Peter has clearly been carrying both the T and the H prions for quite some time, but he shows no symptoms. He claims to have had the disease and recovered from it, despite the fact that no human being has ever successfully fought off a spongiform encephalopathy. Peter did say that all the other humans who had been captured with him had died somehow. Perhaps they were test cases. In any case, Dr. Cottle and I are operating on the assumption that the Cylons infected Peter, then somehow cured him and made him immune."

"Don't want to kill the carrier too fast," Adama observed.

Gaius nodded. "Exactly. Peter's blood contains a third prion. If it has a function, we haven't figured it out yet, but it may be the key. Dr. Cottle and I have made this matter our top priority."

"So," Roslin said, "the fact remains that we have a deadly disease that masquerades as a religious plague along with the other touchy situation on our hands."

"What touchy situation?" Commander Adama asked, clearly concerned.

Roslin gave a wan smile. "There's an entire auditorium full of people who are expecting Peter to sing, but he's obviously not going to."

"Heaven forbid," Gaius muttered.

"We should initiate quarantine protocols," Tigh said. "Stop all ship-to-ship traffic and confine civilians to their quarters until we can spread the cure around."

"Not much point in that," Cottle said from his end of the table. "The prion's widespread by now. Might just as well shut the coop after the chickens get out."

"Are we all infected, Dr. Cottle?" Lee Adama asked.

Cottle shrugged. "Probably. You've all had close contact with Peter or with someone who did. Prion T was created to be easy to transmit. Breathing the same air will do it, really."

Another long silence fell across the room. Gaius felt his own heart beating heavy, pumping the prion to every part of his body. It seemed like he could feel them sliding through his endothelial cells, permeating his brain. Utter nonsense, of course, but emotions didn't listen to logic.

"So we're all dead, then," Tigh said into the silence. "Is that what you're saying?"

Alarms blared. Everyone jumped, including Gaius. Every time that damned alarm went off, it took five years off his life. Sometimes he felt two hundred years old.

"*This is Lieutenant Gaeta,*" crackled the PA. "*Set Condition One throughout the Fleet. Repeat, set Condition One. Commander Adama, please come to CIC.*"

"From one thing or another," Adama said, "we're all dead."

Kara Thrace's pulse pounded in her body while her legs pounded down the corridor. She'd been cooped up in the *Galactica* for two days now, and she was still feeling a little pissed off at Peter for the dinner—or lack of one. She also wanted to throw him down on the floor and get a good, solid frakking out of him. And she wanted him to hold her for a long time and stroke her hair. And she wanted to crack him across the jaw for probably infecting her with some weirdo disease that was going to dissolve her brain into gelatinous goo, even if the cure—maybe—was right around the corner. Peter filled her with dichotomies thick as mud, and Kara didn't like dichotomies. They reminded her too much of life at home with her parents, of her father in particular. She unconsciously flexed her fingers, the ones Dad had broken. Over years, he'd broken all of them.

"You're a little frak-head. A worthless little slut, you got that? Gods, you can't do anything right!"

"Daddy! Please. Please . . ."

"I'll show you what it means to frak up. I'll show you. Go get the hammer."

"Daddy, please. I won't do it again. Please."

"I said, go get the frakking hammer, you little brat. Now!"

Kara stumbled slightly. Her feet wanted to drag. She tried to banish the memory, but it wouldn't go. For a moment, she could only see her father's face. Love and loathing both tried to take command of her heart, and neither would give in. She wanted him to say, just once, that he was proud of her, that she wasn't a frak-up. She also wanted him to beg for mercy, to plead for her to stop the pain she was inflicting on him. It was unfair, and it was wrong that her dad was both father and foe to her, but that's the way it was. Kara set her jaw and quickened her pace toward deck five. Dichotomies.

The solution was simple enough. Out there, in her Viper, she was free. Out there, everything was black and white. Everything she encountered was either a friend or an enemy. No one was both. The certainty and security of that fact brought a rush of exhilaration that not even fear of death could dampen.

A hand grabbed her arm from behind. She wrenched around and found herself looking into Lee Adama's blue eyes. Other *Galactica* personnel rushed and bustled around them, intent on their own Condition One errands.

"Where do you think you're going?" Lee demanded.

She stared, honestly confused. "To kill a bunch of Cylons. You know—bang, bang, kaboom?"

"You're not going anywhere," Lee said. "You're grounded."

"What?" Kara barely kept her voice below a shriek. "For what reason?"

"You were one of the first people to encounter Peter. And you've been . . . close to him."

"You mean I frakked him."

Lee flushed slightly, then got angry. "Yeah. You frakked him. That means that he probably injected you with his little prion."

"It wasn't that little," Kara said with a deliberate smirk.

"Get your head on your job, Lieutenant," he snapped, stung. Kara was a little surprised to find she felt a little bad about making the remark. "You've had this prion longer than most of the people on this ship, which means it isn't safe to put you in a cockpit."

"I haven't shown any symptoms," she said sharply, denying a chilly tinge of fear. "Nothing's wrong with me."

"Yeah? Hold out your hands."

She did. After a moment, the left one trembled just a bit. Kara stared at it. Her entire world shrank to that one tiny tremor. "No."

"I noticed it in the conference room," Lee said gently. He held up his own hand. It trembled ever so slightly. "We can't fly, Kara. Not until Baltar or Cottle finds a cure. Simes is CAG until then."

Without a word, Kara spun on her heel and stomped away. Lee, caught off guard, ran to catch up.

"Where are you going?" he asked.

"To CIC so I can see how the fight goes," she said. "And then I'm going to sickbay."

CIC was busy, hushed, and tense. The steady growl of the dradis undercut every quiet comment. Kara shot the readout a glance. A handful of Cylon raiders was sliding toward a flock of

Vipers. Distorted radio chatter filled the silent spaces. Adama and Tigh stood at the light table in the center of CIC, their eyes also on the dradis.

"Why don't we just Jump?" Lee asked.

"*Colonial One's* Jump computer crashed," his father replied shortly. "They have to reboot and recalculate. It'll take almost half an hour."

"Frak." Lee pursed his lips. "Was it a Cylon virus?"

"Sharon," Kara said without thinking. "She got over there somehow and did it."

"For once, we can't blame the Cylons," Tigh said. "It seems to be an ordinary old computer crash."

"*Galactica Actual, this is Lieutenant Simes. We are about to engage the enemy.*"

The voice was distorted by distance. Kara watched the display as the Vipers closed in on the Cylon raiders. She found herself leaning this way and that, trying to make the Vipers fly in the direction she wanted, like a Pyramid fan trying to get the ball to move a particular way.

"Only six raiders?" she said. "They're just testing us again."

"Which means you didn't need to be out there," Lee said.

She shot him an acid look. He was trying to be nice to her, she knew, but that only pissed her off. Lee was the CAG—or had been until now. He wasn't *supposed* to be nice to his pilots. He was supposed to give an order and watch it carried out. Niceness, however, seemed to be hard-wired into him. It was too bad some of Tigh's bitter acid couldn't mix with Lee's milky niceness. Between them, they might make a fine commander.

The Vipers crawled across the screen until they were nose-to-nose with the raiders. Kara found she was holding her breath.

"*Watch your flank, Mack,*" Simes said.

"*I see it.*"

The soft thump of weapon fire came over the radio, and one of the raiders vanished from the readout.

"Nice one, Mack!"

"Thanks! It was my first piggy bank withdrawal from fighting with a bloody—"

"Shit," Tigh breathed.

"Mack! Return to Galactica immediately!"

"Immediately now once upon a time is flying." On the display, one of the Vipers weaved erratically. A raider dove at it. Kara leaned forward and put out a hand, as if she were one of the Lords of Kobol, able to cup the Viper in her hands and protect it from a distance. Her jaw was tight, and she felt helpless, completely impotent. All she could do was watch. Was this how Adama felt all the time? Her hand was shaking again. The Cylon on the screen dove.

"Mack!"

"Is a great big flying fishbowl full of milk for the cats . . ."

The Viper vanished from the display.

"Frak!"

Kara looked at Lee for a long moment, then turned and fled CIC. She didn't let herself run, quite, but she didn't let anything get in her way, either. People moved out of her way instinctively, like schools of fish scattering before a shark. She refused to let herself think; she just reacted. In a few minutes, she was at Peter's bedside down in sickbay. Restraints still held him down. Kara had mixed feelings about this, too, and she refused to examine them. She was sick of being mixed around like a frakking martini.

A red tube ran from Peter's left arm to a machine. The tube emerged from other side of the machine and ran down to Peter's right arm. Red liquid flowed sluggishly through both tubes. Dr. Cottle stood at the machine, adjusting dials and checking readouts. He and Peter looked at Kara when she came in.

"What are you doing to him?" she asked without preamble.

"Hi," Peter said from the bed. "Nice to see you, too."

"We're taking some blood and plasma," Cottle said. "We won't take too much, and we'll return a chunk of the red blood cells to his body."

"How soon before you find a cure?" she asked.

Cottle blinked at her. "Not right this instant. We're barely—"

"Sure is nice to be treated like a human being instead of a science experiment," Peter put in. "I never realized how much I missed being on the Cylon ship until now. Maybe this is another test of my faith. 'And the Unifier shall walk among the Enemy, and He shall return both changed and unharmed.'"

"Shut up," Kara snapped.

"Kara!" Lee stood framed by the curtains that separated the sections of sickbay. "Are you all right? You took off like—"

"I'll be fine, Lee," she snarled. "Just as soon as the good doctor finds a frakking cure, I'll be even better."

"I told you it'll take a while," Cottle said. He took a drag from his cigarette and tweaked one of the dials. Blood filled four vials. He capped them and picked them up like a bouquet of scarlet glass flowers. "And that's assuming there's even a cure to find."

"That makes me feel so much better." Kara said.

"Will you people quit talking about me as if I wasn't here?" Peter demanded, trying unsuccessfully to sit up. "I'm the frakking Unifier, after all."

"Shut up," Lee said, and Peter sank back into his bed, a defiant look on his face. "Kara," Lee continued, "I wanted to tell you—the Cylons jumped away again. Looks like it was another test. All the pilots are returning."

"Except Mack," Kara pointed out. "If I'd been out there, he wouldn't have died."

"You would both have died," Lee said. "Your hand is getting worse. I can see it from here."

Kara put both hands behind her back like a small child in a glassware store. She could feel one of them shaking, defying all commands for it to stop. How much longer before she lay writhing on the floor babbling junk and nonsense? Anger flared. Peter had done this to her. She knew he hadn't done it on purpose, that he would have stopped it if he could, but that didn't make her feel any less angry. She wished she had just blown the rescue pod to dust. The old saying was true—no good deed went unpunished.

"I'll be able to get out there once I get the cure," Kara said, gesturing at Peter. "If the Doc here would just get off his ass and do some work."

"Stop ignoring me!" Peter howled. "I'm not a thing!"

The sickbay curtains burst aside and the alcove was suddenly full of people. Kara found herself staring down the barrel of a pistol. Lee was doing the same. Cottle's cigarette fell from his lips, and he took a step back from his machine, a startled and frightened look on his face. Kara noted in a flash that the assailants—there were seven of them—all carried service revolvers. Two carried pulse rifles. And all of them wore red masks that covered their faces and hair but left their eyes exposed.

"What the frak?" Lee said.

Cottle moved with astonishing speed. He thrust the blood vials into Lee's startled hands and interposed himself between the intruders and Peter, his patient. "What the hell are you doing? Get out of my sickbay!"

"Freeze, Dr. Asshole!" one of the intruders barked. It was a woman's voice, muffled by her mask.

"Look, I don't care who you are," Cottle said, "but you can't—"

The woman swept him aside with easy strength. Cottle fell heavily against a medicine cabinet. It tipped over backward with Cottle on top of it and crashed to the floor.

"Hurry, now!" the woman said. "Let's do it!"

"What's going on?" Peter asked, pulling at his restraints again. "Frak! Let me go!"

Two of the masked figures holstered their pistols and snatched long knives from their belts. They moved toward the bed, blades glinting in the fluorescent light. Kara's heart jerked and a new fear trilled through her. Her hand continued to shake even as she held it up. The pistol that kept her in place hadn't moved. Peter stared at the blades like a bird hypnotized by a snake.

"You don't need to do this," Kara said evenly. Adrenaline zinged through her like the blade of a hot knife. "Leave him alone."

"I'm afraid we can't, Lieutenant." The leader woman snapped her fingers. The blades flipped down. Peter gasped as they slashed his restraints open. Then he sat up, rubbing his wrists. The two masks helped him off the bed, and Peter pulled the tubes from his arms. A grimace crossed his handsome face, and a thin line of blood trickled down the inside of both elbows.

"Let's go," the leader said.

"You can't take him," Cottle said. "We need him to—"

"Shut up!" said the mask holding the pistol on Kara. "We're the Unity and he's the Unifier. He doesn't belong in a prison. He belongs with his people."

"Listen to me," Lee said in a reasonable voice, his hands in the air, still holding the vials Cottle had given him. "Peter's important to the entire Fleet, not just to you."

The eyes above the mask holding the pistol on Kara flicked toward Lee. Kara took advantage and moved. She swept the pistol out of her assailant's grip and punched him under the chin with the heel of her hand. She felt his teeth crash together, and he staggered backward. Lee dropped the vials—glass shattered on the floor—and grabbed his own attacker by the wrist. In a quick, practiced move, he disarmed his opponent and twisted the man around in front of him, turning him into a human shield. The pair with pulse rifles were fumbling them into firing position, and Kara mentally marked them *civilian*. They were probably more dangerous to themselves than to the people they aimed the rifles at. The remaining two stood next to Peter, apparently unwilling to leave his side. Their pistols were still holstered. Cottle had fled, and he would doubtless raise the alarm, evening the odds considerably.

Kara was reaching down to snatch up her opponent's dropped pistol when Lee stiffened and released his prisoner. The prisoner stumbled away and Lee, looking vaguely surprised, dropped unconscious to the floor. The leader was standing behind him. How the hell had she done that? No time to think about it. Kara's hand closed on the pistol—

—and a heavy foot came down hard on it. Kara stared stupidly down at it even as crushing pain made her cry out. She looked up. The leader's masked face met her gaze with hard brown eyes.

"Don't even," the leader said.

Kara, who was still kneeling, yanked her hand back, feeling the scrape of skin on metal and hard rubber. She tried to punch upward, but the leader caught her hand in a cruel grip.

"Not worth it," the leader said.

"Don't hurt her," Peter gasped.

"We need to go," said another mask. "Now!"

Kara whipped her free hand up and managed to snag the leader's mask just under the eyes. The fabric was soft and stretchy. She yanked downward even as the leader caught Kara's other wrist with terrible strength. The mask snapped back into place. Kara caught only a glimpse of the leader's face, but it was enough.

"Satisfied?" asked Sharon Valerii.

CHAPTER

11

A flash of pain hit the back of Kara's head, and the world sagged. Her muscles went limp as old molasses. She was vaguely aware of her own feet stumbling beneath her as someone half dragged her down an endless series of wavering corridors. Twice she heard gunfire and Peter's voice, and the hand that gripped her arm left bruises that her father would have been proud of. A hatchway closed, and she realized she was on a shuttle. It was small, and red-masked people crowded in tight on the deck plates. The grip on Kara's arm relaxed, and she was allowed to slump to the floor. Her head ached, but at least the world wasn't moving. The deck plates thrummed and sudden motion threw Kara off balance again. She caught a glimpse of blurred whiteness through the canopy up front. Then the view abruptly shifted to a blackness studded with bright stars. They had left the *Galactica*. Kara tried to take in her surroundings despite her wooziness. The shuttle seemed to be a civilian vessel, not military, and it was apparently used for cargo instead of passengers—the only seats were for the pilot and copilot. The back was a large empty space where the red-maskers, Peter, and

Kara squatted or sat. Another wave of pain washed over Kara's head, and she had to stop thinking for a while.

"Where are we going?" Peter asked.

"Into hiding," Sharon said behind her mask. She was flying the shuttle. "I'm sorry, but it's not safe to tell you more right now, Unifier."

"So you guys are members of the Unity," Peter said. "My followers."

"That's us." She turned to the person sitting in the copilot seat. All Kara could see was the top of a head covered by red fabric. "Launch probe."

"Launching." Kara felt a small tremor. "Launch successful."

"Now hang on back there," Sharon called. "I need to do some fancy flying."

The shuttle dipped, and Kara automatically braced herself against a bulkhead as best she could. The armed and masked Unity members all tried to do the same, with mixed results. Two people lost their balance and caromed into other people, who in turn slammed into Kara. More pain exploded across her tender head and her stomach swooped inside her, but she clamped her lips shut, refusing to give her captors the satisfaction of a sound. She hated being a passenger instead of a pilot, and it wasn't any fun being a captive, either. Put the two together, and she found herself poised above a well of misery that threatened to suck her down into cold, dark water like a—

Oh, frak off, she told herself. *You've been in worse positions, Thrace. Way worse. You're alive, and they clearly don't intend to kill you. Those are two major advantages. So work on your next move.*

The shuttle continued to dip and weave. No one was able to regain their balance, and everyone yelped and howled in protest as they tumbled about the shuttle. All thoughts of her next move were driven out of her by force. Kara felt as if she had been tossed into a clothes dryer with a bunch of puppies. Sharon was a better pilot than this, wasn't she? Maybe she was doing it on purpose, a small gibe at the humans.

At last, the shuttle stopped moving. Kara cautiously sat up, pushing aside Peter's leg to do so. "Where the frak are we?" she demanded.

In answer, a hood came down over her head and restraints clamped her wrists behind her. Unseen hands jerked her to her feet and hustled her off the shuttle.

"Hey!" Peter said. "Don't hurt her! What are you doing?"

"We're not hurting her, Unifier," Sharon's voice said. "We're protecting you. We can't afford to let her know exactly where she is." Kara felt someone—Sharon—lean in closer to speak in a low voice as other hands hauled Kara down what was probably a corridor. "The only reason you're still alive, sweetie, is that Peter likes you, and we need his cooperation. But we can probably figure out a way to get his cooperation without you. You're a convenience, not a necessity. Got it?"

Kara clamped her teeth around a retort and merely nodded her head instead. A frakking *convenience?* She'd show Sharon how convenient she could be. Any vestiges of positive feeling she'd had toward the Cylon woman were evaporating faster than water poured on a cactus. Except none of this made sense. Despite weeks of incarceration, Sharon had been helpful, even conciliatory. No matter how much abuse had been heaped on her, no matter how often people called her a toaster or put her in chains or slapped a restraining collar around her neck . . .

Kara grimaced. In that light, maybe Sharon's actions made perfect sense.

Kara's captors and Peter fell silent as they hauled her down a series of pathways, stairwells, and corridors. All Kara could see was red, and it came to her that she was wearing a Unity mask, but it was on backward, so her eyes were covered. She strained to see something—anything—through the finely woven mesh, but couldn't. She tried to keep track of the number of footsteps she took and which direction she turned, but Sharon—she assumed it was Sharon—kept giving Kara sharp jerks, which threw off her count. The dull, persistent ache in her head didn't help, either. Eventually, she gave up, which was probably what Sharon intended. Instead, she tried to figure out what she could about her captors.

The Unity. Louann—or was it Alexander?—had said that there were more people in the Unity than anyone knew. They had to have contacts in the military—it was the only way they could get their hands on pulse rifles and get a shuttle docked at *Galactica* without awkward questions. It was likely they knew how to jam or confuse military scanners, at least temporarily, so they could get away. Kara remembered the probe Sharon's copilot had launched. It probably put out a false signal. It wouldn't fool *Galactica* for more than a minute or two, but that's all it would take, especially if Sharon knew how to switch the transponder codes on her own shuttle to make it look like another ship entirely. A couple of minutes and Gaeta would see through that, too, but once again, that's all it would take.

Sharon jerked Kara again, throwing her off balance and making her take several quick steps to regain her balance. A surge of hatred boiled and hissed inside her like a snake dropped into hot water. How might this little band of fanatics react if they knew the leader of their little expedition was a Cylon? Wouldn't it be fun to watch the fallout if Kara told them? But almost as quickly as it came up, Kara discarded the idea. The fact that the *Galactica* had—or once had—a Cylon in her brig wasn't well known around the Fleet, and it was quite likely that the Unity simply wouldn't believe Kara. Kara had to admit that she'd find it hard to believe. Peter knew, though. He must not have seen Sharon's face. Kara didn't think he'd react well to learning that a copy of his Mistress Eight was one of his . . . rescuers? Captors? Kara was a captive, but was Peter one too? The idea hadn't occurred to her before. Peter had been treated like a captive on *Galactica* twice now—once when he'd arrived and once after Dr. Cottle had determined he was Patient Zero. Would he care that he'd been rescued by a Cylon as long as he'd been rescued? Sharon had once rescued Kara, and at that moment, Kara wouldn't have cared if Sharon was a human, a Cylon, or an insurance salesman. Peter might well think the same thing, no matter what his experiences with his Mistress Eight had been.

There were too many uncertainties. Kara decided to keep her mouth shut about Sharon's identity until she knew more.

Besides, the information might be worth something in trade.

The hands moving Kara along shoved her into an open space that echoed. The hood was yanked from her head. Her hair crackled with static electricity, and bright lights made her squint until her eyes adjusted. They were in a storeroom. Battered plastic crates sat in blocky piles amid freestanding wire shelves. A door in one corner opened into what Kara assumed was a walk-in refrigerator. Harsh flourescents provided stark light, and the floor was cold gray tile. One of the maskers pressed Kara's shoulders with firm pressure until she slid to the floor, her back to one wall. Her hands were still cuffed behind her. Blond Peter stood nearby, surrounded by red maskers. He looked like a sunflower in a rose garden.

"So what's the plan, Petey boy?" Kara asked.

He looked at her for a long moment, and Kara realized she was dreading the answer. Had he really bought into this Unifier thing? And what would he do with her, an unbeliever?

"I haven't a clue," he said at last. "I didn't ask to be rescued. None of this was my idea."

"The Unifier must have a plan," intoned a woman's voice which Kara now recognized as Louann's. "The divine speaks through you."

Peter shrugged helplessly and Kara found herself trying not to laugh. "Looks like the divine took the day off," she said.

Pain smashed through her mouth as the masker standing closest cracked Kara across the face. "Don't blaspheme."

"Hey!" Peter snapped. "I want something clear here—hurting Kara is like hurting me. You got that, buddy?"

The masker instantly dropped to his knees in front of Peter, his fingers trailing the floor in absolute obeisance. A muffled sob came from behind the mask. "I am sorry, Great One. I am ready for you to strike off my head."

"What?" Peter said, startled.

"It is written," Sharon intoned from behind her own mask, "in the book of Glykon: 'And the Heads of those who defy the Unifier shall tumble to the Ground.'"

"Heads will roll, huh?" Kara said.

"Shut—I mean, the consort will be silent," Sharon said, and Kara filed away another fact—the consort had some leeway, even when she was a captive.

"So Petey, I ask again," Kara said, ignoring Sharon. "What's the plan? Now that you're free, what are you going to do? Raise a rebellion? Throw down President Roslin and Commander Adama? Take over a bunch of ships and Jump away on your own? Skulk in the shadows for the rest of your life? What?"

Peter took a step back as the realization of his position finally sank in. He clearly hadn't thought past his rescue. "I . . . I don't . . ."

"You people," said a new voice, "clearly have no idea how to run a revolution."

Kara jerked her head around. Standing near a pile of crates was the dark-haired form of Tom Zarek.

"I'm guessing they ran to another Geminon ship," said Lee. He was still holding a cold pack to his head, even though the Unity had attacked sickbay over three hours ago. Bill Adama studied his son without seeming to and told himself over and over the injuries were minor. Thank the Lords of Kobol for that. A small part of Adama was glad Lee hadn't been kidnapped even while the rest of him was worried sick about Kara—and the Fleet.

"What makes you say that, Captain?" Tigh asked, his voice harsh.

"So far the Unity have been active only on Geminon ships," Lee replied. "That's where their supporters are and that's where they'll find people to hide them."

"We've quarantined all six Geminon vessels," Adama mused. "Including the *Kimba Huta* and the *Monarch*. I want each one of them searched."

"We don't have the manpower to search them all at once," Lee said.

"Why not?" Tigh demanded. "We have lots of marines and the ships aren't that big."

In answer, Lee held up his hand. It shook visibly. Adama's stomach tightened into a cold ball of ice. Lee was getting sick. Adama remembered a time when Lee was five years old and had come down with flash fever. The sickness struck quickly, bringing on high fever and hallucinations, and Lee had been hospitalized with a clear plastic quarantine tent over his bed. Adama wished he could say he had never left Lee's side, but that wasn't true. Caroline, his first wife and Lee's mother, ate, slept, and lived at the hospital. Adama found he couldn't bear to spend more than half an hour at a time in Lee's room. He requested a temporary assignment that allowed him to remain closer to home and he told Caroline that he simply couldn't get away more than that for fear of being brought up on charges of insubordination. The truth was, the hospital room made him feel panicky, and the sight of his son lying there, twitching and muttering to himself under a plastic tent, stabbed him with a fear he could neither identify nor fight. So he blamed his job. Caroline knew Adama was lying about his reasons for staying away but pretended she didn't, and he could see unspoken resentments and rebukes in her eyes whenever she looked at him.

Lee's fever eventually broke, and he made a full recovery. Adama's knees went weak with relief at the news, but his only visible response was to ruffle Lee's hair, give him a quick kiss on the top of his head, and flee the room. Caroline had watched him go. Adama suspected the entire incident was one of the many reasons she divorced him a few years later.

Now Lee was sick again. Various events in the recent past—including the Cylon attack on the Colonies—had forced Adama to become more adept at recognizing and dealing with the depth of feeling he had for Lee, his only surviving son, but that only meant he had to face fears for Lee's safety instead of burying them. Perhaps facing them was healthier for everyone concerned, but burying had been a hell of a lot easier. He watched Lee's palsy-ridden hands and tried not to panic.

"A lot of the marines are shaky," Lee said. His voice remained steady, but Adama detected the slight quiver of fear in it, and it ripped at his heart. "They can't fire weapons until we find a cure for the disease. Cottle and Baltar think Peter is somehow immune to it, which means he's the key to curing it. But . . ."

191

"But what?" Tigh said.

"But they didn't get much blood from Peter before the Unity grabbed him. Cottle gave me four vials, and two of them broke during the attack. That's barely enough for anyone to study, and that's assuming they don't make any mistakes."

Adama and Tigh both fell silent. Adama's mind raced, trying to see options and finding none.

"So you're saying," Adama said slowly, "that the only person who might hold a cure for the plague of tongues is a captive of the Unity, and we're not sure where he is."

Lee nodded reluctantly. "That's the long and short of it."

"Shit," Tigh muttered.

"How many more cats?" Adama muttered to himself.

"Commander," Dualla said. "President Roslin is on the line for you."

Adama sighed and picked up the phone. He had to ask. "Madam President. What can I do for you?"

"I see you've placed the Geminon ships under quarantine," came her tired, breathy voice. "Is it to do with Peter's kidnapping?"

"Yes. We think he's hiding on one of them."

"Hiding. So you think he was in on the kidnapping?"

Adama pinched the bridge of his nose. Frak. The woman was too perceptive for his own good. "I don't know, Madam President. It's crossed my mind, but I have no proof of it."

"Any word about Lieutenant Thrace?"

"I'm afraid not."

"What about the escaped Cylon?"

"Nothing there, either, I'm afraid."

His answers, while short, were carefully polite. Not that long ago Adama would have told Laura Roslin that he was too busy to talk to her, but these days, with her worsening health, he couldn't bring himself to be rude, or even brusque. He wondered if Roslin knew this and was using it. Probably.

"Bill, you're aware that the majority of the algae harvest is still on the Monarch, right?"

"I hadn't thought about it," he admitted. "Why?"

"The algae can't leave the ship now that it's under quarantine. Some of the other ships were counting on that algae, and they're feeling the pinch. And we still need those antibiotics to counter the strep infection."

Adama had a brief image of himself standing in a canyon between two granite cliffs. On one cliff was the prion plague of tongues and Peter Attis. On the other was a bunch of hungry children sick with strep throat. The cliffs were moving steadily together, with him trying to sail a ship between them.

"I'm hoping the situation will be resolved quickly," was all Adama could say.

"I know, Bill. I just wanted to make sure you were aware of everything."

"You're very good at that, Madam President," he said without a hint of the irony he was feeling. Roslin's only response was a small, tired laugh before she hung up.

"Sir," Dualla said abruptly, "I think you should hear this."

And before Adama could respond, she twisted a dial on her console. Music filled CIC. It was a fast tune with a military beat to it. Peter's voice, throaty and strong, sang the lyrics. Peter sang about choices, about religious freedom, and about the need to rise up against oppressors. The song was fast and the chorus was catchy. A few seconds into it, Adama discovered to his horror that he was tapping his foot in time to it. He stopped and glanced guiltily around, hoping no one had noticed. No one had—everyone in CIC was listening to the music. Several people nodded in time to it and Adama caught Dualla humming along with the chorus. He glared at her, and she stopped.

"Where is that signal coming from, Mr. Gaeta?" Adama demanded.

"The *Galactica*, sir."

"What?" Tigh said, coming around to look at Gaeta's screens and controls.

"It's scrambled, sir, and by an expert," Gaeta explained. "So it looks like it's coming from us. I could unscramble it if the signal continues for the next two or three hours and I drop everything else to work on it."

The song ended. *"This is Peter Attis,"* the singer said. *"Earlier today I was kidnapped on the orders of Commander William Adama because of my religious views. Because my followers speak in tongues and because he needed to justify his actions, Adama claimed that I spread a disease. My friends, the disease is a sham cooked up by Sarah Porter and the military to keep me from spreading the truth about the One. The fact that Adama is persecuting me proves that he fears me, that he thinks there is truth to what I preach. Many of you have heard my followers speak in tongues, proof that the One has blessed them.*

"My friends, you've heard me speak of how all the gods are merely facets of the One. The Cylons have a similar belief, a belief in one God. It's the reason they continue to attack us. But belief in the One would shelter us, my friends. The Cylons won't attack those who believe in the One. I call on all right-thinking people to oppose the military's illegal restrictions of our freedom. I call on all people to stand up for their rights! I call on all people to stand up and take shelter in true belief!"

Music swelled, and Peter started singing again. Adama made a curt motion at Dualla, who shut it off.

"Dammit," Adama muttered.

"I don't give a boar's tit if that bastard worships the cockroaches in his bedroom—I want him found and dragged back here by his short hairs," Tigh raged. "We need Attis back on *Galactica* and we need him here now!"

"Do you think he really believes the disease is a sham?" Lee asked. "Or that the Cylons will leave us alone if we believe in his god?"

Adama shook his head and stole a glance at Lee's shaking hand. "Hard to tell. It doesn't really matter, does it? What will matter is whether other people believe him or not."

"Sir," Dualla said, "I'm receiving numerous requests from reporters who want to interview you. Sixteen, at last count."

"Tell 'em to shove their requests up their collective asses," Tigh snarled. "Tell 'em—"

"Thank you, Colonel," Adama said. "I think she gets the idea." He took a deep breath and turned to Lee, his only surviving son. "Are you well enough to lead a strike force?"

"I can't fire a weapon, but my tactics are just fine," Lee said. "Where to? We don't know where Attis is."

"The *Monarch*," Gaeta put in.

Everyone turned to stare at him. He took an unconscious step backward.

"How," Adama asked, "do you figure that?"

"Exhaust trail," Gaeta said. "Harder to trace, but not impossible. I've been working on it since I realized the first signal was a fake. The ships have moved around, of course, and I had to extrapolate a little, but the trail could lead to one of two ships—the *Celestra* or the *Monarch*. The *Celestra* is an Aeron ship and it's small. Hard to hide there. The *Monarch* is a Geminon ship and it has most of the algae harvest on it. He could hold the food hostage if he wanted—another advantage. So I figure the *Monarch* was the shuttle's the most likely destination."

"Well done, Mr. Gaeta," Adama said, then turned to Lee. "Assemble your strike force."

"Much better," said Tom Zarek. He leaned casually back against a bulkhead between two shelving units, his arms crossed. "Raising a revolution is much more effective if you get the people on your side. And having a good fighting song is a real plus."

"You are so dead," Kara growled from her position on the floor. Her hands—still shaking—were bound behind her. "You're going straight back to jail once this blows over."

"Really?" Zarek raised his eyebrows. "What for?"

"For aiding an escaped felon," she snapped. "For inciting riot."

Peter set down the microphone, his face hard. "So I *was* under arrest. Even though they told me that it was a quarantine thing."

"It *was* a quarantine thing," Kara protested. "Peter—"

"There you have it," Zarek interrupted with a grin Kara wanted to smack. "If Peter wasn't arrested, then I'm hardly aiding a felon. And if he *was* arrested, it was done illegally, since he's broken no laws. We still have freedom of speech around here, last I looked. It's not against the law to exercise our civil rights, no matter how inconvenient they may be for those in power."

Peter knelt in front of Kara. "Look, I can't deny it anymore. I'm the Unifier. My time among the Cylons was meant to show that to me, show me that the One exists. I see the One's touch in so many people. The Scrolls say that I'll save humanity with the gift of tongues, and I'm doing it."

"What are you saving us from?" Kara asked hotly. "The Cylons? Give me a break."

"I'm saving us all from lies. Kara, all our lives we've been told about the Lords of Kobol, and they do exist, but not as we've thought of them." He leaned closer, and Kara could feel the heat emanated from his body. His eyes burned with a fervor that until now she had only seen when he was on stage. "We were like children, learning simple lessons. But now we've been thrown out of the nest and into the greater universe. The One will show us the way we need to go, but first we need to believe in the One's existence."

Kara tried to swallow, but her mouth was dry. Peter's handsome face and earnest, hypnotic voice lent credibility to his words. She actually found she *wanted* to believe him, would have been willing to at least consider what he was saying—except that she'd been kidnapped and tied up and her hands were shaking from the prions he had infected her with. His words meant nothing to her now.

Still, he had given her an opening, however small.

"Peter," she said, "your ideas are pretty far out there, but . . . I have to admit that sometimes I wonder how the Lords of Kobol could possibly have let the Cylons destroy the Colonies. Maybe you're right and there's something more out there. I . . . I don't know."

"Of course there is, Kara," Peter said, his blue eyes filling the world before her like a tropical ocean. "You've seen how the One smiles on me and my followers. I'm the Unifier."

"Maybe," Kara said, careful not to agree suspiciously fast. She glanced around the store room. Some of the Unity people had gone off, leaving only two guards behind. They were clearly civilians, and probably not good fighters. A couple of quick moves, and Kara would have one of their pistols. Tom Zarek was standing by himself, watching and listening with an amused expression on his face. He was unarmed and no threat.

Sharon was Kara's main adversary. The Cylon, still masked, was packing up the radio transmitter and jamming device. Where the hell had she gotten that? Must have stolen it while she was wandering the ship. At Sharon's feet lay a large red duffel bag, and Kara had no idea *what* that contained. She had the feeling it wouldn't be fun finding out.

"Look," Kara said, "this whole Unifier thing just seems kind of . . . I don't know." She shrugged and winced. "Ow! Frak, this hurts."

"Here," Peter said, reaching around behind her. His body pressed against hers, but with none of the intimacy they had shared in his room. This time, his touch made her want to throw up. "Let me get those off you."

Kara held her breath as Peter's hands found her restraints. In a few seconds . . .

"Hey!" Sharon grabbed Peter's hands and pulled them away. "She's toying with you, Peter. Unifier. They're all trained for this—get you to trust them, and then when you untie them—pow! You're on your back, and not in a good way."

Peter stepped back uncertainly, and Kara glared at Sharon. "What's your stake in all this, anyway? You're not even . . ." She trailed off pointedly.

Sharon's almond eyes crinkled above her mask. "I want to see the Unifier succeed. The established priesthood feels threatened by anything different, even when it's the truth. Or maybe *because* it's the truth."

"That there's only one god," Kara said.

"That's exactly it," Sharon agreed. "The truth."

The door to the storeroom opened, and some two dozen people entered. Peter turned to face them. Their expressions were alternately fearful, apprehensive, and skeptical. A few looked confident. Some wore red masks, and Kara scrutinized each. Were any of them in the military? Anyone she knew?

One of the masked Unities came forward. "These people want to hear the Unifier speak. They want to hear the truth."

"Of course, my brothers and sisters." Peter upended a crate and climbed on top of it. He seemed to have forgotten all about the truth Kara had wanted to tell him.

Kara strained against her bonds. Even though she knew it was futile, she couldn't help it. "Why don't you tell Peter your own truth, then? Or maybe I should."

"Go ahead." Sharon picked up the duffel bag and set it on the floor in front of Kara. "Just be prepared to pay the consequences."

Kara automatically looked down at the bag's contents. Her eyes widened. "Where the hell did you get missile ordnance?" she asked. Her heart was pounding again. She was sitting bare centimeters away from enough explosive power to wipe out a small ship or punch a hole in the side of a big one.

"There's always someone willing to dicker," Sharon said. "Especially for the chance to get close to the Unifier." She squatted down beside Kara and said softly, "You know what they say, Lieutenant: 'Loose lips blow ships.' Though your lips blow something else."

Kara automatically tried to take a swing at Sharon, and her wrists jerked painfully against her restraints. Peter, meanwhile, was speaking to the crowd.

". . . and know that you, too, are chosen by the One. You are special, part of the force that unifies us all. You can help us end the suffering, end the strife and war. You have the same power I do, if you just believe in the One."

Although he was speaking in a scruffy storeroom in the

bowels of gods only knew what ship, his powerful voice and silvery earnestness made it seem like he was standing on a windswept mountain, preaching to the masses below. The people listened, rapt and staring. When Peter gestured, they swayed in time to it, as if they were an orchestra Peter was conducting. Kara didn't believe a word he was saying, but the power in him was undeniable. She saw the people's expressions shift. Instead of fear or skepticism, she saw hope, and even happiness. The four people closest to Peter fell to their knees. Kara understood exactly what was going on. The civilians in the Fleet had few choices and certainly no control over anything major. They ate what they were rationed, went where their ships took them, died when the Cylons fought them. And the priests could do nothing but offer empty prayers. Peter was offering something better. He made them feel powerful and special, gave them hope for control over their own lives. Kara sympathized, but she wasn't foolish enough to fall for false hope. Not again. Zarek leaned against the walk-in refrigerator door and watched the goings-on, a look of admiration on his face. Sharon watched also, her expression unreadable through her mask.

"Maybe my lips will blow your secret," Kara said to her. "How would the Unifier react to learning one of his followers is a frakking Cylon?"

"You want to tell Peter who I am, be my guest." Sharon gestured at the duffel bag. "But there'll be a price if you open your mouth, honey. Tick tock, tick tock, boom. A boom from Boomer. Get it?"

"You can't set that thing off," Kara said, ignoring the stupid joke. "Not without the access code. And I'm sure as frak not going to give it to you."

"What if I torture you?" Sharon's tone was so idle, so gentle. It made Kara's skin grow cold, and she remembered her father.

UNITY

"Meh," she said, trying to shrug. "Been there. Besides, Peter won't cotton to you pulling out his consort's fingernails."

"It was just a whim." Sharon leaned closer. "I already have the code, sweetie. The guy who gave me the ordnance provided it. I was just frakking with you."

"Sure. Your lies are getting thinner, sweetie."

"Okay. Go ahead and blab about me to Petey-boy. You do, I'll enter the code. Poof! We're nothing but a cloud of bloody debris."

"Don't forget that 'we' includes you."

Sharon shrugged. "I don't have much to live for and so I don't care if I die. What about you?"

"I'm dying already," Kara hissed back. "Plague of tongues, remember?"

"Ah, but you're not a fatalist," Sharon countered. "You think there's a possibility the prions won't kill you. The ordnance, on the other hand, will *definitely* kill you. A chance of life versus a definite death. I think you'll keep your mouth shut."

Kara glared at Sharon but kept her mouth shut as Sharon predicted. A small part of her wanted to shout the truth to Peter and his followers just to prove Sharon wrong, but the rational part of her knew better. She would have to keep Sharon's secret.

For now, anyway.

CHAPTER
12

Lee Adama arrived in the rec room just before the fight started. He was winding his way through the section of the *Galactica* that housed the marines. The entire area smelled of sweat, gunmetal, and old blankets. Corridors were narrow, and the rooms were lined with bunks and lockers. A song echoed through the hallways. Lee paused to listen, tracking the source. It came from the rec room a ways down the hall, and the song in question was the revolution song Peter had broadcast over the radio. An angry rumbling sound provided a background. Lee tensed and hurried his steps.

He didn't need this. He still had a throbbing headache from getting clocked in sickbay. It pierced his skull like a lead stiletto. And a desperate worry twisted his insides so tight, his bones felt as if they would break under the pressure. Kara had been snatched straight out of sickbay a few hours ago and seemed to be in the hands of a religious nutcase. Every detail of the events in sickbay was branded into his brain—Peter's howling, Kara's annoyed expression, the scarlet masks of the Unity kidnappers. He hated to admit it, but those masks had really creeped him out. He couldn't explain why, even to himself. Masks always creeped him out. Once, when they were kids, his brother Zak had found a full-face mask made of translucent plastic. It gave the appearance of a perfectly smooth face with human flesh tones. Zak had jumped around a corner with it on and made ghost noises. Lee couldn't comprehend what he was looking at, this blank-faced thing menacing him just outside his own bedroom. Utter terror had made his bladder let go. Zak had laughed at Lee and Dad had thrashed Zak for it.

And then had come the robotic Cylons.

The Unity were only people, Lee told himself, not inhumanly mechanical Cylons. But you could see robotic Cylons for what they were, and you could identify the human ones once you knew what their faces looked like. They shouldn't be any more frightening than any other enemies Lee had faced. But the masks were still creepy. And he was still worried about Kara. What the hell were they doing to her? She would be both scared and pissed off. A part of Lee smiled at the thought of Kara held prisoner by religious fanatics. Why rescue her? Who cared what happened to the kidnappers?

But Lee continued to worry.

It seemed he worried a lot about Kara Thrace. More than he should. After all, she was just a friend. A close friend. Who was seeing someone else. A religious someone else. Lee's head throbbed again. He had seen the picture of Kara kissing Peter in *Person to Person.* He had closed the magazine carefully, as if it might sprout teeth and snap off his fingers. Then he had pointedly put it out of his mind. No point in thinking about it. Kara didn't matter to him in that way. She was more like a cousin or sister.

Definitely. A sister. Lee shook his aching head, trying without success to convince himself the lie—no, the *statement*—was true and that he wasn't jealous over Peter Attis. He couldn't be. He loved Kara, yes. But he wasn't *in* love with her.

Sure. Of course not.

A few more steps down the corridor, and Lee entered the rec room. The place was crowded with off-duty personnel. A group of eight marines was pounding the table and singing Peter's revolution song. Another group was half shouting at them to knock it off.

"Kill that shit," one of the dissenters barked. "You want to preach blasphemy, do it in vacuum."

"Frak off," snarled one of the singers, advancing on the dissenter with clenched fists. "If you can't handle the truth, get the frak off *Galactica*. The Unifier lives!"

Lee felt his mouth fall open and he halted dead. Unity factions among the marines? That was something he hadn't even considered. Obviously the Unity was spreading farther and faster than anyone had anticipated. Before he could say anything, the dissenter rose to his feet and snapped a punch at the singer's jaw. Taken by surprise, the singer dropped to the floor. There was a tiny moment of silence as everyone stared at everyone else, and then the room erupted into chaos. Fists and feet punched and kicked. Tables and chairs scattered and flew. Lee snatched a phone off the wall.

"This is Captain Adama in rec room seven," he barked. "I need peacekeepers down here. Now!"

The brawl continued. The dull smack of flesh punching flesh thumped through the room, punctuated by grunts of pain and howls of outrage. Furniture crashed against walls and floor. Lee stood in the doorway, unable to halt the fracas by himself. Helpless anger suffused him. He could bark an order for everyone to freeze, but he doubted anyone would hear him, and being ignored like that would undermine his authority. He ground his teeth. The Cylon plague was succeeding in ways no one had anticipated.

"Holy frak! Look!" someone shouted.

And a hole opened up in the middle of the brawl. Two marines lay on the floor, twisting and convulsing. Nonsense fell from their mouths in a stream of babble. The fighting slowed and stopped as people turned to look.

"It's a miracle!" said the singer. "The Unifier's touch brings a blessing."

"It's a disease," shouted someone else. "It's not a blessing. The Lords of Kobol have cursed us for blasphemy."

The two marines continued to babble. One was frothing at the mouth.

"You can't call a miracle blasphemy," the singer said, clenching his fists again. Blood flowed from a split lip. "You can't—"

"Quiet!" Lee bellowed, taking advantage of the semi-calm. "That's an order!"

Everyone in the room turned to look in surprise, noticing Lee for the first time. The afflicted marines convulsed and jabbered, lost in their own private, painful worlds.

"I should have everyone in this room arrested for conduct unbecoming," Lee boomed. "Line up at attention!"

Several of the marines looked defiant and Lee wondered if they would actually disobey orders. What the hell would he do then? But the defiance lasted only a moment. They lined up just as a group of MPs burst into the room. They took in the situation quickly, and the sergeant turned to Lee.

"Sir?" he asked.

"I think we're calmed down," Lee said. "But those men need medical attention. Get them to sickbay. The rest of you need to remain here and make sure the situation stays calm."

The marines stayed at attention while the MPs hauled the two babblers out of the room. Lee walked up and down the row of marines, the broken furniture forming a strange backdrop behind him.

"Hold out your hands, palm down," Lee ordered.

The marines looked mystified but obeyed. Lee watched. Twenty marines held out forty hands, palm down. Two shook noticeably. Another five trembled, and three more started to shake a few seconds after Lee gave the order. Lee kept his own shaky hands behind his back.

"The Unifier's touch," said the singer in awe. He was one of the tremblers.

"No," Lee said. "It's a prion, a disease that Peter Attis is spreading." He pointed at the ten marines whose hands weren't shaking. "Report to the briefing room in ten minutes. The rest of you report to sickbay."

"He's so handsome, Gaius," Number Six murmured. "Have you ever wondered what it would be like to be that good-looking?"

"No," growled Gaius. "It's not an issue with me."

"And he's talented. When he speaks or sings, everyone listens. Even Laura Roslin."

The words popped out of Gaius's mouth before he could stop them. "I'm her vice president," he snapped. "She should listen to me."

"What's that?" Cottle asked from the other side of the lab.

"Nothing," Gaius said quickly. "Just thinking out loud."

Cottle gave him an odd look, then turned back to his instruments. Gaius shot Number Six a harsh glare. She was sitting upright on one of the tables, one knee drawn up, a lot of smooth leg showing under a red dress.

"It must be difficult to be pushed into the background," Six said in a low, silky voice. "It's not fair of them to ignore you, Gaius. You're worth more than that."

"Frak you," he muttered, and managed to wrench his attention back to the protein scanner. So far it was showing very few similarities between Prions T and H and Prion C. He was hoping for *something*, some kind of link between the three. Prion H, the harmless prion, linked with Prion T, the transformational prion, and became the deadly prion. Their link was well established. But what was the third prion for? Gaius knew it was artificial—there was nothing like it in any of the databases, and it was present only in Peter's blood. He hadn't found it in any of the other random samples he had taken from other crewmembers, which also meant the prion wasn't communicable. It was, in fact, rather fragile. Once removed from its host plasma, it fell apart. The samples of Peter's blood and plasma, in fact, had to be kept at body temperature and in near darkness, or the mysterious prion simply melted away. But what did it *do*? It had to be connected to Prion T and Prion H somehow, though it shared no structural similarities. Prions T and H had several similarities that let them hook together like pieces of a jigsaw puzzle so Prion T could unfold Prion H into its deadly form. But if Gaius was reading the scans right—and he was—the mysterious prion had a single marker in common with Prion H, which meant they might hook together in one spot. Gaius furrowed his brow. If that happened, and Prion H linked with the mystery prion, they would form an enormous, ungainly macromolecule. And that would mean . . .

And then Gaius had it. It was so simple, so obvious. Quickly, he assembled slides filled with Peter's plasma. He had to be careful—Cottle had only extracted a few hundred cc's of plasma before Peter's kidnapping. Escape. Whatever you wanted to call it. And some of the vials had shattered on the floor when Lee Adama dropped them. Fortunately, two had remained intact. Now the entire supply rested in a pitifully small collection of sealed test tubes kept in a warmer set at precisely thirty-seven degrees—human body temperature. Gaius took care to return the tubes before the fragile mystery prion could be exposed to temperatures outside its viability range. He would have to hurry, in fact, because the prions he took out of the plasma would only survive a few minutes.

"Onto something, Gaius?" Six asked archly. He ignored her. Cottle shuffled papers from the work area he had carved out of Gaius's lab.

Without bothering to take proper notes or make proper documentation—no time—Gaius dropped samples of Prion T and Prion H into a single slide. Then he slid them under a microscope and watched. It didn't take long for the copies of Prion T to find partners among the Prion H samples. They clicked together like little magnets, and the tightly-wound Ts unraveled, just as Gaius had seen them do a thousand times. His skin crawled with cold worms, and it seemed as if he could feel the same unraveling process happening in his own body. All his life, Gaius had been blessed with a whipcord body that required little maintenance and which held a certain amount of charm, if he said so himself. But in the end, his body was merely a home for his mind. It was his mind that had made him into a celebrity, his great intelligence that had elevated him above other humans. Having such a mind was a terrible and heavy responsibility, and it was his duty to preserve his mind so that the rest of humanity could benefit from it. And now that mind was under attack by a rogue bit of protein that would eat holes in it until it looked like a lumpy gray sponge. It would leave nothing of

Gaius Baltar but a babbling, incoherent fool, and the thought filled him with a cold terror that twisted his gut like a snake.

"All right, you little bugger," he whispered to himself, "let's see what happens when I do this."

With careful fingers, he introduced the mystery prion to the mix and watched carefully. At first nothing happened. The mystery prion floated in the thin plasma, bobbing about the white blood cells, water, and other flotsam like a complicated beach ball floating among the detritus of an ocean shipwreck. Then a mystery prion intersected an unfolded Prion H. Instantly, it linked ribbons with its deadly cousin, forming as Gaius had predicted, a long, lumpy macromolecule of protein. The moment that happened, a nearby white blood cell engulfed the molecule. In a few moments, the macromolecule fell completely apart. The component amino acids drifted harmlessly away.

Exultation swelled in Gaius Baltar, banishing the fear. The mystery prion was the cure to the plague of tongues and he, Gaius Baltar, had discovered it. Pride inflated his chest, and he felt strong enough to punch through a metal bulkhead. See if anyone would avoid his lectures now!

"Are you finding what I'm finding?" Cottle said behind him.

Gaius jumped and jerked away from the microscope. "Gods, you scared the bleeding shit out of me."

"Sorry." Cottle exhaled a stream of smoke. "Just wanted to see what you got."

"The third prion is the key to Peter's immunity," Gaius said triumphantly. "It bonds with the deadly prion and turns it into a form that the body's immune system recognizes as a threat. I just observed a macrophage consume and destroy an unfolded Prion H."

"Interesting," Cottle said. "I just finished examining a bunch of Peter's B cells. B cells produce antibodies, right?"

"I know what B cells do," Gaius said shortly, annoyed that Cottle hadn't acknowledged his breakthrough with appropriate fanfare.

"Just setting the stage," Cottle said, unruffled. "Peter's B cells produce antibodies, but currently they're also producing—"

"The mystery prion," Gaius finished.

"Brilliant," Six commented dryly from the table. Didn't she get cramped from sitting in one position for so long? "Too bad you have to share this discovery with the good doctor, Gaius. The credit should go to you."

Gaius didn't like Number Six very much at that moment, but he had to admit she was right. Cottle might grab credit that belonged to Gaius Baltar.

"So in summary," Cottle said, "if you inject someone with the mystery prion—let's call it Prion C for 'cure'—it bonds with Prion H and changes it into a form your white blood cells crunch down like potato chips. Prion C also convinces your B cells to make antibodies against the transformed Prion H, which further boosts your immunity. You continue to carry the prions, but they don't bother you."

Gaius ran a hand over his face, feeling suddenly tired. "Except our only reliable supply of Prion C was kidnapped by a bunch of religious fanatics. Every time we find a solution, it only reveals another problem."

"Then we'd better get back to work," Cottle said, turning back to his own instruments. "Before we start shaking in our own booties."

The fear took hold of Gaius again. He couldn't afford to get sick—he had to finish his work here or thousands of others would die along with him. A small sob tried to escape and he choked it back. It was so unfair!

"Have you examined your own blood lately, Gaius?" asked Number Six.

"Not half an hour ago," Gaius muttered, wishing she would go the hell away and leave him to his fear and misery.

"Check it again, Gaius."

"What for? Nothing's changed."

"You never know." A small smile tugged at the corners of her red lips. "Not until you look."

Gaius looked at her, but her face remained a beautiful mystery. "Fine," he snapped as loud as he dared. "But it's a waste of time."

He glanced at Cottle to make sure the man was occupied, then pricked a fingertip and dripped several scarlet drops onto a slide. He capped the sample and slid it under a microscope.

"What am I looking for?" he whispered. "What do you think I'm going to find?"

"It's what you don't find that's important, Gaius," Six said from her table. "Go ahead."

He looked. It was a perfectly normal blood sample. Erythrocytes, thrombocytes, lymphocytes, leukocytes. All to be expected.

"What am I . . . *not* looking for?" he asked.

"Keep looking. Focus closer."

A suspicion crawled over him, and he adjusted the focus on the microscope. He spent considerable time searching, and found . . . nothing. He backed away from the microscope, feeling abruptly weak and wrung out.

"No prions," he said in a hushed voice. "I don't have the prion."

"You're observant, Gaius," Six said.

He turned to face her. "But how? No, scratch that. It's obvious how." He started to pace, oblivious to whether Cottle was paying attention to him or not. "In any case of infection, there's always a certain percentage of the population who is naturally immune. I'm simply one of those cases."

"Poor Gaius." Six slid off the table and sauntered toward him. "You still don't believe, do you?"

"Believe what?"

"In miracles." She put his arms around him, breathing her breath into his mouth. "Isn't it clear? God wants you alive for a purpose, Gaius. He took the prion from your blood so you can fulfill your purpose."

Gaius felt a strange combination of uncertainty and gratification. This wasn't the first time Number Six had told him he was special, that his destiny was for something more than puttering around a laboratory and signing paperwork. It was immensely gratifying to hear this. To a certain extent it was a relief, further proof that his own estimation was right—that his innate intelligence and talent made him more valuable, more important than the masses of humanity who scurried through their ordinary corridors living their quiet, desperate lives. On the other hand, it was a little unnerving to think that a Cylon deity—assuming such a being really existed—had its eye on him.

"What purpose am I supposed to fulfill?" he murmured.

"That will come clear in time, Gaius," Six said, backing away. "And in less time than you think."

"Oh, that's helpful," Gaius complained. "Why is it the people who hand out predictions never say exactly what is going to happen? It would be nice, for once, to hear something like 'You'll find an inhabitable planet in a few weeks, so don't worry,' or 'Run for president and you'll win.'"

"Just concentrate on the cure, Gaius," Six said. "It's in the blood."

Gaius was about to argue when a thought crossed his mind. He turned to Cottle, who was still bent over his own instruments and appeared to have noticed nothing. "Peter's blood type is O negative, right?" Gaius asked.

"Yeah," Cottle said. "We caught a break there. O negative is rare, but it's the universal donor. Anyone can receive his blood—and the cure. We're just stuck with the fact that we don't even have two hundred cc's of Peter's blood left."

"We can create more Prion C," Gaius said. "We have the samples. We just need to use the right incubation methods, feed Prion C the appropriate nutrients in the right medium. Shouldn't take more than a few hours. A half-trained beagle could do it. What do you think?"

"That had occurred to me. But I think we need to do more tests first."

"Dammit, we don't have time for that!" Gaius smacked a tabletop in a melodramatic gesture. "Let's just get to work, shall we? You know I'm right."

Cottle looked at him, then shrugged and started pulling petri dishes from a shelf. Gaius was a little surprised he had given in so fast and with so little argument.

"It's funny, when you think about it," Cottle said.

"What's that?" Gaius crossed his arms as he stood next to the plasma warmer.

"Peter's turning out to be the savior he's been claiming to be all along. His blood is going to cure everyone." Cottle set the stack of dishes on a work table and ground out the stub of his cigarette in one of them. "We're going to do all the work, but you know how it always goes. Peter Attis will be famous for saving us while we toil in foggy obscurity."

213

Gaius felt his jaw slowly drop as Cottle laid out the dishes in preparation for the incubation medium. Number Six's soft hands slid over his shoulders, and her warm breath moved against his ear.

"He's right, Gaius," she said wetly. "You and Cottle will labor here in this dim, cramped lab while Peter Attis, handsome Peter Attis, rakes in the glory. If only you could find a cure completely on your own. It isn't fair or right."

The thought made his jaw go from slack to tense. It *was* unfair. How many times had he labored to save the Fleet, and how many times had his hard work gone unnoticed? Once he had spent hours working up calculations on how much food and water the Fleet would use on a weekly basis, and when he had presented Commander Adama with the information at a meeting, Adama had stared at the startlingly high figures for a moment, then turned to discuss the matter with Saul Tigh and Laura Roslin, as if Gaius were a child who had brought home average marks on a report card. As vice president, he had been saddled with idiotic paperwork and given lectures no one attended while people like Kara Thrace appeared in full-color magazines because she kissed a rock star in public. Fury clenched his fists.

"I could do it," he said softly. "A prion is just a protein, and I have a model to work from. Reverse engineering is much easier than creating something from scratch. I know my way around a molecule. It wouldn't take that long to create my own Prion C."

"Except you don't need to," Six pointed out. "Peter's prion will replicate itself in his rare, heroic blood. As long as his material exists, the world doesn't need you, Gaius."

Gaius stared down at the little plasma warmer. It was the size and shape of a microwave oven. The temperature readout on the front indicated that the internal temperature was a precise thirty-seven degrees. A few degrees too hot or too cold, and Prion C would disintigrate. Cottle, meanwhile, was pouring careful amounts of liquid nutrient medium into the Petri dishes. In a few hours, the cure would be ready. The dial that controlled the warmer's temperature seemed to stare at Gaius, daring him.

"Do it, Gaius," Six goaded. "It's the right idea."

"No," he whispered. "People might die in the time it takes me to replicate the original. One person already has."

"Do it," she said firmly. "It's your destiny!" She took his hand and pulled it toward the dial. He resisted, hand trembling, but she was strong, stronger than he had ever been. His fingers found the ribbed surface of the dial. It would be so easy. One little twist, and his position in history would be assured while Peter Attis was forgotten.

"No," he whispered again.

"Yes," Six said, and twisted his hand. The dial slowly clicked counter-clockwise, and the readout indicated a falling temperature. Thirty-six degrees. Thirty-four. Thirty-one. No! This was wrong. Gaius reached out to turn the dial back, but Six's hand snaked out and grabbed his. She wrenched it aside, and he gasped with pain.

"Leave it!" she barked. "Be a man, Gaius! Grab the opportunities God and I send you!"

He stared at her, comprehension dawning. "Did you . . . did you arrange this, somehow? Start this plague of tongues so I could cure it?" His back was now to Cottle, who was still engrossed with the Petri dishes.

"Think, Gaius," Six snarled. "Does anything in the universe happen by accident? Do you think *I'm* here, with you, by random chance? I've told you before, Gaius—you have a destiny, and you can't ignore it. God cured you for a reason. Fulfill your purpose!"

"I . . . I can't . . ." he whispered. But he made no move to turn the dial again, and the temperature continued to fall.

Galen Tyrol held up his hands. Both were shaking. His mouth went dry and fear squeezed his heart, but he didn't panic. Not yet. That would come later, when he was lying in his bunk with the curtain drawn and his trembling hands crammed against his mouth so no one would hear him whimpering in the dark against an enemy he couldn't see, hear, or touch but was coming to kill him nonetheless.

Lined up on the floor in front of him were dozens of people. Deck five—Tyrol's deck—had been turned into an impromptu sickbay because sickbay itself was full. The people lay on stretchers, blankets, towels, and hard, bare floor. Some twitched and writhed and babbled, others lay perfectly still. Two harried-looking medical technicians did their best to tend them, but there wasn't much they could do except try to keep everyone comfortable. Half the Viper pilots were among the patients, as were several of Tyol's people, *Galactica*'s "knuckle draggers." Tyrol squatted next to Cally, who lay on an old rug Tyrol had scrounged for her. She twisted like a dancer whose tendons had been halfway cut, and long strings of nonsense syllables fell from her mouth. He took her cool, squirming hand in his shaking one. The air around her was tainted with the sour smell of sickness.

"I wish I could help," he said. "I'm sorry."

"She doesn't need help," said a man Tyrol didn't recognize. He was similarly holding the hand of a male patient who was babbling just like Cally. "None of them do. They've been

216

touched by the Unifier. When they awaken, they'll have seen the face of God. You should be happy for her."

An urge to punch the jerk in the face made Tyrol's hands into shaky fists. Blasphemous nonsense—and hurtful. Cally wasn't in a divine state. She was sick, and this frakking bastard had the nerve to tell Tyrol he should be happy about it. But he kept his hands to himself and pointedly turned his attention back to Cally. The look she gave him was uncomprehending. She didn't even know he was there. Tyrol pushed down more panic. He liked Cally—as a friend. As someone who worked under his command. Nothing more than that. But the intensity of the distress he felt at her pain startled him. He was the guy everyone came to when something needed fixing. Vipers, Raptors, conveyer belts. Hell, once he'd even fixed a sewing machine. This, however, he couldn't fix.

Abruptly, he got up and strode away. The only solution was to keep busy. Or try to. There wasn't much to do, wasn't much he *could* do with his hands the way they were. Only five pilots hadn't been grounded, but it was only a matter of time. Emergency flights were the only ones running. It meant that the repair crews didn't have much to do, but that didn't matter—with no ships out, Tyrol didn't have much to repair. If the Cylons found and attacked them now, they'd be dead.

Of course, even if the Cylons *didn't* find them, they were dead. No matter what, the Cylons won. Frak.

The escape pod caught his eye, and his feet took him toward it. His footsteps echoed, mingling with the babbling behind him. A little itch at the back of his mind nagged at him every time he looked at it, but he hadn't had the time to examine it much. Until now. Figuring out what was bugging him about it might take his mind off his own impending death—and Cally's.

First he made a circuit of the outside, walking around it and examining every centimeter. It was the standard gray ceramic, no major cracks or visible blemishes. Some scorching from the explosion that had destroyed the basestar. A few scratches, either from the explosion or the landing.

He cranked the door down—it took a while with his hands shaking as they were—and inspected the inside. Nothing had changed. The basic control panel was still there, the porthole was still there, the CO_2 scrubber was—

Tyrol put a quivering hand on his chin, then pulled a measuring tape from his tool belt. He tried to extend it, but his hands shook too much. Frustrated, he flung it against the bulkhead. It hit with a loud clang. His body was breaking down, becoming undependable. Then he set his jaw. He hadn't lost everything yet. He put his arms out like a tightrope walker and paced from one end of the pod to the other, going heel to toe. His body made an adequate measuring tool, and no disease could change *that*. Tyrol counted fifteen of his own feet. After that, he went outside, started at one corner, and measured off the outside.

Eighteen feet.

Ah ha! Excited, Tyrol went back inside. Even assuming the thickness of the bulkheads added up to one of his feet, that left two of his feet unaccounted for. He retrieved his measuring tape and used it to tap on the bulkheads, something even his shaky hands could handle. The bulkhead opposite the door, the one with the scrubber hanging on it, had a hollow ring. Carefully Tyrol examined the scrubber. On the underside, his palsied hands found a switch. He flipped it.

Near the floor, a rectangular section of the rear wall a meter high and two meters long moved inward slightly. Cautiously, Tyrol pressed on it. It gave way, sliding inward and revealing a long, low chamber with a light set into the ceiling. A blanket and pillow lay on the floor. Tyrol's mouth set into a pale, hard line. Someone besides Peter and the dead Cylon had stowed away on the pod.

"I don't know what the hell happened, Commander," Cottle said in the conference room. "All I know is that the temperature in the incubator fell to twenty-eight degrees and all our samples of Prion C fell apart."

Commander Adama's face remained as impassive as rusty iron. "So you're telling me that we have no samples of Peter's blood to work with."

"Yeah." Cottle lit a cigarette with a practiced flick of his lighter. "Frak. I put the samples in the incubator myself, and I'm sure I set the temperature right. But I may have misread the dials. Or maybe the dial snagged on my sleeve and I didn't notice. Hell, I don't know."

Gaius studied both Cottle and Adama's faces, but neither of them seemed to suspect the incident with the blood was anything but an accident. "It could have happened to anyone," he said magnanimously. "However, we do have computer mockups of all the prions. I'm sure, given time and supplies, I could come up with—"

"Let me get this straight," Adama interrupted. "With the samples destroyed, the only source of the cure is Peter himself?"

"That's pretty much the situation," Cottle said.

"Though I'm quite positive I can recreate Prion C," Gaius said. "It'll take a little time, but—"

"Time," Adama interrupted, snatching up a telephone, "is in short supply. Dualla," he said in the receiver, "get Captain Adama on the line."

A few moments later, Adama said, "It's me. I need an update

on the strike force and you need an update on the prion situation. In the conference room."

Cottle excused himself and left. Gaius knew he should follow suit and get into the lab, but he was feeling an utter lack of urgency. If Adama wasn't all that interested in Gaius creating a cure, then Gaius could just trundle along at whatever pace he liked. He was already immune, and his fear of the disease had evaporated. Besides, he wanted to know what was going to happen between captain and commander, so he pulled out a small notebook and sketched amino acids instead. Adama seemed too preoccupied to notice. Ignoring him. Lee Adama arrived after a few minutes and took the chair Adama indicated. Gaius stopped sketching.

"I haven't even been able to round up a dozen people who aren't shaking," Lee said. "And I'm running into . . . other factors."

Adama removed his glasses and polished them with a white handkerchief. In that moment, he looked more like an exasperated grandfather than the commander of a military fleet, though he looked nothing like Gaius Baltar's grandfather. The vain, randy old bastard wouldn't have worn glasses in public if you'd paid him. Gaius wondered what it would have been like to have a grandfather that soaked up the sun in a rocking chair and carved charming little toys out of wood instead of jetting about the world attending conferences and seducing anything that walked on two legs. One of Gaius's earliest memories didn't involve walking in on his parents. It involved walking in on his grandfather and three of his bedmates.

"What other factors, Captain?" Adama asked quietly.

Lee grimaced. "The quarantine of the *Monarch* started up the food shortage again, which is making people unhappy. Everyone in the Fleet seems to be singing Peter's revolution song now, and lots of them seem to think that you're a . . . a tyrant who's trying to step on Peter's civil rights—and on the Unity's. It's making people remember the—uh, the 'incident' on the *Gideon* again."

Gaius added another amino acid to his sketch without comment. It was a challenge, sketching a three-dimensional molecule in two dimensions. The "incident," as Lee put it, had happened while Commander Adama lay in a coma, recovering from the near-deadly wounds Sharon had dealt him. Saul Tigh had taken over Adama's command, and he had sent armed marines to "liberate" food supplies from the recalcitrant ship *Gideon*. An unruly mob had greeted the marines, and the situation quickly devolved into a riot. One marine had panicked and opened fire. Four civilians had died. For days, the media had shown videos of a little girl crying over the bloody corpse of her father. Gaius mentally shook his head. Saul Tigh was crafty in some ways and stunningly stupid in others.

"And I'm learning the Unity has more sympathizers than I knew," Lee finished. "They see Peter as a savior."

"Savior from what?" Adama said in a dead-even voice.

"The Cylons." Lee cleared his throat. "The Cylons seem to have a monotheistic system of belief, and they won the war. Peter is preaching monotheism, and a chunk of the listeners are thinking that our situation would improve if we had the same belief system. It's just as he said on the radio, with the added 'fact' that his touch makes people speak in tongues, and that only makes him more believable."

"I don't give a damn one way or the other about the civil rights of Attis or his followers," Adama snapped. "He has the cure for this prion disease, and that's why I need him in sickbay, whole and unharmed."

"But a growing number of people see the disease as a blessing," Lee countered. "Cure not desired or required. They think they'll recover and be blessed somehow."

"We'll worry about the Unity's attitude toward the plague of tongues after we extract enough blood from Peter to cure it," Adama said. "Get back to assembling the strike force, Captain. Bring Peter Attis back to *Galactica.*"

"I think I'll need two forces, sir," Lee said. "And I'm afraid I'm going to have to use personnel outside the marines. Too many of them are down."

"Whatever you think is necessary, Captain," Adama said. Lee left, and to Gaius's surprise, Adama turned to him.

"You should work on creating that cure, Doctor," he said. "In case we can't find Peter—or in case something happens to him."

Ah. So he wasn't worthy of being ignored after all. "Of course, Commander." Gaius gathered his sketches and rose to go. It hadn't escaped his notice that neither commander nor captain had mentioned Kara Thrace in their final exchange, but it was equally obvious to him that both had been thinking about her.

The group of Unity people ended the final verse of Peter's song just as three of them landed on the floor, twitching like half-dead fish. Those who remained standing cheered and clapped each other on the back. Peter stood on his packing crate, lapping up the attention like a starving cat left overnight in a milkhouse. Several Unity members helped the fallen ones to a place near a bulkhead where ten others squirmed and babbled. Kara watched with a mixture of fear and bafflement. How could these people believe this was anything except a curse? They'd have to be desperate, clutching at straws made of starlight.

She sighed inwardly. How many times had *she* been just as desperate? No, it was all *too* understandable.

Her hands, still tied behind her, were shaking even worse now, and she caught one of her legs beginning to tremble. Fear made her mouth dry. The disease was taking the slower course with her, but it still was progressing. How much time left?

"Left and right of way for fifteen dozen eggs came first—"

Who the frak was talking? No new people were twisting on the floor. It took a moment to realize that the nonsense words were pouring from her own mouth.

"—second in line for muffins and butter with apple pie in the kitchen—" Kara clamped her mouth shut and managed to stop the flow of words. Her heart pounded faster under a fresh spurt of adrenaline. It was happening. It was happening to her.

Not yet, she prayed. *Just let me hold out a little longer.*

Peter was talking to individual members of the Unity crowd now. This was the fourth set that had come in. Tom Zarek, the bastard, remained standing near the walk-in, smug in the knowledge that he had fomented this chaos.

Where the frak was the cavalry? The military knew Kara was missing. Lee had been standing right there when the Unity had kidnapped her. So why hadn't they tracked her down? Kara "Starbuck" Thrace set her jaw. She was tired, so frakking *tired* of having to rescue herself—and everyone else—from everything. It would be nice if once, just once, someone would ride to *her* rescue. Lee, for example. The stupid frak-head was ignoring her, leaving her to face the wolves alone.

Kara pursed her lips and shook her head. Time to get a grip. No one had forgotten her. Least of all Lee Adama and his father the commander. When her Viper had come up missing, Commander Adama had put the entire Fleet in danger by refusing Jump to a safer location until Kara was found. Lee—or someone—would come. In the meantime, it would be better if she were in a position to help whoever showed up. Once again she pulled and twisted at the bonds that held her hands captive. Hot pain made raw ropes around her wrists, and her hands were shaking so much that she couldn't tell if her bonds were getting looser or not.

"Not on a good day for fishing in the watering hole back on—" Kara shut her mouth hard and stopped the flow. How much longer before it became uncontrollable?

Sharon, still clad in her jumpsuit, abruptly knelt down in front of Kara, blocking her view of the goings-on. "I heard that," she said. "Sounds like your mouth has a case of the runs."

"Frak you very much to my own—" Kara clapped her teeth so hard together she was sure she had cracked one.

"Yeah." Sharon reached over and pulled the duffel bag closer to her. The missile ordnance peeped out from the interior in a deadly game of peekaboo. "Now that you've joined the Chosen and are babbling like a lunatic, I think it's safe to let you in on a secret."

"Secret lies within the fallen angels of—"

Sharon pressed a cold finger to Kara's lips. "Shush. Here's the deal." She leaned closer and whispered, "I lied. I don't have the ordnance access code."

Tom Zarek fished a wireless communicator out of his pocket. He listened, then dashed over to Peter and said something to him. Peter stiffened, then disentangled himself from his Unity groupies and got back up on the crate.

"My friends," he said, "I have disturbing news."

The crowd fell silent except for the quiet babbling of those caught in the throes of the plague of tongues. Words bubbled up inside Kara, and she bit her lip to stop herself from joining the babblers.

"I've received word," Peter said, "that a group of marines is burning its way through the hull of this ship."

CHAPTER

13

Gaius Baltar worked quickly in his lab, his movements swift and firm. No sign of the shakes, no desire to spout nonsense. Just him and a pile of amino acids. It was only a matter of putting them in the right sequence, snapping them together like pieces in a very tiny puzzle. It should have been a fine thing to be in control again, should have felt like he was master of his own world. Instead, he was beginning to fear he had bitten off more than he could chew. The prion was far more complicated than he had originally thought. Oh, he could put one together, that was certain. But a mounting alarm was saying it would take days instead of hours, and he was filled with a growing certainty that he would perfect the curative prion only after everyone else was dead.

A computer monitor showed a growing Prion C blown up to the size of a multi-colored octopus. Gaius manipulated sensitive controls, and a microprobe nudged an amino acid closer to the proper position. It touched the prion and attached itself. It seemed to Gaius that he heard a *click*, though the idea was preposterous. He allowed himself a small sigh of relief, then checked his prion against the computer mockup of Prion C and nodded. Perfect so far. He wiped some sweat off his forehead, then dipped the microprobe into a different amino-acid bath, brought out a few samples of the next sequence he needed, and transferred them into the medium that contained his slowly evolving prion.

"Better hurry, Gaius," Number Six said behind him.

Startled, Gaius jerked his hands. The probe skittered sideways and sheared off several amino acids from his prion. They floated off into the liquid medium like fish frightened by a shark. A slow smile slid across Six's face.

"Dammit, that's not funny," Gaius snapped without looking around. "Look what you made me do. That's two hours' work right there."

A hard pair of hands grabbed him from behind and spun him around. "Don't ignore me, Gaius. You know what a terrible thing that can be."

And Gaius lost it. Six had been yammering at him non-stop about being ignored, interrupting him, embarrassing him, slowing or stopping his work. Days of constrained frustration exploded like a cracked pressure cooker.

"Shut up!" he snarled. "Just shut the frak up! I've had it with your petty complaints, your sly comments. If you aren't going to say anything useful, get the hell out of my lab."

Six didn't seem the least bit fazed by this outburst. Her impossibly beautiful face remained impassive, her platinum-blond hair hung in perfect tendrils, her scarlet dress flowed around the perfect lines of her body. At times like this, she *looked* like a robot, or maybe a mannequin. But even here, with him angry and her robotic, he found himself attracted to her. A part of him wanted to fling her to the lab floor and tear the clingy dress away. Sometimes he hated that part of himself. Now, for example.

"I'm not being helpful when I tell you that you're being tracked?" she said. "That within four hours, a Cylon basestar will jump into this sector and wipe all of you out?"

The anger drained from Gaius like blood from a felled ox. "What are you talking about?"

"Someone on board the Fleet is transmitting a signal, Gaius. Once your position is pinpointed, you'll be so very vulnerable. Think of it—an entire Fleet of humans too paralyzed by prions to fight back. The slaughter will have its own scarlet beauty, wouldn't you say? We'll wash away your sins in your own blood."

Gaius stared at her, a cold chill washing over him. He had no idea where Six got her information, but it was always accurate. Back when he thought he had a chip embedded in his head, he had assumed the Cylons were transmitting Six's image straight into his brain, making him think he saw and heard and touched a woman. Since then, he'd learned he had no chip in his head and he had assumed that Six was some strange facet of his own subconscious, a weird waking dream brought on by the trauma of the first Cylon attack on Caprica. It made perverted sense—his conscious mind was so much stronger than a normal person's, so it followed that his subconscious would be equally powerful. That didn't explain the source of Six's information, however. It was possible his own subconscious was figuring out things his conscious mind couldn't and was using Six as a messenger to feed him information that would keep him alive and well. In the end, he supposed, it didn't matter. Six often gave him information he could use. What difference would knowing the source make?

He reached for the phone. "I'll tell the Commander about this. We can Jump to a new location."

"And how will you explain the source of this information, Gaius?" Six purred. "A hotline to the Cylons?"

That stopped him. He paused, confused.

"Besides, Gaius," she continued, "if you check with the Commander, you'll find that more and more of the crew are speaking in tongues. You're short-staffed. Performing a Jump now would be difficult at best. Some ships have no one well enough to calculate a Jump. Another person's hand might shake at the wrong time and . . ." She made a puffing noise and flicked her fingers to indicate an explosion. Gaius felt his stomach knot like tense tree roots.

"So what do you want me to do about it?" he said at last.

"Stop ignoring what's important, Gaius."

"And what might that be?" he said, giving the video screen a curt gesture. "This prion is all that's standing between us and extinction, and I'm *trying* to give it my full attention. Hell, I don't even know if this cure will work. The prion is more complicated than I thought."

Sudden anger twisted Six's mouth into a red sneer. "You think that's what this is about? You think this is about your microscopic problems?"

"Then what is it about?" Gaius raged, thankful he was alone in the lab with the door locked. "Tell me! You've been lording it over me for days now. Just spit it out."

Six grabbed his tie and pulled his face close to hers. He smelled warm, minty breath. "You're ignoring the One," she hissed. "And he's pissed off."

Gaius's mind seized up. For a long moment he couldn't do anything at all except stare into Number Six's face. Was this one of her tests of faith? Six liked to spring these little surprises on him, forcing him to admit to a spirituality that made him feel uncomfortable. She had once threatened to allow the President to learn of his connection to the Cylon attack if he didn't admit to a belief in her version of god, and he had admitted to it. More than once since then, in fact.

At last, his mouth started to work again. "Are you testing my faith again?"

"I'm not. God is. Or the One."

"The One? The One has taken notice of me?"

"Oh, Gaius. Think, for once. You've seen what a terrible thing it is to be ignored. The One doesn't like it any more than you do."

"You engineered everything that's been going on so I could see what it was like to be ignored?" he said in disbelief.

"Peter brought you a message of faith, and you've been ignoring it all this time—and ignoring the One. Now you have the chance to ensure that everyone in the Fleet listens to his message."

"What message?"

"That Gaius Baltar cannot be ignored."

Gaius felt his ego rise to the bait and he struggled to keep it in check. "I didn't catch that part in Peter's song lyrics."

"Because no one else is listening, either. But now you have the chance to make them listen."

"By curing the plague?"

"Oh, Gaius. You think too simplistically. I'm telling you *not* to cure it."

"That's insane! If I don't cure it, everyone will die except me and Peter Attis. Wouldn't we make a fine couple, floating alone through space? Or perhaps you'd care to join us in a ménage à trois."

"Perhaps you should take some time out and pray instead," Six said.

"I'll pray while I work, thanks. Even though it slows me down."

"And what will you pray for?"

"That I find the frakking cure before your people show up to attack," he growled. "It's harder than I thought, and frankly, I'm not sure I can do it in time for it to do any good. Now if you aren't going to help, kindly disappear."

"I'm helping more than you know, Gaius. But right now, I need to tell you a little secret."

"Oh goody. And what might that be?"

Six leaned into his ear and lowered her voice to a whisper. "There is no attack."

He stiffened in shock and outrage. "What? Then why did you tell me—?"

"It was a test of faith, Gaius," she said patiently. "You should have seen that. God wants you alive. Why would he allow anyone to destroy the Fleet unless *you* were saved first?"

"That's outrageous!" Gaius sputtered. "You think you can just toy with me whenever you—"

"If you like," she interrupted, "think of it as God answering your prayer. Or half of it, anyway. Now"—she spun him around and pushed his face back into the microscope—"get to work. And pray as you go."

Commander William Adama looked down at his left hand. It lay palm down on the light table, fingers splayed. Motionless. He stared at it for a long moment. Then a little tremor ran through it. Just a small one. No more than a one on the palsic scale. But it was enough.

"I saw that," Saul Tigh murmured.

Adama carefully and deliberately put his hand behind his back. "Keep it to yourself."

"Keep what?"

Adama gave him a tight smile and Tigh moved on. Then Adama decided to do a quick circuit of CIC. Many of his people were tired, he knew. So many crewmen and officers had come down with the plague of tongues that the unaffected people had to pull double shifts. Dualla had bags under bloodshot eyes, and when Adama wandered by her station, she hid her right hand, but not before he caught the tremor. Dammit! He should send her off duty.

On the other hand, so to speak, he should also remove himself from command. He gave Dualla a nod and continued on his way as if he had seen nothing. As long as she was able to function, he would let her remain at her station. There wasn't anyone to take her place. He thought about calling down to Baltar's lab for an update, then decided against it. Baltar would find a cure or he wouldn't, and interrupting him for a status update wouldn't do anything except delay the man.

Baltar. Adama passed by Gaeta's station with a nod and a hidden grimace. He hated the thought that everyone's health might well rest in the hands of a crackpot who kept up conversations with himself. Adama knew very well that about half the population talked to itself. Adama was in the half that didn't, but he had caught Lee at it numerous times over the years and knew what it sounded like. Baltar, however, didn't simply vocalize internal conversations—he held raging debates that involved full-blown body language. It was as if he were caught up in a child's game of cops and robbers, getting pushed around by imaginary enemies. Baltar probably thought he was hiding it, but Adama had seen him. So had many others. But with quarters so tight and cramped in the Fleet, a new sort of privacy law had evolved. If it didn't involve you directly, you pretended not to notice it. Adama suspected that if they stayed out here long enough, people would go from pretending not to notice to actually not noticing, the way people did in societies that had little or no physical privacy. According to anthropological texts

Adama had read, the tribes of the Numinol Islands on Caprica had once lived in large caves with nothing but lines of pebbles to indicate where one family's living space ended and another's began, and the inhabitants of such caves lived, ate, fought, and frakked with each other in full view of their fellow tribesmen, but only those within the stone boundaries saw or heard a thing. Adama wondered how long it would take before the current tiny handful of human survivors got to that point.

Adama didn't like Baltar's obvious instability and would normally have tossed the man from any discussion group or advisory board, but he couldn't deny that Baltar's knowledge and contributions could be—had been—helpful, even necessary. So Adama went for a middle ground. He ignored Baltar when he could and used him when he had to.

Adama realized he was standing at his light table in the middle of CIC again. He looked up at a monitor that showed a computer image of all the ships in the Fleet. The symbol for the *Monarch* was outlined in red. Lee and his force of marines were burning through the hull even as Adama waited. They were keeping radio silence, which aided secrecy but kept Adama in the dark about the team's progress. He looked down at his slightly shaky hand again and for a moment he was seized with an overwhelming urge to whine. He wanted to whine that the prion infection was unfair, that his only surviving son's life was in danger again, that the only person who could assemble a cure for this disease was a frakking lunatic, that the only other source of a cure was about to be attacked by a military force, that everyone expected him to have answers and solutions to everything when he didn't. For an unsettling moment, he imagined himself with his head in Laura Roslin's lap while she stroked his hair and told him, in his first wife's voice, that everything would be all right. He banished the image.

"Dee," he said, "any way to get an update on Captain Adama's team?"

She shook her head. "Negative, sir. They're still keeping strict radio silence."

"All right," he sighed, "maybe we can—"

Galen Tyrol stumbled into CIC. His gait was uncertain and his eyes were wild. His hands were shaking like butterflies in a windstorm. Everyone, including Adama, turned to stare at him. He tripped and almost fell against Tigh and Adama, who helped him back to his feet. Adama tensed. Tyrol only rarely came to CIC, and never for anything less than a full-blown emergency.

"Commander," Tyrol said in a hoarse voice. "Commander, I found a lost ocean breeze in the tropics for—"

Tigh slapped his face hard. Tyrol stopped babbling and stared at the colonel with startled brown eyes.

"Calm yourself, Chief," Tigh snapped. "Concentrate. What's so damned important?"

Tyrol's expression shifted from dislike to a look of concentration. "I f-found . . . found a peanut in the . . . no. I found . . . in the pod of peas . . . dammit!"

"Can you write it down?" Adama asked in a moment of inspiration.

Tyrol wordlessly held up trembling hands and shook his head. "I was looking in the pod people of Caprican gardens who—frak! It's important to tell the audience that we can't fin mey beldin trassinell—"

Tigh slapped him again. Tyrol slammed a fist into Tigh's gut, then backed away with a look of horror on his face. Tigh bent over the light table, then dropped into a chair, gasping.

"I'm s-sorry," Tyrol stammered. "I'm s-so frakked in the bedroom with Dina melsh zaraform." He shook his head.

"It's . . . it's a-about the Cy—the Cylon. There's someone else cooking my mother's yudin asp terring . . ."

He crashed to the floor, twisting and babbling. Gaeta rushed over and tried to help Tyrol to his feet, but the convulsions were too much for him. He lowered Tyrol back to the floor and picked up a phone to summon a medical team—if one was to be had. Colonel Tigh sat in his chair, still panting for breath.

"What . . . the hell . . . was he saying?" Tigh gasped.

"I wish I knew," Adama replied, and steadfastly turned back to his light table.

"Passive!" Peter boomed. "Your resistance must be passive! Go limp. Block the way. Get underfoot. It will take two of them to drag one of you aside. But don't make any aggressive moves. Don't make a fist or reach for a weapon or even put your hand in your pocket. Don't speak, either. Sing, if you want. Let your faith give you strength. The One will protect us because our faith is true!"

Peter raised a fist, and the people cheered.

"Our love for the One is strong!"

Another cheer.

"We are the Chosen few!"

A third cheer. Peter started to sing his revolution song again. Kara had heard it so many times she was sick of it, but the crowd of thirty-odd swayed in time with the music and sang along. About a third of them wore red masks. How many people were on this frakking ship, anyway? This was the third group of Unity followers Peter was sending out to fight—or resist—the marines. Kara had overheard one of the Unity women mention that this was the *Monarch*, so she knew where she was, though she hadn't been able to escape. She couldn't imagine that the Old Man hadn't quarantined the ship before sending over the marines, and there was no way all these people were part of the *Monarch* crew. So where were they coming from?

The answer, when it came, was obvious. The plague of tongues was no doubt grounding military personnel left and right. Kara suspected few pilots remained steady enough to climb into a cockpit, let alone pilot a Viper on patrol.

Kara scanned the group as they boiled out of the room, and her stomach knotted. Some of these people had brought children with them. The kids sang with their parents. Kara watched, her shaking hands still bound behind her. As the song progressed, a sense of determination filled the room. Kara knew the feeling—it filled her every time she went out to fight Cylon raiders. And she was forced to admit that Peter was doing a good job stirring them up.

"How's it going?" Sharon asked in a patently false chipper tone.

Kara refused to answer. Pent-up words boiled around inside her, pressing against her pursed lips like a riot pressed against a police barricade. Once the torrent started, she didn't think it would ever stop. And Peter—the frakking idiot. He seemed to have forgotten all about her. Gods, what had she ever seen in him? The thought of listening to another Peter Attis song made her stomach ooze with nausea.

"Yeah," Sharon said, as if Kara had answered. "Getting hard to hold it in, isn't it?"

Kara couldn't stand it anymore. "Why . . . are . . . you keeping the barn door open for . . . keeping me here?" she said with aching slowness and deliberation.

"Because Peter loves you, stupid," Sharon said. She was sitting beside Kara, her knees up, wrists resting on them. Between her feet sat the duffel bag and its explosive contents. "Or lusts you, anyway."

"No way for bright red robins to—" Kara bit back the words, took a breath, and tried again. "No. You . . . know I won't . . . give up the fight for freedom that we've—no! I won't give you . . . the access codes. You can . . . torture me, but I'll . . . I'll be . . ."

"Dead before I can torture you enough to get them out of you?" Sharon finished. Then she laughed. "Don't be stupid, Kara. Peter wouldn't let me torture you. Not that he could stop me. It's just I know an easier way to get the codes."

Kara didn't answer. She had a terrible feeling she knew.

Sharon put an arm around Kara's shoulders, drew her close, and gave her a sisterly kiss on the temple. Kara cringed at her touch. Her whole skin tried to crawl away from it. Sharon brought her lips so close to Kara's ear that she could feel Sharon's warm breath.

"What's the access code for missile ordnance?" she asked.

The answer popped into Kara's mind and rushed toward her mouth. She clenched her jaw, but she found the treacherous words spilling out. "Five six eight—no!" Kara clamped her lips shut.

"Five six eight," Sharon prompted.

"Eight chi frak you in the—"

"Now, now," Sharon interrupted. "Try again. "Eight chi . . ."

Sweat broke out on Kara's face and she bit her tongue until it bled, but the words still came. "Omega two four six eight ten twelve fourteen—"

"Nice try," Sharon said. "But ordnance has only six code words. The four-six-eight thing was a silly try at fooling me."

Kara slumped back against the cold wall. Her legs were shaking now and exhaustion pulled her muscles into limp rubber bands. To her horror, she felt tears gathering in the corners of her eyes. Dammit, she wasn't going to cry. Not in front of a frakking Cylon.

"Are those cuffs painful?" Sharon asked like a nurse in a doctor's office. "Make you weepy? Let's see what we can do."

Kara braced herself, expecting a devastating blow to go with the sarcasm. Instead, Sharon reached behind Kara and, with a flick of her fingers, released Kara's hands. Instant anger seized her. She whipped her fists around and smashed them both into Sharon's smiling face.

Or tried to. Her hands and arms wouldn't obey. She managed to get her hands around in front of her, but they only lay in her lap, twisting and flopping like half-dead fish. Her legs joined in the terrible dance. Kara stared down at them in disbelief. She could almost hear her father's voice echo inside her head.

Little slut! That's what you get for frakking around.

"See?" Sharon said. She rose to her feet, the better to loom over Kara. "You're perfectly safe to keep around now. No chance for betrayal. Even if you tell anyone my secret, they'll put it down to babbling."

Meanwhile, Peter's followers finished the revolution song. "Go!" Peter said. "Show them your faith!"

The crowd marched out of the room, many of them still humming. Several people dragged the forms of those who had fallen victim to the plague of tongues. Some were comatose, others squirmed and shook, but all of them would serve to bolster the human barricade. The other people chatted and laughed, as if they were on their way to a picnic. Then the crowd abruptly spread apart, creating a hole around a young woman who was writhing and babbling on the floor. With a cheer that set Kara's teeth on edge, they helped her up and streamed for the door again, taking her with them. Kara was left alone with Peter, Sharon, and Tom Zarek.

"Idiots," Sharon murmured. "They mistake conviction for faith." She took a step away from the duffel, then another. Kara's eyes were drawn to it. Marines might be burning their way into the ship, but the *Monarch* was a big place, and there was no easy way for them to find her unless she could shout for help. And the ordnance might just be the key.

Sometimes missiles overshot their targets, either because the target dodged or the missile's guidance system failed. In either case, there was a small chance that it might hit something else, which meant unexploded ordnance had to be recovered. Or it did in the days before the Cylon attack. Nobody much cared now. Despite this, missile ordnance still carried a homing signal that allowed it to be tracked. It was activated automatically after the missile launched, but there was a manual switch as well. Now that Sharon had untied her, Kara might be able to activate the thing.

If she could distract Sharon. If her body would cooperate.

"What's the . . . difference," she stammered, "between cold snow and hard hail to the—"

"The difference between faith and conviction?" Sharon interrupted. "Conviction comes only with proof. Faith comes from within."

"Does P-Peter think the same wish for a good—"

"Who cares what Peter thinks?" Sharon said. "He's nothing but a toy. Cute, too, and damned good in bed, after he was trained."

"You've never frakked a big baloney sandwich on white—"

"Oops!" Sharon put on a patently false girlish pose. "I've gone and said too much."

Kara gritted her teeth. She didn't care about Peter anymore, or who he might have frakked around with. All she cared about right now was that damned bag of ordnance. "You never," she managed to say without babbling. "Not good enough for him. Be like putting his dick into a toaster slot instead of a Cylon slut who—"

The slap rocked Kara to the base of her spine. She cried out, long and hard, much louder than the blow actually called for. Peter, still standing on his box as the last of his people streamed away, heard the sound. So did Tom Zarek, who was working on some electronic equipment over in a corner. Kara collapsed into tears that were only half faked and covered her face with shaking hands, though she peered through her fingers. Peter jumped down from the box and ran over. Zarek followed.

"What the hell are you doing?" Peter snapped. "Get away from her!"

"She's a mouthy bitch," Sharon said.

Kara managed to raise her middle finger at Sharon. This time the Cylon woman drew back a fist. Peter stepped between them and pushed Sharon back. The move caught Sharon by surprise and she backpedaled several steps, her eyes wide above her red mask.

"I said to leave her the hell alone," Peter snarled. "She's my consort."

"Watch it, Petey-boy," Sharon snarled back. "I don't know who you think you are, but—"

"I *think* I'm the Unifier," he spat. "Do you doubt who I am?"

Kara forced herself to move while Sharon was distracted. She managed to pull the duffel open and locate the switch that activated the homing signal, but her treacherous fingers wouldn't grab hold of it. Twice, she felt the smooth metal of the switch, and twice she felt her fingers slip away from it.

"Don't get a swelled head," Sharon was saying into Peter's

face. "The One may have chosen you, but that doesn't mean you rule everyone you see."

Heart pounding, Kara hooked a finger under the switch. *Come on*, she prayed. *Come on!*

Her finger slipped off. Kara wanted to howl in frustration.

"My followers do as I say because they believe the One speaks through me," Peter said. "Don't you believe it?"

Sharon seemed to realize she was breaking her cover. She swallowed hard and visibly forced herself to take a step backward and bow her head. "I'm . . . sorry, Unifier. I lost my temper. My apologies."

"We all make mistakes," Peter said magnanimously.

Kara made one more try. Her mouth was dry as a raisin. If this didn't work, she was frakked. Her finger found the switch—

—and Sharon saw her. With inhuman quickness, she spun, knelt, and grabbed Kara's quivering wrist. Kara tried to pull free, but her body wouldn't obey. Sharon shoved Kara's hand away with contempt.

"Now just what are you up to with that?" she said.

"That's missile ordnance," said Tom Zarek, speaking for the first time. "What the hell is that doing here?"

"Missile ordnance?" Peter echoed. "You mean a bomb? You have a frakking *bomb?*"

"All part of the plan, Unifier," Sharon said calmly, pulling the duffel bag out of Kara's reach.

"Whose plan?" Zarek said. "I don't remember talking about a bomb."

"It's an insurance policy," Sharon told him. "Those marines won't close with us if they know we have this. It'll keep them at a distance, if necessary."

"We can't blow up the ship," Peter said, clearly shaken. "Shit! Passive resistance, remember?"

"*They* don't know that," Sharon returned. "For all they know, we're a bunch of religious suicide terrorists who'll kill a whole shipful of people rather than be captured. I'm not going to set it off, for frak sake. I'd die, too."

"Bluffs aren't worth the air it takes to make them," Zarek said. "Good players usually call them, and Adama's very good."

"So what? I'm not *counting* on Adama and the marines believing me—us. If they do, it's a nice break and it'll make it easier for us to escape. If they don't, we still escape."

"Where?" Peter said. "How?"

"The less you know, Unifier, the better," Sharon said. "Just in case."

"Wait a minute," Zarek said. "We already discussed this. I told you that the marines won't fire on civilians, so you're supposed to use passive resistance to wear them down and convince them to leave you alone. And if that doesn't work, Peter is supposed to get caught. He hasn't done anything illegal, so he'll become a prison martyr like I was. The press will keep Peter and his music alive until his trial and acquittal. I've already tipped off some of my press contacts about the possibility."

"I'm not willing to go to jail for my beliefs just yet, thanks," Sharon said. "Even if I have a key to the back door." She nodded at the monitors Zarek had set up in the corner. "Check out phase one of the plan, there."

Peter looked torn between the contents of the duffel bag and the monitors Zarek had set up in the corner. At last he said to Sharon, "Don't touch Kara," and strode away. Zarek went with him.

Sharon looked hard at Kara, then calmly reached into the bag.

Kara tensed. Sharon tilted the duffel so Kara could see every movement. Wiggling her eyebrows for comic effect, she deliberately flipped the switch that sent the signal. Kara couldn't keep in a gasp.

"Surprised?" Sharon said to Kara.

And suddenly Kara wasn't. The Cylon's actions made perfect sense.

"I . . . know what . . . mish nar—no. Know . . . your plan," Kara managed.

"Really?" Sharon looked down at Kara, a small smile on her face. "What plan would that be?"

"You don't . . . care . . . care about Peter or . . . galimaufry Alice has a blue—dammit! Or about . . . the One."

"No shit."

Kara shoved hard, and the words spilled out the way she wanted them to for once. "It's a trap. You want the armed force to board and find us so you can blow up Peter and what few soldiers we have who aren't sick and you'll die but just be downloaded into a new body because you don't care anymore that you'll lose your . . . your . . ." She trailed off.

"Lose my what?" Sharon said.

Kara looked up at Sharon, but not at her face. From this angle, she could see Sharon's stomach. It lay perfectly flat beneath her stolen gray jumpsuit. There was no hint of roundness, not even a tiny bulge.

Sharon Valerii—*this* Sharon Valerii—wasn't pregnant.

CHAPTER
14

The acrid smell of burning ceramic scorched Helo's nostrils. It felt strange to be kneeling on the outer hull of a spaceship without a vac suit for protection, but he kept his mind on his job. The marine ship had clamped itself to the *Monarch* like a barnacle and Captain Adama himself had opened the floor hatch, revealing the gray ceramic. Helo kept his hands steady and his eyes on the white-hot flicker of flame that was burning a careful circle through the hull of the mining ship. Goggles protected his eyes. The strike force gathered behind him, bodies tense and weapons ready. Helo could hear their body armor creak as they shifted position.

The final bit of ceramic gave way. Helo jumped back as a human-sized circle dropped into the ship and landed with a loud clang. He extinguished the torch. Captain Lee Adama dropped the end of a cord into the space beyond. The other end was hooked to a small monitor clipped to Lee's belt. It showed a dim, empty corridor.

"No apparent resistance," Lee reported. "Move in!"

Moving with trained precision, the strike force members

dropped into the hole. The first ones scurried out of the way, weapons drawn to cover the ones who came next. Helo and Lee Adama were the last.

"They have to know we're coming," Helo said in a low voice. "Why aren't they meeting us?"

"Maybe they don't want a fight," Lee murmured. "Maybe this'll turn into a game of hide-and-seek." He holstered his rifle across his back and unrolled a long square of paper, specs for the *Monarch.* "Gaeta said that since we stopped enforcing the quarantine, something like ten ships have docked with the *Monarch.* The only place where all those people could be gathering is the main processing area here. But that's just a guess. I wish we knew for sure."

"Sir," Racetrack said. "I'm getting a signal."

Lee spun like a small tornado. Helo wondered if the captain was thinking about Kara like he was thinking about Sharon. "From who?"

"No one in particular." Racetrack held up her radio so Lee could see the readout. "It's a missile ordnance tracking signal."

"Kara," Lee breathed. "She's found a way to tell us where she is and make it look like an ordnance signal."

"I don't know, sir," Helo said doubtfully. "What if the Unifiers really have ordnance?"

"Doesn't seem likely they'd activate the homing device," Racetrack said. "It gives away their position."

A series of clanks and thuds rang through the corridor. Everyone, including Helo, readied their weapons, rifle barrels pointing in a dozen different directions like an angry porcupine. After a moment the noises faded.

"Mining ship," Racetrack said as another set of sounds started up, further away this time. "Lots of weird noises around. Let me get to work and we can get moving."

Helo let himself relax. A little, anyway. Lighting in the corridor was dim, and the whole place smelled of algae and engine oil. Helo shifted inside his flak armor. A belt hung with ammunition and equipment dragged at his waist, a helmet covered his head, and he carried a pulse rifle. The back of his head wouldn't stop itching. The helmet wouldn't let him scratch, which made it worse. Doc Cottle had been too busy with plague patients to look at him, and now Helo was on a strike force, where an itchy head was considered something you sucked up.

Technically Helo shouldn't be here. He was combat-trained, yes, but he wasn't trained to sneak aboard an enemy ship and track down terrorists. But Captain Adama, faced with hundreds of people whose hands shook too much to fire a weapon, had been forced to augment marines with other personnel. At the moment, that included Helo. So far his hands had proven plague-free and rock-steady, though he found himself checking every few minutes.

The search for Sharon had been suspended. No one was available to look for her. Helo couldn't decide if this was a positive or a negative. In the end, he had decided to stop thinking about it altogether. If she turned up, she would turn up.

But he also wondered about the baby.

He was going to be a father. The idea ambushed him at odd moments, like a mugger whacking him over the head and dragging him into an alley. A baby. A little girl or boy who would look at him and say, "Daddy!" First steps, first words. First date.

From a prison cell. How would Adama handle this? It wouldn't be fair to the baby to keep it in a cell, and it wouldn't be right to keep it away from Sharon. Adama would have to make some sort of ruling, and that pissed Helo off. Every other time a baby was born, people celebrated. New life was precious and valued and loved. Except his. His baby would be born in a prison to a lifetime prisoner. His baby would be born to a hated enemy. His baby would endure a life of stigma. His baby's birth would be decided by military law, his parenting held up to military scrutiny. The baby had committed no crime, but already it was being treated like a criminal. Helo got angrier and angrier just thinking about it.

Racetrack jostled Helo's arm, bringing him out of his seething reverie. He almost jumped, realizing how foolish it had been for him to lose himself inside his own head when he was in enemy territory.

"Careful," Racetrack said. She had opened a wall panel and was tearing at the nest of cable inside. "Pass me that shunt, would you?"

Helo obeyed. Racetrack selected a cable and attached the shunt while the rest of the platoon stood guard. Racetrack, an adept ECO, flipped on a portable screen. Helo peered over her shoulder. At first the screen remained blank, but she flicked dials and switches and eventually came up with an image of a large room crammed with people. Several of them wore red masks.

"I've broken into the security cameras, Captain," she reported. "I think we're looking at the main processing area."

"Crowded," observed a marine Helo didn't know.

Captain Lee Adama checked the schematics. "It's also on the only path from here to where the signal is coming from."

"So we have to go through them to get to Kara?" Helo said.

"Looks that way."

"Sir," said one of the marines, "our orders are not to shoot or attack civilians. How are we going to get through those people without attacking?"

Lee Adama looked at the people on the screen, then at the

schematic in his hand, then at the hole in the bulkhead above him. "We're not," he said.

"Commander," said Felix Gaeta. "Lieutenant Edmonson is beaming a direct signal to us. We have video of what's happening on the *Monarch*."

"Put it up, Lieutenant," Colonel Tigh ordered.

Bill Adama turned his eyes up to one of the monitors above his head. Lee was out there, leading the *Monarch* strike in an attempt to rescue Kara Thrace, and Adama had to stand there in CIC and pretend he wasn't worried, that his heart wasn't leaping in his chest, that he wasn't sweating under his uniform. No reason for distress, everyone. The Old Man has everything under control.

He adjusted his glasses and peered at the monitor. It remained blank.

"There a problem, Mr. Gaeta?" Tigh asked.

"Just . . . taking a little longer to get the telemetry right, sir." Gaeta, flushing, worked at his controls, his hands hidden by the rim of the console. Adama knew what was causing the delay, and he kept his face carefully neutral. He shot Tigh a quick glance to let him know that the colonel should keep his mouth shut. Tigh gave a tiny nod in acknowledgment. Dualla busied herself at her own console, as did everyone else in CIC. Their work was similarly slow and laborious and several stations were unstaffed, but no one took note. Yep, no reason for distress. Everything's under control. Ignore the elephant standing beside you. We all know it's there, we all know why Gaeta can't work his console, and we're all going to pretend we don't. The marines will bring back Peter Attis alive, healthy, and chock full of curative protoplasm to cure the disease we aren't talking about. We won't mention that the Cylons could pop up at any time and turn the Fleet into an expanding cloud of gas and debris. We won't mention that the prions are turning our brains to sponges and that our only hopes are the leader of a religious movement that kidnapped one of our best pilots, and a scientist who isn't known for his stability.

A wave of anger suddenly swept over Adama. He was dying, dammit, dying for the second time in as many months. The frakking asshole whose life Adama had spared had repaid Adama by infecting him with a deadly disease, creating a religious cult that fomented chaos wherever it went, kidnapping a pilot who was like a daughter to him, and disappearing into the bowels of a mining ship with the disease's only cure. Gods, Adama had even attended the man's concert. And what an evening that had been. Laura Roslin had clung lightly to his arm like a half-solid ghost, and the two of them sank into lawn chairs set up specifically for them, like a king and queen attending the revels of the commoners. Billy Keikeya hovered nearby like a cupbearer. And gods help him, Adama actually enjoyed the show. The music wasn't his usual thing—as he grew older, the classics became more and more appealing—but Adama recognized good showmanship when he saw it, and Peter Attis had a hell of a voice. Laura Roslin sat next to him, unabashedly enthralled, and Adama found himself feeling pleased and proud, as if he had somehow arranged Peter's rescue and subsequent concert for her benefit. Anything that reduced her pain was, in his book, a fine thing, and no more than Roslin deserved. As for himself, he'd forgotten for a while about juggling cats, about the death of his wife, about Cylon attacks. He'd even caught himself pretending that he was out on a date with a beautiful woman. Adama blushed slightly at that memory. Laura Roslin was the president of the Fleet and a good friend, nothing else. But his treacherous mind, the one that had been hungry for female company for too many years now, planted the idea nonetheless.

But the concert, it turned out, had become a major venue for spreading this plague of tongues and the point of a terrorist attack by Caprica Sharon. Billy had hustled the president away the moment that news came down, and Adama had snapped from civilian mode into commander mode. It was as if an old, heavy weight had smacked down on him with contemptuous familiarity. He had dealt with the crisis, and only later had he realized he hadn't even bid Laura Roslin good night.

And Caprica Sharon was still at large, Adama couldn't spare the personnel to look for her, and gods only knew what she was up to. Still more cats to juggle.

He banished further thought with firm discipline. Right now, he had to deal with the *Monarch* and Peter Attis. The Sharon problem would have to wait.

The picture on the monitor was silent and fuzzy, despite— or perhaps because of—Gaeta's ministrations. A group of helmeted marines, their face plates down and their weapons holstered, burst into a roomful of people. Adama had no way of telling which one was Lee. His muscles tightened. Beside him, he sensed Saul Tigh tensing up as well. Adama understood why. Tigh had been in charge of the Fleet during the *Gideon* incident—the civilians called it a massacre—and Adama knew the man lived under a cloud of guilt over it. Tigh covered it well and acted as if the entire incident had never taken place. Adama wondered sometimes if it wouldn't have been better for him to show guilt or other public feeling about the *Gideon*. There were times when the commanding officer needed to be a god and times when the commanding officer needed to be human. The *Gideon* might have been one of the latter times. Well, it was too late now. Tigh making any kind of public statement about the *Gideon* would only tear open wounds that hadn't fully healed yet.

On the screen, the people in the processing room swarmed toward the marines like ants on a pile of sugar. Several of them wore masks over the lower half of their faces, creating two groups of masked, anonymous people thronging toward each other. Army ants and worker ants, heading for the clash. Adama held his breath. If the people attacked, the marines had the right to defend themselves, but that could quickly devolve into something worse. Another *Gideon* loomed.

But the people just surrounded the marines and stood there, unmoving. The two groups froze, staring at each other. Then one of the marines, the one in the lead, tentatively tried to nudge the woman in front of him aside. She didn't fight back, but she didn't give ground, either.

"Can we get sound on this?" Adama asked. His hands were shaking again, a situation that made his mouth go dry with a fear—

the prion is chewing on your brain

—that he refused to examine closely.

"I'm sorry, sir," Gaeta said. "The security cameras on the *Monarch* aren't wired for sound, and the marines are still keeping radio silence in case Lieutenant Thrace's kidnappers are listening in."

Adama nodded acknowledgment and went back to watching. The marine—Lee?—tried pushing forward again, but the woman still didn't move. Neither did the people standing on either side of her. Another moment passed, and then the lead marine—Adama was more and more sure it was Lee—signaled, and the entire platoon tried to push forward.

The people didn't resist, but neither did they get out of the way. They fell against the marines or went limp or formed human barricades. The marines were easily outnumbered ten to one, and their progress through the crowd slowed to a maddening crawl. Adama recognized the technique, of course. Passive resistance. There was no riot, no attack, nothing the marines could really fight against, but it hindered progress nonetheless. Against an opponent willing to kill, it was almost worthless. The Fleet marines, however, didn't want to kill anyone, and the civilians knew it. It made an effective wall between the marines and Peter Attis, wherever he was.

"Why don't they fire off some tear gas?" Tigh said. "That'd clear the area right fast."

"It would get into the ventilation system," Adama pointed out. "In a ship that small, the gas would fog the entire place in just a few minutes, and there'd be nowhere to run to. Then you'd have a shipful of angry civilians in pain. Bad combination."

"Right, right," Tigh said, clearly disappointed.

On the screen, the marines tried to wade through the mass of people, but were unable to make progress. Every person they pushed aside was immediately replaced by another, and then another. Every so often, one of the resisters fell twitching and convulsing to the floor. When that happened, two of the masked Unity followers hauled the victim into the path the marines were trying to take. The symbolism was clear—the people touched by the One opposed the people who fought for the Lords of Kobol.

"Frak," Tigh muttered. "They're going to have to open fire if they want to get through."

"They have orders not to," Adama said. "And I'm not going to change them."

"Then we're all dead, Commander," Tigh said. "If they don't get Attis back to sickbay, the prions and Cylons win."

251

"I won't have an—a massacre on my watch, Colonel," Adama said, dropping the word "another" just in time. But another voice inside his head said he might need to issue killing orders. A hundred civilians might die, but it would mean the rest would live. He frowned hard. Why did so damn many of his choices come down to letting a few die so many could live? Why couldn't it ever be that *everyone* gets to live?

The marines continued to wade through civilians, making no real progress but also inflicting no casualties. Adama's left hand was seriously shaking now, and he wondered how long it would be before he joined the masses writhing down in sickbay and on deck five.

"Commander, Dr. Baltar is on the line for you," Dualla said.

Hope and relief washed through Adama. If Baltar was calling, it could only mean he'd finished a cure for the plague. He could order the marines to return to the *Galactica*, and Peter Attis could sing and preach blasphemy to his heart's content. End of problem. He felt the weight of stress lift. Even Saul Tigh looked relieved. For once, the solution would be easy. He picked up the receiver with his right hand, the one that wasn't shaking.

"Hello, Doctor," Adama said. "What can I do for you?"

"Commander, I'm afraid I have bad news," Baltar said.

Adama's stomach tightened again, and the weight crashed back down on him as if it had never left. "What is it, then?" he asked with resignation.

"Prion C, the cure prion, is far more complicated than I anticipated," Baltar said regretfully. *"I can eventually synthesize it, but . . . I doubt I can do it before the majority of patients become terminal."*

Adama's insides turned to liquid and he almost dropped the phone. "What are you saying, Doctor?"

"I'm estimating that by now, over ninety percent of the Fleet's

population has been infected with the plague prion and that by the time I've finished creating the curative prion, close to eighty percent of the Fleet's population will have died."

Baltar delivered this news in a calm, flat voice. A thousand different thoughts swirled through Adama's head, making him dizzy. Or was the prion affecting him? He wondered how much time Baltar had wasted calculating how many people would die and how fast, and he wondered if more people would die because Baltar was talking on the phone instead of working in his lab.

"How long before you have the cure, Doctor?" Adama asked, his voice betraying none of these questions.

"Two or three days," Baltar replied.

"Thank you, Doctor," Adama said evenly. "Don't let me keep you from your work." Then he hung up.

"How long?" Tigh asked.

Adama didn't see any point in concealing the truth. "Two days, maybe three."

"But we'll all be dead by then," blurted Felix Gaeta, violating the unwritten rule about mentioning the elephant in the room with a commander who juggled cats.

"Then we'd better hope Captain Adama and those marines bring us Peter Attis," Adama said. With that, he hid his shaking left hand under the light table and turned his attention back to the marines on the monitors.

Nonsense fell in long strings from Kara's mouth now. The only way she could stop it was to bite her lips shut like a child refusing to take medicine, but her treacherous muscles didn't always obey her. Most of her body trembled with earthquake aftershocks, and the moment she stopped concentrating, more bullshit tumbled from her mouth. It wasn't even real words. She could say real words if she worked at it, but she was so tired. All she wanted to do was pass out. Except her twitching, jerking body kept her awake on the cold floor.

Peter sat cross-legged with her head in his lap. He stroked her hair and said things that he probably thought soothing. "Everything's going to be fine. I know it's bad now, but eventually you'll see the One and you'll recover, like I did. You'll be fine. Just fine."

Kara had never wanted to hit anyone more in her entire life.

Sharon, meanwhile, was kneeling over the red duffel bag, dipping tools in and out of the ordnance that squatted inside like a malevolent toad. The red mask still covered most of her face. Except it wasn't Sharon's face. It wasn't the Sharon Kara knew. She was someone else, another copy of Caprica Sharon. Kara should have realized it. Caprica Sharon wouldn't endanger her baby by escaping and trying to commit acts of terrorism. *This* Sharon, a different one, had somehow gotten on board, probably hidden somewhere in Peter's escape pod. There had been one Sharon on it—why not a second? The pod had been searched, but a secret compartment would be easy enough to add, especially since the Cylons had been in possession of the stupid thing for months. And if this Sharon was caught and executed, so what? She'd get a brand-new body and probably spend her remaining days lazing around a Cylon swimming pool bragging about how she put one over on those idiot humans.

The bitch had certainly outfoxed Kara by convincing her to keep silent about Sharon's identity as a Cylon. Black, tarry anger bubbled like pitch, and one of Kara's hands actually managed a fist for a couple seconds before losing it again. Sharon, glancing up from the ordnance, noticed and flashed Kara a quick thumbs-up before turning back to her work.

A monitor set up on one of the shelves showed a troop of marines trying to force their way through Peter's followers. They made almost no headway. The Unity members created a solid wall of bodies five and six people thick. They flung themselves down on the floor. They draped themselves over the invaders like boneless lovers. And the marines clearly had orders not to kill. Or if they did, they hadn't acted on them yet.

"Still silence on the radio," Zarek said. He was fiddling with a frequency scanner, his face serious. "They either know or suspect that we can listen in on what—"

"—*change your orders, Captain,*" said the scanner. Kara's heart jumped. It was Commander Adama's voice. "*Dr. Gaius says he can't replicate the cure prion in time for it to do us any good. Peter's blood is the only cure, and we need him back on* Galactica *no matter what the cost.*"

Kara gasped. So did Peter and Tom Zarek. Peter's blood would cure the plague? Kara's limbs shook with a terrible, all-encompassing palsy, and the cure was standing only a few feet away. Kara wondered what would happen if news of this hit the entire Fleet. She imagined hordes of people stampeding toward Peter, all of them hungry for his blood.

"*I have new orders for you,*" Adama continued on the scanner. There was a pause, and Kara held her breath, knowing what was coming next, praying she wouldn't hear it. "*You are authorized to use force against the civilians. Deadly force, if necessary.*"

"*Sir? I didn't quite copy that.*" It was Lee's voice, and the sound swelled Kara with a bright elation she didn't think was possible. Lee was leading the force that was coming to help her. Help was coming. *Lee* was coming. For a moment, she felt Lee's arms lifting her, holding her and keeping her safe. The hard-bitten part of her, the part that let her survive broken fingers and bruised skin, told her that no one could ever keep her safe, but the part of her that was tired ordered it to shut up. Lee was coming, and she could relax.

If he could get through the civilians.

"I said, use deadly force if you need to," Adama said. *"Peter Attis is your top priority. Nothing else matters, Captain."*

There was a pause. Then Lee said, *"Understood, sir."*

"You frakking bastard!" Zarek shouted at the scanner. "Didn't you learn anything from the *Gideon?"*

Kara licked dry lips. Lee wouldn't shoot unarmed civilians. Would he? But she knew the answer. He would have to. Peter carried the cure for the disease. If sacrificing a hundred people meant several thousand would live, what choice did Lee have? Kara thought about the image of the little kid crying over her daddy's chewed and bloody corpse on the *Gideon* and wondered how many more kids would be crying over their parents in just a few minutes.

"Sounds like our time here is limited," Sharon said, still working on the duffel bag.

Peter stared at the scanner. "What did he mean when he said my blood would cure the plague?"

"I didn't think that remark needed interpretation," Sharon said. "But I'm betting that once word of it gets out, there'll be a whole lot of people wanting to go vampire on your ass."

"People like me," Zarek said coldly. "Frak—this explains . . . Look, are you telling me this is a real disease? I thought it was religious fervor. Your groupies were the ones who came down with it."

"It's . . . it's real," Kara managed to gasp out. "Real service gets good tips for—"

"The plague doesn't need a cure," Peter said. "I was out cold for a while, but I recovered. Everyone else will recover."

But Tom Zarek was already rummaging through a first aid kit. He came up with a syringe. "Let me have some of your blood, Attis."

"You're not a doctor," Peter protested.

Zarek held up shaky hands for a moment, then grabbed Peter by the front of his shirt and shoved him against a wall. He was older than Peter, but his arms were heavy with muscle. "No. I'm just a man who spent twenty years in a prison that taught me a dozen ways to cause someone serious physical pain. You let me draw some blood right now, or I'm going to pound you into a frakking pancake."

Peter shot Sharon a glance, but she just returned his gaze, an amused look in her eyes. He finally nodded. Zarek pushed up one of Peter's sleeves and jabbed the needle into the man's elbow. Peter yelped.

"Watch it!"

"Shut up, god-boy." Zarek filled the syringe despite his shaky hands, then jabbed the needle into his own arm and depressed the plunger. Kara stared hungrily at the syringe, but Peter and Zarek seemed to have forgotten she existed. She wanted that syringe more than anything she had ever wanted. Life in a few cc's of human blood.

"*ATTENTION CIVILIANS!*" boomed a voice from the scanner. Kara didn't recognize the speaker. "*IF YOU DO NOT VACATE THIS AREA IMMEDIATELY, WE WILL BE FORCED TO OPEN FIRE!*"

Zarek tossed the syringe to Peter, who caught it automatically. "You can frak your revolution," he said. "Your religion isn't real, your followers are deluded, and you're as empty as your music. Those people out there are going to die for a cause that doesn't even exist."

Peter looked frantically around the room, as if his world were coming apart. Kara supposed it was. "They're going to kill my people. I should be with them."

Faint shouts came over the scanner. Clearly someone had left their radio open. *"Up with the Unity!"* someone shouted. Someone else started singing Peter's revolution song.

"Not that piece of shit again," Zarek muttered as Peter headed for the main door. "Gods, I can't believe I thought this was a group worth helping."

"Stay here, Peter," Sharon ordered without looking up from the duffle bag. Her voice was cold and brittle as a knife made of ice. "Don't frakking move."

He stopped and looked at her. "Exactly what are you doing with that?"

"I'm putting a timer on the ordnance so we can set it off properly."

"But we don't *want* to set it off," Peter said, growing more and more agitated. "We don't *want* anyone to die!"

"The marines don't know that," Sharon said calmly. "It's a much better bluff if they can see the countdown. And don't try to pull the timer out once I'm done. If you do, you'll have ten seconds to live before the ship-shattering kaboom."

"THIS IS YOUR SECOND WARNING. MOVE ASIDE AND BRING US PETER ATTIS, OR WE WILL OPEN FIRE."

"Why not remove the explosive part, attach a timer to the rest, and bluff with that?" Peter said.

Sharon paused.

Ha! Kara thought, feeling a moment of triumph seep through the fear and exhaustion. *He's frakking got you!*

"There is that," Sharon said slowly. "But I don't think we'll do it that way. We need to move out."

"Move out?" Peter echoed. Kara wanted to roll her eyes.

Peter seemed to spend most of his time repeating what other people said. "We're staying here to confront the marines if they get past my people."

On the monitor, one of the marines looked up at the camera. He raised a pistol and fired at it. People ducked and screamed. The monitor image dissolved into static.

"My people," Sharon said, a smile in her eyes. "I like the way you say that, Peter. As if you own them."

"I don't own anyone." He took a step toward her. "Who are you, anyway?"

"Someone who's telling you we have to get the frak out of here," Sharon said. "Grab your girl-toy and we'll go. Tommy's already left. Didn't you notice?"

Kara, still shaking on the cold floor, managed a glance around the storeroom. It was empty except for the monitors in the corner. They still showed that the marines weren't making much headway against the room packed full of people. Tom Zarek was gone. Kara wasn't in the least surprised. She raised her hands, trying to wave them and get Peter's attention, but she didn't have the coordination. He still held the syringe, and it was half full of blood.

"*THIS IS YOUR FINAL WARNING,*" the scanner said. "*MOVE ASIDE AND BRING US PETER ATTIS OR WE WILL BE FORCED TO OPEN FIRE!*"

"The marines are wrong," Sharon said. "The schematics they're undoubtedly using to get around are telling them that the only way into this part of the ship is through that room your people are guarding. Problem is, when the *Monarch* was modified to take on algae, the workers added another access passageway to make air circulation easier and to simplify transporting goop around, and those changes aren't on the schematics yet. That means we can get out of here just like Tommy did and put the bomb someplace where it'll do some good. It's not close enough to the outer bulkheads here to cause a breach."

"We aren't setting off the bomb!" Peter shouted at her.

Kara mustered all her willpower, forcing her lips to move the way she wanted them to. *"Peter!"* she gasped.

He turned and looked at her. Instant realization came over him. "Frak! I'm sorry, Kara. I'm so sorry." He dashed over to kneel beside her and push up one of her sleeves. Kara felt the sharp prick as the syringe pierced her skin.

But Sharon was already there. She grabbed Peter's wrist and twisted. He yelped and dropped the syringe, though it remained stuck in Kara's arm. The plunger hadn't moved.

"None of that," Sharon said. "We're getting out of here. Now."

"Who the hell are you, anyway?" he gasped.

"The less you know—"

Peter lunged. He caught the bottom of Sharon's mask and yanked. Caught by surprise, Sharon didn't react in time, and her face lay revealed. The mask made a crumpled red beard beneath her chin, though her hair was still covered. Kara continued to shake on the floor, the syringe sticking out of her arm, but she saw Peter's face go pale as milk. His face looked so horrified and stricken that Kara would have felt sorry for him if she weren't twisting in the final stages of a disease he had given her. She looked down at the syringe poking into her arm.

"Mistress Eight," Peter whispered, rising to his feet.

"One of them," Sharon said, also rising.

Cracks of gunfire came over the scanner. People screamed. Kara's blood went cold at the sounds, but more of her attention was focused on the syringe. The needle had pierced her deeply—Peter wasn't a medical technician and had just jabbed it in. A thin bit of blood trickled down the side of her arm. Hers or Peters? Kara gathered her strength. She probably had one chance to make this work. If she frakked it up, she was dead.

"Oh gods." Peter backed up a shaky step, his attention on Sharon. "Oh gods, what have I done?"

"So much for faith," Sharon said. "Or maybe you're swearing to your multiple gods out of habit." She caught up the duffel bag with easy strength and set the timer inside. Kara, still on the floor, couldn't read the numbers, but she heard the familiar beeping of a countdown. "I suppose this is where I bow out. There's a lot more I can do, but not if I'm dead or captured."

Kara made her move. She half rolled, half flopped onto her stomach. The motion drove the syringe deeper into the meat of her arm. It was like being stabbed with a thin knife. Kara bit her lip at the unexpected pain and flopped onto her back again. The syringe fell out of her arm and clattered to the floor. The plunger had been pushed all the way in.

"Resourceful as ever, Starbuck," Sharon said, noticing for the first time what Kara was up to. "Now I *really* have to go."

"Where's . . . groll delk karoledd—frak!" Kara tried again. "Where's . . . real Sharon?"

"I'm perfectly real," Sharon said. "More real than the One. More real than Peter's faith."

"There is no One, is there?" Peter said slowly. He was wrapped in his own fear and misery. The self-centered bastard wasn't even trying to fight Sharon. Not that he had a hope of hurting her, but Kara thought he should at least *try*. "You all just fed that religious stuff to me, made me believe it. But it's all shit."

Sharon cocked her head. "You think so? God exists, Peter dear. How you see God is up to you, really. But we don't care what you humans believe. The prions will kill most of you and leave the rest so weakened that you'll be easy prey. Thanks be to God. And to Peter."

More gunfire over the scanner. More screams and shouts. Kara found that the shakes were already lessening. How long before she could get up and walk?

"I need to get out there and help all those people!" Peter said. "Maybe if I surrender, they'll stop shooting!"

"No, Peter," Sharon said, putting a hand on his shoulder. "You aren't going anywhere."

Peter twisted out of her grip. "I'll kill you," he snarled.

"Will you?" Sharon drew herself up to her full height. Even though she was half a head shorter than Peter, she seemed to tower over him. "I could beat you to death five times before you threw a single punch at me. Now back away."

Peter stared at her for a long moment. *Try, Pete!* Kara thought, pushing herself up to hands and knees. *I'll back you! Or try.*

But Peter dropped his eyes and backed away. Kara's heart sank. Sharon snorted and gave him a contemptuous glance. The crack and pop of gunfire boomed from the scanner, and Kara tried not to imagine bleeding corpses piling up on the deck. Sharon, meanwhile, grabbed Peter's arm. Something metal flashed in her hand. In a single swift movement, she clicked a handcuff to Peter's wrist and snapped the other inside the duffel.

"What the hell?" Peter gasped, shaking his wrist.

"You're a hostage now," Sharon said. "Actually you've always been one—you were just too blind to see it. It won't take those marines long to chew through your people, so let's get moving." She hauled him unprotesting toward the door leading to the other exit—the newly made one, Kara assumed. The scanner continued to spout the cold crackle and crunch of an ongoing massacre. Sharon reached the door. Kara tried to get to her feet, using the wall for support. The cure for the plague was in the hands of a bomb-toting Cylon, and she had to do something. She pushed herself from hands and knees to just knees, then got one foot on the floor. So far, so—

Her legs gave out and she crashed back to the floor. Too much too soon. Sharon laughed at her and opened the door.

"Fight her, you frakking coward!" Kara shouted in a last-ditch effort. Or she tried to. What came out of her mouth made no sense at all.

"See you on the other side, Starbuck," Sharon called over her shoulder. "Wherever that is."

Then main door burst open and a dozen helmeted and face-plated marines poured into the storeroom, rifles at the ready. "Freeze!"

It was Lee's voice. Kara wanted to collapse with relief, but all she could do now was shake. Sharon turned to face them in her own doorway, wrenching Peter around in front of her.

"Go ahead and fire," she said. "But Petey here is between you and me. So how good is your aim? Feeling a little shaky? Want a bit of babble?"

"I said, freeze!" Lee barked. "We've got you, Sharon. There's nowhere to go."

Sharon yanked open the duffel bag and showed Lee the ordnance inside. Peter was cuffed to it, and the timer showed a countdown of twenty-two minutes and ten seconds . . . nine . . . eight.

"Let's play hide and seek, Captain Adama," she said with a winsome smile. "Just you and me. You need Peter alive to cure the plague. I want a shuttle off this ship. Count to a hundred, then come find us to talk about it."

And she vanished into the dark beyond the door, dragging Peter with her.

CHAPTER
15

"Two days' worth of work, Gaius?" said Number Six.

Gaius Baltar continued to peer into the microscope. "That's what I told the Commander. Having you repeat it doesn't change anything."

"Liar. Words have power, Gaius. You just need the right thing to say at the right time."

"Also true. Completely and totally true." He pushed himself away from the microscope and, swiveling on his stool, reached for the telephone. His face was scratchy and unshaven, his clothes were wrinkled and disheveled, but his movements snapped with energy. This often happened to him when he was midway through a project. A sort of manic power crackled through him and he could go for days without sleep—or last for hours in bed.

Six's hand landed on his and pressed them into the dialing pad before he could punch more than two numbers. "Wait. Who are you calling?"

"The president. She needs an update on the situation."

"Don't you think Adama can tell her?"

"I'd rather tell her myself, thanks," he said with a little smile.

She slid her soft hand up his forearm, his shoulder, his neck. A tingle of electricity followed her fingertips, and a coppery taste tanged Gaius's mouth. She leaned down and whispered in his ear, "Call her later. You've been working so hard, Gaius. Don't you think you deserve a break?"

"I have so much to do," he murmured back, though his hands stole up her sides, caressing the cool, smooth fabric of her high-slit dress. "So much work to save the Fleet."

"Will twenty minutes matter in the grand scheme of things?" she said, slitting her eyes like a hungry cat. Her hand reached beneath her own buttocks, opened his fly, and slipped inside. Gaius gasped, then let out a long, rumbling sigh. Her touch made little shudders of pleasure ripple up and down his entire body.

Gaius glanced over his shoulder at the microscope, then at the telephone. He was vice president of the Colonies and their pre-eminent scientist. He was a powerful man with equally powerful appetites, and he needed to indulge them. He *deserved* it, especially after everything he had done for the Fleet. His hands slid up Number Six's smooth thighs.

"Yes, Gaius," she panted against his mouth. "Oh, yes."

His groin tightened, and desire slid over him in a hot rush. He pulled her down into his lap and kissed her, devouring her mouth like a wildfire consuming a forest. He half expected her to push him away, but she met him with a ferocity so powerful, she growled. The sound rumbled in her breasts, and he felt them move against his own chest. His groin ached, and he felt like he could push into her, push *through* her, until the two of them were a single being.

"Twenty minutes?" he said. "I was thinking sixty."

. . .

Lee Adama pointed impatiently at the door. "You six go after her and Peter!" he told the marines who had entered behind him. "The rest of you secure this room. Go go go!"

The marines hurried to obey. Lee pulled up his face plate and ran across the room to kneel next to Kara. She had never been so glad to see anyone in her life. But his hands were shaking. Concern, fear, and relief all mixed together inside her and made her entire body feel weak. Or maybe that was still the plague. Lee gathered her into his arms, and she let him. Hard muscle made a barrier around her, sealing out the rest of the world. For a short, blissful moment, she let herself feel safe and cared for. She felt tears welling up, and she forced them back. Lee looked down at Kara and she looked up at him. His eyes were so blue and full of . . . what? Concern? Love? She wondered what he was seeing in her eyes.

And then he was kissing her. His lips were warm on hers. The move surprised both of them, and Kara's eyes opened wide. A second lasted a thousand heartbeats. Kara wanted this and didn't want this. Too many things could go wrong—*would* go wrong. Best to end it before it began. Kara tensed to push Lee away, but a howl of pain followed by gunfire jerked them apart. Thuds, more shots, another scream. Lee scrambled to his feet and hauled Kara up beside him with an easy strength that left her a little breathless. The other marines in the room had spun and were pointing their rifles at the door Sharon had used. Sharon appeared in the doorway again, holding a pistol to Peter's head. The ordnance was still cuffed to his wrist. Kara swallowed.

"Hold your fire!" Lee barked.

"See what you did?" Sharon said. "Now I have weapons. I said I'd talk just to you, Captain, and to Lieutenant Thrace there. The both of you. Anyone else follows me, I kill Petey. If both of you don't come, I kill Petey." She vanished back into the darkness.

"Frak!" Lee muttered. "Can you stand by yourself, Kara?"

Kara checked. The shaking had ended. She also felt no desire to babble nonsense. Her voice was her own again. She felt weak, but strength was already returning. Lee's hands, however, still trembled.

"I think I'm okay," she said in a tight, tired voice.

"Helo!" Lee shouted. "I want you and the others to check the hall for wounded. And dead."

"Those people," Kara said as Helo and the others obeyed. "I heard the orders on the scanner. You killed them?"

Lee looked at her, and Kara's heart suddenly felt like a bruised apple. A wave of revulsion made her stomach roil. The arm that held her up had just killed a score of innocent people.

Then Lee shook his head. "We didn't hurt a single person. Adama broadcast those orders, figuring Peter would hear them and come out of hiding to surrender himself. We fired into the air to make it sound like we were shooting. People screamed, so that made it even more realistic. Or so we thought—it obviously didn't work."

Relief swept Kara in a powerful wave that weakened her knees. Lee tightened his arm around her shoulders. "It almost did work," Kara said. "How did you get in here?"

"I asked the Old Man to let me bring two forces," Lee said. "I sent one down to the great room as a distraction," Lee said. "The rest of us got back into the Raptor, flew around to the other side of the ship, and burned through over there. That got us around the crowd. We figured the perpetrators would think all the marines were wading through the passive resistance people, letting the rest of us sneak up on them. But we got lost—the schematics are wrong. Eventually, we had to home in on the ordnance signal. Then Da—Commander Adama gave the killing orders, hoping to flush Peter out into the open and maybe distract the bad guys some more. I just wish it had worked."

"I told you it almost did. Peter was about to run out there and give himself up, but Sharon stopped him."

"Yeah. Sharon." He ran a shaky hand over his face. "What the frak is that bitch doing here?"

Helo trotted up. "Sir, we have six dead. She—" He swallowed, and Kara could see the distress on his face. "I'm sorry, sir, but she killed them all. Sharon . . ."

"That wasn't your Sharon," Kara said quickly. Both Lee and Helo stared at her in surprise.

"What do you mean?" Helo asked, his voice full of hope.

"That's another Sharon copy. I saw her close up, and she isn't pregnant."

Helo grabbed Kara's free shoulder. "Are you sure?"

"Absolutely. She—this new Sharon—must have been hiding in a secret compartment on the rescue pod. I don't know what happened to *our* Sharon, but that wasn't her, and I'm betting our Sharon wasn't behind the attack on the concert, either."

The love and hope that crossed Helo's face was so clear, Kara's heart ached for him. She hadn't loved anyone like that since Zak.

Really? said a treacherous little voice in the back of her head. *What about his brother?*

"So where is our Sharon?" Helo asked. "And why did she escape?" Behind him, marines were dragging dead bodies into the storeroom, clearing out the doorway. Some were missing their weapons.

"No idea," Kara said. "But the Sharon who has Peter is definitely someone else."

"Wait a minute," Lee said. "What happened to you? Why aren't you shaking anymore?"

"Peter . . . cured me." She bent down, freeing herself from Lee's hold, and picked up the syringe from the floor. "With his blood. Lee, we have to get him back. He's the only cure for the prion."

Lee visibly relaxed. "Thank all gods. If he injected you, Kara, then we're fine. Your body will start making the cure prion and—"

"No," Kara interrupted. "My blood's AB positive. It's really rare, and I can only give blood to other AB positives. Peter's O negative. He can give blood to anyone."

"Baltar and Cottle might be able to synthesize the cure prion without using your blood," Lee said. Then his face fell. "But not before most of the Fleet dies. Dammit, we need Peter."

"Shit," Helo said. "Nothing is ever easy around here, is it?"

"Sir," Racetrack approached, raising her face plate, "do you want us to go after her?"

Lee checked his watch. "No. She said she'd kill Peter if anyone but me and Kara went in there. Call the Old Man and tell him what's happened. You think you can fire a weapon, Lieutenant?"

Lee's words filled Kara with a new strength. She suspected it was mostly adrenaline, but right then, she didn't care. Her hands were blessedly steady, and the thought of filling that bitch Sharon with chunks of metal made Kara itch to get moving. She held up her hands.

"I'm solid like a rock, sir," she said.

Lee handed her his own pistol and rifle. Helo gave her his kevlar armor, and she belted it on. It felt solid and comforting, despite the stiff weight. Kara accepted an equipment belt and a helmet.

"What do you think her game is?" Helo asked. "There's nowhere for her to go. Now that we know she's on the *Monarch*, there's no escape. Even if the Old Man gives her a frakking shuttle in exchange for Peter, she has to know we'll blow her out of the sky the minute she's clear of this ship."

"I don't know." Lee tried to check the firing mechanism on his own pistol, but his hands were shaking too much and he couldn't get the slide action to work. "Frak!"

"Maybe you should stay here," Kara said. "I'll go alone."

"Like you always do, is that it?" Lee said. "Noble Starbuck, the maverick, on her own again. Well, not this time."

"Lee," she protested, "you're sick. You should—"

"I should get my ass moving," Lee told her. "Sharon—bad Sharon—said she wanted to talk to me and maybe you. We don't know what she'll do if I don't come, so I'm coming."

"Fine," Kara said. "Just keep your pistol in the holster, buddy. You fire with those hands, and you're just as likely to hit me as her."

They trotted toward the door. On the way, they passed the six bodies the others had laid out. Kara carefully avoided looking at them. If there was a friend among them, she didn't want to know it. Not yet.

"Go get her, sir," one of the marines said, and Kara wasn't sure if he was talking to Lee or to her, so she nodded. Pistol drawn, she stepped across the threshold into the blackness beyond.

The darkness wasn't absolute, and her eyes adjusted in a few seconds. They were standing in a metal corridor barely wide enough for the two of them to stand side by side. Something dark and sticky stained the walls and floor, and Kara caught the coppery smell of drying blood. She pursed her lips and felt abruptly glad that Lee was beside her, close enough for her to feel his body heat. The darkness pressed around her, close and frightening. Her heart beat faster and her mouth went dry. Shapes moved just at the corner of her eye, reaching out to pluck at her with cold fingers, but when she jerked her gaze around to look at them, they disappeared.

Kara had never liked the dark very much, even as an adult. She knew exactly why, though knowing the source of the fear didn't make it any less intense. When she was little, her father had used the dark. Like most small children, darkness made Kara nervous, and Dad knew it. He thought it was absolutely hilarious to hide in her closet just before bedtime and bang the door open while she was climbing into bed. His harsh laughter at her screams of terror still echoed in her head. Her pleas for him to stop doing it fell on deaf ears. She needed a sense of humor, she needed to be toughened up. After a while, she took to checking the closet when the lights were still on. Once, she had searched the house, padding around in her nightgown and bare feet, unable to find Dad anywhere. At last, Mom had told her to get her butt into bed and no excuses. Sure she knew where Dad was, Kara had thrown open the closet door. The space beyond was empty, except for her clothes and a few toys. Puzzled, but feeling safer, she had turned out the light and scurried over to her bed before anything in the dark could get her. Something furry shot out from under the bedstead and grabbed Kara's ankle in a monstrous grip. Kara's bladder let go and she almost fainted from sheer terror. The monster, of course, had turned out to be Dad wearing a furry mitten. He had roared with laughter, and then had whipped her for wetting her underwear.

As an adult, Kara knew there was nothing coming to get her in the dark. Or she *had* known that. Now Cylons attacked from the dark of space. And there had been that time a bunch of robotic Cylons had gotten aboard *Galactica* and cut the power. Now the darkness hid Sharon. There *were* monsters out there.

But this time, Kara was armed and armored, and she wasn't alone. Beside her, Lee squinted down the hallway. "Helmet lights?" he whispered. "Or would that give our position away?"

"I think Cylons see pretty well in the dark," Kara muttered back. "We may as well use the lights."

They switched them on, and twin beams of light speared the darkness of the corridor and put sharp edges on the shadows. "Come on," Lee said.

They moved cautiously along the corridor. Their cautious footsteps clanked faintly on the ceramic deck plates, and the damp air smelled of salt water and algae. A part of Kara wanted to hurry, hurry, hurry—the Fleet needed the cure that only Peter could provide. Another part of her urged caution. Sharon might have already killed Peter and just wanted to frak with her and Lee. It wouldn't be the first time the Cylons had screwed around with someone's mind.

The corridor ended in a door that was so new, it still smelled of solder. Lee tried to crank it open, but his hands were shaking too badly, so Kara took over. The hinges creaked, and the sound seemed to boom through the entire ship. Lee flinched. Kara waited until her heart slowed down again before stepping through, trying to cover all directions at once with her pistol. Darkness pressed in on all sides like black cotton, and Kara felt exposed and vulnerable despite the kevlar. Her breathing sounded too loud in her ears, a beacon for bombs or bullets.

The space beyond the door felt big and echoey. Kara and Lee shined their lights around. Huge shapes loomed like black beasts, and catwalks made lattices far overhead. Kara made out trucks and loaders and giant equipment she couldn't name, all motionless, and found herself tiptoeing past them as if they were asleep and the slightest sound might bring them snarling awake.

"I think this is the spot where one of us is supposed to say, 'Let's split up, we can cover more ground that way,' " Lee murmured.

"Frak that," she scoffed.

"Well I wasn't actually going to say it," Lee replied.

Kara smiled in the dark, feeling a little better. A lot better, actually. Having Lee beside her felt good, felt right. They were a great team, both on missions and off duty. And when he had kissed her earlier . . .

She slammed the brakes on that line of thought. They had to find Peter, and fast, or Kara would be one of the few people still alive the next time the Cylons showed up. The thought sent cold shivers over her entire skin.

Something clinked in the darkness above and to the right. It sounded like chains. Kara thought about ghosts as she and Lee both swept their helmet lights across the underside of the catwalk above them. Nothing moved, though Lee's beam was a little shaky. He tried to hold it steady and failed. The light danced around like a malicious fairy. Lee made a small sound in his throat, then coughed, trying to cover it. Kara's heart ached for him. She knew exactly what he was thinking.

"Lee," she said softly. "We'll find her. We'll get you cured."

"I know," he replied in an equally soft voice. "I can always count on you when the chips are down and my hand is shitty." He paused. "*Especially* when the chips are down and my hand is shitty."

Kara slowly reached out, found his hand, and squeezed it. Her heart was pounding as if she were facing a hundred Cylon raiders by herself. Lee's hand was shaking badly, and she couldn't tell if he was squeezing back, but it was warm.

Lee suddenly dropped her hand and swept his light to their right. "You hear that?" he whispered.

Kara listened, still feeling the warmth of his hand in hers. She heard a faint shuffling in the darkness, but her flashlight beam picked up nothing but a giant conveyer belt. "Footsteps?" she whispered back.

"I'm not sure," he murmured. "I can't quite—"

"Why the frak are we whispering?" Kara interrupted. "She knows we're here." She cupped her hands around her mouth. "Hey, Sharon, or whatever the hell your name is! I'm here! Lee too! Get your ass out here!"

Lee flinched, then seemed to realize Kara was right. "Come on!" he bellowed. "Let's get this over with."

"Up here, guys. And no insults, please. I've had a hard day."

Kara's beam stabbed upward toward the voice, and she saw Sharon's face looking down at them through the mesh catwalk two stories above them, not far from the place they had checked earlier. She was kneeling on a kevlar vest and peering over the edge of it. Next to her on the catwalk sat Peter. A long chain was wrapped several times around his body. His hands were tied in front of him with more chain, and the missile ordnance, now minus the duffel bag, was still cuffed to his wrist. He was gagged with a blood-soaked piece of cloth. Kara realized the cloth was a strip torn from the uniform of a dead marine, probably the same one Sharon had taken the vest from. Anger tightened in Kara's stomach like a screw. She thought about taking a shot at Sharon, and instantly discarded the idea. Even if the bullet didn't carom off the catwalk mesh, it would probably just hit Peter or the kevlar vest—a fact Sharon no doubt knew very well.

"Hi!" Sharon called down to them, as if they were meeting to go shopping. "I've got your medicine. It's all here."

"What do you want?" Lee said.

"First, I want you to take off those kevlar vests and the helmets and your equipment belts," Sharon instructed. "Toss them far away. Now! Or I'll slice a piece off of Peter here. Set the helmets on the floor with the lights pointing up so you can see—and I can see you."

Reluctantly, the two pilots obeyed. Kara felt naked and vulnerable once the armor came off, and she had to force herself to toss it into the gloom beyond her flashlight beam. She set her helmet on the floor and pointed the light as instructed. The helmet looked like a decapitated head.

"Now your rifles and your pistols," Sharon said. "And the knives you're keeping in the ankle holsters. Move it! Or I'll cut off a couple of Peter's fingers."

Kara gritted her teeth and tossed her rifle and her pistol away. Lee did the same. He also pulled a knife from an ankle holster and threw that away. It clattered in the dark. Kara wasn't wearing an ankle holster. She pulled up her trouser legs so Sharon could see them. Lee shot Kara a knowing look, and Kara felt a tiny bit better—Lee was hiding more weapons somewhere.

"So you *can* follow directions," Sharon said. "Good. Now take off your shirts. Both of you."

"Our shirts?" Lee said.

Sharon flicked open a knife of her own and gestured at Peter with it. His wide eyes fixed on it. "Do it, Apollo!"

Grimacing, Lee peeled off his shirt. Well-defined muscle rippled in the dim light. Kara, who lived in close quarters with Lee, had seen him undressed any number of times, but never had she seen him strip for a kidnapper.

"Turn around," Sharon said, and Lee reluctantly obeyed. A pistol was stuck into the waistband of his trousers at the small of his back. "That's what I thought. Toss it, Starbuck. And don't get funny ideas while you're doing it."

"Dammit," Lee muttered under his breath as Kara plucked the pistol out of his belt line. Her hand brushed against his back. The skin was warm and smooth, and she remembered how he had cradled her back in the storeroom. His capacity to help her, protect her, was diminishing by the moment, and wasn't that the way it always went? In the end, it came down to just you.

"Now Starbuck," Sharon ordered. "Lose the shirt."

Rather than put off the inevitable, Kara whipped off her shirt and dropped it. The sports bra she wore underneath covered more of her than most bathing suit tops, but still she felt exposed. She caught Lee not looking and knew he was a little embarrassed, even though he was wearing less than she was.

"Turn."

Kara turned, showing she had no weapons. "Okay, fine. We're unarmed and half naked down here. What the hell do you want?"

"A trade, duh," Sharon replied. "Here's how it's going to work. I'm going to send Peter down, and you, Captain Adama, are going to come up. You'll take me to the Raptor that brought you over here and we'll both get in. Then I'll pilot us away. When we're a safe distance from the Fleet—and by that, I mean, 'when you can't blow me out of the frakking sky'—I give little Lee a transponder and shove him out the airlock. I make a jump, you fly out to pick him up, everyone wins."

"Except Lee, who'll be sucking vacuum," Kara scoffed.

"He'll be in a vac suit," Sharon said with exaggerated patience. "Cylons still follow safety regulations. Sheesh."

"Forget it," Kara said. "You're stuck here, with nowhere to go. Why should we deal with you?"

"Because there's only ten minutes left on the timer," Sharon said, gesturing at the bomb. "You better take the deal, unless you want to be licking your plague cure off the walls and ceiling."

276

"So you're giving us Peter?" Kara asked. "I thought the point was for the plague to kill all of us. You kill Peter and the mission succeeds. That's what you were trying to do at the concert, wasn't it? I thought you just wanted to hurt a bunch of humans, but your real objective was to kill Peter after he infected everyone but before anyone realized he was carrying the cure. Though that doesn't explain why you didn't just kill him in sickbay during the kidnapping."

"The longer he stayed alive, the more people he infected," Sharon said. "And it was way more fun watching his followers do what they did. You humans are willing to believe anything that sounds like the truth, even if it's false."

"So why not kill Peter now?" Lee asked. "You put one bullet through his head and a second one through yours. We all die and you get home faster."

"True," Sharon sighed. "But death frakking *hurts*, you know? I'd way rather avoid it."

Kara caught Lee's eye and shook her head. "There's more to it," she said just loud enough for him to hear.

He gave a tiny nod of agreement. "We need to play along," he mouthed back. Then, louder, "So you want to take me hostage."

"That's the plan. I don't think Adama will shoot at me if I have his pretty-boy son Apollo chained up beside me."

"How do we know you won't just kill him and jump away once you're aboard the Raptor?" Kara asked.

"You don't. And maybe that's exactly what I'll do. But you'll still have Peter and the cure." Sharon paused. "Now there's an idea. He could start a new group—Peter and the Cure. Assuming you all survive this. You only have eight minutes and thirty seconds left on the timer." She pulled Peter to her and gave him a kiss on the forehead. "You're so cute when you're tied up. Maybe I'll just keep you anyway."

Above the bloody gag, Peter's eyes were wide with fear, horror, or both. Kara thought about what it would be like to be gagged with someone else's blood and shuddered.

"All right," Lee said. "I'll do it."

"No!" Kara said, stepping in front of him. "I'll go instead."

"What?" said Lee and Sharon at the same time.

"Lee's sick," Kara pointed out. "He's already shaking. Soon he's going to start babbling, and then he'll die. He won't be worth much as a hostage if he's dead. Besides—I've had practice being a hostage already."

"No," Lee said firmly. "You stay here, I'll go with Sharon."

"Actually, I'm the one in charge here," Sharon reminded them from above. "But this is so cute—the two lovers quarreling over who gets to be in danger."

"We're not lovers!" Kara said, with Lee echoing a fraction of a second behind her.

"Sure, sure," Sharon said. "In addition to easily believing a false truth, you humans refuse to believe a real one." She tossed a pair of handcuffs over the catwalk, and Lee caught them. "Starbuck wins the hostage lottery today, I think. Tell me where the Raptor's parked, Apollo."

Lee gritted his teeth. "Aft, starboard side at ninety degrees to the axis."

"Good boy. Now I want you to—what was that?"

Both Lee and Kara froze, listening.

"Who followed you?" Sharon said sharply. "I said, if anyone came with you—"

"I don't hear anything," Kara said.

"No one followed," Lee called upward. "I gave orders."

Sharon narrowed her eyes, then continued. "Just remember I have a knife and about six liters of plague cure up here just waiting to rain down on you. I want you to cuff one end to Kara's wrist, Captain. A little to your right, you'll see the end of a chain. Cuff the other end to one of the links. If you know what's good for you, Kara, you'll grab the chain. And hurry—you've only six and a half minutes left."

Peter made noises around the gag as Lee obeyed. The cuff was cool on Kara's wrist, and she kept swallowing her own heart to keep it from leaping out of her throat. Despite her show of bravado, fear gripped her chest with a cold hand. Lee looked like he wanted to say something but didn't know the words. The muscles on his broad back bunched and moved as he fumbled around in the dim light until he found the chain Sharon had mentioned. He brought one end over to Kara and fastened the free end of the handcuffs to one of the links. It clanked. Kara looked up, trying to trace the line of the chain, but she lost it in the gloom. She grabbed it with both hands.

"Ready-set-go!" Sharon said, and she shoved Peter off the catwalk. Kara tried to shout, but sound died in her throat as she was yanked upward. Chains clattered, and pain wrenched her shoulders. Peter rushed down past her as she flew dizzily up toward the catwalk. Kara got a glimpse of Peter's frightened expression and of the ordnance still cuffed to his wrist. Red numbers flashed, but she didn't have time to read them. Her feet dangled over nothing. Sharon grabbed Kara's belt and hauled her onto the catwalk. Below, Lee was already unwrapping Peter's chains. The moment Kara's feet touched down, she tensed to attack, but Sharon spun her around with terrifying speed and forced both of Kara's hands behind her. The chain clinked again. There was a click, and both of Kara's hands were cuffed behind her.

"Don't try to kick me, either," Sharon said. "I'll whack you over the head and carry you if I have to, and you won't like it very much."

"Is Peter all right?" Kara called over the edge.

Lee and Peter both looked up. Lee had freed Peter from the chain and the gag, but Peter's left hand was still handcuffed to the missile ordnance. The timer was counting down toward five minutes.

"I'm fine, Kara," Peter called. "Gods. Are *you* okay?"

"How do I disarm the bomb?" Lee said. "I don't recognize this setup."

"Well, that's part of the problem," Sharon said. The timer hit five minutes and the numbers suddenly jumped. The minutes counter read zero and the seconds counter read thirty. They were counting backward. "Looks like you got to save your girl-friend's life after all, Captain. And you, Starbuck, get to see both your lovers die."

CHAPTER

16

Kara stared in shock, then fought against her restraints. "No! Lee! Peter!" she cried through the catwalk floor. It felt like she was a mile away from them both.

Peter looked up, stricken. Lee tried yanking at Peter's handcuffs, but they didn't budge. The timer continued its deadly countdown. Lee grabbed it, and his hand shook visibly.

"Pull the timer off and it blows right away," Sharon called down, and Lee froze. "Have fun with it. Come on, Lieutenant." And she began to haul Kara away by one elbow.

"Lee!" Kara shrieked. "Lee!"

Below, Peter's face hardened. Abruptly, he shoved Lee away and sprinted off into the darkness. Lee, still shirtless, snatched up one of the helmets from the floor and pointed its light toward him. The timer, glowing an angry red in the dark, showed six seconds. Peter was already climbing into the heavy metal scoop of a loader. He shot one more look up at Kara. She stared back, feeling completely helpless.

"I'm sorry, Kara!" Peter called. There were tears in his voice. "I'm so sorry."

He dropped into the loader bucket. Lee dove to the floor. Even though she was two stories above it, the explosion knocked Kara off her feet. It was like being slapped by a giant hand. She landed beside Sharon, the latticed metal of the catwalk scraping her bare arms and shoulders. Automatic alarms blared. Sharon recovered her feet first, yanked Kara back to hers, and towed her toward a set of stairs that led downward. The heat sucked the air from Kara's lungs and shriveled her hair. The hot smell of scorched metal stung her nose and acrid smoke clawed at her eyes. Then she heard the scream of tortured metal, and a section of the catwalk behind them crashed to the main floor. The section Kara and Sharon were standing on tilted backward. Kara, her hands cuffed behind her, lost her balance and fell heavily to the latticework. She slid backward with a yelp, losing more skin to the catwalk.

"Frak," Sharon said, and managed to grab Kara by the hair. White pain ripped Kara's scalp and she screamed. Sharon, who had hooked an arm around a strut for support, hauled Kara closer, then managed to get a hand under Kara's arm and yank her along until they came to a level section of the catwalk near the stairs. Kara felt like a bruised bag of meat. She coughed and stumbled, but Sharon yanked her down the steps anyway. Twice she stumbled and fell, and both times Sharon hauled her roughly to her feet.

"Lee!" Kara called over her shoulder. "Lee!"

"Shut up," Sharon ordered. "We have to get to the Raptor."

"I'm not going with you, bitch," Kara spat. "You had that planned from beginning, didn't you?"

"Well, yeah." Sharon opened the door. "You didn't honestly think I'd wreck a plan we've been perfecting for months, did you? This way, Peter's still dead, the cure is destroyed, the only other person whose body makes the prion is with me, and I still have a hostage that'll get me clear of the Fleet. If you're very nice to me, I'll give you a vac suit before I dump you out the airlock, and if you're *really* nice to me, I'll let you put it on first."

"So why did you tell Lee to come along? Why kill him?"

Sharon shrugged. "Someone had to handle the chains."

Kara decided not to respond to this. Sharon shoved her into the corridor beyond the doorway and shut the hatch. The heat vanished, letting Kara breathe more easily. They were standing at a well-lighted T intersection.

"All right, let's see," Sharon said, "assuming Captain good-boy Apollo wasn't lying about the Raptor—and your life expectancy will be really short if he did, honey—we need to go . . . this way."

"I'll frakking kill you," Kara gasped. "I swear I'll find a way."

"Sure, sure," Sharon said, towing her along. "Even if you managed it, I'd be alive and kicking humanity's ass again before long. Not that there'll be much ass to kick now that Peter blew himself to bits and took the cure with him."

"He didn't do it," Kara snarled. "That was you."

"Whatever. Let's see. Left up here, then right, and the ship should be—ah-ha!"

They came across a hole, perhaps a meter and a half in diameter, that had been cut into the bulkhead. Lying on the deck in front of it was a big circle of ceramic. It looked like a mutated round drawbridge. Sharon pushed Kara toward the hole. Kara ducked to get inside and found herself in the familiar interior of a Raptor transport. Sharon also ducked to follow. The moment Kara crossed the threshold, she straightened, spun, and kicked Sharon in the head before the Cylon woman could straighten. Sharon grunted and went down to her hands and knees. All the anger and fear Kara had been carrying with her exploded like a missile. She swept Sharon's arms out from under her with a sweep kick and jumped forward. The back of her foot came down on the back of Sharon's neck. Kara pressed down.

"Now who's the hostage, toaster?" Kara panted.

"Don't call me that," Sharon growled. In a flash of movement, she grabbed Kara's ankle and yanked. Kara lost her balance and crashed to the deck on her side. Sharon scrambled to her feet and kicked Kara under the jaw. Her teeth clacked together and Kara saw stars through an explosion of pain. The Raptor spun around her.

"Frakking human bitch," Sharon spat. "I should shoot you right now."

Running footsteps pounded down the corridor toward the hole and the hatchway that framed it. Sharon started to shut the hatchway, but an arm interposed itself. It was shaking.

"Wait!" said a male voice. Kara was too groggy from Sharon's kick to recognize it, but Sharon seemed to. She let the hatchway open again just far enough to reveal a dark-haired man crouching over to peer inside the Raptor.

"Helo," Sharon said. Her hand dropped to her belt and toyed with a small control Kara hadn't noticed before. "This is a surprise. Trying to delay me long enough for the rest of the troop to catch up?"

"No," Helo said. His dark eyes were serious. "Sharon, please don't do this. Leave Starbuck here."

Sharon looked genuinely puzzled. "Why would I do that?"

"I know you aren't . . . aren't *my* Sharon," he said. "But you have to know how much I love her—you. Please leave Kara here. Everyone over at CIC is too sick to chase you. Leave Kara here."

"So you can try to synthesize a cure from her blood?" Sharon scoffed. "I don't think so, Helo."

Kara tried to sit up, but the pain in her head and her bound hands made it impossible. She could only lay with her cheek pressed into the cool floor.

"Then do it for me," Helo pleaded. "I've talked to my Sharon a lot, and it sounded like all of the Sharons . . . all of *you* . . . share some of the same memories. Don't you remember any feelings for me?"

"Your Sharon never died, Helo, so her memories were never downloaded anywhere. You're just another human." Sharon started to push the hatch shut again. "One who made the stupid mistake of falling in love with a superior being."

A pistol appeared in Helo's hand. "I gave you a chance," he said, and fired.

Sharon, however, was already moving. She ducked, and her foot came up in a sideways kick that slammed into Helo's midriff and flung him backward. He hit the opposite wall with a terrible thud. The bullet ricocheted off a strut in the interior. Kara heard a cracking noise, but lying on the floor as she was, she couldn't see much. Helo slid to the deck, clearly dazed.

"I could kill you, Helo," Sharon said, her hand once again on that strange control at her belt. "But I won't. The plague can take you. Maybe there's something to the whole 'feelings for you' thing after all."

She slammed the hatchway shut, spun the wheel to lock it, and reached into a storage closet to remove a white vac suit. With practiced ease, she slipped it on and sealed the helmet. Kara was too groggy to do anything but lie there. And what did it matter if she fought back, anyway? Lee was dead, Peter was dead, the cure for the plague was destroyed. Almost everyone in the Fleet would die within the next two or three days, and the Cylons would be able to mop up the remaining handful at leisure. A single tear ran from the corner of her eye and down the side of her nose. Everything she had worked to preserve, everything she had fought for, was gone. Her life was a waste.

And you're a waste of life, said her father's voice. *Just a scared little nothing.*

Sharon, fully suited, took up the pilot's seat at the front of the Raptor, and switched on the radio. "*Galactica* Actual, this is Boomer. Anyone over there well enough to give me a high sign?"

There was a long pause. Kara tried to remain hopeful. If there was a way to negotiate her release, Commander Adama would find it. Sharon didn't wait for an answer. She released the clamps holding the Raptor to the side of the *Monarch*, and the bright stars beyond the pilot's canopy began to move.

"*This is* Galactica *Actual,*" came Colonel Tigh's voice, and Kara's heart sank. The man was as diplomatic as a hammerhead shark. "*Just what the hell do you think you're doing?*"

"Hey there, Colonel," Sharon said, as if this were a perfectly normal day. The Raptor picked up speed. "The Old Man too sick to come on the line himself?"

"*None of you goddam business,*" Tigh snapped. "*You just bring that Raptor back, missy, and we'll call it even.*"

"Nah. Thought you might want to know I'm making off with one of your star pilots," Sharon said. Her voice was tinny over the suit's intercom. "Lieutenant Thrace is lying here on my deck, stunned but in one piece. She'll stay that way unless you try to fire on me with those shaky hands of yours."

"*How do I know you're telling the truth?*" Tigh countered.

Sharon got up from the pilot's chair and hauled Kara to her feet. Pain slashed through her head, and she felt warm blood dribble down her chin from a cut she hadn't noticed before. Sharon plunked Kara into the copilot's chair and said, "Say hello, Lieutenant."

Kara remained silent.

"If you say hello," Sharon said sweetly, "I promise to give you a vac suit of your own before I shove you outside."

"Frak you," Kara said.

"That could be a recording," Tigh said.

"Repeat what the good Colonel just said, Starbuck," Sharon ordered. "If you want the vac suit, that is."

"That could be a recording," Kara said through gritted teeth. Every movement only made the pain worse.

"There you are, Colonel. So hold your fire and everything'll be just fine. I'll stick Starbuck here in a suit, give her a tracking transponder, and toss her outside. Once I've jumped away, you can come and rescue her."

The lie was so transparent, even Tigh had to see through it. Kara had no illusions about her eventual fate at Sharon's hands, but the pain in her head made it difficult to think.

"Where's Peter Attis?" Tigh demanded.

"Back on the *Monarch*," Sharon said.

"Where, exactly? The Monarch *is a big place."*

"I guess you could say he's all over the place, really. Boomer out."

A tiny crackle came from the canopy in front of Kara, and a hairline crack ran across the Plexiglas. Kara's blood chilled as she realized what had happened—Helo's ricochet had chipped the canopy and the resulting weakness was getting worse. Sharon, however, didn't seem to notice. She was busy plotting a jump.

"Okay," she said, putting in the final numbers and standing up. "While the computer's finishing that up, you and I have things to do."

She hooked a hand under Kara's elbow, tugged her out of the copilot's chair, and hauled her toward the closed hatchway.

287

"No suit?" Kara said, already knowing the answer.

"No suit," Sharon agreed. "I was lying. Hell, I'm doing you a favor. Better to die now than watch all your friends die while you live."

"Don't do me any favors," Kara said half-heartedly. Sharon's grip was steel-strong and Kara couldn't break the handcuffs. Her mind came up with a dozen ideas, each one more desperate and unworkable than the last. Sharon let go of Kara and put her hands on the wheel that would open the hatchway and evacuate the air. The resulting blast of wind would shove Kara straight out into space. Kara swallowed, trying to hold on to every sensation she could because they would be her last ones. The air rushing through her lungs, the heart beating in her chest, the pain stabbing through her head. It didn't seem fair, having pain as her final sensation. Sharon started to turn the wheel—

—and then another Sharon rose up behind her, both hands laced together in a double fist. Kara stared, not comprehending what she was looking at. The second Sharon brought both hands down on the back of the fist Sharon's head. The thin fabric of the vac suit head covering was no protection, and the first Sharon staggered in pain and surprise. The second Sharon hit her again and again and again, a dizzying rain of blows that thudded against the vac suit. The first Sharon collapsed to the deck.

"Sorry it took so long," the second Sharon said. She was wearing a prison jumpsuit, and her stomach was a little rounded. Pregnant. It was Caprica Sharon. "I had to wait until she was in a vac suit before I made a move."

"What?" Kara said, confused. "Why?"

The Plexiglas crackled audibly. Caprica Sharon spun in surprise. A spider web of cracks was spinning a network across the canopy.

"Oh frak," she whispered, then flew into action. She leaped

behind Kara and snapped the handcuff chain. Kara winced, but she was growing used to pain by now. Every part of her body hurt by now. Caprica Sharon pulled Kara to her with easy strength, and both of them groped through the storage closet for vac suits. The canopy crackled again and the web of cracks grew larger. Kara thought she heard a faint hiss of escaping air. Gods, nothing ever came easy, did it? She should be in the clear now, but she was still struggling for life.

"Could we make it back to the *Monarch?*" Kara asked.

"That canopy's going to go in less than a minute," Caprica Sharon said. "So that would be a 'no.'" She thrust a suit at Kara, who pulled it on with chilly fingers. Neither human nor Cylon spoke further. The first Sharon lay on the floor, still unconscious. A trickle of blood ran from the corner of her mouth. The canopy made a soft popping sound, and this time the hiss of escaping air was clearly audible. An alarm beeped on the console, in case no one had figured out that the Raptor was losing air. Kara checked the fastenings of her suit and reached for the helmet. A slight breeze caressed her cheek, bringing a reflexive stab of fear. A breeze was a fine thing outdoors on a still summer day, but on a ship, it heralded death by decompression. Kara yanked on the helmet, sealed it, and inhaled the rush of plastic-scented air. Caprica Sharon, meanwhile, had put on her own vac suit, but she set the helmet aside.

"What are you doing?" Kara asked, her voice close and muffled inside the suit. The canopy was by now nothing but a network of cracks.

Caprica Sharon wordlessly reached down, unfastened the other Sharon's fabric helmet, and ripped it free. She put it on her own head and fastened it, then shot a glance at the canopy. Now Kara understood. She supposed she should have felt some sort of pity or reluctance, but all she felt was glad relief.

The first Sharon's eyes popped open and she vaulted to her feet so fast, Kara couldn't react. She caught Caprica Sharon by surprise as well. The first Sharon plowed into Caprica and knocked her face-down to the deck with the first Sharon on top of her.

"I'll kill him *and* you," the first Sharon snarled for no reason Kara could see. Who the hell was *him*?

"You can't reach the control while you're in that vac suit," Caprica Sharon gasped back.

The first Sharon got her fingers under the fastenings of Caprica Sharon's cloth helmet. Damage alarms and air alarms blared through the Raptor's cabin. Caprica Sharon couldn't get the leverage to fight back. The first Sharon ignored Kara entirely.

Wild anger roared over Kara. The first Sharon was responsible for everything that had happened—the plague, Kara's sickness, Peter's death, Lee's death, the destruction of the cure. Strength she didn't know she possessed thundered through her. She grabbed the first Sharon's vac suit by the back of the neck and at the small of back and lifted.

The first Sharon weighed less than Kara had anticipated. Startled, the first Sharon came free of her victim with an indignant yelp.

"Grab something!" Kara shouted inside her own suit. Without waiting to see if Caprica Sharon had heard, she swung the first Sharon once to gain some momentum, then flung her straight toward the canopy. Sharon hit the weakened Plexiglas face-first dead between the pilot and copilot chairs. The canopy exploded outward, and Sharon blew into space. Her scream was lost in the rush of air.

A hurricane blast knocked Kara off her feet from behind, and she found herself flying toward the empty canopy. She desperately grabbed for one of the chairs and missed. Then an iron hand caught her ankle. Caprica Sharon, her other hand firmly clutching a handhold, towed her back to safety. Kara caught a glimpse of the first Sharon as she drifted through uncaring vacuum, twitching and clawing at her own face as bloody vapor burst from her mouth and nose. The pain and horror of her expression made Kara look away, despite her earlier feelings of anger and hatred. The Cylon may have deserved the death, but Kara found she didn't want to watch it.

The blast of air was short-lived on such a small vessel, and it died quickly. Once the women were sure neither of them was injured or leaking air, they both carefully climbed into seats, Caprica Sharon in the pilot's chair and Kara in the copilot position. It was unnerving to sit in a Raptor, looking at the stars without a Plexiglas barrier between herself and vacuum. She felt as if she could float off into the emptiness. Maybe she should. Everyone in the Fleet was either dead or dying, and she didn't want to be the only one left behind.

Lee was dead. The thought hit her like a punch to her already-sore gut. Frak. She felt tears well up and blinked them back. Crying in a vac suit was almost as bad as throwing up in one. To distract herself, Kara shot Sharon a glance. The Cylon's face was calm inside her vac suit helmet.

"Thanks," Kara said hoarsely. "For saving me. Twice."

"Thanks for saving me once," Sharon replied with a small grin. "Why don't you radio *Galactica* and tell them we're coming? I have the feeling they won't believe anything I have to say."

Gaius Baltar filled a pipette with fluid from a Petrie dish, prepared a slide for it, and slipped it under the microscope. He peered through the lenses.

"Well, Gaius?"

For once, Gaius didn't jump or yelp or spin around. He had sensed Six's presence before she spoke. "I've been listening to the radio news," he said without turning around. "Quite a lot's been happening aboard the *Monarch*."

"And a lot's been happening in this lab," Six said smugly.

This time Gaius glanced over his shoulder at her. No matter what they did together, no matter what happened, Number Six remained perfectly beautiful. Her white-blond hair was never mussed, her makeup never smeared, her dress never wrinkled. Her legs never prickled with stubble, her breath never smelled of garlic, and the only time she sweated was during sex, which Baltar found a turn-on. She was physically perfect in every way.

"So are you here to tell me something useful or just kibbitz while I work?"

"Work?" She gestured at the incubator. It was the size of a small refrigerator and filled with warm test tubes. "Looks like the machines are doing the work for you."

"Mmmmm." Gaius changed slides and looked again. "I don't suppose you'd be willing to lend a hand."

"Why not call Dr. Cottle in to help you?"

"Cottle is a doctor, not a research scientist. Besides, he's shaking too much to be of any use. Looks like it's just me."

"Chosen by God," Number Six said, "and working like a devil. That's you, isn't it, Gaius?"

"Just hand me that box of syringes, would you?"

"I think it would be more appropriate if I just watched."

"That's not what you said half an hour ago," Baltar teased.

Six smiled. It wasn't a happy smile or a sensuous one. It was the sort of smile Baltar had come to dread over the months. His good mood faltered.

"What?" he asked.

"There's something you're forgetting, Gaius."

Kara was in a frak-it mood by the time the Raptor was safely aboard the *Galactica* on Deck Five, so she pulled off her vac suit helmet and climbed out the shattered canopy instead of exiting through the hatchway. Only five people were waiting for her— the plague was getting worse. Three of the people were combat troops Kara didn't recognize. Their rifles were at the ready, and she assumed they were there for Sharon. The fourth was Karl "Helo" Agathon. His face was pale and his uniform was dirty.

The fifth was Lee Adama.

At first Kara's mind couldn't process what she was seeing. The bomb had gone off. Lee was dead. But there he was. Bruises and burns mottled his face and arms. He had replaced his shirt. A bandage covered one cheek. But there he was. Gladness as wide as a rainbow poured over her, and she grabbed him in a hard hug.

"Ow!" they both said as the embrace aggravated their injuries. They backed away from each other, unable to repress the grins that stretched their faces.

"You bastard!" she said. "I thought you died in that explosion."

"I thought so, too," Lee admitted. "Piece of machinery shielded me. That, and the fact that the bomb went off inside the loader scoop. If Peter hadn't run when he had, I *would* be dead."

"Peter." Emerging sorrow dampened the gladness. "He saved us both, then."

"Yeah," Lee said grimly. "Maybe." And he held up his hands to remind Kara that they were still shaking.

Helo stepped forward and gave Kara a hug of his own, but gently. Then he said, "Was Sharon—*our* Sharon—really on board the Raptor with you?"

"Sure thing," Sharon said, emerging from the Raptor, her vac suit already removed. Before anyone could react, Helo grabbed her in a hard embrace and kissed her. She kissed him back. Kara shot a sidelong glance at Lee and caught him shooting a sidelong glance at her. A moment passed and Lee took a step toward her. Kara leaned in.

Then she kissed him quickly on the cheek. He smelled of metal and sweat. "I'm glad you're okay," she said brusquely.

"Uh, yeah," he replied. "Thanks."

The three marines, meanwhile, moved in on Sharon and Helo, safeties off, expressions tense. Sharon noticed them and stepped away from Helo, hands raised. "Don't shoot. I'm not going to make any sudden moves or hurt anyone."

One of the marines brandished his rifle. "Toas—"

"Don't finish that phrase, soldier," Kara interrupted. "Unless you want a world of trouble from an unexpected direction."

The marine shut his mouth.

"What the frak happened?" Lee said.

"How's the Old Man?" Kara countered.

"Barely functional. Tigh's mostly in charge."

"Aw, frak." This from Sharon. The Cylon allowed the marines to put shackles on her wrists and ankles. Around her neck, one of them fastened a man-catcher—a collar with a stiff pole instead of a leash. Helo watched, a pained look on his face, but he didn't interfere.

"I won't let him hurt you, Sharon," Kara said. "But we all need to catch up."

"The President's already in the CIC conference room with the Old Man," Lee said. "Come on."

They made a strange procession through the corridors of the *Galactica*—Lee and Kara both limping and sore, Sharon hobbling at the end of the man-catcher, the grim-faced marines with their ready weapons. The corridors, however, were mostly empty.

"Where is everyone?" Kara asked. "Down with the plague?"

"I guess," Lee said. "Helo and I grabbed one of the *Monarch*'s shuttles and rushed over here after Helo talked to Sharon—the other Sharon. Helo can still fly, and we were hoping to get him into a Viper or another Raptor, something faster than a shuttle, so we could intercept you. But all the combat ships are down—not enough knuckle-draggers to keep them running. Everyone on the *Galactica* is either too shaky to do anything but lie in their bunks, or they're trying to run three and four duty stations at the same time."

"Have you told them about . . ." Kara trailed off, not sure how much she should say.

"No," Lee said. "I've talked to CIC, but I haven't been up there yet."

Helo muttered something that sounded like, "We're all ass-frakked," but he didn't elaborate. Kara concentrated on staying upright. Exhaustion was weighing down on her like a lead blanket. How long had it been since she'd had a real rest? Or sleep? She couldn't remember. Escaping from the other Sharon hadn't been the end of her problems—or the Fleet's.

CIC was almost empty. Kara counted six people, none of whom she knew, desperately trying to run stations designed for twenty. They barely glanced up as the group passed through on their way to the conference room. Kara swallowed. If a Cylon basestar showed up now, they were dead.

Though the same was true if a basestar *didn't* show up.

The CIC conference room was hushed and dimly lit. At the table sat Commander Adama, Colonel Tigh, and Laura Roslin.

President Roslin's hands were on the table, and they trembled only slightly. Adama, on the other hand, was clearly fighting to keep himself upright and his mouth shut. Tigh was trembling but seemed functional. They all eyed Sharon as the marines herded her through the door. Sharon was keeping her face impassive, and Kara wondered how she felt about being hauled around like an animal. Did she get angry? Or maybe she found all the extra security flattering, along the lines of "only someone truly dangerous rates this kind of treatment." Kara decided that if she were ever in Sharon's position, she'd try to feel flattered.

Everyone took a seat except Sharon, who stood to one side.

"We don't have time for preliminaries, so I'll just ask about the bad news now," Roslin said. Her voice was soft and tired as an old blanket. "I don't see Peter, so I assume he's dead."

Kara gave a reluctant nod, and felt cold fear and hopeless despair settle across the room. "Sharon—a different Sharon—killed him." She briefed them on what had happened to her since the kidnapping and was surprised to learn she'd been gone for less than a day. It felt like a week.

The table remained silent for a moment after Kara's briefing. Adama was sweating with the effort of remaining silent, and Kara wanted to comfort him. Unfortunately, there was nothing she could do.

"Sharon," Roslin said at last. "Tell us what happened to you." Roslin's voice carried an edge of ice. The President loathed all Cylons and had never warmed to Sharon, even after repeated demonstrations that she meant the Fleet no harm and was, in fact, helping as best she could.

"Where should I start?" she asked.

"From your jailbreak," Roslin said levelly. "When you killed that marine and sent the other to sickbay."

"I didn't kill anyone," Sharon said, though her tone said she expected no one would believe her. "The other copy did."

"Thank gods," Helo said with a small sigh.

Sharon gave him a small smile. "She wiped out the guards at the cell and broke me out, but she wasn't offering to get me off the *Galactica* or anything like that."

"What *did* she offer you?" Roslin said.

"Nothing. She said there was a secret compartment in the escape pod on Deck Five and that I'd better find a way to get there and hide." Sharon paused and licked her lips. "She was going to use me as a scapegoat or a distraction or both. Commander Adama would order search teams to look for me, and that would take extra time and resources and allow her to do what she wanted more easily. They also know that I've been helping the Fleet. If I got caught and was blamed for killing the guard, you'd never believe another word I said. My so-called escape was a way to neutralize any further help I might give the Fleet."

"She could have just killed you," Roslin said.

"That would kill the baby, too," Sharon replied. "Not what she—or any other Cylon—would want."

"Why didn't you just come forward?" Tigh demanded. "Let yourself get caught?"

"Him," Sharon said, nodding toward Helo. "She knocked him out just after the escape and stuck a microdetonator under the skin on the back of his skull. She told me she'd blow Helo to pieces if I got caught."

Helo's hand stole to the back of his head. His face was pale. "That's why my head's been itching lately?"

"Probably. I'm so sorry, Helo."

"Is it going to . . . you know . . . go off now?"

"If it hasn't by now, I'd say you're safe," Sharon said. "Like

Kara—Lieutenant Thrace—said, the other one is sucking vacuum, or vacuum is sucking her."

"Why didn't she pop it off outside the Raptor?" Helo pressed. "When I had the pistol?"

Sharon shrugged within the man-catcher. "Who knows? I'd guess she thought you weren't a serious danger to her, and it was more fun to play with you. The detonator was aimed more at me than you anyway."

"Yeah," Helo muttered. "Gods."

"That's what you meant when you said you had to wait until the other Sharon was in a vac suit," Kara said with new understanding. "If she was wearing the detonator on her belt or something, she wouldn't be able to set it off with the suit in the way."

"Yeah," Sharon said. "I hid until I was sure Helo would be safe." She shifted position within her shackles and the chains clinked. "Anyway, I didn't know what to do after the other Sharon sprung me, so I hid for a while. But Chief Tyrol found the secret compartment in the pod, and I couldn't stay there anymore. I snuck on board the Raptor that transported the marines to the *Monarch*. Once you all boarded, I slipped out and tried to get the other Sharon alone, but I couldn't."

"Those were *your* footsteps we kept hearing," Lee said.

"Probably. I couldn't think of a way to get Peter out of there without getting me and Helo killed, so I just waited. Once I realized the other Sharon was going to take Lieutenant Thrace back to the Raptor, I ran ahead. You know the rest of it."

"Nothing . . . matters of state on the steps of—" Adama clamped his teeth together and tried again. "Nothing . . . matters. All dead soon."

That silenced further conversation. Kara bit her lip. The Commander was completely right. Within a day or so, everyone Kara had worked so hard to save would be dead. It would be her, Sharon, and maybe a few other people rattling around in the ships.

Something occurred to Kara. "I can help a few people," she said. "Anyone who has AB blood can get the cure from me. No one else, though."

"That's about four percent of the population," Lee said. "It'll help. Every life will help."

He didn't say what his blood type was, and Kara found she couldn't bear to ask.

"And maybe someone can extract the cure from my blood and help others," Kara said instead. "Tom Zarek was also cured, so maybe we can use his blood, too."

"We'll have to try," Lee agreed. "Though Dr. Baltar said—"

The phone buzzed. Adama looked like he wanted to pick it up, but held back for obvious reasons. Everyone glanced uncertainly at everyone else. At last, Kara reached across the table and snatched up the receiver with her steady hands.

"CIC," she said. "Lieutenant Thrace."

"Doctor Baltar here," said a familiar voice. *"It's good to hear your voice, Lieutenant. How are you?"*

Kara kept her voice neutral. She had been trying to forget that she and Baltar had shared a brief, torrid bedroom session, but every time she saw him, the memory surfaced. She still couldn't believe she had done it.

"I'm just dandy," she said, aware that every eye in the room was on her. "What's going on? Commander Adama's . . . indisposed right now, if you're looking for him."

"Is he there? I know he probably can't talk reliably."

"Yes. What do you want, Dr. Baltar?" She added the latter so everyone would know who she was talking to.

"Just to see if everyone is there. I have . . . I have more news about the plague."

Kara closed her eyes. She didn't know if she could handle more bad news. "What is it?"

"It'd be easier to show you than to tell you," he said. *"If everyone is there, I'll just come up."*

Kara relayed this to the others. Laura Roslin took charge and gave assent. A few minutes later, Gaius Baltar entered the room. His lab coat was neat and pressed, his face shaven, his hair combed, his tie straight. Kara wondered where he found the time and energy. She also noticed that his hands weren't shaking at all. How had he escaped the plague?

Baltar was carrying a tray covered by a black cloth. He glanced at Sharon in surprise but didn't comment on her presence. Instead, he set the tray down at the head of the table and took up a position there.

"What is it, Doctor?" Roslin asked softly. "How much worse can it get?"

"Actually, the news is rather better than you might think." He whipped the cloth aside with a flourish, revealing a row of syringes. The needles gleamed in the dim light of the conference room. "Ladies and gentlemen, I give you the cure for the plague of tongues."

CHAPTER
17

Confused babbling broke out around the table. A fair amount of it was literal nonsense. Commander Adama lost his fragile control and jabbered, a look of shock on his craggy face. Tigh joined in. Until now, his speech had been clear, but being startled seemed to push him over some sort of edge. Roslin and Lee both shouted questions. Only Kara, Sharon, and her guards remained silent, though Sharon's guards stared at the syringes as if they were a rich pile of emeralds and rubies. Through it all, Gaius Baltar stood at the head of the table, his arms folded across his chest, a look of triumph on his face. Kara found herself distrustful instead of glad.

At last, Lee bellowed for quiet and the room fell silent. Or nearly so. Adama and Tigh babbled gibberish for a few seconds before managing to quiet themselves.

"Thank you, Captain," Roslin said. Her body was shaking now. Kara wondered if the plague was worse for her because of the cancer. "Doctor, if those injections will cure the plague, I think you should administer them now. We'll have the explanation later."

"Of course, Madam President." Baltar moved quickly about the room with the tray. He started with Commander Adama, then followed up with Tigh and Roslin. When he reached Kara, she held up her hand.

"I'm good," she said.

Baltar gave her an odd look, but continued around the table. He also injected Sharon's guards. He didn't offer one to Sharon and she didn't ask. Cylons had red blood, that Kara knew—she had seen enough of it over the months—but she doubted it was compatible with human biology.

"You should begin to feel better almost immediately," Baltar said. "The prions fasten onto your nervous tissue early on, and that starts the shaking and the babbling, but they don't do permanent damage until later in the cycle, when the patient is in a coma."

"How, Doctor?" Roslin asked. She was rolling her sleeve back down. "You said it would take you two or three days to manufacture the C prion."

"True," Baltar admitted. "But I found a . . . shortcut in the middle of the process." He paused and made a tiny shudder before continuing. "I had also been operating under the assumption that I would begin to shake as well, which would slow me down. It never happened. I seem to be part of that tiny percentage of a given population that is naturally immune to any given disease."

"Lucky for us," Tigh said.

"Indeed," Baltar said. "Even as we speak, the incubator in my lab is making enough Prion C to innoculate the entire Fleet. I have enough to start on the military—and the government, Madam President. They can handle distribution."

Tigh got up and clapped Baltar on the back. "You're a hero, Doctor. A real hero."

And then everything fell into place. Kara knew. Her jaw tightened and her stomach oozed with nausea. She rose abruptly. "I have to go," she said. "I can . . . I can help with the distribution process. I'll go down to sickbay and see to it. Commander?"

"Dismissed, Lieutenant," Adama said hoarsely. As Kara turned to go, he added, "Lieutenant."

She stopped and turned.

"I was sorry to hear about what happened to Peter," he said.

A lump formed in Kara's throat. Peter had infected her with a disease, aided in her kidnapping, and duped hundreds of people into joining a monotheistic little cult. But before that, he had been funny and kind and fascinating. A few minutes before his death, Kara had hated Peter, found him weak and self-centered. But when the timer was counting down those final seconds, he could have stayed with Lee in the hope that the Captain would find a way to disarm the explosive at the last moment. Instead, Peter had given up the hope in order to save Lee's life. Kara didn't know how to feel about Peter right then, but she did know his bloody death made her sad in a way she didn't want to explore right then. So she nodded acknowledgment to Adama and left the conference room.

Lee caught up with her in the hallway outside CIC. "What was that all about?"

Kara glanced around. The corridor was empty. When people got sick and shaky, they slipped off to their beds to hide rather than collapse in the hallways. "The frakking bastard *lied*."

"Who do you mean? Baltar?"

"No, the frakking High Priest of Geminon," Kara snarled. "Of *course* I mean Baltar. Who else?"

Lee held up his hands. They only trembled the tiniest bit. "His cure seems to be working. I can't tell you how relieved I am. We were all heading for death's gateway, including my dad."

"He lied about how long it would take to make the cure," Kara explained, overly patient. "He said creating the cure prion would take a couple days when he frakking *knew* it would only take a few hours. He lets us all think we're dead, and then he strides in to announce that he has the cure after all, applause and adulation, please. Frak him!"

"That's a serious charge, Kara," Lee said. "Can you—"

"No, I can't prove it," she sighed. "And there wouldn't be any point now." She took off down the hallway again with Lee tagging after her.

"How do you know, anyway?" he pressed. "You haven't even been on the *Galactica* for the last several hours."

"How long does it take to grow a prion?" Kara countered. "I'm betting it takes a couple hours. He had enough on that tray of his to cure everyone in CIC. That means he had the cure prion while I was still with the Unity on the *Monarch*, right? If he had come forward right then, it wouldn't have mattered if we got Peter back or not, and the entire situation would have changed. Peter might still be alive."

"We still needed to get you out," Lee reminded her. "And once word got out that we didn't need Peter anymore, Sharon—the bad one—would have just taken you hostage earlier."

"Maybe," Kara acknowledged. "But Peter"—her voice caught—"would still be alive. Meanwhile, Baltar saves the Fleet."

Lee put a hand on her shoulder, halting her in mid-stride. "Look, we can't know what would have happened. Maybe Baltar lied, maybe he didn't. There's no point in chewing on it right now. We have to get the prion out to the military and then to the public. And you won't be any help by walking this way."

"What do you mean?" Kara asked.

"Sickbay is that way."

Kara managed a small laugh and was surprised at how much better she felt for it.

It was two hours later. Commander William Adama sat once again at the conference room table, but he had managed a shower and a change of uniform. Between that and the lack of shakiness in his limbs and his voice, he felt bright as a new-minted coin. Laura Roslin, also seated at the table, looked more like her old self. He knew the cancer gave her good days and bad days, and she seemed to be having a good day now that the prion had been cleansed from her system. He felt gladder about that than about himself and Lee.

Lee, Kara, and Baltar had set about administering Prion C to Dr. Cottle, his medics, and the rest of the sickbay staff. Once they were well enough, they headed out into *Galactica* proper with more syringes. Adama had ordered skeleton crews for all shifts. The cure worked, but people were still tired and needed rest before becoming completely well.

Once *Galactica* was inoculated, Adama ordered Raptors to carry the cure to the rest of the Fleet.

Unfortunately, casualty reports were also coming in. So far twenty-one people, including five children, had died, and twelve had gotten the cure too late for it to do any good, meaning death would eventually come to them as well. Adama pursed his lips at the report of each new death. Every single life was precious now, and every single death whittled a little more away from humanity's chance of surviving.

Gaius Baltar was also in the room. The rest of the cure had finished incubating and he wasn't needed in his lab anymore. "There's going to be a problem," he said.

Adama sighed heavily. "What now?"

"The *Monarch*, the *Phoebe*, and some of the other Geminon ships are absolutely rife with Unity followers," Baltar said.

"So?" Adama said.

"Oh!" Roslin put a hand to her mouth. "I should have foreseen that."

"Seen what?" Adam said, beginning to get annoyed. Nothing was ever easy on the *Galactica*.

"Peter's death makes him a martyr," Roslin said. "It will only strengthen the beliefs of some—perhaps even most—of his followers."

"And they see the plague as a blessing instead of a curse," Baltar finished.

Adama took a moment to rest his forehead on his now-steady hand. "So you're thinking that they'll resist inoculation. Even though they'll die without it."

"I'd bet a year's salary on it," Roslin said. Adama wasn't sure if that was meant as a joke or not—Roslin hadn't been paid for anything since the attack. Neither had he, come to that.

His tired mind, now overly sensitive to crisis, was already running scenarios. Forced inoculation would take large amounts of personnel and practically guarantee someone would get hurt. It was difficult or impossible to persuade someone caught in the grip of religious fervor. Maybe they could trick at least some of them into thinking the injection was something else?

"This," Baltar said, interrupting Adama's train of thought, "is why I took a small liberty. I hope you don't mind."

"What's that, Doctor?" Adama asked warily. Roslin looked uncertain as well.

At that moment, a knock came at the door. Baltar rose to open it. In walked Sarah Porter, closely followed by two men in priestly robes and another man with a video camera slung over his shoulder. Porter held a double scroll. Roslin kept her seat, but Adama got to his feet.

"Doctor?" he asked.

"You know, of course, Representative Porter of Geminon," Baltar said. "And this is Remus Tal, a Priest, and this is Nikolas Koa, an Oracle. They're also from Geminon."

Greetings were exchanged. Roslin still didn't rise, and Adama suspected she was feeling tired again.

"Some of the people in my jurisdiction are resisting inoculation," Porter said.

"As I predicted," Baltar put in.

Porter shot him a hard look at the interrupting, then continued. "However, Dr. Baltar here has pointed out something which may be of interest in solving the problem." She spread the scroll across the table. Adama put on his reading glasses. They made him feel like a grandfather, but he really had no choice. Roslin got up to join him. Her movements were slow and careful, so Adama resolved to keep this short.

"The Book of Glykon?" Roslin said. "I thought you considered this apocryphal."

"Just between us," Sarah said, "I do. But Dr. Baltar has pointed out something very interesting that just might solve this one last problem."

Kara lay sound asleep in a sickbay bed, dreaming of explosions that hurled chains in every direction. A dark figure loomed over her, and a sixth sense told her this wasn't a dream, and she jerked awake, hands in a fighting stance. Lee Adama backed up, his own hands raised.

"Just me," he said.

"Frak," she said, and sank back into the thin mattress. After injecting maybe a hundred people, Kara's body had finally given out. Darkness closed in and she felt herself falling. She remembered careful hands helping her along until she ended up someplace soft. A bed in sickbay. The place was crowded. Every bed was occupied, and most of the privacy curtains were open. She caught sight of Dr. Cottle bending over a patient in another bed.

"Why am I here instead of in my bunk?" she asked.

"Someone was already sleeping there," Lee said wryly, "so I brought you here. The person who had this bed had recovered enough to walk, so Doc Cottle kicked him out to make space for you."

Kara grimaced. "I feel like I could sleep for a month—and I'm frakking *starved*. Don't ever get kidnapped by the Unity. They don't feed you." Her stomach growled, emphasizing the point.

"I'll see if I can scrounge you something to eat in a minute," Lee said. "Got lots of algae."

"I'll take a big plate of it, as long as you add a steak, some fries, and a hunk of corn on the cob dripping with butter and loaded with salt."

"Maybe after you've had more rest," Lee said. "Even the mighty Starbuck needs sleep once in a while."

"So why'd you wake me up?" she growled. "And how long was I out?"

"Couple hours. I woke you up because there's a news conference coming on I thought you might want to see." He reached up to a video monitor hanging in a corner and switched it on. A well-dressed reporter with braided auburn hair was talking earnestly into a microphone.

"—here on the *Phoebe* where riots have broken out over the military's attempt to inoculate the population against the so-called plague of tongues," she was saying. The picture cut to scenes of angry civilians, some of them clearly in the shaking, babbling stage of the disease, throwing small objects at wary soldiers, who ducked behind shields and dodged around corners. Several carried signs that boasted slogans: PETER ATTIS WAS A MARTYR! WE ARE BLESSED! THE UNIFIER WILL SAVE HUMANITY! THE ONE IS THE ONLY ONE!

The soldiers in the scenes were clearly unwilling to engage the civilians, but it was equally clear that they weren't sure what to do.

"Rioting isn't limited to the *Phoebe*," continued the reporter in a voiceover. "After the explosion on the mining ship *Monarch* killed Peter Attis, the large gathering of Unity members who were opposing the military's attempt to free Attis's lover Lieutenant Kara Thrace—"

Kara bolted upright in the bed. The movement earned a jolt of pain from various injuries, but she ignored it. "How the frak did they learn about this so fast?"

"Hush!" Lee said.

"—refused inoculation," the reporter continued. "Many other Unity members and sympathizers are also refusing to cooperate. President Laura Roslin has enacted a new law requiring all people in the Fleet to receive the injection, which was developed by Vice-President Gaius Baltar. Despite this, Unity members and sympathizers continue to fight being inoculated."

"What idiots," Kara said. "They want to die, that's their business. After everything we've been through to get that cure, I say screw 'em."

"We're talking several hundred people," Lee said. "And several children."

Kara sank back into the bed again. "I know, I know. It's just . . ."

"I know." Lee patted her arm, and Kara realized that out of all the friends she had in the Fleet, Lee probably understood her the best. She felt comfortable with him, even safe. So why the hell did she feel pulled in two different directions about him all them time? Even now, part of her wanted him to take her hand and part of her wanted to shove him away. She settled on ignoring his touch and fixing her attention on the television. More angry civilians vied with uncertain soldiers. Then a newscaster broke in.

"We've just received word that President Roslin will be addressing the Fleet," he said. "We take you to her now."

Billy Keikeya appeared on the screen. He looked pale and wobbly, probably still recovering from the plague of tongues. "Citizens of the Colonies," he said, "I give you our president, Laura Roslin."

He stepped aside, and Roslin, also pale, came on camera. Kara realized with a small start that the background was not the usual podium on *Colonial Fleet One*, but the conference room off CIC.

"Good evening," Roslin said. "By now all of you know of the plague which has struck the Fleet and the fact that we have an inoculation developed by our vice president, Dr. Gaius Baltar. The inoculation will cure those who have the plague and grant immunity to those who don't. However, some people are seeing this plague as a blessing, as the touch of some divine being brought by Peter Attis. These people are resisting inoculation. I am here to tell you that the plague is no divine blessing. It is a prion developed by the Cylons. They infected the late Mr. Attis with it in the hope that as an entertainer, he would come into contact with great numbers of people and spread the plague farther and faster.

"I also know that many people believe Mr. Attis was a person called the Unifier come to save humanity by uniting everyone under a single god. This position seemed to be supported by certain passages in the Book of Glykon. I am here to tell you that this interpretation of the passages is an error. Peter Attis is not—was not—the Unifier foretold there."

The camera pulled back, revealing that Roslin was standing behind the conference table in CIC. The chairs had been pulled away to make room for her and for Sarah Porter and Gaius Baltar, who were standing next her. Baltar looked cool and calm, almost smug. Also present were two men Kara didn't recognize, though she assumed by the clothes they wore that they were clergy. On the table in front of Roslin lay a partially unrolled scroll.

"What the hell is this about?" Kara asked.

"Just watch," Lee said. The expression on his face was rigidly neutral and gave Kara no clues. Was the news good or bad? She couldn't tell, and that annoyed her. Why couldn't Lee just tell her?

"The main passage that the Unity members quote," Roslin said, stabbing a finger at the open scroll before her, "reads as follows: 'He—the Unifier—will save Humanity with the Plague of the Tongue.' This is taken to indicate that Peter Attis would bring a disease that would make people speak in tongues, and this plague would save everyone by uniting humanity. There are also rumors that the Cylons will stop attacking us if we profess to believe in a single god, rumors that further feed the idea that Mr. Attis is the Unifier.

"In light of recent events, I have consulted with Representative Sarah Porter of Geminon and with Remus Tal, a Priest, and Nikolas Koa, an Oracle. They pointed out that Peter Attis and his followers read the Book of Glykon incorrectly, an easy mistake and completely understandable, but a mistake nonetheless.

The Book of Glykon indicates that the Unifier will save humanity with the plague of the tongue. This doesn't mean the plague will be the tool that saves humanity. It means that the Unifier *will save people who have the plague.* In other words, the Unifier will cure—save—the people who carry this sickness. The identity of the true Unifier can now be revealed."

"Oh, frak," Kara whispered. "He didn't."

"Yeah," Lee said. "He did."

Roslin stepped aside so that Tal and Koa could come forward. Between them they held a rectangular piece of gold cloth with two strings at the upper corners. The camera followed them as they solemnly processed to Gaius Baltar, who wore a humble, slightly overwhelmed look on his face.

"The Scrolls of Glykon are clear," Koa intoned. "Gaius Baltar is the Unifier who saved people with the terrible plague of tongues."

"Blessings on Gaius Baltar!" Tal said. "Blessings on the Unifier!"

Kara stared. "Is this . . . are they really doing this?"

"It's the best way," Lee said. "If it works, and Baltar is recognized as the Unifier, people will stop resisting inoculation."

"It's twisting one of the scrolls," Kara protested. "Baltar isn't the Unifier."

"How do you know?" Lee said philosophically. "This might be exactly what the Scroll of Glykon meant. It's hard to save humanity if it's dead."

"—to accept this honor," Baltar was saying from the screen. "I often felt that an invisible hand guided me during my work on the inoculation. I sincerely believe I was touched by a greater power, and I am humbled by this grave responsibility." He paused dramatically. "As the Unifier, I ask my followers to receive my touch and allow the inoculation to continue."

"Turn it off," Kara said. "I'm tired."

Lee obligingly shut off the monitor and turned to go. Kara watched him move away, leave her behind as everyone in her life seemed to do. And suddenly the thought of being alone was too harsh to bear.

"Wait," she said. "Lee, hold on."

He returned to her bedside, a quizzical look on his face. "What's wrong?"

"Nothing." Acting on impulse she reached out and took his hand. "Thank you."

"For what?" He looked genuinely puzzled.

"For coming after me. For bringing me here. For checking on me."

"That's what friends are for, Kara."

"I know." She continued to hold his hand. It was warm in hers. "And sometimes I think you and I . . ."

He leaned down to kiss her. But she turned her head at the last moment and the kiss landed on her cheek. Lee pulled back, looking confused and not a little angry.

"Kara," he said, "I don't know what you—"

"I don't either," she interrupted. "Look, Lee—everyone leaves. Zak. Sam. Peter. I don't want you to join those ranks. I'd rather keep you around."

"I wouldn't leave you, Kara," he said.

"How can you be sure?" she countered.

"Nothing's sure around here," he said, half wry, half sullen. "Absolutely nothing."

"Exactly. Maybe one day I'll feel different, but right now . . ." She squeezed his hand again, then carefully and firmly put it down. Lee gave her a long look with his blue eyes and a hurt look on his boyish face. Then he nodded once, turned, and left.

Something twisted in Kara's chest. Not only had she ruined

any chance of a deeper relationship with Lee Adama, she had also killed their friendship.

You're stupid. A stupid, ugly cow. You don't deserve to be happy. You don't deserve to live. You don't deserve anything at all.

And she couldn't tell whether the inner voice was her own or her father's.

She turned over, squeezing her eyes shut against the tears. Sleep. That was what she needed now. The sounds of a busy, bustling sickbay swirled around her, but the military taught you to sleep through anything, and sickbay sounds were as soothing as a seashore lullaby. She would sleep and forget all about everything. Kara was just drifting off when the clank of dishes brought her awake again.

"What the hell?" She sat up and found Lee there. He was looking at her over a tray of covered dishes.

"Supper," he said. "You said you were hungry." He lifted lids as he spoke. "Algae soup. Algae salad. Algae bread. And for dessert, algae tapioca pudding. Yum yum!"

Kara stared down at green piles of glop, then burst out, "You frak-head!" She scooped up a spoonful of goo, ready to fling it at him, but Lee had already fled, the sound of his laughter trailing behind him. Kara put a hand to her mouth to stifle relieved laughter of her own. Then she sniffed the tray and picked up the spoon again.

The tapioca was surprisingly good.

President Laura Roslin slumped into a chair and leaned back with her eyes shut. The CIC conference room was empty of people except for Bill Adama. Baltar, the clergy, the camera crew, and even Billy Keikeya had left, thank gods, and that meant she could slouch all she wanted. Bill Adama wouldn't tell anyone.

Laura suppressed a snort as she realized that the only two people in the Fleet who she felt comfortable showing weakness to were both named William.

"How are you feeling?" Adama asked from his own chair.

"Like I could sleep for a century," she said.

"Want a drink? I got the good stuff."

She opened her eyes. "No, thanks. That would really lay me low. Wouldn't do for the president to conk out on her way to *Colonial One.*"

A moment of silence fell between them, a comfortable silence Laura enjoyed sharing with him.

"Did we do it right?" Adama asked at last.

"No way to know for sure," Laura said. "I mean, the riots calmed down almost immediately after Dr. Baltar's broadcast, and people are accepting the inoculation, so that's a plus. But declaring Gaius Baltar the Unifier . . . I don't know. He took to the role a little too well for my taste."

"I suspect that part of it will die down after a while. After all, the Unifier has already performed his duty by saving humanity. Nothing else for him to do, really."

And Laura Roslin laughed.

Helo put a hand to the wire-enforced Plexiglas barrier that separated him from Sharon's cell. She sighed, then pressed her own hand to it. Helo tried to pretend they were touching skin-on-skin, but it didn't work.

"Are you okay?" he asked.

"I feel like a dog who slipped her leash for a while and then got thrown back into the kennel," Sharon said.

"I'm going to try to get you out of there, Sharon," he said. "I am. Commander Adama will listen to reason eventually."

"Right," Sharon scoffed. "What do you think's going to happen? That I'll put on my uniform again one day? That Adama and I will sit at a little table together all buddy-buddy and he'll tell me his personal problems?"

"Who knows?" Helo said, trying to remain calm, though his voice was cracking. "It seems like something weird happens every frakking week around here, and you can never tell one day to the next what's going to happen."

"Easy to be optimistic when you're outside the jail instead of in it."

"I know."

"Be honest, Helo," she said, and he detected a hint of nervousness in her voice. "Did you really think I killed that marine?"

"No," he said promptly. "I did wonder how else he could have died, but I knew it wasn't you. Even when other people were calling me toaster-lover and giving me shit, I never thought it was you."

Some of the tension visibly went out of her. "Okay. Thanks."

"I have to go," he said reluctantly. "I have to get some sleep before I go on duty again. I love you."

She nodded. "I love you, too."

He turned and left the brig, not at all sure that he had told Sharon the truth but knowing there was nothing else he could have said.

"No, no, really. I have work to do. Thank you for coming. Really! It's quite all right. Yes, yes. Blessings on you all. I'll be giving a lecture just as soon as everyone's on their feet. Thank you again. More blessings, more blessings! Good day!"

Gaius Baltar closed the door to his laboratory, locked it, and leaned his back against it. Muffled knocks and faint pounding thudded on the metal. A smile stretched Gaius's face. Ah, the price of fame. Never a moment alone, even in his lab.

"That went well, Gaius," said Number Six. She was leaning against the door beside him, but her posture was casual.

"*I* liked it," he said with a grin. "Being the Unifier could have its advantages."

"Even though you lied about how long it would take you to find the cure so you could swoop in at the most theatrical moment and save everyone," she said.

He faltered. "Well, I *did* find the cure."

"And they won't ignore you ever again." Her gaze was hard and penetrating.

"I thought that was the whole idea."

"It was." Six swayed seductively toward him. "How did you put it? 'An invisible hand guided me'?" She put both hands on his shoulders, then slowly slid them down his chest, past his stomach, past his waist. Her voice dropped to a whisper. " 'I was touched by a greater power'?"

He shuddered deliciously as her fingers worked. "Yes. Yes, I was."

"And it's a good thing I reminded you to set up that little display with the priests."

"Yes, it was."

"But you haven't remembered everything, Gaius."

He sighed. "Now what?"

"The other parts from the Book of Glykon. How did they go? 'And the Unifier shall walk among the Enemy, and He shall return both changed and unharmed.' "

"I . . . I suppose that fits me, doesn't it?"

Her fingers continued working on his body, playing it like an instrument of pure pleasure. " 'The Unifier will bring together all

Humans into one Tribe under one God.' I wonder what that could mean?"

"I haven't the foggiest."

"Don't forget the best one. 'And the Heads of those who defy the Unifier shall tumble to the Ground.' "

Her caressing fingers made him shudder. "That has a poetic ring."

"Just so you never forget it, Gaius," she murmured. "Never, ever forget who you are and who got you here."

"I," he said with a sudden grin, "am Gaius Baltar."

He took her into his arms and danced her across the room, swirling in gleeful circles all by himself.

ABOUT THE AUTHOR

STEVEN HARPER lives in Michigan with his wife and three sons. When not at the keyboard writing books and short stories, he sings, plays the piano, and collects folk music. He maintains that the most interesting thing about him is that he writes novels. All four books in his Silent Empire series were Spectrum Award finalists. Visit his Web page at http://www.sff.net/people/spiziks.